The Zafarani Files

The Zafarani Files

Gamal al-Ghitani

Translated by Farouk Abdel Wahab

ARABIA BOOKS

First published in Great Britain in 2009 by
Arabia Books
70 Cadogan Place
London SW1X 9AH
www.arabia-books.co.uk

This edition published by arrangement with
The American University in Cairo Press
113 Sharia Kasr el Aini, Cairo, Egypt
420 Fifth Avenue, New York, NY 10018
www.aucpress.com

Printed in Great Britain by J. F. Print, Sparkford

ISBN 978-1-906697-15-0

1 2 3 4 5 6 7 8 9 10   14 13 12 11 10 09

Cover design: Arabia Books
Page design: AUC Press

Deliver us from evil

File 1

Containing Profiles of Certain Subjects
Residing in Zafarani Alley; Information Drawn
from Sources Who Are Closely Informed
about All that Goes on in the Alley

1

S aturday evening, first of Sha'ban. Usta Abdu Murad, having
completed the evening prayer at al-Hussein Mosque and having
attended the religious observance organized by the Broadcasting
Service on the occasion of the beginning of this Islamic month, came
finally to a decision about something over which he had been hesitat-
ing for quite a while. He hurried toward the room of Sheikh Atiya on
the ground floor of house number 7 in Zafarani Alley. Usta Abdu is
employed as a driver by the Cairo Transit Authority. Before joining the
said Authority, he drove cars for hire, in which occupation he held the
following positions:

> In 1949, after discharge from military service at the end of
> the Palestine War, he worked as driver of an intercity taxi-
> cab, transporting passengers between Cairo and Alexandria.
> The cab was a 1949 Ford that could carry seven passengers,
> and was owned by a sackcloth merchant in al-Khurunfish

by the name of Hagg Abu al-Yazid. Following a dispute that arose between them, Usta Abdu found himself unemployed. After three months of unemployment, he went back to work, this time driving a Cairo taxicab. For ten years he got on well with the owner of the cab, a good hagg who was a dealer in plumbing supplies and who always talked about his good fortune: how he had left his village in the deep South and walked all the way to Cairo, and how God had bestowed upon him so much of His bounty that he had now become one of the select few who sold and installed plumbing supplies, sinks, toilets, and the like. In addition, the good hagg also owned a truck and a number of taxicabs. Usta Abdu liked his job because of the different passengers he got to meet and the conversations he had with them. He would frequently recount the incident that had befallen him during the war when he was engaged in a bitter fight against the Jews in a Palestinian village called Majdal. He still bore the scar he had received just below the knee. He would describe how it had felt as the shrapnel penetrated his skin; how he thought he had died; how he moved his limbs; and how he came to. Only once did he ever show anyone his scar, and that was when two young men rode with him from Heliopolis to Saqiyat Mekki and seemed friendly. One of them even moved onto the front seat, to sit next to him. That pleased him immensely.

In 1957, Usta Abdu began employment with a private bus company. He worked on the Sakakini Square–Citadel line. He did not give up the cab, however, but drove it for hours at the end of his bus shift.

It is not known exactly when he married Sitt Busayna, but it is an established fact among the inhabitants of Zafarani Alley that the two made their acquaintance in the taxi. Whenever this was mentioned by the women, they would lower their voices and grimace in disgust upon pronouncing the word 'taxi' (thus implying that he had not asked for her hand from her family). The women would also allude to yet another facet of Sitt Busayna's life, namely her work during the Second World War as a dancer and her amassing of a fortune estimated at four hundred Egyptian pounds, a sum that had tempted Usta Abdu to wed her. She had bought for him, before the wedding, one suit, three pairs of trousers, five shirts, a number of socks, and underwear. Some people, but not many, claim that he had married her before the Palestine War, then divorced her after his return, and was now living with her in sin. Others maintain that he had not divorced her, and that the 'isma, or right to divorce, lay in her hands, and that she often beat him. Even on his way back from work every afternoon, he already looked as if he was afraid of her, as he walked quietly along the alley with head bowed, glancing neither left nor right, and speaking to no one, as though in a hurry. The kids of the alley would sometimes taunt him, shouting and sticking out their tongues. He never scolded them or even reacted at all. He just seemed scared and did not even complain to any of their parents.

This particular night, however, the first of Sha'ban, Usta Abdu did not enter his own house but, instead, went on right to the end of the alley. Zafarani, it should be noted, is a dead end that leads nowhere. House number 7 stands at the far end, and it is here, in a narrow room tucked under the main staircase, that Sheikh Atiya resides.

Usta Abdu entered the room and sat on the floor in front of the sheikh, whose head almost touched the sloping ceiling. The sheikh stroked the beads of the rosary hanging from his neck and said, "Well?"

3

The Usta spoke quickly and, just as his wife had instructed, came straight to the point, saying that his marital life was in jeopardy, that his home was falling apart, and that he didn't know what to do. He was no longer able to fulfill his conjugal duties, and this had already lasted a week. When he was engaged to be married, but before signing the contract, his fiancée, as she then was, had asked him specifically, "Can you water the soil, daily?" Refusing to believe his nod of affirmation, she had tested him thoroughly. For many years, apart from the days of her period, he had not ceased. She would fall ill and lose weight if he failed to mount her each and every day. This passing of a dry, unproductive week had been terrible, especially since his condition was showing no signs of improvement. He was getting so tense and his nerves were so bad that he now thought twice about going home. He feared she might give in to temptation because she had a fiery temper and her patience, in the present circumstances, had worn very thin. He said that he had tried folk remedies, bought herbs from al-Hamzawi, and had followed the advice of an old cab driver he knew who has had great experience in life.

The sheikh's eyes gleamed in the dark. Usta Abdu heard the sound of paper being shuffled. The sheikh was making calculations, mumbling in a childlike voice. The Usta dared not raise his head, but the sheikh seemed to be paying him no attention. The paper kept on being mysteriously shuffled about. If, Usta Abdu whispered with humility, he could not find a cure, his wife would kick him out. After a period of silence the sheikh said: "Come to me on the morning of Friday after next, at the moment of sunrise."

2

Sayyid Effendi al-Tekirli is an employee of the Department of Public Trusts. He often comes into the alley accompanied by other effendis who wear prescription glasses, and golden cuff links, and clean, shiny shoes. Some of those effendis carry handsome briefcases that, according to several Zafaranites, are worth twenty Egyptian pounds apiece. Various questions have been raised, from time to time, concerning those gentlemen: Are they his relatives? Are they just influential acquaintances? Some of them hold important positions of a certain 'special' kind inside those ministries and departments and Sayyid Effendi's relations with them have helped to resolve a good many of the alley's little problems.

When Sitt Wagida sought his advice, for instance, he did not hesitate to help her son, when his schooling was complete, to get into a vocational training center, where after only a short time he would leave with mastery of a skill or a trade, thus saving his family a lot of money and even helping with their expenses. Whenever the sewage pipe exploded Sayyid Effendi would immediately make a call, and in no time at all, workmen would arrive in great numbers to remove all the filth and clean the whole place up again. When a scorpion stung Aliya, daughter of Sitt Khadija, the Sa'idi woman, he went with her to the hospital and, on coming back, she told everyone how he had spoken to the doctors and the nurses as if he were a state minister or a director. Sayyid Effendi is the only one who can restore power to the alley within minutes of a cut. Many of the locals speak of the way in which he dials the telephone and of the rhythm of his voice as he shouts his distinctive "Hello!" He is the only one who is allowed to make calls at any time he wants from the telephone at Me'allim Daturi's café.

But in spite of Sayyid Effendi's many services to the inhabitants of Zafarani, he does not mix with them, and nobody knows what his apartment looks like from the inside. Some assert that he owns a refrigerator, a water heater, and a cassette recorder. But none of the women can eavesdrop on him because his apartment is situated on the top floor of Umm Kawsar's house, which is fifth on the right as you enter Zafarani

Alley but, as it stands opposite the low house belonging to Hagg Abdel Alim, which only has two stories, his apartment faces a wide, empty space.

On 8/4/1971 Umm Sabri conveyed to Sitt Busayna an important news item: she had seen Sayyid Effendi enter the house accompanied by a dark man wearing a white galabiya and 'uqal, speaking Arabic with a foreign accent. Sitt Busayna tsk-tsked and said that his beautiful wife still continued to ignore Zafarani women, and that whenever she stood on her balcony, even for a short while, she spoke to no one and wore a look of disgust. Umm Sabri said, "Homes are built on secrets; if she insists on acting so uppity and stuck up that she won't even greet her neighbors, what's keeping her in the alley? Why doesn't she move to a more sophisticated neighborhood where she can visit with uppity people like herself?"

The women of the alley keep their eyes on her and watch all her movements whenever she stands on her balcony, or hangs out her wash to dry, or looks down holding a bucket of water, waiting for passersby to leave Zafarani so she can empty it out. Each time she walks the short distance between her house and the alley entrance, the women discuss her clothes, trying to guess how much they cost and wondering who sewed them. They also discuss her strong perfume, and her hairdo gets a lot of attention as well. But it is her figure, tall and luscious as the green shoot of a plant, and the way she walks that make everyone look at her with the greatest of admiration.

Last year, Oweis the baker swore that, just as he had been getting ready to haul the dough racks from Hasan Effendi Anwar's house, he had seen a long car stop in al-Hussein Square and Sayyid Effendi and his wife had then got into it. Hasan Effendi's wife remembered what her son Hassan had told her: that as he came home late from the cinema one night, he had seen both of them get out of a red car. Oweis had told her the car was white. When she related what she had heard to her husband, he scolded her, telling her they should keep to themselves and that it was none of their business what Sayyid Effendi or anybody else for that matter rode or got into. He also asked Hassan, his son, not to convey such news again.

Sitt Umm Nabila would meanwhile listen warily to what was being said; she didn't like gossip as she feared the consequences for her daughter Nabila, especially since she was not yet married. However, she couldn't help remarking on the empty liquor bottles that she noticed in the garbage being collected by Abdu al-Wahati, the sweeper. He, when questioned, told her that the bottles had come from Sayyid Effendi's apartment. She then replied that Sayyid Effendi was a good sport to allow his acquaintances to spend the evening in his house, and that they did nothing to annoy the neighbors.

Just lately, during the last few days, several strange, new events had been noted. Some of these things were nothing extraordinary for Zafarani Alley. The inhabitants, for instance, were used to being woken up, late at night, by a quarrel in one family or other; somebody might go and stand on a high balcony and threaten to jump off, or might heap insults onto the entire alley when they were really aimed at the people they lived with. Certain families were notorious for this sort of behavior and certain quarrels stood out as memorable in the recent history of the alley. Among these, for instance, was the series of acrimonious fights between Zannuba, the nurse, and her husband Umar, who had worked as a conductor for some time and who had been fired, though nobody knew why. Equally memorable were the quarrels of the Umm Sabri family and those involving Farida the White shouting at her husband Hussein the Radish-head. Farida's shouting was usually quite funny and the neighbors loved it, especially since it was harmless. It was even more entertaining when Farida rejected the playful amorous advances of her pygmy husband. If he protested and left the house in a huff, she would stand on the balcony, stick out her tongue at him, and then spray him with water. As soon as he disappeared around the corner, she would start up a conversation with one of her neighbors as if nothing had happened.

The alley dreaded Sitt Busayna's quarrels, however, because she knew the greatest number of insults and obscenities and had the ability to deliver them in vast quantities in the shortest possible time. Sometimes she attacked her opponent physically by laying her flat on the ground and beating her with her slipper on the most sensitive and private parts of the body. Neighbors did not let quarrels go on for long, though, and more often than not would go over to the house of the family concerned and spend hours with them. Each member of the family would then list all the things that were bothering him or her. Sometimes people threatened to commit suicide and would actually proceed to pour kerosene on themselves or attempt to jump from windows. On occasions such as these, everyone rushed to the scene where the screaming was loudest. That was how the most intimate secrets in Zafarani Alley usually came to be known. That was the norm. For the screaming however, to be coming from Sayyid Effendi al-Tekirli's apartment was doubly interesting.

In its first few moments, Daturi thought the voices were coming from Qurqur the musician's house, but the voices seemed different and the very manner of the screaming itself was such that he shifted his huge body and opened the window, while trying to trace the noises to their source. To his utmost amazement, it turned out to be Tekirli. Meanwhile Atif, the college graduate, who lived on the third floor of the same house and who was interested in Tekirli's wife, reported that when he had heard the loud voices and the sound of dishes breaking, he had gone to peer out of his window which overlooked the inner courtyard, and from which he could catch even the slightest movement inside the house, since, not being near any passing cars or trams, and with the shouts and noise of the kids usually dying down at dusk when they went home, there was deep silence in Zafarani at night. Tekirli's voice was coming through, loud and clear, as he responded to someone who was speaking so fast that Atif couldn't make out the exact words, especially since the man had a strange accent. These are some of the things that Tekirli said: "I am not responsible for this." "I will not give you back one single penny." "You're the one with the problem!" Over the next few days, these quarrels came to be repeated many times over, with loud voices coming quite clearly from Tekirli's house. On the fourth day, Atif, and Me'allim Daturi, and Hassan son of Hasan Effendi Anwar, and Umm Suhair all heard the soft, tearful voice of Tekirli's wife: "I've had enough. I can't take it anymore. I just can't."

3

Name: Hussein al-Haruni, also known as Radish-head

Occupation: Grocer; also works as *meseherati* of Zafarani and neighboring alleys; he inherited the job from his father.

Place of Birth: Number 3 Zafarani Alley

Current Address: Number 3 Zafarani Alley

Distinguishing Marks: Height 127 cm; head elongated, curved, pointing upward, narrowing at the top like a sugar cone or radish; eyes round like marbles, pupils always cast down as if in consternation; lips parted, and sometimes visible, a very fine line of saliva threading its way from mouth to chin.

Marital Status and Some Relevant Developments: One Sunday morning, toward the end of December 1957, Hussein Radish-head had been sitting outside Daturi's café. It was sunny and the streets were empty. A white girl had come along carrying a kerosene-filled can (it was later learned that she was doing some shopping for household things). The said white girl smiled at another girl coming the other way and asked about the seamstress who had sewn her new dress. Radish-head was forced to lean slightly forward to see the white girl properly. He filled his eyes with the sight of her and noted that her face was scattered with freckles. He turned to Me'allim Daturi and asked: "Whose daughter is this?" After casting a leisurely glance the me'allim replied, "Would you like to marry her?" Hussein's lips parted even wider; he clutched the mouthpiece of his hookah, nodded, and loudly expressed the wish that this would happen. Thereupon the me'allim imparted some further information. He told him that her name was Farida and that she was the daughter of Police Corporal Hadu'ah, a good man who loved al-Hussein, and who never harmed anybody or informed on anyone. He did not use narcotics either, in spite of working at the Darb al-Ahmar precinct, which had jurisdiction over Batiniya, which everyone knew was filled with hashish and opium dealers—a fact that presented him with plenty of opportunities for getting free highs. He was the father of seven: three boys and four girls. Daturi said that the corporal would not refuse him anything, that he would even welcome it, since Farida, his eldest, was the pride and joy of his life. On that same Sunday, and before any further steps could be taken, Radish-head went up to the rooftop where his mother, Umm al-Khair, lived in a room that she herself had built.

Nobody knew Umm al-Khair's real age. Her body was so bent that her head almost touched her feet. Some people claimed that she was over a hundred years old and that she already had her green teeth, popularly presumed to presage death. She never mixed with the neighbors or stood around with the other women. Sometimes she crossed the alley on her way to visit one holy shrine or another. From her neck hung a bag made of sturdy cloth, the contents of which nobody knew. She would disappear for days on end and no one would notice.

Sometimes, however, while the inhabitants were standing on their balconies, they would have the weird sensation of being watched. They would raise their heads and, with a shudder, their eyes would meet those of Umm al-Khair, whose head seemed to survey the whole alley and, with the fence hiding her body, appeared to be floating there, detached. The neighbors would wonder how her bent body had managed to straighten up. Standing there in that fashion she never said a word or nodded any greeting, but spent hours looking in one single direction. Everyone thought it was himself alone she was watching, looking at just him or her personally. Some of the neighbors would feel obliged to close their windows and balcony doors, yet when they looked again some time later, they would still find her there in the same position. But then she would disappear for days. Sometimes she would come to a halt on her slow walk along the street and look up at someone, who then, in turn, would flee.

She was all the family that Radish-head had. He did nothing without telling her. She never responded or answered his questions. Perhaps he gathered from her features or movements or sensed from certain signs that she had said yes or no. Anyway, when he told her about Farida, she made no apparent movement, yet he still hurried enthusiastically to Daturi and told him that his mother had approved.

When the news of Radish-head's impending marriage spread, there were various reactions: some women showed dismay, especially Umm Sabri and Umm Hamada (who died four years ago), both of whom were mothers of at least one daughter or more. Radish-head did not look like much, but it was well known that he was rich and extremely stingy. He was never seen wearing anything other than his one galabiya, of which it was said that, should he ever take it off, it would stand up on its own, from all the dirt that had collected in it. He had inherited from his father a whole house in Zafarani Alley and another in Darb al-Farrakha which, rumor had it, he intended to tear down so as to build a huge apartment building. He had also inherited the grocery store located in front of Darb al-Masmat Alley. The most important item in that grocery store was a large glass container filled with big pickled limes that had split with age; even the pips had become soft. At one time, when things were cheap, he would sell them for three piasters apiece; now he sold them for five. He spent long hours and much effort preparing these limes and considered their pickling a secret that should never be divulged.

His most precious possession, however, was a huge warehouse located under his house in Zafarani and extending God knew how far. Its entrance was like a tomb—and haunted, it was said. It branched out into several warehouses, all of them underground. Radish-head used to go into it at any time of the day or night. The warehouse was full of furniture, rugs, hats, old picture frames, mirrors, books in unknown languages, records, wooden boxes inlaid with ivory and mother-of-pearl, iron tools, electric elevators, and coal-fired stoves. In one deal, Radish-head brought out a huge motorcar engine and charged a merchant four hundred Egyptian pounds for it. It was said that the warehouse contained cars of different models, that he even had in there the very first automobile that had ever entered Egypt. The inhabitants once saw him hauling some huge metal object. When asked what it was, he said it was the smokestack of a train.

Radish-head usually closed his grocery store on Sundays and Fridays and went to the auctions, where he would get his stuff. All the owners and managers of private and government-run auction halls knew him. Everything that he bought he brought back to the warehouse. In 1954 some trouble-maker once made a report to the Gammaliya police station that he suspected a pharaonic mummy, ancient gold jewelry, and cadavers for medical students were to be found in the warehouse belonging to

Radish-head. For some reason the complaint was turned over to the directorate of political police, which duly raided the warehouse on a Thursday evening. They fetched Radish-head, who most unhappily unlocked the huge locks and the big steel bars. No trace of mummies or cadavers was found. The commander of the raiding force said there were indeed numerous pharaonic relics inside, but when these were examined they turned out to be reproductions that were permitted to be bought and sold. Several rumors about the incident of the warehouse search were circulated. Some people said that Radish-head had somehow managed to close off whole sections of the warehouse so that even the most careful searcher would not suspect the existence of other passages or rooms. (Some even suggested the existence of an underground tunnel running under all of Cairo, beginning from the warehouse and ending in the Dahshur desert.) It was said that Radish-head had bribed the commander of the raiding force with a huge sum of money to make his misleading report. It was also said that a force of guardian jinn hid everything in the warehouse from all human eyes except those of Radish-head. Some people, however, said that the government had learned of large quantities of gold in the warehouse vault and that was the reason they didn't want to draw attention to it, but that they were keeping Radish-head under permanent and strict surveillance to prevent him smuggling the gold out of the country. The government considered that gold to be part of the strategic reserve of the national economy. It was reflected, they said, in the budget of fiscal year 1955, and the factories that were built later on were only made possible thanks to that peculiar gold cover.

After the political police raid on the warehouse, the grocery store had remained shuttered for seven days in a row, which Radish-head spent inside the warehouse putting his possessions in order. Nobody saw him for an entire week, which meant there must have been sources of food and water inside; otherwise where else did he get what he ate and drank all that time?

It was also rumored that Radish-head collected coins as a hobby. He had an account with the National Bank, al-Azhar branch, but because the bank kept its customers' accounts confidential, no one could find out how much his account contained. He always told those who were close to him that he never saved, even though everyone knew he kept large amounts of currency in his house. But he was telling the truth; he collected money, but didn't save it. He kept whatever metal piasters—round or with holes in the middle—he could get his hands on. These he put in a big can until it filled up. Some nights he would bring out a washtub and empty the cans of piasters into it, listening to the sounds of metal hitting metal, arranging the coins in rows, adjusting their positions, writing letters and words with them, making mysterious geometrical patterns. Later it was learned from Farida that he kept a can full of hexagonal two-piaster pieces made of pure silver that had totally disappeared from circulation because each of the coins was worth more than fifty piasters due to its silver content. He had another can full of round gold coins that he counted once every fortnight, then washed in rose water. He had coins dating back to the Ottoman empire, and some dating even further back to Mamluk times. He had Indian coins, Ethiopian coins, and Chinese coins, all made of gold or silver.

All the women of the alley knew of Radish-head's untold wealth, and each wished he would propose to one of her daughters. Umm Sabri invited him to her house and spread out a banquet for him, for he loved to be invited to lunch or supper; not only would he save the cost of a meal, but, being wifeless, he was under no obligation to reciprocate. Umm Aliya once said jokingly to Sitt Busayna that perhaps the real reason Radish-head was afraid of marrying was that he would lose his excuse for not returning invitations.

14

Then suddenly, one day, three horse-drawn carts carrying furniture entered the alley. One of them carried chairs and a fully assembled armoire in which there were hanging brightly colored galabiyas and dresses. Another cart carried pillows and rose-colored covers and a tray on which sat three full covered earthen water jars. Radish-head soon appeared on the scene and began to supervise the moving of the furniture. When the porters were done, a quarrel broke out between Radish-head and the drivers of the carts over payment. In point of fact, Radish-head was not being unfair, because the carts had not come very far, yet the drivers were insisting on double tips since it was not every day that they moved bridal furniture. The quarrel did not last long; Radish-head caved in and gave them what they were asking—a very rare occurrence in his life.

The arrival of the furniture, accompanied by drum beats and the shrill, trilling ululations of joy, as were customary, was considered the culmination of a long phase of discussions and negotiations with the bride's family. At the beginning, Radish-head had offered to provide the furniture himself from his own warehouse in return for not paying a dowry. Police Corporal Hadu'ah welcomed this idea, for if he were paid one hundred Egyptian pounds as a dowry, he would have to add double that amount to it, and this was difficult for him. The mother of the bride, however, rejected the idea, saying that her first joy shouldn't begin her new life with old furniture. Radish-head countered by saying that he was willing to pay fifty Egyptian pounds, one bank note, for the bride. The mother was visibly perturbed. She said her daughter was worth much more than that. After a lot of give and take and numerous discussions in which Me'allim Daturi also played a part, it was decided that Radish-head would pay eighty Egyptian pounds and would be responsible for furnishing the kitchen, providing the tea cups, the drapes, a full service of chinaware, forks, spoons, knives, and one mattress. He told Me'allim Daturi that he had a gold leaf bed on which, for many years, one of the eunuchs of the royal palace had lain (in other words, no woman had ever slept in it). From the moment Radish-head had got hold of that bed, he had been determined not to part with it under any circumstances, and in spite of the high prices he was offered by antique dealers. He told the me'allim that he was going to set it up and sleep in this bed and the new one on alternate nights. When Daturi told him he could do whatever he liked, but not to talk about what went on in his own house, Radish-head nodded obediently.

Two days before the wedding ceremony, a problem arose: Farida was only fourteen years old. Daturi, however, went to a Health Department physician and paid him five Egyptian pounds in return for which three years were added to Farida's age. Thus she became a seventeen-year-old bride. One week after the day of the consummation of the marriage, the women of the alley started whispering among themselves that Farida was still a virgin. It was not known how this news spread. Young men added several details. They said the girl was afraid to lie beside Radish-head because his eyes glowed in the dark and his running saliva disgusted her. They talked of how she had hated him from the very first night because as soon as they were alone, he had proceeded to examine her all over, feeling her arms, counting her teeth, tapping her knuckles.

Some of the whispers reached Daturi's ears and he called Radish-head over and told him what was being said. Radish-head said the girl was still young, that she didn't know anything about these matters, and that whenever he approached her she cried and he backed away, embarrassed. Thereupon the me'allim tapped him on the knee and said, "Crying is a sign of consent." He told Radish-head that he should do that which would silence those tongues. He said that he had never made a match that failed, and that he had his own name to protect. On the following day the windows of the newlyweds' apartment remained shut; the grocery store remained shut; and the iron bars across the doors of the warehouse stayed in place. The alley's inhabitants whispered, "Radish-head is settling his account."

Three days later he emerged, heading directly for his grocery store. Several women went to pay a visit to their new neighbor. She offered them the traditional sharbat fruit drink and she looked sweet and fresh. But Umm Sabri told Umm Suhair that very evening that the bride was but a child, that she was not yet mature, but giddy and careless. Umm Suhair said that while it was true she was white and her eyes were as green as lettuce leaves, she still had freckles all over her neck. Umm Nabila pointed out that the bride was thin, that her body was frail, and that for women like her neither the prescriptions of apothecaries nor fattening medicines could do any good. Umm Aliya lay especial emphasis on her sharp, long nose. Sitt Wagida, the Bannan woman, Rhode, and the wife of Hasan Effendi Anwar all agreed that her legs were skinny. Zannuba, the nurse, noticed something that had escaped the attention of everyone else who was present, namely, that the drink offered to them didn't have enough sugar in it, which meant that she was no good at housekeeping. At that moment they were all unanimous on one thing in particular, namely, that her youth and inexperience made the performance of her marital duties, such as the sweeping of floors and cooking, a highly doubtful proposition. She could not, they asserted, last long.

In the days that followed their visit, several phenomena were observed by the women of the alley. Farida not only kept away from her female neighbors, she seemed to ignore their very existence. A case in point: Farida failed to greet Umm Suhair even though the latter was right there in front of her, just across the narrow alley. This had prompted

Umm Suhair to shout at her own daughter (four years old at the time), "Suhair, you're just a little cop's kid!" which was obviously an attempt to pick a fight since Suhair's father was in fact a carpenter and not a policeman, as was Farida's. It was also observed that Farida tended to befriend little girls. One Tuesday afternoon, for instance, Umm Yusif happened to hear the sound of children playing noisily on the staircase. She opened her apartment door and shouted to scare them away, as their racket was threatening to disturb Tahun Effendi Gharib, "who toiled all night long and could never sleep a wink in this stinking alley." As usual, she prayed to God to free her family from Zafarani. Hardly had she finished her prayer when she caught sight of Farida running about and playing with the other children. Another case in point: Umm Aliya conducted a very thorough interrogation of her daughter, who confessed to the following: Farida had called her over and had given her a piece of candy; the two of them had gone up to the roof and, in full view of Radish-head's old mother, they had drawn lines on the flat roof with white chalk; Farida had then fetched an old, empty tin of shoe polish; and the two of them had begun hopping along on one foot, pushing the shoe polish tin across the squares drawn on the roof; in short, they had played hopscotch.

As days went by, however, Farida began to visit some of her neighbors. Her demeanor during such visits was described in various accounts as: "merry," "laughing," "showing no care or worry about tomorrow," "no complaints about being short of cooking oil or sugar," "not once did she lean over to whisper a request to borrow five piasters." Farida had no qualms or reluctance about broaching any subject at all. So, when Umm Suhair enquired how her husband was doing, she started describing all his affairs in her childishly merry way, divulging valuable information which was very quickly circulated and thus brought a change in the prevailing image. Upon hearing some of the details,

Hagg Hanafi, the cattle prognosticator, usually hired to tell the sex of an unborn calf, said that God had made it up to Radish-head several times over from His bounty. Umm Suhair said that what Farida described was beyond all expectations and estimates, and she remarked on the way Farida walked after her marriage. Umm Sabri said she had met Farida at Muhammad the greengrocer's and noticed that her wallet was full of money. Certain facts were established after intensive surveillance was successfully conducted, on account of her proximity, by Umm Suhair. A meticulous inventory of the clothes hung out to dry on the clothesline revealed that the number of expensive see-through sets of underwear came to more than twenty, and all were imported. As for dresses, Umm Suhair, losing count, came to the conclusion that they were innumerable.

One Wednesday morning, Sitt Busayna suffered a tremendous anxiety attack when she saw a small cart entering the alley, pushed by a man wearing a shirt, a pair of pants, and a pair of sandals. On the cart was an electric washing machine. She displayed signs of stifled vexation; the washing machine would now be the central conversation piece among the women of the alley. They would go over to see how it worked and what it did. Sitt Busayna had always made a point of being the first person in the alley to buy modern appliances. No matter how much time passed, the inhabitants of Zafarani would never forget the very first radio set that had been introduced into the alley in 1951. On Umm Kulthum concert nights, Sitt Busayna would place it on the sill of the window overlooking the alley, having called Abu Ghazala, the electrician, to install an electrical outlet next to the window so that the whole alley could listen. Sometimes, however, when Sitt Busayna had had a row with one of the women, the radio was her means of making her displeasure and anger public: it made no sense for her to turn on the radio for one of her enemies. When that happened the men would protest, Was it any fault of theirs? Hasan Effendi Anwar would say, "You are goodness itself!" Whereupon she would feel satisfied, since any compliment bestowed loudly upon herself would be considered a dig at her rival. She would declare that for the sake of the genuine, noble Zafaranites—and not those alien upstarts who plagued Zafarani, at this, the end of time, those dregs whom even the dirty neighborhoods had spat out—for the sake of the good, loving, caring people who had built the alley brick by brick, she was going to turn on the radio.

The alley could also not forget that it was Sitt Busayna who had first introduced the butane gas oven. When it came home accompanied by a procession of children, she stopped at every house to explain to the women its advantages and the way it worked. When it was time to change the tank, she would shout loudly from her window, calling one of the boys to run and make the delivery man hurry up. Sometimes, while engaged in a conversation with one of her neighbors, her voice would suddenly grow louder: the potato casserole was in the oven and she had to go in to watch it.

Sitt Busayna did not wait long. One month after the arrival of the washing machine at Radish-head's house, a cart carrying a washing machine of a different model entered the alley. Sitt Busayna declared in a chat with Sitt Altaff that her washing machine was unequalled, that it was expensive, and that only four such machines could be found in the whole land of Egypt: three were in the palaces of the rulers and the fourth was in her house. When she got to that part, her voice grew deliberately louder while Farida stood on her balcony. Radish-head's wife, however, paid no attention to the intended provocation. In the evening, Qurqur the musician told Tahun Effendi that Sitt Busayna's four-hundred-pound savings had considerably dwindled with the purchase of the washing machine.

In the summer following Radish-head's marriage, the alley was caught up in a serious contest. Early one morning, as she went out to buy fuul and milk, Umm Suhair saw Radish-head wearing a new coat and walking along with his wife; behind them was a man carrying two suitcases. Umm Suhair murmured a morning greeting to them and asked where they were heading. In a childish tone of voice Farida said they were leaving to spend two weeks at a summer resort. The news spread like wildfire throughout Zafarani, becoming the major topic of the morning conversations conducted from balconies and on staircases. Someone said that it was one of the portents of the Day of Judgment, since Radish-head had never in his life gone to a cinema or a theater or an amusement park. How could he then bring himself to travel and part with the money needed for a summer resort? Daturi said, "Love works miracles!"

The news caused great perturbation to Sitt Busayna, who immediately laid the blame on her own husband Usta Abdu, reminding him of her suggestion two years back—that they go for a week to a summer resort to rest their bodies. Usta Abdu didn't answer. He couldn't swear that she had made any such suggestion. She told him anyway to tell this story to everybody he met. She thought of going to one of her relatives just to disappear for two weeks and then come back to say that she had been in the summer resort of Ras al-Barr. But that appeared too obvious; everyone would say that she was jealous of Radish-head's wife.

Sitt Busayna could not sleep that night. The following day she quickly did the round of her neighbors. She attacked Farida, who had introduced new heresies into the alley. She proclaimed that going to a summer resort was a sinful disgrace because women uncovered their breasts and thighs and because on the sands of the beach reprehensible and dirty abominations took place. She lowered her voice when she said that the young girl had turned the head of Radish-head and persuaded

21

him to travel. There, in the summer resort, she would be with him on her own and it would be easy for her to fool around with the young men. In the alley she was under the watchful eyes of the honest and righteous inhabitants. But at the summer resort everything happened under the very noses of the most experienced of husbands. Sitt Busayna said that if Farida were truly upright, she would have taken her old mother-in-law along. It wasn't enough that she had driven a wedge between her husband and the old woman; he had to leave his mother by herself, suffering under the painful burden of her hundred years. She asserted to everybody that Radish-head had begged his wife to let his mother go along; that he had said that, if they left his mother behind, she might die alone and be eaten by cats and rats. Farida, Sitt Busayna added, had categorically refused. Why? To fool around in the resort without supervision. At dawn yesterday, the old woman had groaned and moaned for a long time and Sitt Busayna had felt such pity for her. The women of the alley, she urged, must all unite to face this disgrace. It was enough that Radish-head had gotten away and married from another alley. Umm Aliya interrupted Sitt Busayna's ranting, retorting angrily that if the likes of Radish-head were to propose to her daughter offering their weight in gold for her hand, she would never accept their proposal. Sitt Busayna thought to herself: This woman is feigning rejection now, but she had worn out her shoes chasing after him to marry her daughter Aliya, even borrowing three Egyptian pounds to buy a goose, ghee, and vegetables when she spread out a banquet for him.

Sitt Busayna's visits to her neighbors continued, daily. Once she even forgot and visited Umm Yusif twice on the same day, telling her the same story a second time. On realizing her mistake, she knew it could spoil her objective, but that didn't stop her. Throughout the following days she showed extreme zeal and passion in her appeal to the alley to boycott the little slut. In front of Muhammad the greengrocer's, Umm Nabila told Umm Yusif that Sitt Busayna was the last person one would expect to be so zealous in defending the honor of the alley, considering her past of dancing and well-documented debauchery. Saying no more, she requested Umm Yusif not to repeat what she had just said, to keep out of trouble.

Two weeks after Radish-head and his wife had left, Umm Suhair heard noise and commotion in Zafarani, early in the morning, and she looked out of the window. The windows of Radish-head's apartment were open. She shouted to inquire who was there. Who could tell? Perhaps burglars were busy at work. She heard quick footsteps on the tiled floor of the apartment and then Farida looked out, smiling, her white skin having acquired a bronze tan. Umm Suhair gave her a very warm welcome. The news reached Sitt Busayna around ten o'clock, since she didn't get up as early in the morning as the other women of the alley. It was said that this was a habit she had acquired during her career as a dancer during the war. She learned of Umm Suhair's warm welcome and her saying literally that the alley was dark when Farida was away and that the light had returned when she returned. Sitt Busayna also learned of Farida's visit to Umm Yusif—a visit that lasted three hours—but she had no idea what took place during the visit.

Here are some of the details of what happened during that visit: Farida took two bags, one filled with chufa and the other filled with sesame and roasted chickpea brittle, to her neighbor Umm Yusif and told her about the summer resort, how they went into the sea in a secluded area, how they went in just far enough that the water covered her breasts. Farida laughed as she told Umm Yusif how she pressed her husband's head down in the water several times and how he kept flapping his hands about like a fish that was not quite dead. She also said that he did what shouldn't be done, in the water. Umm Yusif expressed surprise.

Farida said that he had wondered whether it could be done and then went ahead and did it; they had sat facing each other in the shallow water near the beach, then he came up close to her, and although their heads appeared separated to whomever might look at them from the beach, their two bodies were perfectly welded together down below. She said that it was very exciting, the very best time they had done it, ever. He bought her whatever she desired. She ate a kind of ice cream called kluklu and some grilled Suez shrimp. Once as they were out on a walk at sunset they were hassled by some young men, one of whom wondered how such a monkey could beget such a houri, and that made her laugh. She laughed again as she related the story and nudged Umm Yusif on her knee, saying, "They thought I was his daughter!" She also told her that in the evening they didn't go out; he would always pull her to him early in the evening and not leave her until dawn. Farida laughed with childish coyness. Umm Yusif wondered whether that took place everyday in the summer resort. Farida said that that had been happening daily since the wedding. At the beginning, the whole matter seemed meaningless; her husband would be drenched in sweat and his breathing would get heavier as he made love to her, while she would amuse herself by sucking a piece of candy or hitting him on the back in playful rebuke every now and then or asking him to tell her a joke. Strangely enough, he did whatever she asked him to do, but he never stopped; she got used to that.

Umm Yusif listened in amazement at the simplicity with which Farida was saying those things, visualized what she was hearing and said to herself: Oh God! You do indeed give your secret to the weakest of your creatures! Farida said that her husband had enjoyed himself enormously and had told her that any time she wanted to travel, he would close the store and go off with her. Umm Yusif laughed and said that her going away didn't please certain people. Farida was somewhat surprised. Umm Yusif added that some of the women of the alley had no love for other people and wouldn't just let them be. Among those was Busayna the dancer; nobody was safe from her tongue. She was a foul-mouthed tramp who threw her melaya to the ground and wouldn't hesitate to take off all her clothes in any fight she got involved in. Since Farida's departure, she had not stopped badmouthing her. Umm Yusif hesitated when she noticed that Farida showed no interest in what she was saying, but she added that Busayna had called Master Hussein an improper name. She pursed her lips, saying that she couldn't repeat that name since she saw in him a good man who provided everything that his household required. Farida interrupted her with quick movements that shook her body as if she were a child tugging at her father's arm to buy her some candy. "For the sake of the Prophet, please, please tell me." Umm Yusif asked God's forgiveness and said, "She called him 'Radish-head.'" Farida paused to think for a moment, then she burst into loud, merry laughter. It was no laughing matter, responded Umm Yusif, and if she herself were to hear somebody use such words to describe her own husband, she would most certainly rip him apart. Farida pictured her husband entering the house with his eyes fixed on the floor. She saw him with her mind's eye getting up at night to gaze at his money. Sometimes, when he was preoccupied with something or other, she would slip her fingers under his armpits, and tickle him. Then he would lose control, and start writhing with laughter. How well that name suited him!

In the afternoon, Umm Suhair called out to Farida. Farida had begun to enjoy her visits with the women, listening to stories and catching up on the gossip. She took some candy with her. Umm Suhair said that was an unnecessary expense. Farida answered simply: "Take it, please." Umm Suhair exclaimed as she was taking the disks of sesame and roasted chickpea candy, "God's blessings on the Prophet! God protect her! God save both of them! Grant her your blessings, Oh Sayyid!"

After a short conversation, Umm Suhair told Farida that there was something she wanted to share with her. Once again Farida listened to what Busayna had been saying about her. What surprised Umm Suhair was that Farida didn't show any reaction, but suddenly got up because, as she said, she was expecting some friends. Outside, three girls wearing school uniform were waiting in the alley, and they shrieked with delight when they saw she was back.

Sitt Busayna learned that everything she had said had reached Farida's ears, together with yet further things that she had never actually said. Stifling her vexation, she postponed her vengeance on the whole lot of them until some later date. She wished that brat of a girl would show some sign of hostility; then she would really show her. She would let off all her anger and wage one of her most violent battles. She would have a brawl that would be a landmark in the history of the alley for years to come. Farida's interest in the whole matter, however, was confined to the nickname 'Radish-head,' and when she chanced upon Busayna in the alley and remembered that it was she who had given her husband that nickname, a spirit of mischievous merriment took hold of her and she bowed her head in greeting, but Busayna ignored her, drawing out her lips in contempt. What really bothered Busayna was that the girl was ignoring her provocations, which she took to be an act of defiance that must be answered and crushed.

Farida no longer called her husband anything but Radish-head. One night she said to him, "I love you, Radish-head." He clapped his hands, kicked his legs high in the air and said with glee, "Say it again!" She repeated: "I love you, Radish-head," and he became even more ecstatic, even though earlier in the day he had had problems because of this very description. Some boys had shouted, "What's up, Radish-head?" He had turned very angry and chased them but couldn't catch a single one. An impish boy named Hamdi had broken away from his playmates and came up to Radish-head, telling him that the leader of the group was Marzuq, son of Umm Marzuq. Radish-head had immediately gone to the Gammaliya police station and asked the officer in charge to take down his statement. The officer had then sent a policeman to bring Marzuq in. When the boy's mother saw the policeman with papers in his hand, she had cried out, "I'm ruined!" She went to the station and offered herself in place of her son. She wept and begged Radish-head, reminding him of his future children. He had insisted on pressing charges and proceeding with measures that would send the boy to a reformatory, because he had almost lost his life on the boy's account. At that moment a policeman had come in, holding Marzuq by the collar of his galabiya. Umm Marzuq had cried out: "By the life of Sitt Farida!" Radish-head had seemed confused for a moment. The officer, noticing his reluctance, asked him: "Would you like to drop the charges?" He nodded an affirmative, whereupon the officer turned to Marzuq and told him to go kiss the head of his uncle Hussein. The boy approached fearfully; he didn't have to reach up that far because they were almost the same height. Later he swore to his friends that Radish-head's head felt like a turnip.

The incident received mixed reviews; most people protested that Radish-head had possibly endangered the little boy's future, subjecting him to a possible beating at the police station. Such a beating could well leave him with a fright that would stay with him the rest of his life, no matter how long he lived; it might even cause him to be ill. The comments encouraged Marzuq, who lay in ambush for Radish-head to walk under their balcony, and then doused him with the water that had collected in the tray beneath the water cooling jars. Farida happened to be standing nearby and saw her husband get wet. She rose on her feet, winked when she saw him shivering and insisted mischievously that he should take a cold bath. She wished her friends had been there to see his long underpants and his fear, like a small boy's, of the icy water. Two days later, Marzuq threw a cabbage stalk at him, whereupon Radish-head went to Me'allim Daturi, asking him to intervene to protect him. The me'allim summoned Umm Marzuq and demanded that she put an end to these acts of aggression that might provoke Radish-head to retaliate. Umm Marzuq promised to restrain her son, for she was all alone without support, as her husband had deserted her and she couldn't go to the police station again and see that officer, "the one with the stars."

In later months and years, Farida grew into a mature, splendid female, the mother of two daughters, Nashwa and Mervat, who bore no resemblance whatsoever to their father. When the family went out together the mother and daughters looked like sisters, they were so close in age. Their father, meanwhile, looked more like a stranger who was just accompanying them. Farida kept her childish manner and often joined her daughters in their little games. The two girls had no respect for their father and, whenever a slight dispute arose between their parents, they automatically took their mother's side. As for Radish-head, he showed no signs of age; his hair was still black, his gait, his weight, and his stature were neither more nor less than they had always been; even the expression on his face as he confronted the world remained totally unchanged. Yet now the inhabitants of Zafarani could swear without perjuring themselves that not one of them had seen Radish-head leave his house once throughout the last three days. What was also certain was that not one of the neighbors had inquired about his absence; Umm Suhair who lived in the house opposite to him did not inquire; and Umm Yusif mentioned not a word.

It should also be noted, moreover, that quite a number of the other windows in Zafarani had not been opened in the last few days; not even the window of Atif the bachelor, whom the alley had become accustomed to seeing standing there just before sunset every day, summer and winter, wearing his suit. It seemed as if certain extraordinary concerns were keeping the inhabitants apart. What was indisputably certain, and supported by several of the historical sources as well as the oral accounts of old timers, was that this was an occurrence without precedent in the history of Zafarani. On the fourth day of Radishhead's non-appearance, he suddenly came out of his front door and made his way up toward the end of the alley. He had only ever walked along that part of the alley twice before in his whole life: once to offer condolences upon the death of Hasan Effendi's grandfather, and the second time to look at an old chaise longue whose owner, the late Amina, had wanted to sell when things got tight for her. He paused a little in front of the last house, then crossed its dark threshhold. A voice mysteriously rose up if as if from underground. "Enter in God's peace." As he stepped inside the room, he heard Sheikh Atiya say that he knew all that Hussein al-Haruni had come to tell him, that he would say nothing further before next Friday, and would do so only if he came at seven minutes before sunrise.

4

Eight o'clock on this evening, a Wednesday, was a decisive hour for Atif the bachelor, employee of the General Authority for the Planting of Vegetables, law school graduate, the only college graduate in Zafarani, living by himself in a three-bedroom apartment on the third floor of house number 5—or as the inhabitants of the alley called it, Umm Muhammad's house, although she was not in fact the landlady. It was named after her because she always sat outside the front door, sometimes chatting with the women of the alley. The actual landlady was Umm Kawsar, the Alexandrian, who lived in Birguwan Alley and came round only once a month, on the fifth, to collect the rent.

Now Atif the bachelor is peeping through the holes in the wooden shutters that cover the window. Part of the paved surface of the alley and the opposite house are visible. The lamp light annoys him. He wishes the alley were as dark as it usually is most nights, even though it is he who most often volunteers to replace the lamp to keep the alley properly lit. The boys don't leave a lamp whole for two days in a row. While playing, one of them will kick the ball and break the bulb, then they all run away, even though nobody ever does anything to them. The most that can happen is that someone will yell at them, cursing their grandfathers, their fathers, and their mothers for pushing them out into the alley to get some peace and quiet at home. Now he wishes the lamp were broken. He can see watermelon rinds, vegetable waste, a broken basket. Years ago the lamps were gas-lit. He still remembers a man who used to carry a long ladder that he leaned against the wall to light the lamp. Sometimes he didn't show up and the night would prevail unopposed.

Now Atif's heart is beating fast. He swallows hard. Rhode is coming down the alley; he goes to the apartment door and opens it quietly. He listens for the sound of her slippers on the stairs but hears nothing: she is climbing carefully. If some woman stops her she will have all kinds of excuses ready. When she knocks on the door they will both go straight into the bedroom. The first room is empty but for a desk, three chairs, and a shelf containing a few books. Going directly to the bedroom will cut out the stage of moving from the study. He will ask her to sit on the bed. For a few moments he recalls how he had become acquainted with Rhode. He knows that in all his comings and goings, his every movement is being monitored and the slightest glance at any woman will be held against him, since he is the only bachelor in the alley.

Sometime during the first few months after he had moved to Zafarani, Hagg Hanafi the cattle prognosticator had come to him. He had suggested that Atif bring his mother over from the village to live with him, to look after him and keep him company. Atif had responded with hostility and since that time nobody has ever mentioned the idea again. When the inhabitants learned that he was a respectable employee and a college graduate they showed him due respect, and he in turn did nothing to upset them. As time passed, he noticed that the women of the alley all watched him intently every day as he left each evening just before sunset, wearing his suit and his glasses with his hair glistening in the faint, departing light of the day, walking slowly until he disappeared around the corner.

It was usually at that time of the day, with the passing of daylight, that the women came out to their balconies or windows, to talk or stare at the alley, where there was no new movement and where strangers seldom appeared, since it was a dead end. The women would make guesses about Atif's destination. Once Sitt Busayna said that her husband, driving his cab in the afternoon one day, had been hailed by three young men and two women. He was surprised to see that Atif was one of them. He gathered from the conversation that they were all heading for someone's house, and because of his long experience as a taxi driver he realized what kind of a party they were going to have. Atif didn't recognize him and appeared to be the merriest and the most shameless of the bunch. Usta Abdu was so amazed that he thought it was somebody else, but he saw Atif's face well in the rearview mirror. In another story, Umm Yusif said he had been seen with a very beautiful girl on Fuad Street. Umm Suhair commented that this was natural for somebody his age. He could do whatever he liked outside Zafarani, so long as he observed decorum with his neighbors and didn't hurt their feelings. Umm Yusif, in yet another story, later said that she had seen him kissing that nurse girl at the Martyrs Hospital. Sitt Busayna did not scruple to ask about the circumstances under which Umm Yusif had seen them. She had gone to the hospital, she replied, to get a penicillin shot on account of her tonsillitis. When she entered the hospital around three-thirty, the place looked deserted. It was supposed to be closed from three to five, but Fikriya, the nurse, lived in Shubra, and instead of going home and coming back at five she stayed at the hospital. If someone came for an injection she would pocket the two piasters if the shot was intramuscular, three if given intravenously. When Umm Yusif went in, she didn't find Fikriya in the hall and, because she went to that hospital frequently, she knew she must be in the dressings room, for the two examination rooms were usually locked and only the doctor had the keys. Umm Yusif crossed the little corridor leading to the dressings room, which had originally been the kitchen of the apartment, and there her heart had almost jumped out of her chest: she saw Master Atif bending down over Fikriya, clasping her in his embrace, kissing her as they did in the movies: sucking her lower lip while she was sucking his upper. Sitt Busayna gasped, "Son of a bitch!" and left hurriedly to relate the story to Umm Suhair, for whom she added yet a further scene in which she uncovered the nurse's bosom, with Atif's hand covering her right breast. Sitt Busayna did not fail to note the admiring tone in which Umm Yusif spoke about Master Atif.

Some women of Zafarani harbored secret resentments toward Atif because he ignored all the treasures contained in the alley. At the beginning, they had said to themselves that he had studied at the university and that it was natural for him to go out with pretty girls. But Fikriya was dark and ugly and a nurse. The truth was that Atif took good care to protect his reputation in spite of pressure from his friends. On one occasion when they were out with some girls, they had had a hard time finding an apartment to take them to, but Atif had adamantly refused to offer his own.

About six months earlier, as he had gone out one morning, he had met a young white woman with big eyes, carrying a bowl of fuul. As she passed by, he had resisted a mysterious urge to look back at her. He spent the whole day haunted by her sad, velvety glance. There was a vague similarity between her and Rahma that he couldn't quite pinpoint. Was it the way she walked? Was it the glance itself? He had watched all the women of the alley in his solitude, but had never noticed this one before. Who was she? On the following day he had encountered her again at the Sidi Marzuq Mosque. Things were quiet on the street; there were just a few school children and a man who looked like a bus conductor, since he carried a leather pouch with tickets in it. Atif slowed down a little as he drew next to her, and her feminine presence seeped through to him. After five days of silent encounters she came to a halt ahead of him and unwound her melaya, and he caught a glimpse of her short house dress beneath. Slowly, she began to rewind the melaya around her body more securely. Did she resemble Rahma in her way of looking at you? Their glances met and she said faintly, "Good morning, Master Atif." Fire ran through his blood. She walked on ahead of him, past the fuul vendor, the dairy store, the Bayt al-Qadi gate. She turned at Qurmoz Alley and he said, "Good morning" and she said, "Happy morning, Master Atif." Her voice pierced his body. That slight weariness in her eyes slid into his very marrow. She said her name was Rhode, daughter of Umm Sabri, and that he had not seen her before because she had been living in her own house in al-Darb al-Ahmar. But it was now no longer her house. She had been divorced by her husband, Abd al-Rasul the dye-house worker. Encounters like this, brief and quick, kept taking place in the Qurmoz archway. Once he had held her arm and the melaya had slipped from her shoulders. She had begged him to avoid a scandal, telling him she was at his disposal—but only discreetly. How could that be done with all those sharp prying eyes on all sides of him? He had decided that the quietest time in the alley was soon after sunset. The balconies would be empty.

Rhode could leave her own house, walk to Gammaliya Street, then turn back quickly toward his house. Umm Muhammad was usually asleep by nightfall; Ali the ironer didn't get home early and his peasant wife closed her door, fearing the city.

Atif was now opening the door to his apartment. As much as he wanted to embrace her, he also wanted to look long into her eyes, to look for that vague similarity and that mysterious meaning that kept eluding him. He embraced her and she whispered, "I am yearning . . . very much." She flung her melaya on the bed, uncovering two alabaster thighs, strong and firm. She moved a little to give him space. When she offered him her lower lip, his heart began to pound. But what was this? Before, with other women, he had never been this slow to react. All the others had been casual adventures with no continuity, women he didn't know and on whom he had had no claims. He had almost risked ruining his reputation there under the archway all for the sake of a hug or a kiss. Now, all that was missing was for him to get started. The warmth of her body was reaching out to him, but . . . . Perhaps things might happen after he pressed his body against hers. He kissed her eyelids, grabbed at the end of her dress; she moved her body to help him undress her. She pushed her awakened breasts to his chest. But what was happening? He moved away. He was facing a condition that was hitherto unknown to him. "What's wrong? What's wrong with you, Master Atif?" Her voice was thick with desire. He said: "I'd rather we talked a little." He seemed like a train without an engine, a face without a nose. He could hear her trembling and burning. Until now he had never had any trouble handling these flames. Rhode realized the difficulty of the situation. She had to slow down a little, in spite of her body's growing intoxication and the warmth of her breath, which was getting out of control and turning into light, erratic panting.

34

Since Rhode had come to Zafarani, no man had touched her. Before, it had been easy for her to visit Me'allim Farghali the fruit grocer. She had gone to him often while she lived with her husband. But since she had met the ustaz, she had had no thoughts of the me'allim. She did not respond to the advances of Hagg Nassif the bakery owner. The ustaz had filled her heart and mind. After that first morning greeting, the day had passed in a long dream in which she had relived his unhurried walk, picturing to herself his finger as he pushed his glasses up. She had looked out the window, bursting with joy. She and she alone had been given this effendi's glances, his conversation, his touch in the archway. She had often envied those girls hanging on the arms of effendis, girls in high school walking next to their boyfriends, their cheeks red with shyness and ecstasy. When she was their age she had had nothing but misery and hardship. She remembered once passing a park and seeing a young man and a girl sitting on the green grass. She remembered the white handbag that the girl had placed next to her. She had wished she could go to a park with a man—not Me'allim Farghali, not Hagg Nassif, but some other man whose features she could not make out at the time—a man who was kind and who would whisper a few words in her ear and make her blush. She would give herself to him willingly; one who would not undo his long underpants as soon as they were alone and just collapse on top of her. Would Atif Effendi ever be willing to go out with her to a park one day? Wouldn't he be ashamed of her melaya? How she would love to tell her ex-husband Abd al-Rasul the dyer about it. He had fed her nothing but a steady diet of humiliation. With him she had moved from one set of dark rooms to another. He had yelled at her every morning. He would throw her ten piasters and she would ask how she was supposed to manage on so little. He would shout that his daily wages were seventeen piasters; was he expected to strike the ground and cause watermelons to appear?

Did he mint money? Wasn't it enough that he had neither his breakfast nor his lunch with her so that she could manage and thank God? Had it not been for Me'allim Farghali and her few visits to Muhammad the bookseller, who lived behind al-Azhar Mosque, her mouth would have rotted with hunger and milk would have dried in her breast and her son Sayyid would have died. Muhammad the bookseller liked to look at her naked. He would ask her to stand in front of him and would pass his tongue all over her back and grieve: How can all this beauty receive such humiliation? As for Me'allim Farghali, he would say, after slipping a twenty-piaster piece in her hand, that no woman had given him as much pleasure as Rhode did. Then he would give a disgusting belch.

She wished she could tell all this to Atif. All of the men had expressed great admiration for her femininity, but he remained silent, lying next to her, lifeless. His nakedness pleased her. Now she had reached the point of no hope and began to feel relieved. After he had undressed, she no longer saw the halo that had crowned him when he was outside. His body looked skinny and his legs were very thin. But from now on she could boast to herself that she was the mistress of Atif, the college graduate. She didn't know the nature of his job nor the name of the ministry or organization for which he worked, or even the kind of education he had. His college degree was enough. It is true that she wouldn't be able to announce their relationship publicly, but merely repeating the details to herself would give her great satisfaction. If Muhammad the bookseller or Me'allim Farghali met her by chance, she would apologize for not going with them. She would say that she had become acquainted with a young man who had a college degree and who was a government employee, that he was very jealous, and that he had promised to take her to a park. No. She would say that he went out with her every day to the parks, that they sat on the bank of the Nile, that he held her hand and whispered in her ear. Perhaps Me'allim Farghali would make fun of her, and sadness might appear in Muhammad the bookseller's eyes. She would quickly say that he would marry her, that he had introduced her to his mother, and that preparations were going on as they would in any respectable marriage. She wished she could say all that to both of them as if merely uttering it would make it happen. But now she had to work harder to please him. At noon today she had used up half a bar of scented soap that she had borrowed from Farida, Radish-head's wife.

Atif was now looking at Rhode with eyes that were filled with intense distress, as he longed for something to stir. Scenes of what he had been hoping would happen flashed before him. He wished she'd stop rubbing up against him and stroking his back with her fingers. He whispered, "Get up; get dressed." He saw her slender waist, the roundness of her hips, her long straight thighs and her firm breasts unaffected by her abject poverty and by the rough handling of a brutal husband and still others of whom he knew nothing. What was going on? What if his friends found out? What would he think of all this later, after she had left? How could he now walk down Zafarani? She said she'd come again. He cried out, "Wait!" He got up, covered himself with the bed sheet, reached into his jacket pocket, and offered her a whole pound. Her eyes grew wide with hurt and that look of weariness. She said, "You shouldn't, Master Atif."

5

Sheikh Atiya asked Oweis the baker to tell him two things: first, a detailed account of what had happened to him since he had come to Cairo; and second, the name of his mother. The second request seemed so easy, and he was about to utter it first, when the sheikh's eyes lit up in the darkness of the room. Oweis imagined he was seeing two round prayer beads glowing in the dark in place of eyes. He requested first to be heard.

Oweis said, with fear beginning to take hold of him, that during the last few days a certain condition had befallen him—a condition that prevented him from taking advantage of a job that he had held for the past few months. This condition made him like a woman. At that point the sheikh's voice sounded strange, as if it was coming from a very large room filled with layers of thick smoke. Oweis could not see in front of him. The sheikh asked about the number of days in which he had not functioned as a man. Oweis replied, "Seven."

He said that he had suffered a great deal for a long time, that he had had difficult occupations since leaving his village in Upper Egypt at the age of sixteen. He had come to Cairo on foot. On the way he had picked cotton, harvested wheat, climbed date-palm trees tied to a rope to harvest the dates. He had tilled the earth, moved water using a shaduf, carried stones from the river bank to the big boats, pressed cotton with his feet and inhaled the white dust. When he arrived in Cairo he had gone to Café al-Salam in al-Hussein, where people from his village tended to congregate. In the village they had told him the opportunity to make a living was wide open in Cairo. Perhaps luck would come his way and he would strike it rich, like some of the men of the village who had left it barefoot and become big merchants. One of them, Ibrahim Bey, was now constructing government buildings. He was living in a house with a garden in Manyal al-Rhoda, and was now hard to see, he was so busy and so often out of town. Outside his door stood two guards who stopped anyone trying to go in. He had a cook and a specialist who created some kind of sweet delicacy that he was fond of and frequently fancied. On his finger he wore a ring worth one thousand Egyptian pounds. Oweis recounted how he had continued going to the café and the me'allim refused to accept any money from him when he ordered. That was the way the me'allim treated people from his village: he waited until they got a job and then he collected the money they owed. They say that Ibrahim Bey still owes him ten piasters, and that he says he will never pay that ten piaster piece back, and will always remain in debt, in order to learn a moral lesson and go on fearing God. Ibrahim Bey came to the café whenever he visited al-Hussein Mosque. He would sit on the mat-covered bench, smoke the hookah, and weep for the simpler, good old days that were free of all these big worries.

Oweis said that the me'allim pumped anyone newly arrived from the village for information and the latest village news: Who had died? Who had been born? Who had married? Who had been murdered? Had any new houses been built? How about the roads? Were they still the same? When Oweis mentioned something about the new house built by Hagg Abu al-Fadl, the me'allim inquired about the number of stories it had, the color of the paint, the shape of its entrance, the thickness of its walls, the water closet. Was it built with an outhouse like all the rest of the village buildings or did the house have its own water closet inside? Oweis had never actually been inside the house; the likes of him would dismount if they were riding and came within sight of the Hagg. But he still gave a detailed description of the house anyway. He justified it by saying he had seen the house before it was occupied, when he had gone in carrying a big wooden box containing he knew not what. The me'allim was touched; he shook his head in sadness. He said that when he visited the village he wouldn't recognize it; everything was changing; nothing remained the same. Over the next few days the me'allim asked Oweis to repeat his description of the new house. He inquired how it was supplied with water, the shape of the wheat stores inside, and what it would look like from the Imrans' house next door.

Oweis continued to describe the house every day, until Me'allim Snaibar, who owned the bakery at the entrance to Zafarani, came looking for somebody to deliver his baked goods. It was Oweis's good fortune that someone else had just arrived from the village, which made it easy for the me'allim to let him go and introduce him to Hagg Snaibar. And thus it was that Oweis left the confines of the café, which had been the only place he knew. He no longer slept on the pavement of al-Hussein Mosque; he now slept in the bakery. In the morning he would open the door and the cold air would rush in, dispelling from his chest the smell of the soot, the low ceiling, the remnants of leavened dough, the bran, and the sawdust. Then the children would come and order dough racks. At the beginning he had asked the children to wait so they could accompany him. But within two weeks he knew the houses and inhabitants by name, as well as several from other alleys who had dealings with the bakery. And then it was enough for a child just to come and order a number of racks for, say, Sitt Kawsar in Darb al-Rusas for Oweis to nod his head and say, "I'll be there." Once the risen dough was baked, he would set off around midday bearing the hot, delicious loaves on trays made of palm fronds. The customer usually gave him half a piaster or a fresh loaf as a tip. Sometimes, if he got up before daybreak, he would hear muffled pounding coming from a Zafarani house. Then he would immediately know that Umm Suhair or Umm Yusif—depending how hard the pounding—would be baking that day.

Oweis got used to sleeping at the bakery; he was no longer upset by the pitch dark, the crawling of soft insects, the running of huge rats, or the stories the inhabitants told of the 'ifreets that lived in that very bakery. He had once spent the night in a watermelon patch, and in the morning had sensed something coiled in his underpants; reaching with his hand, he had found a huge snake that had sought refuge in the warmth between his legs. Umm Yusif asked him on several occasions how he liked sleeping in the bakery. She told him that an 'ifreet had once blocked her husband's path. Her son Yusif, meanwhile, had once

40

met a policeman who asked him where Zafarani Alley was, and when he replied that he was there in it now, the policeman had laughed and fled. Yusif had been terrified to see that the policeman had bare legs with hooves like a goat. Umm Yusif had gone to Sheikh Atiya to obtain an amulet that would counter the effects of shock in her son; had it not been for the good sheikh, the boy would have gone crazy.

Oweis said that his conversation with Umm Yusif had aroused him; especially when she stood there in her nightgown revealing her firm breasts, or when she bent down to help him lift the wooden dough racks. When she sent her son over with a plate of watermelon, his sleep suddenly caught fire; he remembered the stories told in his village about the women of Cairo and how they couldn't resist the men from Upper Egypt. Then, when he saw her boy Yusif buying loaves of baked bread from the store, he grew alarmed. He asked whether they no longer did their own baking, and Yusif replied that they had run out of their own homemade bread, and that they would be making it again the following day. Umm Yusif usually kneaded her dough twice a week. Several days had now passed. He had been anticipating the moment when she would call him into her apartment, and imagined how he would pin her down, and listen to her sighs as she passed her fingers through the hair on his chest. But in fact, when he did go to her apartment, he had no sooner crossed the threshold than he realized that the gift of watermelon meant nothing after all. So when he went on to Karima in Musa Alley and she joshed with him, nudging him in the chest, he decided not to miss this opportunity. When she invited him in to catch his breath, his legs began to shake, and he threw himself on top of her, but his heart almost stopped beating when she started to scream. He kept trying to embrace her as he recalled a scene in a movie he had seen at Cinema al-Kawakib, where the hero embraced a woman who first resisted him and then at a certain moment her hands suddenly relaxed and closed her eyes while the audience shouted their admiration by hurling obscenities at nothing in particular.

Oweis went back to the bakery, sorely beaten, his head swollen. Hagg Snaibar promptly slapped him and kicked him out. As he was leaving he overheard some woman wondering: Who'd have ever thought that Oweis . . . . Someone else replied that Oweis had often taken fallen women to the bakery at night. As darkness fell he found himself without shelter. Later that night he went into Zafarani; the bakery stood at the entrance to the alley, occupying only a narrow strip of land there, although inside it extended over into Masmat Alley, which really made it separate from Zafarani. He climbed to the top of the stack of dough racks, weeping when he remembered that another's hands had stacked them. He slept on top of that stack till morning. The people of his village had advised him to save some of his earnings for hard times, and so he had set aside some of the money he had made, three pounds. He put the money in a handkerchief, tied it in a knot, and secured the handkerchief to his upper arm. He had had to use a few piasters from the sum that he had been hoping would soon grow to twenty pounds. His dream was to buy a pushcart, painted in two colors, red and white, on which he would paint a puppet and women wearing melayas. In front he would write Allahu Akbar (God is Great) in big letters and paint the country's flag. He would sell ice-cream in the summer and hot boiled chickpeas in the winter. The kids would crowd around him and he would ask them to stand in line. He would set aside a corner to display that red candy which contained surprise prizes. The cart would enable him to rent a room, go back to the village, and come back married to one of his cousins.

On the seventh day after his firing, Oweis bought thirty piasters' worth of corn ears, which he had roasted in a distant bakery in Guwwaniya Alley. He had remembered the Bedouin who came from

Nazlit al-Simman, in the Pyramids district, riding a camel laden with a sack of fresh corn on each side: he would roast the corn at Hagg Snaibar's bakery and make his way through the alleys, beginning with Zafarani, and before sunset he would cross al-Hussein Square on his way back. Oweis had long been watching him and he discovered that he managed to sell both sackfuls of roasted corn in less than an hour. This was what tempted Oweis to buy his own corn. He now recounted how he had hawked his corn for a piaster apiece. By nightfall he had sold twenty ears. As time passed the corn began to get cold; he reached in his hand and felt inside the sack. After the late evening prayers he started to call, "An ear for half a piaster!" That night his anxiety was unbearable. Later he learned that the Bedouin had been coming to the neighborhood regularly for forty years, and that hawking merchandise required practice and talent, just shouting was not enough.

Oweis went back to Me'allim Abul Ghait's café. He saw him sitting in the same spot on the wooden bench, smoking the hookah, watching the customers, calling the waiter to take an order here or help a customer there—a guardian of his customers' pleasure. Oweis told him that a woman had tried to seduce him, and when he refused she had screamed and drawn a big crowd, that he had had terrible difficulties and been forced to return to his village. He added, lying, that he had just returned from the village. The me'allim was pleased. He said that Awad had arrived two days earlier, but was an idiot who didn't know anything. Oweis described the houses and the roads just as he had seen them a year before, and if he remembered that someone had once said a house would be built in six months, he would say it had already been built. When, however, he began to describe the road leading from the bridge to the village, he said the canal leading to the basin of the water pump was still there. The me'allim expressed surprise, as somebody had told him two months earlier that the canal had been filled in and a wider canal had been dug, and that children were now swimming in the new canal. Oweis insisted that the canal was still there, that he had seen it before he left that very morning, that the dust of the trip was still on his clothes. He asked the me'allim to look and see for himself. The me'allim thought a little then asked with sudden interest about the scent of the figs at the bend near the bridge, and the speed of the water flow into the basin of the water pump. Oweis said that the scent of the figs was very strong especially at night and could be smelled from far away, that the water was flowing at its usual speed. The me'allim shook his head, exclaiming that time kept marching on, that things were changing all the time, that Great, Almighty God alone had the power. He kept repeating it when Oweis told him that a stranger had gone to the village, selling red sugar near the bridge. The me'allim was dismayed: Where had this stranger come from? What was his village? What was his name? Oweis said he was unknown to all. The me'allim was upset: Was the village going to be opened up to total strangers? That was merciless Time for you.

Two days later Abul Ghait sent Oweis to the nearby Bazar'a agency, where he worked as a porter, moving soap boxes and rolling oil barrels across the street from the warehouse to the plant near al-Nasr Gate. On the street, children from Zafarani would call him "Uncle Oweis" and he would say to himself: "These will be my customers when I sell corn and chickpeas." Once again he was consumed with desire for Umm Yusif's body, especially whenever her galabiya got caught between her buttocks. He was fired from the agency a short time later. No reason was given.

He next worked in a paper store where he bundled old newspapers and tore off book covers. Then he worked as a servant in a restaurant, as an assistant to a carpenter who made barrels on Amir al-Guyoush Street, as a helper in a copper tinning shop, listening the whole time to the owner's complaints about the dearth of work after aluminum had become so popular and so available—a complaint to which Oweis was most receptive. He worked as a dishwasher at Galal Restaurant on Bayt al-Mal Street, as a worker in the old Khurunfish dye house, where he stirred indigo in basins and carried the fibers up to the roof and hung them on poles. Sometimes he begged at the mulids of Sidi al-Bayyumi and Sidi Marzuq. He joined the crowds forming around men who came to al-Hussein Mosque bearing loaves of bread filled with cooked fava bean sprouts in fulfillment of pledges or for other religious reasons. He ran after the cars carrying the couples who had just been married at al-Hussein Mosque. What he saved from all these endeavors came to no more than six Egyptian pounds. This sum looked even smaller when a carpenter who made push carts told him that they now cost more than fifty pounds. He never lost his hope, however, of one day owning a cart.

Oweis said that God had willed that his toil should end after four years of misery. One day, as he was sitting at the café, a man wearing noticeably clean clothes approached him. He said he was Me'allim Dawny, owner of the famous public baths, al-Ahrar, and that he saw promise in Oweis and was offering him a job coveted by many; he would be clean, eat meat every day, and have a free room on condition that he stayed at the baths all night long. He would get a salary like government employees and his job would be easy and pleasurable: every night he would meet a number of respectable effendis, some of whom held very prominent positions and the fate of a great many people in their hands, while some of them were even celebrities who appeared on television and who were regularly interviewed on the radio—which made their coming to the baths a strictly confidential matter. If he pleased one of them really well, he might perhaps receive a big tip, a whole pound for instance.

Oweis accepted immediately. He ate two pigeons and scrubbed his skin in hot water. In the evening he was alone with a white effendi who had a smooth, soft body and who didn't speak a word, but heaved melodious sighs. A week later he learned that a room was available for rent in the house of Usta Rummana, the politico, and that the rent was thirty piasters a month. He went right away and rented it from the landlord, Sergeant Major Sallam, who did not seem to remember Oweis or his scandal with Karima. He paid sixty piasters—a month's rent and a deposit. He now had a key to a lodging of his own.

On the first of the month he was struck by how small his salary was: Me'allim Dawny paid him one pound. He then found out that the respectable customers had already paid such huge sums that they rarely gave any tips. He had to pretend that he was content; many men would have loved to have his job. One pound was a tiny sum, it was true, but it guaranteed his ability to pay the rent, go to the movies twice a month, and eat a piece of basbusa and a plateful of kushari every week. These two particular kinds of food he made a point of having because he thoroughly enjoyed them, even though the me'allim would give him whatever he asked for. In the beginning the latter had questioned Oweis elaborately about the kinds of food that made him feel strong sexual desire, and he had replied: cow's feet. As for the fish that the me'allim insisted on giving him, it made him sleepy. He once heard Me'allim Dawny tell one of his clients that Oweis cost him a lot because of the high price of meat, especially those sheep's feet that he preferred, but that he had to be liberal with him so that he could satisfy his noble customers.

Oweis recounted how once, as he entered Zafarani, he had encountered Umm Yusif, who asked how he was, and whether he had married? She said she had heard all about what happened with that skinny Karima girl. She poked him in the chest; he was blind; the fruit was right in front of him but he didn't pluck it. He laughed, and his burning desire for sleep and rest evaporated. He said his eyes were never closed to the sight of apples. She laughed, saying, "Oh, by God, Sa'idi, you've learned how to talk." She whispered: "I'll wait for you at eleven tonight." He remembered how when she bent over, the outline of her panties showed under her light dress. He had long desired to squeeze her body—hers in particular. But he didn't go. He could have taken an hour or two off from the baths, but he didn't go. When he lay down in his room he folded up his garment and put it under his head as a pillow. Something was bothering and depressing him, preventing him from thinking of Umm Yusif. He was no longer ecstatic: Would his job make him impotent with women? He felt afraid. Was he about to change and become like one of his clients?

The following day he went with a client who, it was said, held an important post in one of the newspapers. After this first time, the client told Me'allim Dawny, "This is the very one I have been looking for for years." Nobody had pleased him the way Oweis did. The me'allim said that he had exerted a great deal of effort and had looked everywhere until he had found Oweis and chose him from among many to sleep with His Excellency, that he was going to set him aside so that he wouldn't exhaust himself with the others, that he was going to forbid him to sleep with just any client. The client replied, "So, from now on, he's my man," and the me'allim replied, "Most certainly, Your Excellency." Oweis knew that the me'allim said the same thing to all the clients, counting on Oweis's ability to serve seven of them well every night.

On the first night of Oweis's impotence, His Excellency the journalist was annoyed. He asked, "Is there no hope?" Oweis strained himself to no avail. His Excellency the journalist summoned Me'allim Dawny angrily. The me'allim swore many oaths that he hadn't offered Oweis to any other client despite all the tempting offers that had come for him, especially that night. When same thing happened two nights in a row, the me'allim screamed and slapped Oweis in the face as he shouted, "You've eaten a whole foot and a whole kilo of meat. A kilo that I myself can't afford to eat!" On the third day he fired him. Oweis went to al-Hussein University Hospital, where he was examined for three piasters. The doctor determined that his organs were all in good order. Perhaps Umm Yusif had cast an evil spell against him for standing her up, for he had once left behind at her place a piece of cloth that he had used to place between his head and the wooden dough racks when he carried them. So she now had an 'athar' of his to use against him.

All this explained why he had now turned to Sheikh Atiya for help. He said that he was tired of toiling for his living, that Cairo had crushed him ever since he arrived. He needed only a little more money until he had enough for the cart. He would then quit the baths for good and seek his livelihood on the road.

Oweis fell silent. The sheikh's eyes were glowing. The sounds of Zafarani did not reach inside the room. The sheikh said, "Go on." Oweis said that he wanted nothing more than a little security. Only one person from Zafarani frequented the baths, a young man by the name of Samir who was one of the lewdest and loudest. Oweis said that he was homesick for his village and would love nothing more than to be on the 8:00 a.m. train home. True, he had seen some hard times in the village, where sometimes he had been reduced to accompanying other men and waiting for them to have tea so he could have some as well. But all the hard times of the village were nothing compared to one single day of the previous week. All he wanted was to live modestly, and the cart would enable him to do just that. He said that another woman had given him a significant glance in the alley just that morning.

Oweis paused for a moment. He wondered: Should he mention the name of his mother now? The sheikh said, "Go on." Oweis said that because of what he had seen at the baths, he now thought everybody on the street was either going to the baths or coming from the baths. He said he now felt too ashamed to go to Abul Ghait's café. Once again Oweis fell silent as if something mysterious had robbed him of speech. He couldn't look at the strange features, the baby voice coming from the body of an old man. Was one of the jinn speaking through him? Sheikh Atiya said, "Answer my second question." Oweis said he was prepared to serve the sheikh, buy things for him, carry him on his back if he wanted to go from one place to another.

"Answer my question."

Oweis responded loudly and promptly as if caught by surprise, "My mother's name is Tahiya."

The sheikh told him to leave and to come back the very instant the sun rose on Friday.

A Preliminary Report on the Condition of Hasan Effendi Anwar

Hasan Effendi Anwar constantly boasts of two things that he repeats over and again: he has never set foot in a police station, either as plaintiff or as defendant, and he has never borrowed or lent any money. When he goes to al-Hussein Mosque to perform the Friday prayers or the dawn prayers in Ramadan, he prays for the success of his two sons, Samir and Hassan, the fruits of his life, and for curses to be visited upon those in the department who conspire against him, and upon those on public thoroughfares who bother him or disturb his sleep. Sometimes he might invoke the name of the same person twice on the same day: in the first prayer he might be against him; but then, if he should meet him and let go of his ill feeling, he would duly pray that God not accept his first prayer. It happened, for instance, one day that he came face to face with Sayyid Abul Mu'ati, director of the section in which he worked. Hasan Effendi, in an audible voice, said, "Good morning, sir," but

Sayyid Bey did not stop nor did he return the greeting. Hasan Effendi was overcome with a grief so intense that four cups of black coffee could not dispel it—a rare occurrence, since he was accustomed to drinking only one cup of coffee as soon as he arrived at the office and a second before he left in the afternoon. Why hadn't Sayyid Bey returned his greeting? He was a good, punctual employee who had never taken a single day off in all his long years of service, had never been late even by one minute, nor did he use any excuse or pretext to leave before the official signing out time. His files were a model of good order. Had someone badmouthed him? Had someone fabricated a lie about him and conveyed it to Sayyid Bey? Was it because he was only a high school graduate? That must be it. Sayyid Bey had graduated with a college degree in commerce, whereas Hasan Effendi had only graduated from a commerce high school. When Hasan Effendi reached that point in his thoughts he almost choked with emotion. He decided to go to Abdel Azim Effendi, his schoolmate and colleague at work. He picked up a file containing some official papers that would suggest to anyone who saw him in the corridor or on the staircase that he was going from one office to another to take care of some unfinished business. He stood at the door of his colleague's office (for, after a long battle and well orchestrated intrigues, Abdel Azim Effendi had been able to get his own private office in a room that had been a kitchen before the government took over the building). Abdel Azim Effendi was able to score an even more sweeping victory when he succeeded in having a telephone installed in his office, which he then placed on top of two huge volumes of the Standardized Commercial Dictionary. That day Hasan Effendi had had no feelings of jealousy. He told Ashur, Gabir Hifzi, and Husni Disuqi that what Abdel Azim Effendi had achieved was a triumph for all veteran employees who had intermediate diplomas and who had served the government for many years. He said that as soon as a college graduate started on a job they would give him a desk with a thick glass top and sometimes even a telephone with a direct line. When his colleagues went to congratulate him, Abdel Azim Effendi told them that he would not rest, that he would have no real joy in life, unless and until he got a telephone with a dial from which he could call any number directly, with no need for a switch operator.

That same day, Hasan Effendi wrote several memos in which he requested that a telephone with a dial be installed on his desk, as it was urgently needed for his work. He thought at the time that perhaps he would get lucky and actually get a telephone with a dial, in which case he would have gone one step better than Abdel Azim Effendi. If, however, he should fail in this, he would at least get an ordinary extension phone which would place him on an equal footing with Abdel Azim Effendi. A long time passed and still no telephone!—in spite of his repeated requests and his point of referring each subsequent request to an earlier one by writing the number in a very prominent place at the top of each letter. At the same time, he applied to the National Telephone Department to install a telephone in his apartment. He was told that there was a very long waiting list and that he would need an 'intermediary.' Hasan Effendi went to see a former chief of security from his village, who gave Hasan Effendi a business card to hand to a relative, who in turn sent him to a friend who knew a high-ranking official in the ministry of communications. A year after he had filled out his application, he got the telephone. He considered this a triumph: on the one hand, he was the only person in Zafarani who had a telephone in his apartment; on the other, he was the only intermediate degree employee in the department who had a telephone at home. He printed new cards with his name and, in a corner, his telephone number in Arabic and English numerals. He gave out the cards to his friends and colleagues and asked them to call him any time. As soon as he arrived at the department in the morning he would call the house. Sitting there among his colleagues he would call to find out what was being cooked, even though it was always he who bought the vegetables, the meat, the ghee, the oil, and all other provisions for his family.

On the morning of Eid al-Fitr, Hasan Effendi called Sayyid Bey at his house, congratulating His Excellency on the occasion of the Eid, and saying that he was calling from home. Sayyid Bey's voice was cold and lacked all emotion. The whole conversation lasted only a few minutes, but Hasan Effendi remained agitated all day long. His wife noticed that his hands shook when he held a glass or a spoon. It was a serious step, talking to Sayyid Bey at home. Would he embarrass him? Issue a warning? Hasan Effendi's excuse was that it was Eid.

Now here he was sitting in front of Abdel Azim Effendi, asking after his colleague, then saying that one was at a loss to understand certain directors. Abdel Azim Effendi raised his head and asked what had happened? Hasan Effendi said that some directors had no respect for the long experience that one acquired working for the government. Abdel Azim Effendi shook his head, saying that he had indeed recently witnessed certain directors doing strange things. He had been surprised last week when his telephone had rung. He had said hello, and had been shocked when a voice at the other end said, "Abdel Azim?" He immediately recognized the voice of one of the young directors—his telephone being of such a good quality that one could distinguish voices clearly. He replied, "Abdel Azim Effendi, if you please!" The young man wondered what difference that made, and Abdel Azim Effendi replied that it made a big difference, that he should learn how to address people of his age and station before lifting the receiver, and promptly hung up. Hasan Effendi—absolutely certain that his colleague was lying—said, "Well done!" and sighed, hoping for things to get better. Then he added, "Ah well, Abdel Azim Bey, there are four things you should never trust: money, no matter how plentiful; rulers, no matter how close to you they are; women, no matter how long you have lived with them; and Time, no matter how good it has been to you."

Hasan Effendi then left, convinced that his colleague shared his resentment toward Sayyid Bey, even though they had not even mentioned him by name. He knew how cautious Abdel Azim Effendi was. The whole department knew that, as soon as he arrived at the office, he would get out several sheets of white paper, a pencil, and an eraser and write, in the right hand corner of every sheet, four lines, one below the other:

The Ministry of Production
Department of Efficiency and Care of Products
Cost Division
Incoming Mail

Then he would very meticulously compose replies to various letters. He was so well known for being good at composing official communications that the director general of the department one day summoned him and told him to write a memorandum on blue paper to submit to His Excellency the minister. Abdel Azim Effendi spent eight hours working on it; this entitled him to overtime, but he never requested it. Until now he has told no one the content of the important memo despite many attempts on the part of his colleagues to make him do so.

Hasan Effendi returned to his desk, the lump in his throat less thick. In the afternoon he headed for al-Hussein's resting place. There, at the mosque, he recited many prayers against Sayyid Bey and begged his beloved, his intercessor, al-Hussein, Master of the Youth of Paradise, to realize his wish, if only once: that the undersecretary or the director general would summon him and tell him to write a memorandum, as had happened to Abdel Azim Effendi, or thank him.

He told his wife what had happened, adding a few embellishments: that he had shouted at the directors and told them he was better than them, that he had ordered those new college graduate kids to get out of his office. Sitt Saniya raised her hands and prayed for curses to be visited upon Sayyid Bey despite her husband's talk of his tough stand and his contempt for the director, which was so deep that Sayyid Bey had had to turn to Abdel Azim Effendi and ask him to beg his colleague to respect the director in front of the other employees.

As Hasan Effendi and his wife ate, he asked about their sons, Samir and Hassan. We note that he bragged about them constantly. They did not go out without his permission; if they saw him on the street, they kissed his hand. They never played in the alley, nor did they go to climb the Darrassa Hills. Samir's name was on the honor roll in his preparatory school, and on one occasion at the parents' council meeting the principal gave him a medal. Sometimes, while talking about his two sons, Hasan Effendi suddenly remembered the evil eye, especially when sitting with Abdu al-Burtuqani and Awad al-Rammah at the Café al-Club al-Asri, since each of them had a son who had dropped out of school. The son of the former had run away from home to become an actor in a troupe that performed in mulids. The latter's son liked riding bicycles so much that the owner of a bike shop got him to work there. When he remembered this, Hasan Effendi would tell a story about Samir or Hassan misbehaving, and Samir's not performing his prayers regularly, which made him beat his son more than once.

That was indeed true: Samir did not perform his prayers regularly. His father one day summoned him to his room and closed the door. He said he couldn't imagine Samir, who was so quiet and who blushed if he spoke loudly, disobeying the commands of God. It was then that Samir confessed that his clothes, sometimes . . . and he paused. The father understood. He didn't accept his excuse, however, and told him to bathe, always. On the following day he went to Sheikh Atiya and asked him to prepare an amulet for his son Samir, whom he thought had been cursed by the evil eye.

Hasan Effendi always asked how Samir and Hassan were doing. Did each take his schoolbag to school? Did either receive any letters? Two years ago he had seen an envelope on top of the radio addressed to "The Honorable Brother, Mr. Samir Hasan." He was stricken with panic that a letter had been sent specifically to his son. He read it and trembled all over; its writer requested Samir to write, "In the Name of God, Most Gracious, Most Merciful" a thousand times. Hasan Effendi almost choked. He asked his wife when the letter had arrived and whether Samir had read it. She replied that the letter had been unopened, so how could he have read it? Cautiously Hassan Effendi closed the windows, brought out the little alcohol burner, lit it, burned the letter, gathered the ashes, and flushed them down the toilet, then flushed the toilet several more times.

Who knew? Perhaps one of those secret societies was trying to recruit his son. He thought of locking Samir up at home for a month, but such an action would draw attention. He talked to Abdu al-Burtuqani about a letter received by the son of one of his colleagues at the department, who had come to him not knowing what to do. Al-Burtuqani expressed his apprehension: that was a well-known method; the letters would keep coming, the assignments would grow more and more demanding until the son found himself a member of a society or an organization fighting against the State and the whole of society.

Hasan Effendi's heart trembled like a small wet dove. He passed many sleepless nights. Every footstep in the alley after 1:00 a.m., he thought, belonged to men coming to arrest Samir. He would then take a flashlight to his son's room to make sure he was in bed. Who knows? Maybe they had put somebody else in his place. He also hurriedly moved his books to his own bedroom, writing on each of them clearly: "This book belongs to Hasan Effendi Anwar, an official government employee." The books dealt with Sufism or war. The presence of books about war, he feared, might raise certain questions, the subject matter, albeit very vaguely, having something to do with a military coup. So he added one more line to what he had written on the military books: "I purchased this book because one of my hobbies is learning about the history of wars. I developed this hobby during the Second World War."

Every day thereafter Hasan Effendi would ask his wife if any letters had arrived. She would answer in the negative and he would make her swear that this was indeed the case and she would swear and he would fall silent. His wife would proceed to tell him the news of the alley and what she had seen when the vegetable cart entered the alley, the price of zucchini and onions, rising inflation. She would begin to relate a conversation she had had with one of the women when he would tell her he would rather she kept away from the women of Zafarani, since keeping to oneself was a form of worship. Besides, the alley attracted people of all kinds; now for the first time a bachelor was living there, one who would have been able to entertain women in his apartment had it not been for the alert, high-minded inhabitants of Zafarani. His wife remarked that Atif was polite and a college graduate. Hasan Effendi reacted as if boiling water had been poured on him. He shouted that of all God's creatures, college graduates were the most rotten and the most ignorant; a sixth grader of the old days was much more conversant and well-versed in the sciences than today's PhDs. His wife tried to calm him down, and after a few minutes he lowered his voice. The people were not used to shouting coming from his apartment. Here it must be pointed out that Hasan Effendi lived in a two-storied house which was the third on the right as one entered the alley, not counting Hagg Snaibar's bakery.

Hasan Effendi had been born in the alley, in the house next door to the one where he now lived, and which had been boarded up for a month as a prelude to being torn down and its inhabitants evacuated to Madinat Nasr. Hasan Effendi's family had lived in that house for a very long time. His father had left him half an acre in the village and a vacant lot next to the house which, it was said, his father had bought for one pound several decades before. His friends suggested that he sell the half acre and invest the proceeds in building a two-story house on the vacant lot. But Hasan Effendi didn't like the idea. True, a half acre was worthless, but it made the people of the village remember him and made it possible for him to consider himself a landed gentleman among employees who had nothing but their salaries. Some time later he heard the children shouting, "Let's play in Hasan Effendi's ruin!" which he took to be a bad omen. So he decided he would build the house. But how, since he couldn't bring himself to sell the half acre? It seemed al-Hussein had responded to his prayers, for a few days later he met Abdu, a contractor from his village. He told him that all he had was one hundred Egyptian pounds in Post Office savings. The contractor said that would be fine, and he'd give him a twenty-year mortgage with simple interest. Hasan Effendi didn't make up his mind right away. He related what had happened to his wife, to his friends, to Abdel Azim Effendi, and to anyone who chanced to be praying next to him at al-Hussein Mosque. Four months later he had made his decision. And one year later he had moved into his present house, the second story of which he rented to al-Daturi.

Hasan Effendi thought the new house brought him good luck, since Hassan was born to him nine months after he and his wife moved into it. After his marriage, he had seen many doctors who had all confirmed that their childlessness was his fault. Yet apparently the house-moving treatment worked, although after Samir arrived, Sitt Saniya was no longer able to conceive. Hasan Effendi praised God and devoted all his time and care to his sons. When they were little, he often left work on the sly to look in on them at home, then went back and signed the departure record book. He drew up a precise plan for raising them and keeping them away from bad people. He noted, with satisfaction, that they didn't go out very frequently; that none of their classmates visited them or whistled for them under the balcony; that they didn't stand around on the street corner. Samir was now in secondary school. As for Hassan, in a few months he would receive his secondary school diploma. Their getting into the university was an essential objective, since he himself had experienced at first-hand what those with only an intermediate education went through.

Hasan Effendi often closed his eyes and imagined a big sign with bold lettering that said, "Doctor Hassan Hasan Anwar, Doctor of Medicine, Fellow of the Royal College of Surgeons of London." Only when he saw his son's name there in al-Azhar Square, would he know the meaning of real relief. If one of his acquaintances complained of something, he would then be able to give him the address of Doctor Hassan Hasan Anwar and would answer his interlocutor's question: "Yes. He's my son." Then very slowly and deliberately he would take out his card and say, "When Hassan sees this card, he will take extra care and find an earlier appointment for you." Sayyid Bey would ask him to put in a good word with the doctor, and Hasan Effendi would forget everything that had previously taken place between them. That was right, for one did not gloat where sickness was concerned. He himself would dial the number, talk to his son, and tell him to take good care of Sayyid Bey, his wife, and his children. He saw himself heading toward the office of the director general of the department requesting permission to take one day off. The director would give him the permission, but would express surprise; he would say that this request was news and deserved to be published in the newspapers. At that point Hasan Effendi would drop his head in embarrassment and, in a humble voice, would say, "My son, Doctor Hassan, is going to England for two years." The director would congratulate him, and he would go with his wife and Samir to the airport, Hassan would wave to them, and then the plane would carry him away. He wouldn't be able to bear that separation, and had already begun to worry about it while completely failing to understand why he would need to have sexual intercourse with his wife on the day of Hassan's departure. He would read the society column in the papers: "Sayyid Bey thanks the humane Doctor Hassan Hasan Anwar." "Abdel Azim Effendi thanks Doctor Hassan Hasan Anwar who, after God Almighty, is credited with his recovery."

As for Samir, Hasan Effendi hadn't yet settled on a specific profession for him. He had once asked him what he wanted to study and Samir had blushed, like a girl, and answered softly, "Anything, Daddy." Samir was causing him anxiety. Several months ago, Me'allim Daturi had whispered to him in that sleepy voice of his that Samir had been seen in Umm al-Ghulam Alley, in the company of a young man of ill repute whose name was Mahdi. Samir had cried a lot and swore that he didn't know anybody by that name. On the following day his father bought underwear in two styles. His wife was surprised; there was no need for all these clothes; the kids had enough. He said that one of the employees had distributed the clothes, that this employee was supplementing his salary by selling such things, so he had bought the short underpants for Samir and the long ones for Hassan. A week later he went to the kitchen, turned on the light and began to empty the laundry basket. He held Samir's underpants up to the light, saw the congealed yellow stains, and went back to bed, relieved and reassured of his son's manhood. Now Hasan Effendi had gone to bed at midnight and was staring with open eyes at the dark ceiling, recalling the day's events in his own journalistic composition. He saw a red banner and several headlines:

FLAGRANT AGGRESSION AGAINST HASAN EFFENDI ANWAR
GRAVE INCIDENTS AT EFFICIENCY DEPARTMENT

- Hasan Effendi moving fast in confronting Sayyid Bey
- Abdel Azim Effendi expresses total sympathy and declares support for Hasan Effendi's position
- Important Meeting

Hasan Effendi this evening received Me'allim Daturi at the permanent headquarters of his home. Following the meeting, the me'allim stated that he had requested the conference in order to discuss the turmoil in Zafarani and the phenomenon of marital quarrels that has arisen during the last few days. He exchanged points of view with Hasan Effendi Anwar, and both agreed that quiet times were behind us for good and that the time of people of goodwill and friendship has likewise passed.

Hasan Effendi then gave the weather report and continued to compose newspaper articles until sleep overtook the contents of his paper. It was a fact that for several years all his efforts had been devoted to raising his children. As for his wife, she was quite absorbed in her two sons and had lost interest in her conjugal duties, which suited Hasan Effendi perfectly, since his health was not as good as it once had been, a long time ago. Now such duties on his part required great effort—herbs and folk preparations from Hamzawi and such. His wife looked after him, was kind to him and keenly supervised every aspect of hygeine; she would be as cross as a little girl if she smelled cigarette smoke on his breath. Hasan Effendi did not fall asleep right away that night. He heard shouts and continual crying. He composed a big headline:

DISTURBANCES AND TURMOIL IN ZAFARANI

All the information available on Sheikh Atiya is uncertain. A number of stories are told about him, but they are all secondhand accounts. Nobody can establish anything on the sheikh's date of birth. The old timers, such as Sergeant Major Sallam Abu Hafiz, who retired twenty years ago, and Amm Abdu, the cotton-candy vendor, all remember him as part of their ancient, faraway childhoods. Sergeant Major Sallam, remembers, for example, that his sister failed to produce children after her marriage. Two years passed and her husband grew worried, especially since his family had been putting great pressure on him. Two months after the wedding his father had already asked him, "How is it going?" It is customary among certain families to inquire about these things so that if the wife proves barren, she can be divorced without further discussion. But the husband would not let her go. They had a hard time with doctors, but it was no use. Umm Sallam said she was going to turn to a blessed sheikh who lived in Zafarani (at that time the family lived in al-Darb al-Asfar Alley). The mother accompanied her daughter and took one of the husband's handkerchiefs with her. Sergeant Major Sallam went with them—he was eight years old at the time. He can still remember how his mother and sister went in to see Sheikh Atiya in his dark room. He remembers the glow of the sheikh's round eyes. He cannot remember any incident earlier than that one; it is his earliest memory. The event appears to him far away, belonging to a different era. What he is sure of now is that he saw Sheikh Atiya as an old man then, and that is why he is certain that today the sheikh must be over one hundred and fifty years old. When he remembers the sheikh, he does so with awe; thanks to him his late sister gave birth to four sons, three of whom died, but the fourth of whom lived to have many descendants.

Bannan says that he has never seen the sheikh leave the house, but, when he turned to him seven years ago to prepare an amulet that would soften the heart of his only son, who went to Europe and forgot his parents completely, he saw that the sheikh was a very old man who had a beard with gray in it. Seven months later, his son sent him a letter. Some people explained the length of time that elapsed between the making of the amulet and the arrival of the letter as the result of the great distance between father and son—a fact that affected the potency of the amulet. The son kept sending a letter every year or two enclosing a money order in a small amount that they could cash at one of the banks, but he never wrote an address or reply to anything that they sent to him. The neighbors explained that the son kept on moving from one place to another and pointed to the different postage stamps on every envelope. The mother believes that the sheikh's blessing will one day bring her son back. He will knock on the door, and when she opens it she will see her son in the flesh and he will rest in her arms and cry out, "Mama!" and she will kiss him and he will whisper, "Being away has killed me," and after the neighbors leave, he will rest his head on her knee and tell her all he has been through. Radish-head's mother was once seen going to the sheikh's room. Several years ago, she told Sitt Wagida that the sheikh had blessed her when she was a child. Sitt Wagida seized this opportunity of the ever-silent woman speaking and asked if she remembered the sheikh. She said, "How could I not, when he is blessedness itself?" She remembered what had happened to Sheikh Hussein, the landlord of the house where the good sheikh was now living. At first he had refused to give him the room, and the sheikh had been forced to sleep for two nights in a row in the abandoned lot on which the house of Umm Nabila, the teacher, now stood. Then Sheikh Hussein . . . . But suddenly the old woman fell silent and looked about her in anger; since then, she has not spoken to Sitt Wagida again.

On the occasion of al-Hussein's mulid, the Sufis and leaders of their orders converge upon the alley. Some stay with inhabitants of Zafarani while others stay outdoors in the alley. During the mulids, the sheikh disappears. His name is well known in Egyptian villages, hamlets, and neighborhoods. Third-class passengers in Upper Egyptian trains are familiar with an old man who walks in the aisles reciting verses containing the names of all the saints and holy men in Egypt, and among them he mentions the name of Sheikh Atiya, resident of Zafarani. The following are some of the accounts circulating about various aspects of the sheikh's life:

Some people assert that the sheikh will witness the Day of Judgment with his very own eyes. In some accounts it is related that he was born with a full beard and that before coming out of his mother's womb, he had recited verses from the Qur'an. His mother died as soon as he was born. Some people say that he first came into the world in Zafarani, others that he settled in the alley after much wandering. The people will get up one day and not find him in their midst. Some have heard his voice chanting verses from the Qur'an on rainy winter nights. A number of inhabitants have seen him go out in the alley on the coldest nights.

His acquaintances include people from different races. The Moroccans visit him on their way to Mecca for the pilgrimage. Zannuba, the divorcée who lives on the only floor above the sheikh's room, has heard dignified laughter reverberating during their visits. She has seen Indians and heard the sheikh greet them as "cousins." Black people and men with Chinese features who spoke Arabic have also visited the sheikh.

The inhabitants of the alley have never seen any food going in or leftovers coming out of his room. It is said that the jinn are in his service; they fly to heaven, eavesdrop on what the angels are whispering about people's destinies, and report what they hear to the sheikh. In 1944 he told Sitt Umm Samya that the sun of the following Friday would not rise on her son. And indeed his soul ascended to heaven one hour before sunrise.

The grandsons of Sheikh Hussein say that a crippled religious scholar arrived one day, carried on the shoulders of a Nubian Azhar student. At that distant time in the past there was no housing shortage, so the landlord didn't think of renting the room located under the staircase and which in fact had only been created when the buildings had been divided up. The slope of the staircase forms its ceiling, while the room itself drops down about two meters below street level. Upon entering, one has to descend five steps. The room has no windows and is almost triangular: its southern wall is wide, measuring about four and a half meters across, but then it narrows right down, so that its northern wall is no more than three quarters of a meter across. Its floor is covered with shiny paving stones—exactly like those with which Zafarani Alley itself is paved.

Sheikh Hussein refused to rent out the room, saying that he had sworn never to shelter a bachelor in his house. The crippled sheikh and the Nubian friend who carried him left. The following day some frankincense and perfume merchants came along and begged him to rent the room to the ascetic cripple. They said that they had gone to great trouble to convince him to enter their stores and stay there, if only for a few moments. Sheikh Hussein said he had sworn never to rent lodgings to bachelors, and besides, he didn't understand this insistence on his room in particular. They said that as far as his being a bachelor was concerned, that was irrelevant in his condition. As for the choice of the room, that was one of the secrets about which he shouldn't be questioned. Sheikh Hussein asked them to give him until the following day.

That night, after evening prayers and after shaking hands with the man to his right and the man to his left as was customary, he was surprised that one of them addressed him by name. It was a dignified old man with a gray beard who begged Sheikh Hussein to give his room to Atiya, the good, devout man. Then he whispered, "That is no way to treat someone who has come so close in his communion with God." On the following day they both came, the Nubian student and the sheikh, and went up to the landlord. Sheikh Atiya stayed alone with him for some time, and from that night on he never left Zafarani. On the following morning the Nubian student came with a pushcart. A number of the alley's children gathered to see what the Nubian was moving: some old books and a big brown box.

Sometimes people talked about him, wondered, made inquiries, then suddenly fell silent. Their silence would last for months, until something that might be completely insignificant occurred, when the talk would start up again and grow. But at no time would the feeling leave the people that the sheikh was close to them, that he watched over them, and knew just what was going on among them. The Zafarani women were fond of attributing miraculous feats to him. They said that he was married to a female jinn of splendid beauty, that he went to different parts of the world, transported on the back of a demon.

One of them maintained that she had opened the door to his room but couldn't see him there. He was capable of assuming different shapes—perhaps he was disguised in the form of this passing black cat. When someone suddenly realized that they may have gone beyond the bounds of the acceptable in their conversation, and as others remembered the dark stairs that they would have to climb on their way home, they would whisper, "By God! He is full of blessedness," and change the subject.

The inhabitants undoubtedly feared Sheikh Atiya; they hadn't forgotten the catastrophes that befell those who tried to do anything to him. In the year 1942, for instance, when air raids against Cairo were at their most intense, a number of burglars, under the cover of the blackouts, became very active. They had apparently heard rumours about the contents of his room—the jewelry, the sapphires, the emeralds, and the pearls. They were not scared by the stories of a bottle in which an 'ifreet was imprisoned and who could be set free if one of them accidentally knocked over the bottle, or at the command of the sheikh himself. Three of them attempted to burglarize the room; two stood outside while the third stepped in. Hardly had he taken four steps when he shrieked and fell to the floor clutching his belly. His two accomplices fled, scared by something—perhaps the sounds he was making, his long, drawn out wailing screams; perhaps the dark of the night. In the morning the inhabitants of the alley found a man who looked disfigured as though a giant hand had twisted him about, and who was still gripping a dagger and keys and a bag made of red and yellow striped cloth. They tried to make him move but he couldn't, so the police had to carry him away in his statue-like condition. It turned out that he was a fugitive on the run from a huge number of convictions.

Other events created an aura of caution and fear around the sheikh. This had intensified seven years ago when the sheikh disappeared; his strange visitors stopped coming and his door remained shut. Before disappearing, he had told his visitors that he was going into seclusion because he would be absorbed in a great mission. At the beginning, people were full of conjecture. It was said, for instance, that he would turn the stones of the houses into gold, distribute drops of the water of elixer among the inhabitants of Zafarani so that none would ever die and fill the houses with so much purified honey, bread, and cheese that no one would ever go hungry. Some people expressed fear. How could any good be expected from a cripple who couldn't even move? Hearing this sort of talk, others chided them and demanded they take back their words. As time passed, people forgot everything that had been said about the sheikh's lofty mission. Zannuba the divorcée saw his door always closed. When children went into the courtyard to pick up a stray ball that had landed there as they were playing, they would always glance at the door and quickly run out again. Some of them would avoid hiding in the courtyard when they played hide and seek. It was true that the door was locked, and that there was no sound of the sheikh's voice at all from within, but a vague feeling still weighed on adults and children alike each time they turned toward or thought about that door.

One month ago, a Nubian had appeared. Zannuba saw the door ajar. Somebody said that the sheikh had come back from a long trip during the night when everyone was asleep. There was a rumor that he had come back angry, which struck fear in the hearts of certain of the residents, especially the old timers. In any event, Usta Abdu had been able to find no one else to resort to in his calamity except for the sheikh. He was even optimistic; if his impotence had stricken him three months earlier, he wouldn't even have found the sheikh and couldn't have sought his help. By Friday evening, the number of those who had visited Sheikh Atiya had reached six men and one woman, all from Zafarani. He told them all to come the next Friday before sunrise. The seven were:

1) Usta Abdu, driver, Transit Authority
2) Radish-head
3) Oweis the baker
4) Ali the ironer
5) Tahun Effendi Gharib
6) Rhode, daughter of Umm Sabri (who brought with her a handkerchief, saying it was an 'athar' belonging to a young man she knew who had been stricken by a limpness of the nerves)
7) Qurqur the musician.

File 2

Certain Preliminary Events that Took Place on a Friday

When Ali the ironer entered Sheikh Atiya's room and saw Oweis the baker, his surprise was mixed with embarrassment. His feelings were slightly tempered the moment Radish-head arrived, since the latter had all his life avoided entering his neighbors' homes, to such an extent that when the time came to collect the Eid gifts for the meseherati, he would stand out in the alley holding a basket and would send his young daughter to collect the cookies or what little money was due to him. His expression changed, however, as his heart quickened. He realized that he had been exposed and decided not to utter a word about his condition in front of any of these people. When Rhode came in she murmured, "In the name of God . . . God's will be done. . . ." Her steps were uncertain and she stood away from the men, looking at Sheikh Atiya, praying that he would not expose her. She had never heard of his being hurtful to anyone in this way before. When Usta Abdu entered, wearing his khaki uniform with the logo of the Transit Authority—a horse with wings—on his chest, all those assembled felt fairly certain that they had all come for the same reason. What surprised them was Rhode's presence. Why had she come?

Their heads were bowed down and the silence was heavy. What each of them feared above all else was that the sheikh might address himself personally in such a way as to reveal his condition and make him the object of shame. Usta Ali began to sweat and his back broke out in goose pimples. Some of them finally gathered enough courage to look at the sheikh. In point of fact, they all began to look at him, therefore it is now possible to draw a quick, realistic sketch of the sheikh: he is short, no taller than a child of eight; his shoulders are narrow and his pelvis wide, perhaps because his crippled legs are folded under his body; his head is sunk in such a way that he seems to have no neck, but rather three rings of flesh, one above the other; his face is oval, swollen, or so it appears, especially since he has no wrinkles; his mouth is small and his lips are pursed; his eyelids are heavy and his skin is flabby. He looked as though, if someone grabbed him and pulled, he would stretch out like taffy; this gave his whole face a strange shape that contrasted with his small, gray beard. He resembled a fetus that has been aborted yet has still managed to grow. As for his eyes, they were perfectly round, and glowing green.

Set out before him were several engraved brass vessels. To the left stood four wooden boxes piled on top of each other. The darkness of the room was penetrated by a light from an unknown source. Qurqur the musician reckoned one could read a book with small print without difficulty. Perhaps it was this strange light, coupled with other factors, that inhibited them from staring long at the sheikh. There was something that repelled their eyes, preventing them from looking for more than a moment in his direction. When he raised his head, they realized that the sun was rising at that very moment. They listened to his slow voice that seemed to emanate from all over the room.

"Your number is not complete yet." He twirled his thumbs round as a little bulge appeared and disappeared under his galabiya. Oweis recalled Sheikh Salih, the headman of his village, sitting on the large bench in front of the little mosque, looking constantly in one direction as his thumbs also went round each other in circles.

"I am not going to speak in detail until seven more come. Some have been exempted, but I want fourteen men; one of them must be Atif, son of Hasanain Guda."

Rhode trembled. Hot fear crawled under her skin. She dreaded a scandal.

"I want the men only. Some may object, but you will find that, what each of you complains of, what each of you has told me about in secret, whoever you turn to, he will also have it as well."

Beginning of the Day

The men stayed where they were. The whole matter looked too complicated and none of them could act alone. They all followed Sitt Rhode with their eyes as she left the room. Why had she come? Oweis was about to say, "Each of you is suffering from the same thing as everyone else," but he didn't say a word and kept his distance from the rest. One must be polite after all, and not get close to the most prominent Zafaranites. This was the first time he had ever found himself with several of these inhabitants.

He was an outsider; when he had first arrived, he hadn't talked to anyone in Zafarani, hadn't sat at the café of Me'allim Daturi, and hadn't visited anyone in the alley. Then the incident with the woman in Darb al-Rusas had made them look at him with annoyance. But he had been forgotten again as soon as he rented his room, because he slept the whole day and nobody ever saw him on his way to work at the baths at night.

Whatever happened today would merely be a prelude to other things. He recalled a distant morning in the village when he had once been awakened by a scream in Abu Missallam's house. He had leapt up and run through the first rays of the sun that were starting to spread over the village. Faydallah had been killed as he slept in the watermelon patch. Everybody in his village had known that Abu Missallam's family was entitled to kill a member of the Awadallah family. In just the same way, things would not simply come to an end in Zafarani when they all went back to the sheikh the next day.

Ali the ironer meanwhile said they should act quickly because time was very limited and they all had to go to work. Usta Abdu was about to ask each of them what had brought him to Sheikh Atiya, but he was afraid of being asked the very same question himself. Each was denying what the others were there for. He didn't know, he said out loud, who else they should go to, but Sheikh Atiya's mentioning Atif Effendi by name made it clear that someone had to go and ask him. At that point Tahun Effendi looked at Usta Abdu, since he, among all those present, was the closest to him in status. True, Usta Abdu was a bus driver while Tahun Effendi was a train engineer, but they both worked for the government. Tahun said he would talk to Atif and suggested, by his tone and the way he pointed to his chest, that he felt fully capable of discussing things on his level.

He looked at the others. Radish-head didn't try to hide his disgust at the fact that circumstances had forced him into Oweis's company. His features alone, however, could not contain the full extent of his irritation. He peered at him sideways, then moved himself away, and then moved himself back. Three times, he gave a sigh of impatience. He was determined to do whatever the situation required to restore his faculties so that he might calm Farida down, who was beginning to jeer at him openly, so much so that two days before she had grabbed

72

a glassful of water and poured it down his back. He hadn't dared to chide her; he had already been sufficiently humiliated. Usta Abdu pointed to him: "How about you?" Radish-head would go to Tekirli, he said, and invite him.

Ali the ironer was secretly amazed. How could sweet Farida, who was so many years younger than Radish-head, stand her husband? Two months earlier he had himself delivered some pressed dresses to Radish-head's apartment. When Farida had opened the door for him and he saw her bare arms and her body shimmering behind the see-through gown, he had swallowed hard. Oweis the baker also looked at Radish-head from a distance, cursing the money that forced a pretty, green-eyed woman to live with a man like that. He now recalled her bending to help him lift the dough racks, revealing her small, firm breasts and her smooth armpit as she raised her arms.

As he had gone back down the stairs, Umm Yusif had deliberately begun sweeping the staircase; quite obviously this uppity Tahun Effendi did not satisfy her. Regret touched Oweis's soul; he had wasted all those golden opportunities for pleasure with Umm Yusif. As soon as this curse was lifted and as soon as he had saved enough money, he was going to buy his pushcart, quit the baths and the effendis and their nightly debauchery, and pluck his pleasures in the gardens of Umm Yusif, Farida, and the wives of all those who were now ignoring him, hiding their problems with arrogance and false pride and holding themselves aloof.

The usta said he would talk to Me'allim Daturi, and Qurqur said he would find Ashur the carpenter. At that point Tahun Effendi said they ought to bring in Hasan Effendi Anwar and his two sons, as he was one of the wise men of the alley. Who should approach them? They realized that the only one without an assignment was Oweis the baker. Was it proper to send a depraved, unemployed baker to an employee who had been serving the State for the last thirty years? Radish-head announced that he had to go and open his store. Usta Abdu pointed out that nobody was left but Oweis. Oweis raised his hand in greeting. Ali the ironer said that Oweis was quite a talker, and once again Oweis raised his hand in greeting.

Tekirli

Tekirli knew Radish-head and had heard of his mysterious warehouse and of his relationship with his wife Farida through the gossip that his own wife had gleaned across the balconies, and by noticing Farida once or twice making funny faces at her husband as he was leaving. Yet he affected coldness and asked, "Who are you, sir?" Radish-head regretted coming to this soft man with the effeminate voice who had not even invited him in. However, as the popular saying goes, "That which forces you to swallow something bitter is that which is even more bitter." He had to be nice to him in order to persuade him to join the group the next morning. Tekirli enquired about Sheikh Atiya. Radish-head was quite surprised: How did he not know about him when the whole of Zafarani lived by his blessing? Tekirli had been choked with annoyance for several days. The previous night the scandal had almost erupted publicly. He had had a fight with one of his guests and Nadia, his wife, had been forced to separate them. Why did Sheikh Atiya want him? Maybe he was going to tell him to leave the alley.

These sheikhs had spies who supplied them with accounts of what people did, whereupon the sheikhs would confront the people concerned—and it all looked like a miracle to the likes of Radish-head. Then a thought far removed from anything connected to the situation hit him: How did Radish-head kiss his wife? Anyone seeing her would never believe that she was married to this ageing, open-mouthed man. If a rich old Arab were to fall in love with her, he'd pay her thousands

74

to seek a divorce or a hundred pounds for one night's pleasure, plus a gift such as a bottle of perfume or a transistor radio with a cassette recorder. But what was to be done when the Lord, in His wisdom, gave earrings to those who have no ears?

Tekirli had this habit of appraising women by what could be paid to each for a passing pleasure. As he walked down the street he would say to himself: This one is ten pounds; this one is worth five. Radish-head was now telling him that other men were going to the sheikh. Was he going to expose him? Perhaps the sheikh was going to relate incidents and summon people. Tekirli recalled that a number of the men who had visited him recently had been very . . . tense. One of them, a technocrat, complained that he had never experienced this before and demanded his five pounds back. Tekirli had said that he was not entitled to a refund; he had been left alone with Nadia, who had taken off all her clothes, leaving on neither slip nor panties, and she had played with him and indeed fondled him more than was usual—which had cost her some effort and for which she deserved a generous tip. As for his success or failure, Tekirli was not responsible for that. Perhaps the inhabitants of Zafarani were eavesdropping on them as they were always trying to do, especially with that Atif living downstairs. Tekirli had observed his lustful glances at Nadia. He was going to confront the sheikh firmly and decisively and hint at his close ties with influential men. He would do something positive; tonight he would ask some of these men to kick the sheikh out of the alley, especially since such trickery and deceit were against the law. He would hint that the sheikh might start spreading rumors about them—something that would damage their reputations since, as that other saying goes, "The bullet that misses you can still give you a headache." Tekirli hid his agitation and in a soft voice told Radish-head that he'd go with them to see what the sheikh wanted. He would force himself to get up early. So, where would they meet?

Atif

Atif felt scared about facing the night alone, and so he went out on his own, to escape the dark. He feared the gloomy, gray colors, the echoes of distant conversations, the ghosts, perfume, and remnants of crowds on streets that he had once walked in the company of his love. He sought refuge from the night in the crowds, drifting aimlessly with no particular destination in mind. He looked at shirts, watches, feminine things. He would have liked to hurry, but instead he dawdled over the perfume bottles, the delicate watches, and the colored fabrics on display for ladies in the shops. Now he just gazed and looked without buying. Who would he give sweetheart gifts to?

Before her twenty-fourth birthday, he had gone to visit his friend Farid on the outskirts of the city and asked his advice about what he should give her. Farid had suggested a dress; his wife had suggested a watch. He had liked her idea. He had a hard time making up his mind in front of the shop windows. When he finally did make his decision he went in, and the salesman asked him whether he wanted it for the evening or for work. He told him that shiny, decorative watches were good only for the evening. Practical watches, however, never left the wrist. He selected a watch that was in-between and took it back to show Farid's wife, who really liked it, whereupon he said, "Please keep it," to which she replied, "May you live long and give her many things."

Before, whenever he made his way to her house, his steps always felt lighter, the pavement softer. The roads leading to the house always looked wide and the air clean and the passersby lovable. He always wished he could talk to the passenger sitting next to him on the bus, to the conductor, to all the passengers. When the doorman of her building stood up for him, he gave him a ten-piaster note. That day, she had put her arms around his neck and hurriedly called her mother to show her Atif's gift for her birthday.

Atif would no longer walk around the streets leading to Rahma's house. In the first moments of the night, he would see a girl, hunger for love, but keep on going, surrounded by an invisible fence which kept him apart, and then he would lose his way downtown.

Atif was now back at home, resigned to the coming of night. His sorrows had multiplied, become a heavy burden, but he was confined; he did not want to go out. If Farid heard of this, he would consider it a portent; how could Atif spend three days without going out at all? He did not think of going to the hospital to squeeze the nurse Fikriya in his embrace as he had done once, but never again. Perhaps Rhode was thinking of him now with surprise, or even contempt. She had yielded to him without resistance; she had closed her eyes and opened her lips. He had been surprised by hearing Rahma's voice in hers, the echoes of their nights and the meals they had shared. When he saw Rhode, when they met in Qurmoz Alley, he had noted sadness in her big eyes and she had appeared to want him. The moment she entered his bedroom he had been certain that his days of wandering the streets, the agonizing loneliness in the midst of crowds, the chat and the gossip, the whisper of girls, the offers of vendors, and the begging of beggars were gone for good. Rhode hid nothing and he desired her. He had decided to tell her what had happened with Rahma. But his impotence made him reluctant to tell her how his love had ended. She would think that his inability with her was the reason Rahma had left him.

If he were to tell his friends, they'd say it was an ordinary matter, that there was no need to get upset; he had proven himself, they could testify to that. A fear, however, was gripping his heart; what had befallen him was more than a temporary symptom. Perhaps shame prevented him from going out. He imagined Rhode looking from her window, whispering to herself or to one of her friends: this handsome effendi, the college graduate, this big, tall man . . . can't. Now the night weighed heavily on him.

A knock at the door.

He was afraid that Rhode might come; perhaps she was looking around and over her shoulder now, smelling of cheap scented soap. He wished she'd leave. Was he going to add another failure to the first? If only she'd leave him alone until he identified the source of this calamity. He had tried by himself yesterday and the day before yesterday. No use. He was assailed by successive waves of memory that he couldn't keep back; he was unarmed, succumbing to the dark. What more could the night wreck? Ordinarily he would be watching the street from his balcony, or leafing through a detective novel. But from the moment he returned home his back had been glued to the wall; time seemed heavier at the end of the day, as if everything that had happened in his entire life had taken place in one day, the day that he was now watching depart.

More knocks. A cough. Some men. Who? He wasn't expecting anyone. Waiting in the office was pure anguish. It seemed to him that he had but to raise his head and he'd see her standing at the door, with the laugh she had kept from childhood.

Who?

A short, thin man whom he'd often seen as he came and went in the alley.

"Tahun Gharib, train engineer with the Railway Authority."

Atif wondered about Sheikh Atiya. Who was he? Why was he summoning him? At the door Tahun repeated his plea that Ustaz Atif not miss the appointment. He himself had had to ask for a day off, even though it created a mess in scheduling; he would have to forego driving the Upper Egypt train on which he had been working for some time. When Atif closed the door and returned to his spot, he was trembling. Tahun's eyes were still gazing at him from the depths of the darkness, eyes filled with irony, that were intimating clearly: We're all in the same boat.

Hasan Anwar

He was descending the staircase of his house. He had awakened his two sons early lest they be overtaken by the sun and would thus spoil the meeting. He couldn't turn down a request from Sheikh Atiya, even if it was conveyed by Oweis the baker, with his shameful acts. Seldom had the good man requested that anyone go to him. Often people from the countryside came to him from faraway villages, only to discover that he was in seclusion and they had to leave empty handed. Hasan Effendi's two sons were wearing their finest clothes, as if they were going to the Eid prayers.

They did not greatly enjoy their father's company; they had to walk in a certain manner and he often forced them to visit relatives and stay a long time, sitting there quietly. On the street, if he saw an acquaintance, he would hurriedly take a few steps away from his sons, then turn to them and call them over to shake hands with one of his colleagues. He would point to Hassan saying that he was a senior in secondary school and, God willing, was planning to go to medical school. As for Samir, he was about to finish preparatory school and intended to enter the school of engineering. His bragging about them didn't escape Hassan, though it didn't bother him either. Samir, however, was embarrassed; to him his father was like a clown—undignified. He told his brother that their father was exhibiting them like monkeys. Hassan was surprised; he replied that their father had worked hard all his life and had a right to brag about them.

Hassan and Samir were now exchanging glances; they had stayed up late studying and had hoped to sleep in a little more, especially since they were in the reading period preceding their exams. Other men from the alley were standing in front of the sheikh's room. Samir was apprehensive: What if the sheikh were to tell his father about his relations with Atwa, the falafel maker, and Mabruk, the Azhar student?

The presence of Oweis also scared him; he had seen him once at the baths. That day he had only taken a bath. Did Oweis remember him? Samir did his best to avoid eye contact.

They were now shaking hands, exchanging anxious glances. Tahun stood there, very tense. Atif was pale, his arms folded across his chest, while he kept shifting his weight from one foot to the other. Oweis looked energetic. Tekirli stood apart from the others, ignoring them. Tahun said that sunrise would be at exactly 6:04, that he had contacted a friend of his at *al-Nidaa* newspaper who had told him the exact time the sun was expected to rise. It was now 6:03. Hasan Effendi said his watch pointed to six o'clock sharp. Tahun Effendi insisted that his watch was very precise; that it had been acquired by a friend of his who worked at the airport, who had purchased it from the duty-free shop there. He relied on it to check the times of arrival and departure from the different stations, and that was added proof of its accuracy. He finished his explanation with a smiling glance at Tekirli and Atif. Later on, when each of them, alone, recalled what had taken place, neither could determine who it was who cried out, "Come in, please."

(Summary of what was said by Sheikh Atiya at his meeting with fourteen males from Zafarani Alley; it should be noted that he made his statement from behind a faded light brown curtain.)

Without any preliminaries, Sheikh Atiya said that he was fully aware of the condition of those standing before him and the condition of all Zafarani males: they had lost their virility for the time being. Some of those impaired (he used the word 'impairment' many times) had never been men to begin with, and the new situation would not change them in essence except for certain manifestations that in their case had no origin or form:

- Any male whose feet touched the ground of Zafarani would be impaired.
- Any child born from now on in Zafarani would be, a priori, a loser.
- Any Zafarani woman who slept with any man, anywhere in the world, would make him impotent, without regard to nationality or religion.

He said that he had excluded one Zafarani man and one Zafarani woman for his own secret reasons, and that he would never reveal their names. He said that all those who frequented Zafarani Alley would be affected by the spell; he explicitly mentioned those who talked on Hasan Effendi Anwar's telephone, and anyone who shouted in adjoining alleys and whose voice could be heard by the Zafaranites. Anyone who stood outside the alley and loudly called out or made fun of a Zafaranite would be impaired. Also impaired would be anyone who tried to harm any child, woman, or man from Zafarani and any person who tried to enter the alley, whether from under the earth or through the air.

He said that what had befallen them would be cured by neither physical nor psychological treatment.

He said that what had stricken them was only the beginning.

He said that his spell was powerful, mobile, all-enveloping, pervasive and long-lasting; that he had prepared it for reasons of his own and for processes that would be revealed in due course. These processes would not be restricted to Zafarani but would come to include the entire world—all existing things, and all creatures. What impelled him was his contemplation and reflection on conditions and destinies, on reasons near and far. No one but he knew the secrets of the spell; no one but he could undo it. No other spell could counter or weaken the potency of his spell. What he had prepared was the first of its kind, unique in its power. He would heed no one. Anything anyone said would be in vain and any effort would be for naught. They were to leave and keep themselves informed of what he had to say and what he would disclose to them. Nobody was to come to him. Only Oweis would visit him twice daily, at sunrise and at sunset—to receive his messages and convey them to the rest.

Appendix to File 2

What Took Place on Friday and Subsequent Days

Rummana

It should be noted that none of the inhabitants of Zafarani went to work that day. Until 4:00 p.m. none of the usual sounds—the morning chats on staircases or across balconies, the scattered shouts that were usually heard from time to time, a woman ordering her son to put a pot on a table or return something to its place—not one of these sounds could be heard. The clotheslines were completely bare. A large number of children were observed leaving before nine o'clock in the morning. It was later learned that they had been given more pocket money than usual. Most of them went to Cinema al-Kawakib, which showed four movies back-to-back until 4:00 p.m. Some of them—the older ones—went off to ride rental bicycles. Zafarani suddenly lacked the usual noise of children. The elementary schools had closed for the holidays some time earlier and the inhabitants had become used to the children's noises. None of them played sock-ball soccer. Not one grabbed another by his clothes or shouted until his mother looked down from the balcony and gave him instructions: "Hold him by the collar! Take that stone and beat him with it! Hide over there! Beat him! Beat him!" Nor did the other mother then look down from her balcony so that a violent quarrel would ensue, perhaps ending up with the men getting involved after coming home from work.

The silence of Zafarani was noticed by the street vendors who entered the alley. Not one single woman bought anything from any of them. Nor did Umm Suhair call them over. Umm Suhair would usually stop every vendor and loudly ask what he was selling, even though the man's voice was hoarse from shouting his wares; then she would haggle over the prices but yet she rarely ever bought anything. That was why many of the vendors ignored her—not in the sense of not answering her; that they dared not do, for she was not above greeting anyone who annoyed her by pouring a bucket of dirty water on him—but they would answer her questions without enthusiasm and use their arguments with her as a way of advertising their prices to the other women. Umm Suhair did not even look out, even though the windows of her house remained open. This surprised the eleven vendors listed hereinafter:

- Three: the first, Bayyumi, is from Bulaq al-Dakrur; the second, Abdel Hadi, is from al-Utuf; the third, Wanis, is from Upper Egypt. They all sell vegetables.
- A fabrics peddler whose name is Haridi and who lives in al-Hamzawi al-Kabir. He carries bundles of fabrics—batiste, flannel, and pique—and a wooden measure that he keeps under his arm.
- Fusduq, the sweet-potato vendor; always seen in Darb al-Farrakha Alley at nightfall, sleeping on his cart.
- A woman who sells sour milk, carrying it in a skin placed inside a basket on top of her head; splendid figure; beautiful voice; comes on foot from the direction of Shubra al-Khayma; name: unknown.

- A cotton-candy vendor; did not sell anything in Zafarani on account of the absence of children.
- An itinerant tinker called Amm Radwan; rumored to have spent some time in the loony bin. When he goes up to a house to mend a stove, he sits on the landing and the women sit around him, eyeing him in fear. They try to get him to talk about his experience in the hospital, but he doesn't speak much. He may sing suddenly, or cry, then stop as suddenly as he began. It is said that the reason he lost his mind was his love for his wife who ran out on him twenty years ago. He is thought to be quite virile, and many women are thought to have had sex with him when their husbands were away, tempted by his virility and feeble-mindedness, for who would believe that his wife would let a crazy idiot like him sleep with her? Some of the women give him money or food. It is said that he once got mad at a beautiful woman from Guwwaniya Alley whom many would love just to look at. He stood in the middle of the street shouting at the top of his voice: "Woman, I slept with you, you . . . ." Nobody believed him, not even her husband. This encouraged the other women. There are those who are certain that he is per-fectly sane. Some tell how they heard him one night in al-Watawit Alley scoffing at those who thought he was mad. Only God knows the truth.
- To the above should be added the mailman.

At 12:05 p.m. one of those who had been away came back; it was Usta Rummana, the political prisoner, also known as the politico. Everything he saw looked new to him. He wondered how he could have forgotten certain features of the alley, despite being able to recall them so vividly while in jail. When he had left the headquarters of the Supreme Security Authority an hour earlier, he had begun to imagine the way Zafarani would welcome his return: A woman's shout, "Usta Rummana is out!" Umm Suhair would come out on her balcony and, with her huge body, lean out, shouting "God is great! God is great!" His neighbors from way back would shower him with the family feeling that he so missed. All his prison mates had gone back to their wives; but he was not coming back to a family. He imagined the succession of neighbors visiting his room, saying, "God be praised for your safe return!" And he would respond to the greeting twice. The first time to himself, his heart whispering: What safe return? and the second one audibly: "May God keep you safe."

Had the inhabitants moved to other alleys? News from Zafarani did not reach him inside because nobody corresponded with him. In his absence, one of his relatives had come every two or three months to pay the modest rent to Sergeant Major Sallam. In previous stints he had lost the rooms he'd rented and what little furniture he'd bought. The cruelest thing facing someone leaving jail was to have no shelter, especially these days when people had so little sympathy for each other. He was now climbing the stairs slowly, his heartbeat slowing. Ali the ironer's apartment door was closed, and he had no idea who was living in the room under the staircase. The heavy silence reminded him of the cells in solitary confinement, the prison-within-the-prison where all the sounds of the world were banished except for that train that he used to hear twice toward the end of the night. The first time, at exactly 2:00 a.m., it sounded remote, adding new layers to his melancholy. The second time it sounded closer; he heard the wheels as they crossed the gaps in the rails. Now he was opening the door to his room: dust, cobwebs, rust, tight clothes, lime-wash on the glass of the only window. He sat on the edge of the bed, his hands gripped between his knees. What had happened? The silence was getting heavier even though the noise in the alley usually increased around that time. The sounds of ball-playing used to get so loud that he would have to go down and ask the boys to play a little farther away so he could sleep. It was as if the whole of Zafarani were taking part in a funeral procession somewhere.

At two-thirty a radio played the music of the afternoon newscast, the first loud sound that had been heard in the alley since sunrise, aside from the vendors' calls and the noise the children made in their almost collective exodus. Some of the children had preferred to play on the swings in al-Hussein Square and drink fruit juices at Kharalambo's in Ataba Square. These ones began to return around three o'clock—almost in time for lunch. At around four o'clock Rummana imagined he heard someone shouting, but couldn't tell where it was coming from. Maybe all the good Zafaranites had moved to other places. That was natural, even though it saddened him and aggravated his loneliness and reminded him of the passing of time and the accompanying changes. While his own life had been constrained in a relentless pattern, many variables shaped the lives of others. The city now looked different; he had noticed a tunnel which carried cars in both directions; the red buses looked strange to him. They had torn down the old buildings in al-Hussein Square and put up new ones. But that was nothing compared to the silence that surrounded him in Zafarani. Perhaps it would have been better if he had come via Bayt al-Mal Street and passed by Daturi's café. But he had chosen to enter the alley from the side street of Umm al-Ghulam.

At four-twenty, Rummana heard the voices of Sitt Busayna and Usta Abdu. The people of Zafarani were used to their constant bickering and fighting and, although their arguments were an eternal backdrop to life in the alley, the first sign of raised voices was enough to bring the women out to the windows, especially Khadija, the Sa'idi woman who never left home without her husband the carpenter. These quarrels relieved the monotony of her life, especially since she didn't have a radio and her husband didn't allow her to go watch television at the apartment of Sitt Farida, wife of Radish-head, who had been the very first to install the familiar metal antenna on her balcony. But Sitt Khadija didn't go out to her balcony to look when Sitt Busayna's voice was heard, and that was strange.

What happened in Sitt Busayna's apartment was only learned about later. Immediately upon leaving the sheikh's room, Usta Abdu had gone back to his wife and, without giving her a chance to wash her face, had insisted on doing it there and then. She lay down, legs spread. Who could tell what might happen? Knowing nothing of the sheikh's announcement, she was taken by surprise. What was now happening? He had been failing every day for a whole week now and she was fed up with him, but here he was, resuming his strivings.

Who knew what might happen now? Perhaps the sheikh had meant himself, when he said that only one man in Zafarani would be able to manage it. She was extremely aroused and had reached a degree of intense burning excitement, but he was unable to put out her fire. When he finally gave up completely at three o'clock, he told her what had happened. She refused to believe him. She said it was just an excuse. From now on, she could not keep someone who was a man only in name. He said it wasn't his problem alone, that what had happened to him had happened to everybody else as well. She punched him and he shrank in terror. In the past when that happened, he would at worst run away while she chased him, or he'd return her blows. Twice he had bitten her on the shoulder and the buttocks. He now looked so small in her eyes, as she held her slipper with its wooden heel; his pleading eyes had provoked her. She was cruel to him for reasons she couldn't even name; perhaps because he kept flailing about all day long like a fish, and all to no avail. He raised his hands to protect himself like a child and began to scream even before she touched him. Suddenly she threw the slipper down and went out on the balcony. He, in the meantime, could not stop screaming. She announced from her balcony that some bastards whom Zafarani had sheltered for many years were now harming others. She would not put up with it. If some people thought their amulets were invincible, there were others who had even stronger amulets. Zafarani had been humiliated enough since it had allowed those who had no families, and no grace, to play with its destiny.

Usta Rummana the politico listened in amazement. What was happening? He looked out of his narrow window just when Busayna stopped to see what effect her words were having on the alley. Nobody had gone out to hear her; she caught a glimpse of Rummana and addressed him, saying that there were no real men in the alley, that all that had already happened and all that would happen to them now was fully deserved because they had lost their manhood a long time ago. What was going on? He went back to his room. He avoided looking at any woman for long, so as to prevent potential accusations. He looked up at the wooden beams supporting the ceiling. Busayna knew him well, yet she hadn't said a word about his return, hadn't congratulated him. He smiled sardonically when he heard her saying that there were no men in the alley.

At about five o'clock Tekirli went to see Atif. It is not known what took place in that meeting, but Tekirli was also seen before sunset talking to Tahun. He told them he was preparing to take counter-measures through his acquaintances. Tahun wished him success but seemed reserved, unwilling to speak. Tekirli, on the other hand, did not hide his annoyance.

Sunset. Children's noises. Balconies without women. Umm Suhair, who used to tell anecdotes and stories, had not appeared. Atif had not gone out on time for the third day in a row. Hasan Anwar's windows had not been opened. Under Sitt Busayna's house, the old woman Latifa came out and sat facing her husband, al-Bannan, an old worker in a coffee mill. They always talked about just one thing—their son Ismail, who had left years ago. The last letter from him had arrived five months before; he had told them that he had passed through the port of Alexandria but couldn't leave the ship. With the letter he had sent twenty Egyptian pounds. Latifa had ululated and Zafarani had spread the news from the balconies and during the nightly supper conversations between the women and their husbands. Now old Latifa was talking about her son's favorite things: he liked tea sweetened with lumps of sugar and didn't like fine granulated sugar; he liked to drink tea twice a day. In the morning he would dunk bread into it, and he would drink tea again when he got up from his siesta before sunset. Until now she had continued to make tea at the same time. She kept his bed empty, making it afresh every morning as if Ismail had slept in it the whole night. Months ago one of their relatives had come from the village. Al-Bannan had suggested that he sleep at their place, for he was an old man and the hotels around al-Hussein were expensive and uncomfortable. She refused to allow this; for someone else to sleep in Ismail's bed was a bad omen. Al-Bannan was obliged to pay the hotel bill for his relative two days in a row, at great cost to his meager finances. They both imagined Ismail coming in. The mother would be awakened by something sounding like knocks. Her heart would shake like a slaughtered dove and she would cry out, "Who's that? Ismail?" In disappointment she would press her hands to her head when she discovered that the sound wasn't knocks on the door but something else, far away. Now they were sitting, facing each other, not knowing what was going on in the alley, thinking of nothing but Ismail; perhaps he was at the ends of the earth, or perhaps he was coming up the alley by Hagg Snaibar's bakery, heading for their house. At nightfall they went inside to continue their vigil.

The sound of a qanun being played started coming from Qurqur's house, then it was intermittent, and then it stopped altogether. A child began crying. A loud voice started chiding him. A voice then began crying out, "Oh God!" It seemed that Sergeant Major Sallam and his wife had gone out, because Usta Rummana didn't find them when he went downstairs and knocked at their door. He saw a man wearing a galabiya, squatting down in front of the room under the staircase. The man raised his hand in greeting: "Your servant, Oweis the baker." The usta asked about the sergeant major and his wife. Oweis said he hadn't seen them, that they must be in their room. Rummana replied that he had knocked many times at their door but nobody had answered. Oweis laughed; the sergeant major was very old and surely must have given up all that a long time before the spell was cast, so why had he closed the door? "What spell?" asked Rummana, and Oweis replied that the whole alley knew, the usta must have just returned from a trip. Rummana said that he had indeed come back from a trip-like absence. Oweis asked why he had come back to the alley on this particular day. The usta asked what was going on—this was not the Zafarani he knew.

Oweis remained impassive; perhaps the sheikh would get angry if he learned of this chatter. Other inhabitants could speak as much as they liked. For him, however, things were different. The sheikh had chosen him to convey his messages. Oweis's hopes were haunting him again; perhaps the sheikh would help him get a pushcart. . . .

Rummana was puzzled by Oweis's sudden silence. Why was everything so strange? What was this spell? As he left the house, Rummana saw Tahun Effendi, who knew him well. He had often stopped to talk with him about communism and socialism in the past. Tahun had spoken of a way he'd discovered to arrive at universal socialism. He believed it

91

was necessary for thousands of people—the poor, crushed masses—to work in solidarity and in absolute secrecy. They would begin by digging a huge network of tunnels interconnected with other tunnels in which they would hide during the day and leave at night to loot palaces and rob banks, storing the loot in the depths of the tunnels. The rich would be forced into abject poverty as a result of the theft of their fortunes, bit by bit. Then they would be recruited to join the tunnel dwellers who, once they had achieved control of all the earth's fortunes, would spring back into the light of day and build a world free of poverty and disease. Tahun Effendi said a group of strong men would be in charge of the mission and they would be the ones to supervise the redistribution of wealth. Money would be banned; a few specimens would just be displayed in museums. Money was the root of all evil. Besides, it reflected the stupidity of human beings, since one banknote had a value of ten piasters, which was not enough to buy even a pack of cigarettes, while another banknote of exactly the same size had a value of a hundred pounds or a thousand dollars or ten thousand francs, which might buy a whole automobile. The era of these symbolic paper notes would end with the achievement of universal socialism; any human being who worked would be given food and drink. He said that he had prepared detailed plans and little booklets that explained the theory of the tunnels and how to go about making and organizing them. His work as an engineer with the railways would enable him to put out the call. Right now, however, he shared his views only with those who were closest to him, and Usta Rummana was close to him because he too believed in an ideal. Although Tahun disagreed with Rummana's ideas, he respected him nonetheless. To prove what he said, he would refer to various books, including some by Marx and Lenin. He would also mention Rosa Luxemburg and then fall silent, as if his knowledge of the name alone was proof of the most profound understanding of Usta Rummana's own ideology.

Rummana's eyes now met those of Tahun Effendi, but the latter did not stop, nor did his face light up. Instead, with a panic-stricken look, he ran into his house as if escaping. The usta was surprised. Had jail changed his appearance? The cobblestones of the alley were shining under the streetlight; there were zucchini peels, potato skins, and torn-up paper in front of Umm Sabri's house. He slowly headed for Daturi's café. Daturi was there as usual, sitting in silence. If he talked, it was usually about the apartment building that he was planning to build on land he had not yet selected or bought. For many years Daturi had been talking about that building, so much so that some customers had offered him cash as a pledge on the key money. They begged and begged him to accept it, but he would shake his head and ask them to wait. All he would agree to take was one month's rent as a security deposit. He knew that some people had to sell their furniture to get the sum necessary for key money. Some of the customers tried to get him to give his word of honor, but he refused, deciding to study, case by case, all the applications to rent an apartment in his building. It didn't make sense for him to deny an apartment to a bride living apart from her bridegroom. Rumors began to spread that the me'allim would only rent to newlyweds, but he denied it.

Usta Rummana was now at the café. Nobody welcomed him; nobody noticed him. His feeling of loneliness gave way to a strong sense of astonishment. In the past, Zafarani people had greeted him and had not been afraid to welcome him, since to them he was a hero who had defied the government and gone to jail. What had happened to them? Ali the ironer, who lived on the floor immediately below his, was sitting there saying that the spell could only have been prepared in India. A few months before, he had seen three Indians enter Zafarani after the sheikh had ended his seclusion. Someone asked whether it was true that one man would not lose his virility. Rummana asked what was going on.

Daturi noticed him there and in a slightly raised voice which, compared with his usual tone of voice, sounded like shouting, he called out, "Who's that? Usta Rummana? God be praised for your safe return!" They embraced. Usta Ali shook hands with Rummana. One young man, an outsider, asked who he was and Usta Ali said that Rummana had been away for as long as a trip to India would take. The young man replied that one could go to India and return in four days, but Rummana had been away for four years. Usta Ali said that India was much farther than people imagined. The young man laughed. He said that the usta attributed everything to India. Usta Ali said that without the secrets of India, none of what had taken place in Zafarani would have come to pass. Rummana now felt depressed, perhaps because this was the hour that the guards usually made their daily inspection. They would then turn their keys in the huge locks and the doors would remain locked until morning, and even though the door of the cell only opened on to the central ward where the doors were yet more massive still, the prisoners used to beg the guards and bribe them with cigarettes to keep the cells open, if only for a few more minutes. The men in the café looked furtively at Usta Rummana.

Daturi shook the mouthpiece of his hookah and said to Rummana, "Couldn't you have stayed away or gone somewhere else? Why did you come back to Zafarani?"

Tekirli

On the Saturday morning Tekirli told his wife he was going to consult Rushdi Bey, the legal expert. She raised her eyebrows. She looked so beautiful and fresh; that was how she always looked when she got up. If any of his acquaintances could see her now, they wouldn't think twice about paying whatever he asked. Nadia tried to remember the man of that name. It was Rushdi Bey, who hadn't visited them for some time because he had been away in Europe, and had come back a month before and inquired about the "apple," although Tekirli hadn't told her at the time. She bit her full red lower lip and he smiled. He told her that he would remind her who he was. Gradually his voice lowered to a soft whisper and he said it was the short fat man who only looked at her naked body then shrank away into a corner of the bed, crying, sighing, and gasping in regretful sorrow.

Nadia bowed her head and closed her eyes. Her face was covered with shame. He came so close to her that his mouth almost touched her ear. What pleasure did he find in relating the details? He would begin quietly then his voice would tremble and his body would shake while his soft voice penetrated her veins. Sometimes he suggested to some of his clients that he watch part of the intercourse. Usually he would first go into the bedroom on his own while Nadia sat with the client in the living room, drinking some of the liquor that the client had brought. Tekirli in the meantime would be sweeping the floor of the room, changing the sheets on the bed, smoothing over the little wrinkles, lighting the rose-colored lamp on the nightstand, trembling as he anticipated what was about to take place. He would look around him, call out, stretch Nadia out himself and undress her, bit by bit. Some clients preferred to undress her themselves; one high-ranking official actually demanded that she put her clothes back on when he saw that she was naked. If Tekirli was allowed to watch, he would sit on a low chair and put his hands flat on his knees, his forehead moist with sweat as he followed every quiver of her body, gnashing his teeth when she closed her eyes; he would leave the room dizzy. He would be highly excited whenever he saw her toes twitch with pleasure.

Now Tekirli was trying to recall everything that Rushdi Bey had done, how he had only licked her nipples; all the details of the last three visits were still vivid in his mind. Suddenly, however, the pleasure of relating these details was lost. Nadia's eyes were still closed; that was how she always listened to him. The way he whispered aroused her more than any of those men. When he whispered like that, she forgot the alley and the women; she forgot going with Tekirli to some of the acquaintances whose social status prevented them from coming to Zafarani; she even forgot the hassle she suffered from rich old Arabs. There was only one person that Tekirli didn't mention: that was Nabil, the university student who visited almost a year ago and paid only one pound, which angered Tekirli so much that he never brought him back again. In her husband's absence, however, Nabil visited her many times.

Nadia opened her eyes slowly; something was causing Tekirli's voice to tremble. What was the matter with him? She clasped her hands before her breast; throughout her life with him she had never uttered a single word against him, even during the early months of their marriage and his nightly agony. Had he now lost the ability to talk as well?

Suddenly Tekirli got up, declaring that it was necessary to take the severest measures against Sheikh Atiya. He was going to turn the whole world against the sheikh. He had talked to Radish-head, Atif the college graduate, Tahun, and Ali the ironer. He looked at her apologetically; circumstances were forcing him to mobilize all his forces, and by condescending to talk to those whom he had long despised, he would make them more daring in moving with him. Now he was provoked. Bringing a client home had become risky since the spell affected anyone whose feet touched Zafarani. If that happened repeatedly it would lead to a scandal. But with someone like Rushdi Bey, there'd be no risk since he usually stopped at touching. There were not many like him though.

Nadia was afraid of one thing only: that Nabil might come. The reason for her fear was not Tekirli, who couldn't stand seeing him—whenever she mentioned him he yelled at her, demanding that she never talk about that "little pupil" again. Then he would embrace her; he was jealous. She was quite surprised, but said nothing. Every night he would bring her five men, sometimes seven. Some of them really loved her and brought her gifts, wrote her love letters, and held her hand and pressed it with real passion. And yet he couldn't bear to hear Nabil's name. From the moment Tekirli had set eyes on him he had had a strange feeling. He saw a mysterious affinity between his wife and Nabil, as if he were her brother; the way he whispered to her scared him, as did the way she looked at him. Now she was afraid that Nabil might turn up. She had seen the spell in action; real studs who had been servicing her for years became impotent in her arms—a strange powerlessness created a barrier between two bodies about to unite.

Tekirli didn't ask her what she was thinking about; he was used to her long silences, when she'd fix her eyes on one spot in the room. She decided to risk everything; she would go to Nabil. He lived in the dorm. Which building? Which room? That she didn't know. She wouldn't give up hope of finding him. She would say that she was his sister who had come from the village. She must prevent his coming here. Tekirli was kissing her now. She got up to see him off.

Two years earlier, Umm Suhair had chanced to be coming down from the roof where she had left an old rug overnight in the open air and had caught sight of her. She had cried out, "A morning of beauty, bliss, and flowers to the bride!" and Nadia had blushed. Throughout the day, Umm Suhair had done the rounds, making visits to say that with her own eyes she had seen Tekirli kissing his wife. Sitt Busayna commented that this was one of the customs of the gentry. Farida, however, wore a dreamy look in her eyes and said they were perfectly matched to each other. Sitt Busayna referred to some rich relatives of hers who lived in a palace in Zamalek. Once when visiting them she had been surprised when one of her relatives had kissed her. It was a light kiss that barely left an impression. She felt confused and didn't know what to do, but the young man had moved away as if nothing had happened. Later Umm Suhair told Farida that what Busayna had said was a bunch of lies; that the young man she had mentioned had to be one of those punks left over from the legacy of her old cabaret dancing days. As for Sitt Khadija, the Sa'idi woman, she said that her husband had never kissed her, but that sometimes he would move his mouth close to her cheek and stretch his lips forward to make a smacking sound, using his tongue and not his lips. Did that count as a kiss?

Tekirli realized that he had to be careful. Everybody in Zafarani had his own calamity, it was true, but now everyone's eyes would be open more widely. It would be enough for the inhabitants of Zafarani to get to know just one aspect of his life to ruin his reputation for ten years. He suddenly stopped at the entrance to the house. Oweis the baker was coming from the direction of the sheikh's house and stood right in the middle of the alley, planted his legs wide, cupped his hand around his mouth like a bullhorn, and called out:

"People of Zafarani! People of Zafarani!"

Daturi

What Oweis said reverberated not only through the whole of Zafarani, but it became the subject of heated discussions at Daturi's café as well. The content of the message was even discussed in other cafés in the same neighborhood, such as Café al-Salam and Salih Safiha's café and the café that belonged to Umar Birwaz, relatively far from Zafarani, which meant that the story was constantly growing bigger. By the end of the night it had reached the ears of a young man who lived in Bayt al-Qadi and who was a student-at-large at the Faculty of Arts, Department of Journalism, whose interest was piqued and who said he would talk to the editor in chief of the daily where he was interning, since he thought it was a "scoop." Some of the regulars at Daturi's café had sounded sarcastic as they discussed what they'd heard, but Oweis's announcement now tempered their sarcasm somewhat. A real panic broke out among the men living in adjoining alleys. Me'allim Daturi would not answer any questions; he was now quite impassive and seemed indifferent to everything. Yet he was listening hard to everything that was being said. He had often listened to the conversations among transients or, as café owners called them, "roving" customers. He sometimes only came in in the middle of a conversation, and would remain outwardly impassive while thinking fast as he tried to make sense of what was being said. His hearing was so sharp that if he wanted to hear a conversation between two people in the midst of all the noise, he wouldn't miss a syllable. Once, Hagg Abdel Mu'min, the coppersmith, one of the devotees of al-Hussein, came to the café with a hearing aid that he had brought from Hijaz which was skillfully hidden in the frame of his prescription glasses, with no wires attached. Daturi expressed an interest and asked several questions; he inquired about the possibility of focusing on one specific sound among many. The hagg said that was impossible since the hearing aid magnified all sounds at the same time without distinguishing one from another. Daturi's enthusiasm then ended abruptly and he praised God for the blessings of sight and hearing.

Now Daturi heard strangers relating Oweis's pronouncements, casting aspersions on Oweis and even questioning his identity. One of them said he was a lost soul who had no family; another disagreed, saying the sheikh had been preparing him for this task for a long time. A man in a turban wondered: Could the memory of this illiterate man retain exactly what the sheikh had said? A young man asserted that an illiterate person usually had the best memory, and the proof of this were those peasants who made the most complex calculations using only their fingers without making mistakes. Daturi exhaled thick smoke. He was annoyed. It was his alley, the alley in which he had lived all his life, where he was born, which he loved, and about which he said that each stone and each tile contained a piece of his flesh and a part of his life. It was the alley that he would defend jealously whenever an obnoxious stranger entered or an impudent vendor passed through it. Pointing to the dust of Zafarani, he would say it was a vitamin that nourished his blood; he would never leave it. Were the good, sweet old days of Zafarani gone forever? The men going together to perform the dawn prayers at al-Hussein or their nightly gatherings— was all that gone too? What a pity! Zafarani was the talk of the town, his customers and those of the other cafés. Perhaps even the papers would jump into the fray and the whole world would begin to talk. Zafarani's nakedness would be exposed and gentle discretion and modesty would be lost.

One customer said the sheikh was about to reveal terrible scandals affecting those who had moved against him. Another wondered: Did what went on among the people actually reach him? A policeman laughed, saying that he couldn't wait for those scandals, but then suddenly he stopped. Who knew where it would all end? Perhaps the spell would affect those who mocked the sheikh or badmouthed him. Another topic drew the attention of the whole café and was raised by all those who talked about what had happened. It was the strange order that Oweis had repeated seven times, namely, that Zafarani inhabitants had to comply with a new system: bed at 8:00 p.m. at night and no leaving the alley before 7:00 a.m. in the morning.

A heavy weight slowly began to descend on Daturi. What the customers and the strangers didn't know was that the alley's elite had gone to Oweis the baker at about 4:00 p.m. and begged him to ask the sheikh to revoke this rule, since it would affect their livelihoods. Tahun had been driving the night Upper Egypt–Cairo train for the last twenty years; this required leaving the alley at 8:30 p.m. If he followed the sheikh's instructions he would lose his job. As for Hasan Effendi, he hoped an exception could be made in the case of his two sons, Hassan and Samir, since they both stayed up late studying and when their lord, Sheikh Atiya, learned of their diligence and industry he would surely bless them and permit them to stay up. As for himself and his wife, they were committed to carrying out every letter of every word that their lord and master said. Usta Abdu hoped his wife would be exempted because she was used to staying up late and he himself had to come home late because of his work as a taxi driver at the end of his shift at the Cairo Transit Authority. Ali the ironer explained his own position, pointing to the customers who insisted on getting their clothes back, pressed, the same night because they went to work early in the morning and had only a few changes of clothes. He said he would only truly rest if he emigrated to India, but until that happened, he was hoping to be excluded.

Oweis had listened politely and promised to convey what they said honestly. Apparently Tahun didn't completely trust Oweis's ability to convey the messages and had asked him to repeat them. Oweis had answered gruffly that he would not miss one word. They all hesitated a little, then retreated from his room. At the door they met Rummana the politico. Usta Abdu said, "You would have been better off in jail." Rummana replied that he didn't believe what was being said, that it was certainly just clowning on the part of a senile fool who was trying to impose his will on Zafarani by deceit. At that point Hasan Anwar's hand stretched out in warning, and he winked in the direction of Oweis's room. No need to rock the boat.

Daturi sat sadly recalling what had taken place, and listening to what was being said around him: "Has Zafarani fallen so low?"

Radish-head

He had forgotten himself in the warehouse, he said, and he asked Oweis to tell the sheikh how sorry he was to have stayed out past the curfew. He promised to honor it the following day. He would close his store early despite the financial loss he would incur by forgoing late-night customers. Many heads of families used to stop by the store on their way home from work and buy supper for their children: cheese and halva or eggs and bastirma. From the expression on the face of each father he could tell how he was doing financially and how much money was in his pocket—those trembling, uneasy glances at the merchandise: what food to buy and what could he do without?

Farida now sat eyeing the tray of basbusa that he had brought home for the first time in ages and wondered whether he had done this because of the sheikh's instructions too. He said he had bought it from al-Khudari, the famous pastry maker who used real ghee and who stuffed his baklava and kunafa with hazelnuts and walnuts. She carried the tray in clenched fingers, turning it right and left, and inquired why he had been late in the warehouse. He said curtly that he had been looking at a few things.

Farida did not insist on knowing what he did at the warehouse, knowing it would be pointless to ask. She had enquired many times about the contents of the warehouse, but he always evaded her questions. Whatever he bought at the auctions he always took straight to the warehouse. Only once, a few months after the birth of her daughter Nashwa, did he come home late one night carrying some pictures. She remembered his tired eyes; he placed the pictures on the rug and on noticing that they were covered with a heavy layer of dust, she asked him to move them into the hall so they wouldn't dirty the furniture. He went out and she followed. He undid a leather strap around the pictures. He didn't touch his tea and didn't wash his face. He took the frames one by one and with the sleeve of his galabiya wiped the dust that had collected on the glass. She remembered some of them: a picture of a little harbor where some boats with folded sails were anchored; a narrow street shining after rainfall. The one picture over which he lingered a long time was that of a woman with a round face and big eyes, with a faint smile on her lips, and a man with a thick mustache behind her, his fingers curling over her left shoulder. Her face looked like the faces of the actresses she had seen in the old movies of Muhammad Abdel Wahhab. As for the man, she couldn't tell whether he was an Egyptian or a foreigner. Radish-head had tsk-tsked, looked at the picture, passed his fingers over a hasty signature inscribed at the bottom, and looked sad. She had asked, "Did he know them?" He said he didn't know a thing about them, that the picture was dozens of years old, that they must have turned into decomposed bones by now. Suddenly he bent, holding the picture, saying they were a bride and bridegroom. She saw an arrangement of white roses touching the woman's chest and noticed a pair of long white lacy gloves on her hands, and pinned at the breast a delicate brooch.

That day she had looked at Radish-head and wished she could run out, get a bucket of water, and pour it on the pictures. But the intensity of the attention he lavished on them, which was no less than the attention he gave to the money he emptied into the tub and then arranged anew, made her stop thinking of playing. She had left him and gone to bed. When she got up a while later, she had found herself alone. The hall was lit and Radish-head was sitting in the far corner with the picture of the man and woman in front of him. She watched him for a few minutes. He got up, put the picture where he had just been sitting and then moved to the other corner. She made an angry gesture with her hand and went back to bed. She imagined him inside the warehouse gazing at the old things he had bought from a street vendor, an antique store, or an auction.

Now, however, Radish-head sat staring ahead, afraid to make eye contact. If he went to bed he might have to try. He was thinking of the nights to come. Would Farida put up with it, especially as what the spell did to women was not clear? True, if any of them—except for one—slept with any man he too would be affected by the spell, but did those women affected by the spell still have their own desires intact? What did Farida's anxiety and her pretense of being asleep last night mean? What if she found herself forced into another man's arms? Even if no man could push himself inside her body, she would still be naked. A strange idea haunted him: Which man was it who would see her nakedness? In whose arms would she bury herself? Whose chest would she bite? Who was he? Where was he now? How big was his organ? As a child he had wondered about the girl he was going to marry: Where was she? What was her name? What did she look like? After his wedding he had thought: Where had she been playing on the Friday of the week he had turned eighteen when he had not yet seen her? What day had it been? A Wednesday? A Sunday? Or . . . . He was certain that tonight she was thinking of something very specific: the one man in Zafarani who was still fully virile. Some customers had mentioned the subject, but he had avoided them by taking down some cans from the shelves.

Farida nudged him in the chest: What's the matter with you? Tonight he appeared to her much smaller than on any previous night, all withdrawn, as if he were afraid of a sudden attack by something or someone. He pointed to the tray of basbusa. She pursed her lips. A thin stream of icy cold sweat was trickling down his back. He wished he could rush away to his warehouse, turn on the light, and sit quietly in front of the antique costume collection. Earlier that evening he had sat for a long time in front of a formal black suit from the inside of which hung a short sword with an ornamental hilt. In his head he had drawn a picture of that unknown pasha, imagining him getting close to his wife as if he were going to deliver a speech to the Senate, then taking off his fez to reveal a bald head, then unbuttoning his suit and standing there naked. He had tried to imagine the ecstasy of sex on the face of that dignified pasha.

Farida embarked on the frivolity he had been dreading—pushing her fingers into his ribs. "Stop it, Farida; shame on you." She stopped suddenly and sat facing him, an abrupt seriousness on her face. Her silence tormented him. He asked about the news of Zafarani. His voice was low and she could see how humiliated he felt. She said that Oweis had shouted out an announcement that the sheikh had turned down the requests of Tahun, Hasan Anwar, and Usta Abdu. He had said that Zafarani had a special law and a design different from all others. Radish-head was interested; he asked her to recall exactly what Oweis had said. She said that she hadn't forgotten a single syllable because he had repeated everything three times. The whole alley had looked out of their windows: the men, the women, and the children. Not a single sound could be heard except that of Oweis's voice. He had mentioned Tekirli's name, announcing that the sheikh intended to expose his secrets within two days. Umm Suhair said that the sheikh's curse would strike Tekirli and his wife on account of what had happened. There had been rumors at noon to the effect that Tekirli was coming from the direction of al-Hussein Square accompanied by an engineer from City Hall and some workers, heading for house number 11 in Zafarani in order to examine it, as they had been informed that it was about to collapse and therefore had to be evacuated and its inhabitants relocated to some new neighborhood, such as Matariya or Madinat Nasr.

Radish-head said the sheikh's blessing would prevent the house from collapsing. He said it loudly, hoping that it would somehow reach the sheikh's ears. At the same time his heart beat faster. He was anxious to hear the news from Farida, and was secretly hoping that Tekirli would succeed. Farida said that three men who didn't live in Zafarani had appeared in front of Daturi's café. They had told the engineer and the workers that any man whose feet touched Zafarani would lose his virility. The engineer showed no concern because he was familiar with the tricks of landlords. This was only the latest. One of the men standing nearby remarked that the landlords lived somewhere else, far away, and never came to check on the house because its total rent came to only one Egyptian pound, the rent of Zannuba the divorcée's room. As for the sheikh's room, no rent had ever been collected for that. Nevertheless, the engineer insisted on going ahead, encouraged by what Tekirli had said about the trickery of landlords.

The workers were afraid. One of them reminded the engineer of what had happened to a colleague of theirs when they had started tearing the tomb of Sidi al-Halwagi, while widening al-Hussein Square: no sooner had he raised his hand holding the pickax than it had turned stiff and become paralyzed. If this had occurred at the tomb of a holy man who had died some time ago, imagine what would happen with this sheikh who was still alive! By this time a large number of passersby had gathered; nobody knew where they had heard all the minute details about what was happening. The engineer became confused; averting his gaze to the engagement ring on his right hand, he told Tekirli that he had to notify the higher-ups in his department.

Tekirli grew angry: How could an engineer who had studied in Europe believe such superstitions? The workers were refusing, came the reply. Tekirli took one pound out of his wallet and waved it in front of them, but they turned their faces away. One of the passersby shouted at Tekirli that it was unfair to cause them to lose their virility in Zafarani. A voice was heard loudly saying, "It must be because the effendi himself is not a man." Tekirli shouted at the engineer, threatening to tell the director in person about what happened. The engineer shrugged his shoulders and said he would request that someone else be sent. Besides, no previous records mentioned any defects in the house. He said that it was suspicious that he had only received personal instructions from one of the directors.

In a few moments Tekirli found himself alone; even the passersby had moved away, as if the sight of a Zafaranite was enough to make them lose their manhood. As for the three strangers who had appeared at the beginning, nobody saw them again. Ali the ironer had asserted that they were Indians. Umm Suhair had then announced that the sheikh's special powers were now clear for everyone to see. Radish-head nodded his head in agreement and secretly regretted Tekirli's failure. He asked about the other news of the alley. Farida said that Busayna had quarreled with Sitt Zannuba the divorcée, but that it was a short quarrel; Busayna had called Zannuba a "lost woman," whereupon Zannuba had cried and that made the people pity her. The reasons for the quarrel were not yet known. A radish vendor had entered the alley, but when they told him about the spell, he had run out again. At about 3:00 p.m., three women wearing black had appeared and asked about somebody called Farag, but nobody could tell them anything. The mailman had not made his round of Zafarani, a matter which caused al-Bannan and his wife some puzzlement. Leaning on each other, they had walked from house to house inquiring if anyone had seen the mailman. They told Farida that sometimes he got lazy and threw the letters in front of any old house, relying on the fact that everybody in Zafarani knew everybody else. Farida denied receiving any letters, and Al-Bannan and his wife had left her house arm in arm.

Farida suddenly fell silent and Radish-head wished she would continue to speak, even to play about. He was puzzled by her features, which had suddenly fallen as still as the portraits he stored in his warehouse. He didn't know what he was going to do. He was hoping the sheikh would bless him. The sheikh was bound to give special consideration to those who had obeyed him; surely he would favor them over the others. Now he had to find something to occupy Farida so that his glances were not crushed when they met her eyes.

He went to the steel safe in the wall, opened it, and took out a black briefcase. He slowly drew out bundles of banknotes. Not long before, the same amount had fitted inside a small envelope. When the order banning one-hundred-pound notes had been issued he had been terribly upset and had had to buy a leather briefcase to hold the amount that had once fitted in an envelope. Strangely enough, he had kept one of the one-hundred-pound denomination notes, even though he was fully aware that it had no value. He had complete sets of the money used throughout the last century. Now he was breaking into the bundles slowly, moistening the tip of his finger and beginning to count, adjusting here and there an upturned note. He looked at Farida from the corner of his eye; she didn't get up as she usually did, nor did she snatch up a ten pound note to hide in her bra and which he usually had to struggle hard to snatch back from her. Even if she were to snatch ten notes now he wouldn't try to get them back. He thought of giving her twenty pounds, but he preferred to wait until she asked.

The door opened and Nashwa, their daughter, entered. He closed the briefcase quickly. He did not exchange tender words with his two daughters; he was certain they had no respect for him. Nashwa came up closer and said that a lot of people were predicting that the exams would be difficult, that she was weak in the English language, and that was why she was hoping her mother would give her some money—because Ustaz Akif, the English teacher, had decided to offer a tutorial to a group of students after the end of classes. Her mother could come to the school to obtain the schedule of those tutorials. By that, of course, she meant that Radish-head could do so, but the two daughters were accustomed to not talking to him directly. Whatever they needed they

108

would ask their mother for in his presence. That annoyed him. He had once scolded Farida because she had brought about this mutual aversion between him and the girls. She had responded frivolously, springing to his shoulders, fondling his head.

Now he was looking at Farida, asking her how much those tutorials would cost. Nashwa, addressing her mother, said they cost five pounds a month. He took one note from the briefcase and gave it to Farida saying it was a ten pound note to pay for the tutorial and to buy dresses with what was left. Mechanically, Farida took the money and gave it to Nashwa who said, "Thanks a lot, mother." Farida said she herself would go to the school to pay the money. It was usually she who dealt with any school matters involving parents. Years before, Nashwa had come home in tears one day, saying that Radish-head had gone to the principal and argued with him over a quarter pound's worth of revenue stamps that the school had charged and that he wanted back. The teachers had made fun of her and her classmates had taunted her about her father's head and his running saliva. She demanded that he not go back again, otherwise she would refuse to attend school. Since that day he had acquiesced to Farida on this issue.

Now he was hugging his briefcase, saying that he had applied at the Telephone Department for a telephone. Farida was indifferent, even though she was hardly accustomed to surprises from him. Previously, when Hasan Effendi had received his telephone, she had urged and nagged to no avail. Now she remained silent. The tray of basbusa remained on the table, untouched.

Oweis

Sitt Busayna had a suspicion that Oweis the baker was the one exempted from the spell's effect. Her evidence for this was his closeness to the sheikh and his obvious virility. She decided to try to get in touch with him secretly, but should that fail she was willing to approach him in broad daylight. She regretted not having established a close relationship with him when he had frequented her house to take away her dough and bring back baked bread. She remembered, happily, that she had once given him a loaf of bread and a piaster. No other woman had been as generous as she. Khadija the Sa'idi woman used to count her loaves several times and Umm Yusif often shouted that several were missing. As for her, she had never hassled him, and now she had to beat the other women to get to him. None of them was as good as she was at what she did; she had worn out quite a number of men in her embrace. Perhaps there were questions about her marriage with Usta Abdu. How could such a short man who walked hurriedly, as if afraid of receiving a sudden slap on the face, satisfy her? But whoever asked such a question didn't know his secret: it was his ability to remain in her embrace for two hours at a time. He had never failed to fulfill his duties before; the spell had turned him into a useless pillow. Oweis must not get away.

The same idea was haunting Umm Yusif and today she tried to attract his attention; she had prepared the way some time before by accusing him of being shortsighted when he had embraced Karima and was kicked out of the bakery. He had never come to her, but she was determined to find a way. At night she imagined Oweis's broad shoulders through his galabiya, his muscles swelling as he lifted the dough racks, and a sweet numbness would overcome her body. Oweis had not changed; his neck had not started to slump between his shoulders as her husband's had. On the contrary, his voice had lately grown louder as he addressed Zafarani.

The truth was that Oweis paid no attention to her or to anybody else. He would go to his room, lie down and, with wide open eyes, would gaze up at the sloping ceiling that was formed by the staircase of the house. He would be gripped with panic as he recalled the way the sheikh's voice had reverberated from all around: from above, from below, from the ceiling, from the floor tiles. He now found himself in a situation completely new to him; something that he used to hope others would not ask of him. It was the same kind of feeling that he had had when he was alone with the respectable effendis, sleeping with them and treating them with the utmost respect; and when one of them asked to be beaten or insulted, he had done so only as someone following orders. The people of Zafarani thought he was happy because of his assignment, but in fact he felt fearful being connected with it. If he were to make an unintentional mistake, what punishment would be meted out to him? In his youth he had heard of a sheikh who had the power to transform a man into stone or into an animal. Some people used to avoid black cats and dogs out of fear that they had human souls, that their owners might have transformed them into animals. He was afraid of making a mistake, although he didn't know what kind of mistake he might make.

Oweis felt that he was being watched the whole time, that even his dreams were known to the sheikh. Yesterday he had dreamed that he had stepped forward and ripped away the curtain, and then bent over the sheikh's neck, which had shrunk down between his shoulders. Yet his face had looked very strange; it had combined the features of an infant with those of an old man who fixed him with a mocking look. He had leaped awake in panic, imagining there was someone else in his room. He heard breathing and saw a shadow. How would he face the sheikh after this dream? And there was another thing: he was not used to staying in one small place. In the village he used to move in the fields, sleep on the banks of irrigation canals, go deep into the corn fields, go to the market towns, to the small villages, making a living here and there. Now his village seemed so far away, his childhood even farther—the way he had moved from house to house on top of the straw and the firewood of the roofs, the silos of wheat and doum—this was the way the women of the village also kept on the move to avoid being seen by strangers in the streets. He remembered the way he always used to sit on the waterwheel, watching the water pouring from the scoops, his nostrils filled with the smell of green fava beans. As a child he had thought the well was very deep. When he grew up and sat on top of the wheel itself he saw that the well was shallow and very small—he had had just the same feeling when he visited his uncle's house in al-Tulaihat after an absence of many years. He saw that the courtyard was in fact narrow and the walls were low. Everything that had appeared big and endless to him as a child was smaller when he grew up. He felt sad and missed his childhood, where there had been no obstacles and he could enter any house he liked and mistakes had not been punished.

Those were faraway days, lost like the sad songs of the camel drivers that he had waited for many a time on the bridge: "If you come from Mazata, tell me which way to go. I want to go to Mazata. I've got no money, though; I've got no money, though." Their singing would begin suddenly and end suddenly and he could not keep up with them, run as he might.

Now he couldn't go to Me'allim Abul Ghait's café. The sheikh had told him not to leave the alley, ever. Two weeks before he had gone to the me'allim, who looked pale and didn't even greet him. Someone who had recently come from the village had told him that his grandmother Nigma's house had collapsed and a builder had bought the debris. The me'allim wept hard and long; he said his childhood was scattered over all the bricks of that house. In it he had listened to the stories about the jinn and the 'ifreets. A piece of his life had collapsed with the house. Oweis kept away; he no longer thought the me'allim was a little weird. He himself didn't own a house or a palm tree, but a yearning for the village was still burning within him. It was now so far away. He was more afraid than any other resident of Zafarani of the sheikh. What if he made an unintentional mistake?

Perhaps Oweis was being transformed in a mysterious way because of what was taking place around him. This morning he had noticed Umm Yusif's eyes; if he had seen the same glances when he went to her house to carry the dough they would have made him burn with desire. Perhaps the sheikh was placing temptations in his path to test his patience and loyalty. He was still hoping to own a cart; perhaps the sheikh would reward him by giving him one. He fantasized about the sweet days ahead in which he would rush up and down the alleys, selling ice cream and boiled chickpeas. Oweis left his room, trying to keep the village, the cart, and Umm Yusif out of his thoughts so that he could absorb what the sheikh was about to tell him. The alley was quiet in accordance with the new instructions, whereby its inhabitants were not allowed to rise before 7 a.m. He was afraid of oversleeping; if he had been given this assignment after his work at the bakery it would have seemed easier, but the time he had spent at the baths had changed his routine. Perhaps some of the inhabitants were watching him from behind their windows. He heard footsteps behind him, but it was an illusion no one was there.

The door to the room stood open. He uttered a greeting and the sheikh's voice came out as if it had originated inside his ears, as if it were a voice that a man would hear without seeing anyone. The voice told him to pay attention, for what was about to be said was long.

File 3

Containing Some of the Quarrels that Took Place in
Zafarani, Some Incidents, and Memoranda

First Quarrel

At about 10:00 a.m. Tekirli headed for Oweis's room. As soon as he appeared, a number of inhabitants looked out of their windows. This embarrassed him greatly. From her balcony, Umm Suhair declared that she had never liked or trusted that Tekirli man, that she had always had her suspicions concerning those visitors of his. Those suspicions had been confirmed when his wife had kept to herself despite the Prophet's injunction that we look after our neighbors—even unto the seventh one. The previous year, Suhair had gone upstairs to borrow a cup of oil but had come back before she had even knocked on the door, saying that her heart was not at ease. Suhair was a pure, chaste virgin who had sensed the foulness and would not pollute her hand by shaking it with the whore. Umm Suhair added that the likes of the Tekirli woman pretended to be shy, as if they had not reached puberty; yet the very smallest gesture—the flick of a hand or an eyelid—would reveal whoredom in all its ugliness. She thanked God that Tekirli had not helped her own nephew to enroll in a vocational training center when she had asked for his help. Had he talked to one of his acquaintances, perhaps the boy would have come to harm later on. Sitt Busayna discussed the very same subject with Umm Nabila.

Tekirli had approached Oweis shaking a finger at him; he would pay for what he had said today. He grabbed Oweis by the collar and several children shouted, "Tekirli is beating Oweis!" Some of the women had sent their children out to keep them apprised of what was happening and the children did a wonderful job. They had reached the first flight of stairs without Tekirli noticing them. Their shouts stirred some of the inhabitants. Sergeant Major Sallam was now coming down the stairs followed by his wife. He shouted, "Halt, effendi!" Usta Rummana looked out of the window then came out and proceeded to separate Oweis and Tekirli. The sergeant major declared that what Tekirli was doing was improper. Tekirli's face turned so red that those standing nearby thought it would explode. He shouted out, in language that was close to Classical Arabic, why they were defending that miscreant of a knave—were they in league with him? Sergeant Major Sallam shouted back in a strong, loud voice incongruous with his weak frame: "Do you know whom you are addressing?" Tekirli didn't answer and Sallam declared that he was an old soldier, one of the king's men. Did Tekirli know what that meant?

Usta Rummana tried to hide a smile while his soul quivered, as he was about to hear echoes of the old reality: the sergeant major was going to talk about his long history of service at the palace—his job as the bodyguard of one of the princesses, and his finally ending up as a cook at the royal palace, accompanying the king on his domestic and foreign travels, tasting the king's food. A few women began to arrive. Zannuba the divorcée pointed to Oweis saying, "He has more honor than that one," gesturing toward Tekirli. Zannuba added that, just as the saying went, "He couldn't handle the donkey, so he'd come to punish the saddle." The sergeant major narrowed his eyes: that was no way to describe the sheikh. Tekirli interrupted her, saying he was going to reveal the truth about the wicked wizard. Hardly had he finished when the sergeant major, his wife, Zannuba, and the children all started shouting at him. Usta Rummana didn't understand what their protest was about. Tekirli backed away—he had never faced so many people before—shouting that he was going to take measures that would amaze the alley. The sergeant major was provoked into shouting back: "Do your worst!" Zannuba made a pointed implication about the alley's desire to be rid of the pollution, and the children shouted and pointed at him.

Usta Rummana felt sad. It seemed to him that he had been ambushed after getting out of jail. Ordinary things usually look so strange to the eyes of someone newly released that it would take a while before equilibrium returned to his life and he could function. The situation in Zafarani shocked him. He would not have believed what he had heard, had he too not found himself impotent when he went to visit Nabawiya, whom he had known for a long time. She had patted him on the shoulder in a kindly, motherly way, saying that it was being away from it for so long, that she would find him better next time. He felt certain, though, that it would be no use for him to go again. So far he had not begun to panic, as things were not yet clear.

Sitt Busayna arrived and the people standing around made way for her. She had heard that Tekirli had gone to the police station to fetch a policeman to take Oweis away. And that was why she was now suggesting that Oweis go with her to her place where no power could touch him, since she knew the sergeant at the police station, and he would turn everything against Tekirli. Umm Yusif somehow managed to hear what Sitt Busayna was saying; she shouted from her nearby window that Oweis was already safe, that no creature on earth could touch or harm him. Besides, the sheikh protected all Zafaranites. Zannuba nodded in agreement while Busayna boiled with exasperation.

Comment

Oweis did not stop, but continued until late in the evening to relay all the details of Tekirli's life that the sheikh had uncovered. In view of the uproar these revelations caused and the far-reaching effects they had, we sum them up as follows hereinafter:

By noon, Zafarani inhabitants had learned the following details of Tekirli's life: He was twenty-nine years old. His father had died when he was four. His mother refused to remarry, for Tekirli's sake. For a long time she dressed him in a girl's dress and called him Samira for fear of the evil eye. Until he was sixteen years of age, he slept next to her in the same bed, and if he wanted to go to the bathroom at night he'd wake her up to keep him company. He would be very shy if he spoke to a woman in front of her, and he didn't dare look at a woman on the street. Despite that, he was very cruel; when he went out with Nadia, his wife, during their engagement, she noticed that he plucked up grass by the roots, trampled on flowers, and described passersby as ugly. He could not keep a pen for more than three or four days; he would begin by biting on it, then twisting it, and would not rest until he had broken it to pieces. His married life was calm because his wife was anxious to avoid quarrels. His soft voice breaks off the moment he gets angry. He smashes pots and plates, eats the slivers, throws himself on the carpet and bites the edges, imagines himself holding an iron bar with which he would rape the women passing by. He has never had sexual intercourse with his wife. He offers her to men of all kinds.

All afternoon Zafarani listened to Oweis, who went out into the alley several more times. He said that what was happening to them was the nucleus of what would be happening to the whole world, and that as soon as things were under control here, this situation would be expanded and would spread; he who was ignorant today would have knowledge tomorrow, and he whom facts and conditions escaped tomorrow would be aware the day after tomorrow, until the day arrived on which everyone, every tongue would be speaking of what was happening, would learn the lesson and respond, and thus the world would be changed. A heavy silence descended upon the alley and the gloating in the eyes of the Zafaranites turned into fear and puzzlement. Umm Suhair anxiously thought: Who is next? The sheikh knew everything, lived with every family, counting every breath and movement. As the proverb goes, "Every tree will be shaken by the wind." The inhabitants were beset by uncertainty. Maybe each of them would get up one day to find the most intimate details of his life on every tongue. Besides, what did the sheikh mean by talking about the world and changing it? How many months and years would that take? Apparently it was going to take a long time.

In the afternoon Oweis spoke, quoting the sheikh, about Nadia. She was the youngest of four sisters: two of her sisters are married and the third is engaged to a man who works for an airline. This last sister is quite promiscuous and has had sexual relations with many men, especially young men from Arab countries. The previous day she had met her fiancé at 6:00 p.m. and when he tried to put his arm around her waist she had scolded him, even though at 5:00 p.m. she had been stark naked and her voice had gone hoarse with pleasure in the arms of a young man from Bahrain. Nadia had made no effort to meet men; her loneliness was made worse by the fact that she had failed to pass her preparatory school certificate exams three years in a row. Her parents had gradually lost interest in her. She didn't go out with her sisters unless she was invited. When eating she would turn her face away from people. She couldn't tell the difference between one kind of food and another. She didn't buy her clothes herself; she just wore whatever they bought for her. She never started a conversation or got into arguments. That was what Tekirli's mother liked most about her, and what led her to pick Nadia as a bride for her son. For, as she put it, "No one had heard her say anything." And even though she remained a virgin for some time after the wedding (until Tekirli broke her hymen with his finger), she never complained to her mother. When her sisters kidded her she would simply bow her head, and this made them kid her more. When Tekirli gave her the option of separation, she embraced him in tears saying that anything at all would satisfy her, that it was enough for her to see him and hear his breathing as he slept, that she didn't want to go back to her family. They would make her a servant, forcing her to mop the floors, chop onions, and clean bathrooms, and nobody would ask her to join them in watching a movie on television or going out. With him she was in her own house, she said. He began to bring men home. The first one to sleep with her was a high-ranking official in the Department of Public Trusts; he paid five pounds and one kilo of kebab and kufta. Then came a bailiff working for the courts, and he paid two pounds. Then they came in droves. Tekirli chose them carefully and made sure not to bring home men who had paunches, because she didn't like those. Tekirli would look at the client through her eyes to see if he would appeal to her. She didn't object; she actually devoted most of her time to spoiling her husband. In truth, she was a very kind and tender woman; she cried when she saw a beggar and tears came to her eyes if she heard a sad story. At Bab al-Khalq she once saw women chained inside a paddy wagon and this saddened her. Contrary to appearances she was not standoffish and would have loved to visit her neighbors, but her situation and the cruelty of her husband made that out of the question.

At sunset Oweis announced the names of some of Tekirli's visitors and listed the services they had rendered in return for enjoying his wife. He described her body and mentioned certain marks. He talked of Tekirli's objective: earning ten thousand Egyptian pounds by the sweat of his wife's vulva. Of that sum, he had so far made three thousand four hundred pounds. There were other bits of information about Nadia, but these were pitiable and he wasn't going to divulge them.

The Second Quarrel

This one took place on the same day at 1:00 p.m., after Oweis had finished recounting Part Two of the Tekirli story. Busayna went out for a short while and came back with slow steps. She looked at Umm Yusif's window with tremendous annoyance; had it not been for her intervention, the men standing nearby would have convinced Oweis to go with her. Umm Yusif was working toward the same end, and Busayna's annoyance fired her imagination so that she was certain that Umm Yusif had already won him, tasted him, enjoyed him, and smelled the sweat of his virility. So Busayna decided to pick a quarrel with her. She passed along the alley slowly on her way back, in the hope of seeing Umm Yusif and picking a quarrel with her for any made-up reason. But the two windows were closed—a fact that fired her imagination even more. What was happening behind those windows? She headed for her apartment on the third floor, where she would be out of range of any dirty water that might be aimed at her. Besides, by standing on the balcony looking out at the alley, she would be looking in one direction—a much better position than if she were standing between the houses which would have forced her to keep looking both right and left. The quarrel proceeded as follows:

Busayna called out loudly to Umm Suhair, who lived across the street from Umm Yusif. Umm Suhair loudly answered in the name of God, hoping that everything was all right. Busayna declared that no good would come to this God-forsaken Zafarani so long as hearts were ungrateful and women who were more like scorpions than people nested there. Umm Suhair realized that this was the prelude to a quarrel; a number of women looked out of their windows. Khadija the Sa'idi woman ran to her window in joy, repeating excitedly, "A quarrel! A quarrel!" Busayna noticed that Umm Yusif's windows were still closed, so she cut short the usual preliminaries which led into every quarrel she fought. She declared that that harlot of a woman, whose tongue was fit to be a leather strop, that wife of the train stoker . . . . The truth was that Tahun was not an engineer as claimed by this whore daughter of a harlot who persecuted him and prepared him different food from the food she prepared for her children . . . . The sheikh's anger was not without cause; the man was good and pious and would never cause anyone harm for no reason.

At that point Umm Suhair made a gesture, Sitt Umm Nabila shook her head, Zannuba the divorcée clapped her hands and shouted, "Wow! . . . Wow!" and still Umm Yusif didn't open her window. Busayna shouted that some women who had never been properly satisfied by their husbands before the spell were now losing their minds, and she pointed her arm in the direction of Umm Yusif's house. She clapped, repeating, "Wife of the stoker! Wife of the stoker! Women of the alley! Alley of the women!" She wanted them to be her witnesses against the wife of the stoker who exposed her bare breast when she looked out of the window, who didn't wear any underwear, and who badmouthed her even though she had lent her five pounds when she turned to her in tears begging her to save Tahun . . . Tahun, the stoker! Tahun, the stoker, because part of his inventory was missing and he had been given the choice: pay up or go to jail. She had regretted it later because good people told her that Tahun al-Mathun al-Matahni al-Matahini had stolen part of that inventory and sold it in the junk yards of Wikalat al-Balah. She regretted bailing out a thief who had stolen the government's money. The harlot had winked at Usta Abdu, and because he was a faithful husband he had told her what had happened and she thought she had an excuse: her husband had been affected by

121

the spell and she was trying with everyone hoping to find out who was still virile. What she had learned this morning, however, she would never accept silently.

Stillness. Umm Yusif did not respond. Khadija the Sa'idi woman was certain that if she did, a really big quarrel that would help her cope with her loneliness would ensue. Umm Yusif, after all, also had a talent for heaping abuse that was not to be sneezed at. So it seemed there was some mysterious reason making her take such abuse from Busayna in silence. Umm Suhair was certain that Busayna was holding something back. Busayna was now leaning almost her entire body over the balcony, waving with her shoe, declaring that she would beat Umm Yusif on her most sensitive private parts.

The Third Quarrel

At 2:30 p.m. the following day, Atif was approaching Sergeant Major Sallam with slow steps, his eyes full of shame, and his face very pale. He was surprised to hear a scream and he trembled. He expected strange things to happen in Zafarani these days. The sergeant major peered out of his window, turned and looked round behind him, then climbed onto the iron railing. Atif had to stop walking. He was confused; what should he do? The sergeant major, seeing nobody else, addressed him, declaring that he'd had it with his wife because, after a whole lifetime together, she had dared to intimate that he was a liar. As he spoke, his wife appeared and began tugging at him, asking him to be reasonable. Atif was annoyed; he wished he had come past ten minutes earlier; if he had gone faster he would have been in his apartment by now, taking off his clothes and washing his face with cold water, away from the disturbance. The sergeant major continued to address him: all his life he had served kings—two kings and three queens. No king had ever put anything in his mouth unless he was sure that Sallam had tasted it. He had entered all the palace rooms, even those that prime ministers and heads of political parties had never seen, and even the decorations room, which housed the most magnificent jewelry and the most precious weapons. He had an old back issue of *al-Musawwar* magazine that had a photograph of His Majesty the king wearing a horseman's outfit and leaning on a thoroughbred Arabian's neck. Who was holding the horse's reins? Who? "It was I. I, Sallam!" It wasn't his job, but the king had been a little out of sorts so he had summoned Sallam to bring the horse. The king had whispered some words to him—words that until now he has always refused to repeat and would only repeat to God on the Day of Judgment if He asked him to. And now his own wife was suggesting that he was a liar. His wife screamed for help as he pushed his body forward. At that point Atif huried his steps; he had to go upstairs anyway, and this way he would avoid the glances people were now turning on him and it would look as if he had done a good deed.

Atif went upstairs quickly. Rummana the politico was trying to open the door. Atif said that Sallam's wife was afraid that if she left him by himself for a moment he would jump. Rummana smiled; he doubted that. Atif expressed surprise; the sergeant major was indeed poised on the railing. Rummana shook his head, took a step back, then rushed forward, hitting the door; dust fell off the door's upper opening. On the third try there was a tremendous noise and both men fell into the room.

The alley's inhabitants saw Rummana and Atif holding the sergeant major's arms. All eyes were on Atif the college graduate, who was concerning himself with Zafarani affairs for the first time. Nabila the school mistress expressed unmistakable admiration, even though she was standing on her balcony and thus relatively far from the scene. When they had managed to remove him from the balcony, the children shouted, "Hurray! Hurray!" In the hall, Qurqur the musician stood in readiness. The sergeant major continued to shout, wondering how he could go on living after his wife had accused him of lying. Rummana patted him on the shoulder, then asked the wife to stop crying.

Qurqur asked what the story was and the sergeant major replied that what had happened was horrible. Qurqur repeated his question and Sallam said the story had begun ten days earlier, or rather, it had really started seven years ago, and in fact, to be really truthful one must say it had started fifty years ago. It had to do with Sallam's very close relationship with the crown prince, who was now exiled in Europe and whom he had loved dearly and accompanied on all his trips except those abroad—not because the prince hadn't let him, but because he couldn't stay away from the son of the daughter of the Messenger of God—al-Hussein. He pointed to a photograph hanging on the wall next to the entrance showing an old, gray-bearded man with calm eyes and Turkish features highlighted by a short fez. Atif tried to remember the man whose likeness it was. It seemed to him the picture had been cut out of a glossy magazine. He noticed the serenity in the eyes of the man in the picture. An idea occurred to him: that man never knew insomnia. Rummana hid a smile. He had not recognized in the picture any of the crown princes of the days of the monarchy under which he had lived and during which he had been jailed. They turned their eyes away from it when the sergeant major raised his hands and recited a prayer in which he begged God to protect the crown prince who was away from his land and to continue to give of His bounty and to reunite them soon. After his prayer he looked calmer.

Sallam turned toward them at the very moment that Atif had finished making some calculations. The picture was at least thirty years old, the man in the picture was about seventy; if he were still alive today he would now be over a hundred years old. The sergeant major wished he could show them the crown prince's signature on the back of the picture but that wasn't possible because of the stupidity of the man who had made the wooden frame and glued it over, hiding the autograph forever. Three days ago he had seen the prince in a dream. The prince had looked tired and said, "Homesickness is killing me, Sallam," and Sallam had told him, "God preserve you, Your Highness." At that moment a Nubian servant had arrived carrying a silver tray with a pair of prescription glasses on it. His Highness loved silver, wore only decorations made of silver; the sheath of his sword was made of pure silver; all his gold decorations and medals he kept in a special case; his pistol was made of Indian silver. He wore that pistol under his jacket in such a way that its handle would show through the leather holster if he pushed it just a bit. At that moment, Atif, in his mind's eye, saw that prince, his hands clasped behind his back, walking in the hall of his palace, wearing his formal suit. As the valet helped him take off his clothes, the whole pistol appeared. It had an engraved handle—a small circle with the name of the prince in the middle. The sergeant major said that the Nubian servant had taken the glasses from the tray and offered them to the prince, who had then given them to Sallam to wipe before he put them on. "What is the meaning of that dream?"

Yesterday he had asked Oweis to ask the sheikh about the meaning of the dream, and Oweis had brought back the sheikh's answer: the sergeant major was soon going to witness an important meeting. He didn't say with whom. But the sergeant major was now awaiting an invitation from the crown prince to go to him, to counsel him in his perplexity, to keep him company in his loneliness. Sallam was going to attach one condition: that the prince return to Egypt so that he might meet his maker here, close to the beloved, the master of all martyrs, al-Hussein.

Those present exchanged glances of surprise. The sarcasm disappeared from Rummana's eyes. Qurqur the musician thought about the fact that the sheikh would answer someone who asked him a question. Atif was still imagining the prince wearing his pistol when the sergeant major rushed into the bedroom and came out clutching an old gun. His life had no value now that his wife had contradicted him.

Qurqur asked God's protection and Rummana just stared. As for Atif, he gazed at the long muzzle and the hand holding the brown, wooden handle inlaid with ivory. He saw it aimed, threatening some unknown person; he saw a finger touching the trigger; he saw the gun on the night stand next to his bed. The wife screamed, "The gun! The gun!" Slowly Rummana began to measure with his eyes the distance between himself and the sergeant major. Qurqur asked him, "Would you be happy to die an infidel?" The woman kept screaming, "The gun! The gun!" Would he accept death as an infidel? Slowly his hands came down to his sides. Atif's eyes followed the movement as he saw himself sitting with Rahma, with her eyes that belonged to an eternal childhood. She had asked him, "Why do you carry a gun?"

The sergeant major agreed to give up the idea of suicide. Qurqur asked the woman to kiss her husband's head. She said that she loved him and appreciated his grief for his friends, the kings and princes, but that he had misunderstood her. Rummana shouted as he winked at the sergeant major, "See?" Atif wondered about the price of the pistol, the country where it was made, the hands that had carried it. Had a fatal bullet come out of it? What year? What day? What moment? Who had it killed? He was startled when the sergeant major moved toward him, the pistol almost touching him. Qurqur said that the reunion would take place soon, as the prophecy of the sheikh would never fail. The word 'sheikh' had a special ring to it at that moment. They all remembered what had happened to them. Qurqur could no longer brag about maintaining his sexual prowess past the age of sixty. He thought quickly: He must invite Atif the college graduate to listen to his music. He would ask him to invite his friends; he was sure of his ability to win their admiration with his talents, although they had gone unappreciated so far.

He was going to win some highly sophisticated listeners, not the stoned ones at weddings, or the drunkards to whom one tune was much like another and who were moved by neither sad melodies nor dancing ones; all they did was bray whenever the dancer showed a centimeter of thigh.

Atif was afraid to ask any of them about their condition since the spell had been cast; he would wet his pants if he did. What restrained them all was that everybody was suffering the same thing. The sergeant major's wife was still crying. Atif now saw Rahma; her hands were turning the beer glass. After she drank her cheeks became rosy and her eyes gleamed like two beads in a rosary, emitting a soft, sweet light in the dark. A short while later, words would begin to flow from her lips and he would listen in joy as she talked of her little things. Joy would overwhelm him and he would rest his chin on the palm of his hand and listen. Her face would glow, and he would watch the gaiety of her eyes while the river water turned to rays of light and the tree trunks into echoes. When he had shown Nabil her picture for the first time, Nabil said she was a child. Atif told him she was over twenty-one, that she was a woman whose soul guarded the innocence of the first years of life. Nabil had been astonished: that's a rare rose.

Qurqur said that it all had ended well and it would please him to invite Atif Bey and also Usta Rummana and Sergeant Major Sallam to listen to his music. Rummana said that he was indeed in need of music, that he had heard much about Qurqur's genius from Me'allim Daturi. Qurqur was pleased and he looked at Atif as if to say: Did you hear that? The sergeant major stood stiffly, saying in a slow tone that he accepted, with full appreciation, the invitation extended to him by Qurqur. A concentrated grief made its way through Atif's heart as if a drop of hydrochloric acid had gone through it; had this invitation been given him six months ago, he would have taken Rahma along with him. He said he was ready to go at any time. His voice sounded weak; he had tried to hide a very deeply felt sorrow that almost spoke on its own through his eyes. The shame in his voice didn't escape Rummana, who attributed it to the spell. Atif noticed the sergeant major's gun, and the curve of that thin piece of steel that defined the space in which the trigger could move. They heard a knock at the door, and the sergeant major said, "Come in." In stepped Sitt Latifa, wife of al-Bannan, barefoot, hiding half her face behind a black shawl, her tired glances directed sideways. She begged them to excuse her, but had any of them seen the mailman? Had he left any of them a letter to give to herself or their uncle al-Bannan, who was so old he couldn't climb the stairs?

The Fourth Quarrel

Hasan Anwar, most uncharacteristically, was heard yelling at around 7:00 p.m. From the few words that the neighbors could catch, they concluded that he was quarreling with his younger son, Samir. This came as quite a surprise to some of the inhabitants, as until now he had never been heard to raise his voice, either at home or at anyone else in Zafarani. The Zafarani residents had trouble following because they weren't used to this kind of yelling; it sounded as if he was shouting in Classical Arabic.

Atif listened as he sat on his bed, succumbing to the descending black night, unable to see any details of the room since his eyes hadn't yet adjusted to the dark. A light trembling was causing pain in his heart. He didn't feel that his own body was really present, rather he was merely a collection of images near and far, whispers, odors, and words that once had been said and stayed in his mind forever. Hasan Anwar's voice snatched him away from that hard, thorny siege of memories.

Tekirli also had to pause for a few moments while taking off his clothes. He looked at Nadia and said, "Hasan Effendi is beating his son." She said the alley was possessed. She cited the sergeant major's attempted suicide and how he would have died had it not been for the intervention of Atif and Rummana. The two names sounded strange to Tekirli's ears; he thought his wife was pronouncing them with affection. He decided to ask her before he went to bed why she had mentioned these two names in particular. She said that Umm Sabri had insulted a woman who was selling cottage cheese; she had attacked the woman, who left her cheese bowl behind and ran away, scared, but Radish-head had carried it for her as far as the bakery. She said that old Basyuni al-Hagrasi, the former plainclothesman, had quarrelled with his son Luli and his daughter-in-law Safiya. He had come out of the single room where they all lived and begun to address the windows and the balconies, announcing that his daughter-in-law was begging him to sleep with her, that she was a lost woman and that any man in the alley could sleep with her for one piaster. After the return of Luli, his son, Basyuni poured kerosene over himself. Latifa the old woman and Umm Muhammad prevented him from lighting it. Once again Tekirli felt some anxiety; his wife was relating the news of Zafarani in detail. Had she gone out? Had she met someone? Her face turned totally red as she said that she hadn't left the house, that she had sat the whole day on the sofa and when she grew bored she moved to the other sofa across the room. Tekirli said the people of Zafarani were evil and that a number of high-ranking officials had now been informed of what was taking place in the alley. One of them was quite upset and had said, "This is very serious." Tekirli said the people of Zafarani were cowards; when they were showing submission to the sheikh and his servant Oweis, some of them had sent unsigned complaints to several government departments and an official had shown him one of those complaints.

He said that he had asked several real estate agents to find another apartment for them.

At that moment a woman's intermittent screams were heard. The woman was Hasan Effendi Anwar's wife—a kindly, polite, wise woman. She was separating father and son. Hasan Effendi's veins were about to burst: he was facing, for the first time, impertinent opposition. At sunset he had called his two sons and told them that they should go to sleep at 8:00 p.m. to obey the sheikh's instructions until the crisis was over. Here he had lowered his voice until it almost became a whisper: at noon today he had met a pious man for whom the clouds of unknowing were drawn aside and to whom he had resorted in several previous crises. The devout man told him that relief was soon coming to the alley; the sheikh would lift the effect of the spell from three Zafarani residents. These of course would be chosen by the sheikh from among those who obeyed his commands and who had faith in him both publicly and privately. The sheikh had great plans that Zafarani, the neighboring alleys, the city, the country and the whole world would duly come to know. These plans would be known in every place where people congregated.

It must be pointed out here that Hasan Effendi was so overjoyed by what the man had said that he forgot his standard prayer as he circumambulated al-Hussein's tomb: to protect him from entering a police station, neither to borrow nor to lend, in addition to yet another prayer he had planned to say against Sayyid Bey, who had done him a tremendous wrong. Sayyid Bey had summoned him to his office and Hasan Effendi was so pleased with this invitation that he looked at three of the young college graduates who had joined the department recently. Perhaps Sayyid Bey would assign him some task or another. This would give him the right to sit, tired, in front of Abdel Azim Effendi and tell him that Sayyid Bey had singled him out and entrusted him with so many tasks that he was exhausted. Abdel Azim had once told him a story that left him quite shaken: some memoranda were overdue, so Abdel Azim Effendi had come to the office on a Friday. He had come hoping for neither overtime nor a bonus. At around noon he was surprised to see Sayyid Bey enter the office; in fact he didn't notice him at first because he was so immersed in his work.

He didn't believe his eyes and uttered some confused greetings. He even dared to invite the Bey to sit down—something that simply was not done. He was surprised when His Excellency began to ask him about some job or other, then about his children and his health. On the following day Sayyid Bey wrote a memo asking for a ten-pound bonus for Abdel Azim in view of his diligence and loyalty. Hasan Effendi spent whole days dreaming of something like that happening to him. He would meet Sayyid Bey's arrival with an impassive face and would ask him about his health and how he was doing. On the following Friday he went to his office, skipping the Friday prayers for the first time in many years. He took off his jacket as proof of being immersed in his work. He didn't go to the bathroom for fear that Sayyid Bey might come by while he was in there. Twice he dozed off with fatigue and was afraid Sayyid Bey might come at a time when his eyes were closed; he would look odd. On the following day he told his colleagues how he had spent the whole day finishing some late work. They listened to him with indifference. One of them mocked him, observing frankly that he was only trying to imitate Abdel Azim Effendi. Hasan Anwar pounded the table: "That's a lie, a lie!" and without thinking, he said that Abdel Azim had not come to the office by chance but had known in advance of Sayyid Bey's intention to go to the office that day. Everything he said reached Abdel Azim, magnified. The latter said that he was saddened by what he had heard because Hasan Effendi was his schoolmate and was not the kind of man to harbor feelings of hatred. Why then had he made up this lie? Besides, such behavior undermined the unity of intermediate degree holders at the department. The matter almost reached Sayyid Bey after some of the college graduates related the story. Hasan Effendi was distressed since he had no intention of harming the cause of intermediate degree holders. At any rate, he went to the office on the four following Fridays but Sayyid Bey didn't show up.

Now, the day before, Sayyid Bey had summoned him. He had pointed to three sheets of paper and asked why it was necessary to have a telephone installed. Hasan Anwar's face shrank up. He read a line from the last memorandum: "Urgent needs of the job call for installation of a telephone." Hasan Effendi gestured with his hands several times. He imagined one of his colleagues entering and seeing him like that; he would have a heart attack. Sayyid Bey shouted, "What urgent need when your job doesn't require contacting the outside world at all?" Hasan Effendi said he wanted an extension telephone to contact his colleagues in other divisions. Sayyid Bey shouted, "But you are requesting a telephone with a direct line!" He revealed very white teeth and said that this laziness was unbecoming of an old employee, and that it was unacceptable deviousness. As Hasan Effendi turned to leave he heard the sound of paper being torn up.

Outside the office Hasan Effendi saw four employees and one messenger. He wrote a memorandum asking to be transferred to another department. Before finishing it he tore it up quickly; it would bring him trouble. If one of his colleagues saw what it said he would report him. He was faced with other difficulties; some of his colleagues passed by but didn't speak to him. That hurt him. Before leaving he spoke in a loud voice to Rashwan the messenger, while the other employees were gathered at the elevator.

Rashwan was the oldest messenger in the department and he commuted to Tanta every Thursday. Hasan Effendi loudly asked him to pray for his two sons, Samir and Hassan; Samir was going to be an engineer, God willing, and Hassan was going to graduate as a medical doctor. He wished everybody had heard what he'd said. He wished he could tell Sayyid Bey of his late father's insistence that he go to a secondary school in preparation for college. Family circumstances, however, like those of all the noble families to whom the times had not not been merciful, did not permit. He convinced his father that he should enroll in a commercial school and continue his education after he had graduated and had worked for a time. But over the years his intentions fell by the wayside, especially since he had become an avid reader and discovered Sufism.

When the Second World War broke out he had followed the battles, bought *al-Ahram* every day, clipped all news of the fighting, and mounted the clippings on white, ruled paper. From the beginning he had taken Hitler's side. He obtained a big picture showing the Fuehrer looking handsome as he clasped his hands in front of his chest. He kept the picture in his bedroom. He was sure that Hitler had not died: where was his body? He was secretly certain that Hitler had come to Egypt, that perhaps he was living in one of the provinces in a home for the disabled, that he would appear at the right time to open warehouse number 13, which contained tremendous weapons of mass destruction. Hitler would overcome his enemies and become master of the world. Hasan Effendi wished Sayyid Bey knew how he kept himself constantly well-informed about military matters by reading and how his friends had sought his counsel about the events of the war; this could be testified to by Awad al-Rammah, Abdu al-Burtuqani, and Hagg Abboud, God have mercy on his soul. Throughout the Western Desert battles he hadn't had a moment of quiet. He would open the newspapers and say, "If Rommel had advanced here rather than going around, he would have achieved victory." When Rommel began his retreat, Hasan

Effendi asserted that this was not due to any fault of his genius but to a shortage of materiel. On the day of Rommel's funeral he was sad; he considered himself responsible for Rommel's demise since certain obstacles had prevented the two from meeting. When the first announcement on Monday 5 June 1967 was broadcast and he heard the announcer saying, "Israel has attacked our airports throughout the Republic," he told his colleagues: "We've lost the war."

If only Sayyid Bey knew of all this, his tone would change and he would perhaps invite him to talk it over. He would press the red button and when the messenger came in, he would say, "Coffee for Hasan Bey." Had he finished his education, he would have been an undersecretary by now or a chairman of the board. He had given all that up for the sake of learning. Then he recalled that he hadn't gone to college so as to ease the burden on his parents. Who would remember that? Everything was forgotten. He wiped two tears away quickly so that none of the employees would see him. Hadn't Hitler struck his own forehead several times? Such moments were beyond the comprehension of Sayyid Abul Mu'ati.

Hasan Effendi was puzzled. He had requested that a telephone be installed in his office a year ago. Why had Sayyid Bey summoned him to his office only today? Had somebody told Sayyid Bey some lie about him? He wished he could get up and call home and ask Umm Hassan what she had cooked and tell her that he was going to be a little late at al-Hussein, so that everyone would know that he had a private telephone of his own.

The day, however, did not end well. It was learned that His Excellency would make a surprise tour of the offices during the few minutes remaining before closing time. The files were brought out again from the desk drawers, ladies' handbags were hidden away, some employees came back from in front of the elevators, and there was an abrupt end to the state of anxiety among those left in the offices when each would ask, "How long before closing time?" Even Hasan Effendi tried to overcome his annoyance by taking out an old memorandum and rephrasing it. He thanked God he had not gone to Abdel Azim Effendi to complain about his troubles. Some minutes later he heard the bey's voice: he knew that Hamdi, the secretary, was with him, as were al-Husseiny, head of the Remote Assignments Division, and al-Tawansi, head of the Permanent Inventory Division; Abdel Azim was not yet high enough to accompany the bey on his tour of the offices.

Hasan Effendi didn't know why he had suddenly been gripped by the frightening thought that Sayyid Bey might ask him about what was happening in Zafarani. The entire old neighborhood district knew the story: the news was like a stone tossed in a pond where the ripples grew wider and wider until they touched the banks. If he was asked about it he would dissolve like a burst bubble. Sayyid Bey, however, didn't come into his office. Al-Tawansi came to him and informed him that the bey had decided to rearrange the desks to accommodate the maximum number of employees in this office, in order to reduce expenses at a time of war. It was decided to give the room over to the young women who had recently been appointed so as to reduce their contact with the male employees. He told Hasan Effendi to put everything he normally kept on his desk into one of the drawers and close them firmly so that it could be moved into the hall. At this point in his long life he was going to be the guest of the typists! His struggle to put his desk in the most prominent spot in the hall was doomed in advance because their boss, Tabuny Effendi, was already there. What if his two sons were to hear of this decision? Sayyid Bey was tightening the siege around him, was trying to humiliate him, to make him lose those privileges he had gained after such a long struggle.

Retreat is sometimes the best offense. Slowly he collected his papers and looked at the room in which he had spent a considerable part of his life: treetops and a huge unfinished building were visible through the small window. He must not be provoked. In situations like these he recalled what he had read and he would stand up straight, thrusting his chest forward as he walked, as if he were reviewing a division that was standing there to salute him. So, he lost an excellent post. What was it worth compared to what Hitler lost? How did he behave when the Russian armies came from the east and the Allies from the west? What did he do when the siege around Berlin was tightened? He didn't lose hope. He didn't collapse. He didn't raise the white flag of surrender. He tried to bring his armies back to break the Berlin siege, to push the invaders eastward and throw the Allies into the English channel.

That is how he should withdraw, proud of his long history with the department and of his clean file never sullied by a bad report. The blow aimed at him was terrible; it came at a time when he was facing an unknown threat against his virility and that of his two sons. Was he now going to move into the hall, to be within reach of all those passing through the corridor? He must prepare himself to face what could be even worse; the cafeteria servant might one day come and put the beverage tray on his desk, then take the tea cups and the coffee demitasses to serve them to those sitting nearby. He would not chide him; patience could absorb all these shocks. If he were to respond nervously, perhaps the other side might resort to a suicidal attack; perhaps Sayyid Bey might order him transferred to a faraway branch. Hold your ground. One day Hitler's absence would end; his aides, hiding in the east and in the west, would appear, and he would regroup his divisions and send them to the four cardinal points. Then he would tour the world and he would know from his intelligence service the names of those who had kept faith in his return, those who really cared for him. Where would Sayyid Bey be then? How would he face the Fuehrer? Hitler would execute him in the most horrendous way; he would dissolve him alive in lime. As for now, Hasan Effendi must seek a truce so as not to be transferred and thus leave Samir and Hassan without proper supervision. Their mother is kind and so she can't watch them properly. They might deviate.

Hasan Effendi Anwar was now looking at his two sons and telling them what he had heard from the pious man at al-Hussein. That was a good omen, undoubtedly. The spell would be lifted from three persons, and if they carried out everything the sheikh ordered, it would hasten their cure. They must go to bed at 8.00 p.m. "Impossible," said Samir with such abruptness that the tenderness in his voice was completely absent. Hasan Effendi's eyes popped out; a sharp buzzing deafened him: his younger son, whom he held up as an example, whom he mentioned before his older brother! Was that the way he answered his father? The shock was so great that he asked in a low voice: "What do you mean, Samir, my son?" Looking at him with impudent eyes he replied that he would not go to bed at 8:00 p.m. and would not obey any superstitious nonsense. Not obey? It was a dangerous concept. Samir was refusing to keep to the straight path until the crisis was over.

The most painful thing is an insurrection coming from those closest to you, your most faithful lieutenants. Then the hemorrhage is internal and difficult to detect and stop. His shy son whose name had appeared on the honor roll more than once was now talking back to him using foul words. He shouted, "This is an order!" Samir got up and declared that he couldn't go on living in such an atmosphere. Hasan Effendi shouted, "Boy!" The boy's mother was watching a situation the likes of which she had never seen before. Her son was pointing at his father and saying, mockingly, that he wanted them to go to bed at 8:00 p.m. He looked at his brother and told him to stop being a coward. Blood was now boiling in Hasan Effendi's veins: he no longer knew what he was saying and was looking around the room for something to throw at this rebel. He overturned the chairs, broke the glass of the little cupboard; things fell down. His wife cried out, "Samir did not mean that!"

He moved about the room more frantically. Actually he wasn't looking for anything in particular, but was hiding his puzzlement and pain behind a feigned attempt to find something with which to discipline the boy. Samir shouted that he didn't care. Here the neighbors heard Hasan Effendi's voice: "You are no longer my son."

In the alley Daturi stopped to listen to the noise. He didn't look around or up; his head inclined toward the ground: now even Hasan Effendi, the noble, kindly, princely man of Zafarani whom nobody had ever heard raise his voice before. What had happened? What was happening to Zafarani? Silent tears found their way out of his eyes in the dark. "I disown you to the Day of Judgment." Hasan Effendi's wife began to slap her own face as she cried, "We are ruined!"

Hassan's body grew as stiff as board. Several images kept forcing their way around in the father's head: Sayyid Bey tearing up the three sheets of paper; Abdel Azim Effendi on the telephone, then putting down the receiver slowly, exchanging a friendly smile with Sayyid Bey; a young college graduate waving nonchalantly; the cafeteria servant putting the tray on his desk. Four things you should never trust: money, no matter how plentiful; women, no matter how long you have lived with them; rulers, no matter how close to you; and Time, no matter how good it has been to you. The principal praising Samir; Hitler; Goering's planes dashing about; holy people crying, bewailing the beautiful, quiet past, safe and free from storms; a commander whose name he did not remember beating the ground with his hand; he had been surprised by the penetration of his ranks; the penetration had taken place. If only Samir would come, in his usual polite way, and say, "Forgive me, Father," he would pardon his son and forget all his infractions. However, something enormous was happening; a single moment in which the whole of destiny was decided. Samir's sudden outburst had dumbfounded his mother; she had pushed him toward the wall to show her anger and to keep him away from his father; he slipped out of her grasp and headed for the door. On the staircase Samir announced that he would not stay another minute in Zafarani. Daturi, still standing there, repeated to himself, "Children turning their backs on their parents? I weep for you, Zafarani." Umm Suhair told her husband, "Samir has run away." "Samir who?" he asked. "Samir, son of Hasan Effendi."

The Fifth Quarrel

In the afternoon of the following day a conversation between Rhode, daughter of Umm Sabri, and her elder sister developed into a shouting match—a matter that aroused the curiosity of the Zafarani women. They went out onto their balconies trying to follow what was happening even though most of them had been busy discussing the instructions from the sheikh which had been recited aloud that morning. He had told all Zafarani people to replace 'good morning,' 'good evening,' and indeed all greetings with a single sentence, and whoever deviated from that sentence would be stricken by all kinds of calamities. It was said that the sheikh would turn anyone who crossed him into stone, that he would cause breasts to grow on the chests of men.

Rummana the politico tried to decipher the sinister meanings behind the new greeting. Umm Suhair repeated it many times over until she had memorized it; Khadija the Sa'idi woman asked her husband to repeat it about a hundred times until she was satisfied that he knew it. Farida, Radish-head's wife, wished her husband would make a mistake so she could see what might happen to him. Umm Yusif thought that going to Oweis would now be justified; she could ask him about the real meaning. In his room she could be alone with him, bury her face in the hair on his chest, smell the sweat of his manhood. All the houses in the alley were repeating the phrase; Hasan Effendi reflected on its letters as he listened to his wife during the short spells he spent in the apartment before going out again to look for Samir. Daturi sat in front of his café, not saying it but mulling over its meaning: "Time to flee." Al-Bannan suggested to Latifa, his wife, that they write to their son so that he could use it too. She said, sadly, "Do we know his address?" Atif's reflections on the phrase moved beyond the mere words to the exegesis that Oweis had announced: it was the time of flight from one era to another and from one condition to another. Destinies would not be determined according to wishes and impotent desires and wasted efforts that took lifetimes and exhausted whole generations. The speed of flight would determine the realization of hopes and the actualization of dreams. Gone were the eras of human stagnation; a new age had just begun: the age of mobility, change, flight from the impossible to the possible, to what was actually accomplished, not what was probable or improbable.

The people of Zafarani were busy reflecting on these ideas, especially after Oweis had expounded on them that afternoon, and so it seemed strange that a quarrel should arise now. For the first time the two sisters were heard loudly exchanging words. The alley was used to watching Umm Sabri's family when it was quarreling with another family. A quarrel like that could not be ignored, even if it erupted during a wake. The truth was that the seeds of the present quarrel could be traced back to the last few days which had witnessed a reconciliation between Skina, the elder daughter, and her husband, Kamal al-Qadusi. The reconciliation had taken place a few days before the sheikh's declaration, and it had taken the efforts of many good friends and a lot of work by Umm Sabri. Throughout the previous two months she had been upset by the fact that both of her two daughters had come back to stay with her at the same time. Each of them was bored and tried to occupy herself by doing the housework or cleaning the windows or helping Khadija the Sa'idi woman, who called Skina over to slaughter a sickly chicken because she was afraid of seeing blood. Skina also helped Umm Suhair with making her dough; she was strong, had a broad chest and full thighs, and could never sit still. Rhode was silent, always thoughtful. Umm Sabri was always busy, going to the wakes of people she knew and people she didn't, her voice reverberating through the loudspeakers. In the morning she would go to one funeral or another, address the women, and tell religious stories and sermons. She took part in the setting up of weddings and the preparation of the brides by performing various personal grooming services and counseling. But no matter how much she tried to occupy herself there would always come a particular moment when she would look at Rhode or Skina. Seeing Rhode in particular was unbearably painful because she knew what it meant to yearn when a woman had no mate. She admired her daughter's beauty and often asked to look at her big eyes, to Rhode's embarrassment. Umm Sabri was quite experienced in women's ways. She liked Rhode's figure, her waist, her full firm breasts, her firm belly which had seen only one pregnancy. She once insisted on seeing her daughter's body, but Rhode never took off her clothes in front of anyone. So one time, when she went to the bathroom to bathe, her mother winked to Skina, then knocked hard on the door saying that if she didn't urinate immediately, she'd explode. Rhode knew that her mother had kidney trouble so she opened the door and turned to face the wall, bending down and tucking her arms between her thighs to hide her chest and the front of her body. Her mother began to scrutinize her, taking her time, and Rhode understood. She asked her mother to hurry up because she would catch a cold. Her mother looked pleased, and hoped that the right man would soon come along.

Umm Sabri felt sad that time was passing her divorced daughter by. Rhode suffered a great deal; she had never complained of her husband's poverty, especially after Muhammad had begun to kick inside her womb. At the beginning of her marriage, she had suffered from the dampness of the room and the water seepage during the winter. When she went out and sat at the entrance of the house to watch people coming and going, she would tell herself that things would improve when she turned twenty-five. The time between eighteen and twenty-five seemed too long. All she wanted was that God provide her husband with a job in one of those modern factories; then she would be able to buy her own copperware, a little armoire from Hagg Fuad the cabinetmaker, and make a rose-colored satin quilt, and then they would settle down in a room with its own bathroom, on a roof, any roof, so that she could always sit in the light. How she hungered for the light, the sun!

During the first year of her marriage, her dreams seemed simple and within reach. The passage of time and the periods of unemployment that her husband went through left a bad taste in her mouth. When he found work in a nearby dye house, his wages dropped and he told her frankly that he couldn't feed her. She frequently went to see her mother, holding her baby, and when her mother asked how she was doing, she would praise God and thank Him; she didn't want her mother to worry. Then she'd wait to eat lunch after sometimes being hungry for two days.

During those hard days, Rhode got to know the fruit grocer and the Azhar student. She remembered continually glancing over her shoulder on her way to either of them. Then, one day at noon, she had seen Atif, the college graduate, going into Zafarani. Very early one morning she had left her house, her legs shaking, and on her way back she had slowed right down until she caught sight of him approaching, with his sunken eyes. After he passed, the morning had clouded over. She didn't know what had come over her; she recalled in sorrow a sadness that she had never known before, not even in times of acute hunger, a sadness that was both tender and painful and one that she could not explain. Perhaps it was the calmness of his face or that mysterious grief etched into his features. Was it that which had made her deliberately slow her walk and sway her hips? But what good could it do anyway? Merely thinking about it was impossible. She had no idea how to get closer to him. If anyone could read her mind, they'd think it outrageous and silly: did she have to choose Atif, the college graduate? Even Nabila, the school mistress, had failed to attract his attention.

Only five days later, however, the moment arrived when she overcame all her shyness and said, "Good morning, Master Atif," and he had answered her. She saw that sadness that only she could detect. She was filled with a joy and a light far more brilliant than she had ever dreamed of feeling or basking in on the rooftop. She was not afraid of him; she saw from his drooping shoulders and from the way she remembered him when she was alone that he was somehow subdued. In the Qurmoz archway he had gripped her shoulders. She didn't ask him to stop; she didn't even feign an objection. It appeared quite natural to her that he should think of her body from the first moment. She would start their relationship, take him into her embrace. At a certain moment he would whisper in her ear; and she would listen to his quickening breath and would stroke his back. She would be embracing Atif, the college graduate, the dream of the women of the alley. She would ask him why he looked worried and she would try to understand what he would say. In the archway she said, "I am at your disposal, but discreetly." In the archway she had put her finger on what she had thought at first was an illusion; she was sure the effendi was subdued, perhaps because of some calamity that had befallen him, or because he was upset by something. When he embraced her in the archway, it seemed as if he

143

were seeking refuge in her from she knew not what. He didn't assault her as the fruit grocer had. He seemed like a child who was seeking security; involuntarily she said, "My darling," as if she were addressing her son. She wished she could quickly be alone with him. She wasn't going to play games or beat around the bush; she wasn't going to hesitate to offer him all she had, and when ecstasy had reached its peak and relaxation set in, she was going to look him in the eye and tell him all about her life, the nights of waiting for Abdu, her husband, as he came back with bread and falafel, reeking of acids, indigo, and the rotten odor of dyes. She was even going to tell him what had taken place between her and the fruit grocer. But if she were another woman, would Atif still want her? If Umm Yusif went to him would he reject her advances? Wasn't he a young man who needed a woman? What reassured her, though, was that what she had sensed and felt could not be sensed by another woman, that unseen links had joined them, and that her blood was mixed with his. Rhode was haunted by a secret wish: to sit with him some day in the sun on the green grass, in a distant park where nobody knew them. They would talk and sometimes just sit there in silence. A sorrow gripped her: this wasn't going to happen. Even if he were to ask her to meet him, she wouldn't have a galabiya to wear under her torn, black melaya. She would ask nothing of him, but would offer him all she could.

She would wash his clothes, clean his house, and let him inhale the aroma of home-cooked food as he came home in the afternoon. She would clean the windows, arrange the glasses and the plates in the kitchen. She would know her place and not go beyond it. When she went to him, therefore, she was very cautious, fearing the sharp tongues of Zafarani. She avoided Umm Muhammad, who always sat in front of the house. When she finally entered his apartment, it looked as though the sun never shone there. The tiled floor was bare, gray with a big red square in the middle. The subdued house and its sadness seemed part of the sadness that she had seen in Atif's eyes. When he took off his clothes, she stretched her body to meet him. She was overcome with kindness. When he became damp all over with sweat and moved away she wasn't annoyed. It was strange that she wasn't even tense, although two months had passed since she had last slept with the fruit grocer. She reached with her hand but he pushed it away. It seemed to her that she understood why he was subdued and she remembered something that she always repeated: this world does not give in every way; if it gives in one way, it takes in another. She was not annoyed. When she began to put her clothes back on, she pushed her breasts forward, felt her buttocks, hoping to arouse him from a distance but he just buried his face in the pillow. She wished she could hold his head to her chest, whisper to him, rock him, but she was afraid of his reaction.

On the following nights he began to go out at irregular times. She had heard Umm Suhair saying that one could set one's watch by the time he went out every day. What did he think of her? Would he now stop everything? For the first time she was going after a man driven solely by her heart, by the anxiety that gripped her whenever she was away from him, by waking up every morning from a sweet dream: that she was sitting with him in a park bathed in sunlight. Yet anxiety was now gnawing at her; what she thought had just begun, was it already over? Was it because she had perceived his broken spirit?

After the developments in Zafarani were announced, she had remembered his muffled whisper, "This has never happened to me before." Hope stirred within her afresh like the first movements of a fetus in the womb: to her, the spell made a strong reason to continue what had begun. She was not attracted to him by mere desire. His simplicity, his talking to her would be substitute enough for the moments of ecstasy. She waited for him on the Friday at the entrance to the alley; she had decided to follow him and speak to him in al-Hussein Square. She wouldn't pay any attention to the other men and women. But he didn't go out; he stayed at home. She felt deeply unhappy; he had shown no interest in her. Maybe he felt justified in his own mind after the spell.

During the last few days Rhode had resented staying at home, sitting in one corner of the hall where she slept with her child and her mother. Her glances seemed to be lost in her surroundings. Once she entered the only bedroom, where Skina and her husband slept. Skina glared at her sister, but Rhode didn't notice. She seemed to be looking for something. At first Skina thought her sister wanted to talk to Qadusi, her husband, but when she looked at her face, she rejected that idea.

Once her relationship with her husband had returned to normal, Skina had been very careful not to lose him again. The recent developments in Zafarani had turned her bed into one of thorns and pebbles. She had not yet reached thirty and yet she had already been married three times. She had been fifteen when she was married to her first husband, Lutfi the goldsmith, who furnished two rooms at al-Utuf al-Guwwaniya Alley with running water and electricity and bought her a radio. But his mother kept on at them until, one year after the wedding, when Skina was sixteen, she had managed to wreck their life together. A year later, Sabri, her brother who worked in Alexandria, had told her that a Libyan man was looking for a wife and had been agreeable when Sabri had mentioned his sister.

Umm Sabri was overjoyed. Soon the news spread all over; it was said that the bridegroom was very rich, that he was going to send Umm Sabri a radio, a television set, and a dress of pure, natural silk. The whole matter was concluded in three days. The bridegroom did not come to Zafarani; he stayed at the Parliament Hotel in Ataba Square. Umm Sabri groomed her daughter and, accompanied by Umm Suhair,

Busayna, and Umm Nabila, they went to the hotel. At dawn Skina and her husband took a car to Libya. When the women went back to Zafarani they made fun of the bridegroom. Umm Suhair said that even if they were to give her his weight in gold she would not allow him to marry her Suhair. Busayna said that he stood on two feet: one in this world and one in the other.

Many days passed and no presents came to Umm Sabri. During the month of Ramadan, Zafarani was abuzz with news that Skina had sent her mother one sheet of rolled dried apricots and one kilo of American apples. Sitt Busayna felt reassured as time passed, for at the beginning she had been afraid that Skina might send some modern appliances that might suddenly raise Umm Sabri's status. The truth of the matter was that the mother herself was disappointed but, because she feared the women's gloating and mockery, she made a point of talking about the luxury in which Skina was rolling. She told them her daughter had honey and feta cheese for breakfast and ate meat every day. The women of Zafarani were skeptical: if what she said were true, she would have had something to show for it, but her black galabiya had not changed.

Umm Sabri was distressed when Skina's letters stopped coming. Then, two years after Skina had left, Hagga Fawqiya, Umm Sabri's close friend, came to her. She came in shouting "In the name of God!" and some prayers, and said that a messenger had come from Libya and told her how her own daughter Husniya was doing, and had also given her news about Skina, which Husniya, who lived in the same town, had passed on: Skina was unhappy. It was not enough that her husband was a very old man and of no use, she was also harassed by his grown sons and daughters, who treated her as if she were a maid; they counted the loaves of bread, kept track of the tea and the sugar. Umm Sabri was alarmed; she rushed right away to Sheikh Atiya, who had not yet entered his period of seclusion. His answer confirmed the news Sitt Fawqiya had conveyed; he said Skina was suffering and having a hard time. That same day, Umm Sabri went to Sitt Khadija's husband and asked him to write a letter to her daughter, asking that she come back immediately on account of her mother's illness. She didn't mind Skina being alarmed; she was more afraid that they wouldn't let her leave if it were just a routine letter.

The contents of the letter soon became known in the alley. The women shook their heads and winked in understanding; what they had predicted had come true. Busayna said she knew an upper-class lady who lived in a palace surrounded by a garden in Abbasiya whose daughter had a western education and did not speak a word of Arabic, but knew many languages and was a stunning beauty. She was engaged to a wealthy man from a black country. He paid a big dowry. After she left with him they had no news of her for a long time. Her mother was so concerned that she chartered a plane to see what had happened to her daughter. She came back in shock; the man liked his pretty, light-skinned wife and one night he liked her so much that he ate her. Umm Suhair said that this fate was justly deserved by those mothers who sold their daughters, that her Suhair would never leave Egypt, and that when she married would live close to her mother; Umm Suhair would even consider letting her live in a bedroom in her apartment. Umm Nabila asserted that what had happened to that wealthy bride had been doomed to happen. She had heard a lot about those cannibals, as her daughter, Nabila the schoolmistress, who was also studying at the Faculty of Arts in the English Department, had told her about the Niam-Niam who ate people.

A month passed, and Sitt Umm Sabri's letter had still not been answered. She sent another letter, then a third and a fourth. Five months later Umm Sabri saw a stranger enter Zafarani and read all the house numbers. She called out from the window and asked what he was looking for. He said he was looking for Umm Sabri. She shouted, "At your service, Umm Sabri." The women all looked out of their windows and balconies, but because Sitt Busayna lived at the end of the alley, she had to ask Umm Nabila what was going on, and Umm Nabila told her that a man had come to Umm Sabri to say that her daughter would arrive at dawn.

Nobody saw Skina when she came back, and she didn't appear at the window. When the neighbors went to welcome her back, they just sat in the hall and didn't enter the room because she was sick. The truth of the matter was that Skina had suffered some difficult years and had horrible memories when she returned. For a long time she seemed not to want to mix with the women or go out. When Kamal al-Qadusi came, a year after her return, and proposed to marry her, she was afraid. Her mother reassured her, though, saying the bridegroom was guaranteed, that she had made the necessary inquiries and that it had been proved that he was of good moral character and had a secure job that paid about seven pounds a month, in addition to working in the afternoon in a paper store.

Skina appeared anxious to protect her new marriage; she knew the agony, the sense of loss that she suffered when her relationship with a man came to an end. She had faced fear of the unknown when living in a faraway country that almost belonged to a different planet. While away she had kept thinking: Who would want her now that she was damaged goods? What she wanted now was to enjoy quiet and calm in the arms of a real man. She longed for that nightly tête-à-tête in that closed box of a room, and in return she would be willing to put up with any number of hassles from her husband. She would tell him about what she had seen when she went out to buy things; she would use his arm as a pillow and stroke his bare shoulders and chest with her fingers.

In the early days of her marriage she had thought peace of mind was attainable, but then Qadusi revealed something that he had previously kept hidden: he thought that she had saved some money after her stay in Libya. He kept asking her and pestering her. He looked everywhere in the house for a purse containing money or a savings passbook. With every question she became annoyed, but she didn't get angry. She might be about to choke, but she never raised her voice. What was painful to her was seeing herself always as the object of someone's greed; in Libya it was the greed of the old man and his children; here her husband wanted that imaginary fortune which she had never received and which she didn't have. She suffered a great deal and eventually became convinced that he had proposed to her only because he was certain that she had a fortune. The most irritating moments were when, in bed, he would suddenly whisper, "Where's the money?" He tried everything; he went to Sheikh Atiya hoping he might say where the money was. He prepared in his mind what he would tell the sheikh about the reasons for his interest; he wanted to open a store selling old newspapers, which he would run on his wife's behalf without touching a penny of her money. But he was unable to meet the sheikh, since by then he was in seclusion.

Despite Skina's patience, several quarrels blew up. They disagreed over matters that would be trivial to others: her going over the budget by one or two piasters or leaving the kerosene stove burning with no food or water on the flame. His face would turn red and sometimes he would tear at his clothes and she would slap herself in the face because he didn't have another shirt or another galabiya. He would beat his chest, run to the hall knocking down everything in his path. Then he would suddenly turn around, snatch up his shoes, push Skina and her mother out of his way, and run out. The first time she was quite alarmed; she cried over her misfortune and misery for a whole night. All her mother's attempts to calm her failed. She said that he would be back sooner than she thought. And indeed, he came back the next day, exhausted. When she settled in his arms he cried and asked her to forgive him; he had wronged her, but she didn't know the humiliation he was suffering in his work, or how hard up and in what financial straits he was. He embraced her and was about to kiss her hand. She became tearful and her body trembled with emotion like a little dove. Suddenly she heard him whispering, if she'd only tell him about her savings, everything would be fine. She trembled still more and her eyes flowed with tears.

A few weeks later they had another fight. That time he stayed away for three whole days. She went out looking for him in the cafés around al-Hussein hoping to come across him by chance, then she would be kind to him and apologize, even though he was so hard on her, and she would accompany him home. But it would be impossible to find someone again like this, by chance. She went to Sheikh Atiya and found his door closed. At the end of the day, Qadusi came back looking angry and expressed no regret. She had to humor him; she washed his feet in warm water and salt. Later she got used to his moods and escapes. After he returned, she would declare that it had all been her fault. Her mother would side with Qadusi while secretly winking at her daughter. Skina would say she was ready to take any punishment that he wanted to mete out to her. She did not want her life to fail, especially as she was now the mother of two children and getting on in years. If she were divorced again, who would take her as a wife?

It seemed that Qadusi too had realized this, so he now got angry for the slightest reason, and at the first sign of a dispute he would run off. After their last quarrel he had spent more time away than ever before. Umm Sabri's efforts to entice him back took a whole month; she went to his work, begged his colleagues, and implored some of the people from his village. He finally returned with her to find that the number of people in his apartment had increased by the arrival of

Rhode, who had been divorced by her husband, Abdu the dyer. Then a few days later, Zafarani was subjected to the spell. As usual he blamed Skina; had she agreed to move with him seven years ago to the room he had found in Guwwaniya Alley, he would have been spared this fate. But she had refused. Why? Because she wanted to stay close to her mother. He asked angrily, "What, aside from misfortune, had she gained from staying with her mother?"

When she heard what her son-in-law had said, Umm Sabri noted calmly that if his memory had been better, he wouldn't have asked such a question: when he had found the room, he didn't, at the time, have the key money. Her voice began to break when she said she had sacrificed a lot for the two of them; she had left her own bed for them and slept on the tiled floor of the hall so that they might enjoy each other; she saved the best food for them and deprived herself. Had Qadusi forgotten that? She began to cry. Qadusi was confused, but he wanted to appear indifferent to the tears. It was the first time she had ever cried; an extraordinary event. She was a valiant woman, stronger than men, and did not neglect any ritual event. He continued to shout for a little, then he rushed out the door.

As soon as he had gone, Umm Sabri stopped crying. She said, in a serious voice, that he was suffering a crisis and that it was she who was having to put up with it; she was going to appeal to the sheikh's servant, Oweis the baker. She had heard rumors that the spell would be lifted from three of the men in Zafarani. She would exert all her efforts and recruit all her old contacts among the sheikhs and the pious women disciples to intercede with the sheikh to lift the spell from Qadusi.

That night he returned early just as he had been doing since the spell was imposed on the alley. A new worry, however, was now added to Skina's troubles; she noticed that his glances had begun to turn toward Rhode. His tone of voice when he talked to her sister caught her attention. Rhode looked distant. She looked out of the window a great deal, and no sooner had she returned from some errand than she discovered she had forgotten to buy something and would go out again. Accidentally her eyes would meet Qadusi's. Who knew what was going on? Perhaps he was thinking of trying with her; she looked pretty to him and firm, perhaps she could give him . . . perhaps she could cancel out the spell's effect. And because the house was so small and one could always see from one spot what was going on in another, Skina kept Rhode under constant surveillance.

Today, Skina came out of the bathroom to find Rhode entering the bedroom. Had it come to that? Rhode seemed surprised to see Qadusi in his underwear. She was confused. Skina didn't say anything, keeping her anger to herself. After her husband had gone out she asked Rhode what she had wanted from Qadusi. Did she have any illusions about him being any good? How could anyone be any good when the whole alley was under the spell? Rhode was shocked and her voice was soon heard declaring what she thought of Qadusi: that if he was the last man on earth, she still wouldn't have him. Skina alluded to Abdu the dyer, whose rotten smell was so stifling.

Rhode was stung by Skina's words, and she decided her sister must be silenced. What would Atif say when he heard about the shouting? He would say that not only was she poor and uneducated, but also insolent. Skina looked quite vicious, with her disheveled hair, and making insinuations about the amounts of food devoured by Rhode at every meal and the noise made at night by her son which prevented her husband from sleeping and made it impossible for him to go to work feeling well in the morning. She talked about her constant drudgery, how she cleaned the house and prepared the food, went to the co-op and desperately struggled for four hours at a stretch in the midst of the crowds that blocked the store to get one kilo of fish for sixteen piasters. And who gobbled that up? Rhode, who had no other care except combing her hair and going out.

The people of Zafarani predicted that the quarrel would lead to blows. Sitt Busayna followed it with interest, and because of her relative distance from it, had to inquire from Umm Nabila several times. Realizing that the cause was Skina's jealousy over her husband, a strange thought occurred to her: Would Skina be jealous over an impotent husband? Had she found the only man in Zafarani at last? Would she be able to cure her insomnia, her nocturnal shortness of breath, and her tossing and turning? She would turn her attention to Qadusi from now on. Nabila the schoolmistress came out, shouting a few semiclassical Arabic phrases to find out what was happening. People were supposed to be quiet during the day since nobody had any time at night thanks to the 8:00 p.m. curfew. With such quarrels going on, she could not keep up with her university studies. Turning back to her apartment, she glanced at Atif's balcony.

Umm Suhair threw a look to Farida with mockery in her eyes, silently alluding to Ustaza Nabila's talk and her constant references to her university connections. The quarreling suddenly stopped. It was later reported that the wife of Ali the ironer, who lived opposite Umm Sabri, had seen Rhode collapse in tears. Skina had apparently appeared reluctant for a few moments, then she had gone over to her sister and embraced her. The sound of her crying was clearly audible. The sergeant major's wife observed that Zafarani was possessed by the jinn.

The Sixth Quarrel (did not materialize)

This took place on the same night that the sheikh issued new instructions, which included certain requests that could be considered commands. Everything attributed to him was taken by the people of Zafarani extremely seriously. Some of the instructions sounded weird, but there was no protest or even surprise. Nobody opposed him openly. Certain objections would arise in people's minds, but these were not made public. In fact, there were actually attempts to suppress these objections on the part of the very people in whose minds they arose. Who could tell? Maybe the sheikh was aware of things invisible and things below the surface. The instructions given out that night had included a number of important points that could be summed up as follows:

- All quarrels were banned so that quiet might prevail in Zafarani, in wakefulness and in sleep.
- Breakfast would begin at the same moment and would take the same form for everyone: it would consist of fuul and milk.
- The sheikh issued a warning to those leading futile campaigns against him. For the first time, he said that the pimp Tekirli had been prowling around the house where the sheikh lived, adding, however, that he hadn't moved one step in the direction of his abode. He said nobody should think he was capable of stopping what was taking place; this was impossible, for could anyone stop what was happening all over the world? Could the time of flight be stopped?

It was rumored that the sheikh would inflict unspeakable harm upon any who opposed him. In addition to suppressing their virility, he might also transform them—something of which he was quite capable. For years now Zafarani had been talking about two strange stones that stood in front of the bakery, both resembling a big block of ice and tapering off at the top, suggesting a human shape. The customers of the bakery avoided touching these stones or sitting on them even when the place was crowded, as it especially became during the period just before Eid al-Fitr, when large numbers of people would wait for hours to get empty racks for their cookies. The local stories related that each of these stones was originally a human being with whom the sheikh, for some reason, had grown angry and turned into stone. One was a woman and the other a man, and if you came near them at dawn, you could hear the sound of sobbing and weeping coming from the stone on the left.

Radish-head was in the grip of frightening and disturbing thoughts; for the first time his private world was being affected by external factors that were new to him. Previously, he had only ever been moved by the loss of money or by missing a chance to acquire something precious to add to the collection in his warehouse. Farida's childish silliness never bothered him. In point of fact, it sometimes pleased him. Throughout their marriage he had fulfilled his duties: he had provided her with food and sex until the spell changed everything. Farida and Nashwa were still out; bedtime was approaching. What should he do? Should he stay up for them and disobey the sheikh? Or should he go to sleep, in which case he wouldn't know when they came home? He had had to change his routine, and this resulted in losses for him. He had always closed his store in the morning while he went to auction halls, antique dealers, and second-hand stores. The street vendors knew him well. He was always happy whenever he came across some old, empty bottles or an ancient typewriter or book bindings that were torn away from their books or brass ink wells or statues fixed to wooden bases or old ledgers loaded with figures. He usually finished his rounds at about one o'clock in the afternoon and took his purchases straight to the warehouse. Then he went home and had his lunch.

His grocery store, meanwhile, depended on late-night customers. Several years earlier he had noticed that the grocery stores in the neighborhood closed their doors at 11:00 p.m. Many people who wanted to buy an item or two, or supper for their children after that hour and up until 2:00 a.m. could find none but Radish-head's store still open. Staying up late made his job as a meseherati easier. He didn't know what would happen when the month of Ramadan came. Would the sheikh permit people to stay up past the curfew? Besides, his was the only store that sold beer. He knew his beer customers well; most of them drank after coming back from their night's work.

It was a familiar sight to see Radish-head's store well lit in the middle of the dark narrow street and next to it a wooden bench on which sat two or three men talking to Radish-head, who opened his mouth only rarely; some would drink a whole bottle while others drank by the glass, and he preferred the latter because he made three more piasters a bottle that way. Some of the beer drinkers talked to him all the time as they sat, speaking slowly with long pauses as they drank. And in spite of his silence, they would be quite relieved and grateful that someone was listening. Radish-head would sometimes be moved by what he heard, but no gesture or movement betrayed his feelings.

Tonight, however, he had to close his store and go home early; he lost his night customers. He had noticed that since news of what was happening in Zafarani Alley had begun to spread, the number of men frequenting his store was shrinking. He heard Hagg al-Sunni, who sold bread in the store next to his, say that if a Zafarani man touched something and somebody else touched that same thing he would fall under the spell. It was rumors and stories like this that had led to the fall in customers. He was also vexed at being unable to find the time to make his rounds of the antique dealers; every moment that he wasn't searching meant that something precious and rare was being picked up by someone else. What consoled him, however, was that he was better off than the others. Tahun Effendi had to stay at home and ask for sick leave since he had been unable to change his hours. Nobody paid any attention to him despite his nimbleness and the precise information he had compiled over the years on ministers, governors, chairmen of boards, high-ranking officials, and army officers. Every time the name of a high-ranking official was mentioned in front of him he would immediately list the man's education, his degrees, his family and that of his wife, his friends, and the posts occupied by his family members. Now he was at home speaking loudly from his window about a project that must be started immediately, and declaring his intention to inform the sheikh of its details so that he might supervise it.

Two days earlier, as Radish-head was coming down the stairs, Tahun had opened the door to his apartment and begun to talk about the closely guarded secret that he was going to divulge to his dear neighbors. He talked of tunnels that could be dug and that could lead to total equality between the poor and the rich. Radish-head listened to him impassively, and when Tahun had finished he continued on down the stairs as if he hadn't heard a word.

Tahun looked out of the window all the time, talking to the women neighbors. Umm Yusif was rarely seen looking out these days. Usta Abdu was no longer capable of taking Sitt Busayna's abuse; his wife was now very upset because he was still impotent and as useless as a rag or a piece of old furniture. She tried everything with him, using various methods. She went to sheikhs who wrote amulets and magic formulas; nothing worked. The news spread across Zafarani that Usta Abdu the driver had run away. Many tried to predict what would happen to him. Would he escape the spell by fleeing the alley? Some answered by quoting what the sheikh had said at sunrise: the effects of the spell would not leave a man. Others expressed sorrow, saying he would remain under the spell all his life. After lifting the spell the sheikh would show no leniency to those who had left Zafarani or rebelled against him, like Tekirli, who was saying openly that what he was about to accomplish would save everyone. Usta Abdu had lost his chance to be one of the three who, according to the whispers making the rounds of the alley, would return to normal in a few days.

Dark thoughts were assailing Radish-head now, a feeling that it was possible for unexpected things to happen. When he went to the antique dealers, when he combed through those neglected heaps, in the debris of Time, there was always that vague certainty that he was going to find something dazzling, mysterious, unknowable, but very, very rare, very, very precious. When was he going to find it? He didn't know. What he expected now was 'a tremendous change in his life. Several thoughts would take hold of him, but he would try to slip away from them as he reflected on the hassles that had begun to circumscribe his life as a result of the new conditions. As of tomorrow he would have to carry a bowl to Umm Suhair to get breakfast for his family. He would pay Oweis three times more than al-Bannan, or Zannuba the divorcée, or Ahmad the carpenter, Khadija's husband. The sheikh's instructions had stipulated that each resident of Zafarani would pay a sum equal to what he usually paid for breakfast every day. He made an exception for Radish-head, Atif the college graduate, Nabila the schoolmistress, and Daturi; each of them would pay fifteen piasters. Radish-head couldn't remember ever having breakfast at home before. His mouth would be dry in the morning; then at 10:00 a.m. he would usually have a cup of tea in the first café he came across.

As of tomorrow, he would have to have his breakfast at exactly 8:15 with the whole alley. The last few days had made him realize that he could get used to just about anything. Even the most difficult things seemed so only at the beginning. Now, he could hear the old clock chiming, one flat, faint chime that evoked a certain smell, maybe the smell of the corners of the hall that never saw sunlight, or the wood of old chairs. It reminded him of an older time. His heart beat faster; only ten minutes remained before Zafarani bedtime. He thought of closing the windows and turning off the lights in the two rooms, not cheating or attempting to circumvent the sheikh's commandments, but . . . but he was overcome with fear of what might happen.

As he was pulling the shutters closed, Radish-head looked out for the first time in his life, awaiting Farida's return. Zafarani was lifeless; the homes were possessed by something. He raised his head and for a fraction of a second saw Hasan Anwar standing out on the balcony, upright, wearing the military uniform he had bought from him. Hasan Effendi had come to him the day before and addressed him in a formal manner. He asked for an awe-inspiring military uniform. Radish-head had lit up with enthusiasm; he went to the warehouse and came back carrying a complete uniform: a greenish-yellow suit; on the shoulders, two circles of orange thread that were still bright. The chest of the jacket was loaded with bright medals and blue crosses. The pants were wide around the thighs, then tapered toward the ankle. The cap gave no clue to the nationality of the suit's long-departed owner. On the front of the cap was a big eagle with spread wings. Hasan Anwar was genuinely over-joyed, and his joy grew yet greater when Radish-head presented him with a wooden stick whose tip was covered with a goldish yellow metal. Radish-head asked fifteen pounds for it. Hasan Anwar knit his brow; he said he would pay him ten now and the rest on the first of the month. He agreed to sign an I.O.U. for the remaining five pounds and gave a military salute.

Radish-head didn't care. Everything he saw these days was puzzling. Nothing was more strange than his impotence and his confinement at home. Decay had penetrated his very backbone, distorting his spine. He was assailed by countless little thoughts like the flashes of a strobe light. He saw Farida in a stranger's house, naked. He saw her face, noticed what the ecstasy of orgasm did to her features. She turned around in some room. Where was that room? What was the address of the house?

Who saw her as she entered? She put her feet down, felt for her slippers, gathered her hair on top of her head. She asked some man to turn his head until she had finished putting on her clothes. She combed her hair and he got up, aroused by the touch of her slip, as if he hadn't been making love to her all night long, had not felt every part of her body. She made a faint gesture of resistance. The heat sceped through to him as she whispered, "I'm late."

Radish-head could not possibly know where she was. He remembered what the sheikh had said: "What afflicts the men shall afflict the women, all except for one." What if Farida had been saved from the spell? And if she hadn't, would she reveal what had befallen her, whether the stranger had been successful or not? Would the spell prevent the roaming of the hands, the feeling of the breasts and the buttocks? Radish-head paced to and fro, thinking of going upstairs to his mother on the roof, of opening the balcony door and watching Hasan Anwar. Would he end that strange watch of his at eight o'clock, or would he disobey the rules? He thought of hitting the wall with his fist, of screaming, of going down to his warehouse. Was it possible that his wife and daughter were in league together? Had they agreed to go their separate ways, each doing her own thing, and then meeting somewhere to come back together? He sat stiffly on a chair next to the apartment door. The clock struck eight; it sounded like a catastrophe. What's done is done. Tomorrow he would run to Oweis to declare how sorry he was.

Before the clock struck nine, the door opened. He looked at Farida and Nashwa and his heart sank; Farida looked satisfied. Her daughter crossed the room and Farida said, "Time to flee," and he repeated, "Time to flee." It seemed to him that ordinary greetings had been given only in very ancient times, that they belonged to dead languages. Farida's strides were quick; she tried to move away from him. He didn't say a word, didn't speak to his daughter.

161

Their relationship was tenuous. He would often look at her as she passed in front of his store asking himself: Is this really my daughter? The bed squeaked under his wife's body. Slowly he stretched out next to her. A cold silence filled the void. A few minutes later he said, his eyes glued to the ceiling, "Being later than eight can be dangerous." She said she was not very late; she could not leave her daughter by herself with a teacher who was really a stranger. Radish-head was gripped with pain; he was about to cry out, What teacher? Hadn't she said she was going to have her tutorials with a group? He remembered the ban on shouting and that it was after bedtime, so his words came out half chewed through his teeth. She said her daughter had made arrangements with a female teacher, but those plans had fallen through because the teacher was too busy. She had approached a number of other teachers, asking them to come to the alley, and one had actually agreed, but some bastards intercepted him the first time he tried to enter the alley and in the end he didn't dare. After a long search, a teacher agreed to tutor her in his own house. Farida didn't trust him alone with Nashwa, so she had gone with her. There was silence.

Radish-head's head was now boiling. Where was the teacher? Was he a bachelor? Didn't the mother look more enticing than the daughter? Was the daughter protecting her mother? His reactions had always been too slow when sudden things were involved. During the night he tossed and turned. It seemed to him that the mother was sighing in too relaxed a manner. Old images flashed before him: her joy during the days after the consummation of their own marriage, her eyes lighting the whole bed, the sighs, those purrs of satisfaction, the joy at discovering the sources of pleasure. On the following day he cut short his daily rounds and decided to confront her. In his mind's eye he saw the teacher embracing her, bending her body slowly while Nashwa waited in the hall. Never in his life had he taken a violent stand, but now he shouldn't hesitate; the two of them had to endure the present crisis.

He knew women who had remained faithful to their men after the latter had been sentenced to life in prison. What had happened to him hadn't happened to him alone; the whole of Zafarani was suffering. The men did not object in the hope of being saved.

At the entrance to the house, Tahun called out to him and he was obliged to stop. Tahun told him that the pimp Tekirli had sent an account of what was happening to a newspaper, that a reporter had come to Daturi's café to try to find out more, that a student at the Department of Journalism had informed the editor in chief in charge of his internship and that he was gathering the news. These two, however, had not entered Zafarani and nothing had yet been published. Tahun said that two detectives from the Special Security detail were making enquiries in the neighborhood about what was happening; it seemed that the government had caught wind of the news. Radish-head shook his head and was about to go in when Tahun pointed up. Hasan Anwar was standing there wearing the military uniform, holding a short stick that he pointed upward and downward every now and then.

Quickly Radish-head went in. He stood in front of his wife; his heart beat faster and faster. He made a point of not looking around the room so that she wouldn't think he was looking for some man who might be hiding there. Of that he was certain. Then she asked what was going on? What was wrong with him? What had happened? He looked at her. All the words he had prepared and that constant reel of images, day and night, were now receding. He didn't know what was happening. Perhaps it was his fear of matters escalating until a shouting match ensued, which the sheikh had banned; perhaps it was because he felt he needed her now and couldn't imagine her being away from him. He was upset at himself for being so weak, but he had grown accustomed to her presence, the way she talked, the way she looked, her smell. He needed her now more than ever before.

Farida was surprised. He looked up. Oh God, how beautiful she looked now! She stifled a laugh so as not to provoke him. She was not used to his coming home early. His voice reached her, calm, with a strange tone of humility and resignation. He said nothing had happened to cause her to worry. The truth of the matter was that he had found a splendid work of art, but that he hadn't had enough money with him, so he had come home to get it.

Memorandum Number 1

From: Old District Police precinct

To: Supreme Security Authority

Re: Strange Events in Zafarani Alley

Preliminary investigations by the secret police detail attached to the precinct force indicate that strange things are happening in Zafarani Alley. For many days now, nobody has been able to enter the alley—except for its inhabitants. The reason cited is claimed to be a spell. The effect of the aforementioned spell, to cut a long story short, is to rob men of that which is dearest and most precious among their possessions, namely, their sexual capabilities. This situation has resulted in several government employees being unable to perform their official duties. Several reports have reached us, which we shall sum up hereinafter:

- A report from the employees of the Department of Electricity (Collection Division, Old District Branch) concerning their inability to read the meters of the inhabitants of Zafarani Alley for the month of March. The branch is hereby requesting an urgent resolution of the matter, otherwise it will have to cut off power to the whole alley.

- A report from the Department of Antiquities (Inspectorate of the Old District) regarding the inability of Antiquities

164

Inspector Suad Abu Zeid to enter the alley to conduct routine inspection of item #43: the remains of a house of the second Mamluk era that contains plaster moldings, marble slabs, and wooden panels. The Inspectorate requests that the Security Department take immediate action to protect said item or to enable inspectors to enter the alley without coming under the alleged spell.

- Complaint from a certain Tekirli against a certain Sheikh Atiya and some inhabitants of Zafarani.

- Complaint from Usta Abdu, driver with the Transit Authority, against his wife, Busayna al-Shariti, in which he accuses her of evicting him from his own apartment and seizing his belongings.

- Complaint signed "Men of Zafarani" requesting protection for their womenfolk from certain professional pimps who have begun to frequent Daturi's café. Preliminary investigations have also indicated that the said Sheikh Atiya has begun to impose his whims on the people under the spell; that he has imposed a strict schedule for sleeping and waking. This has conflicted with the interests of certain inhabitants, as, for instance, in the case of an employee of the Railway Authority. The sheikh has, likewise, forced the people to eat specific foods at fixed times and has started a broadcasting service to the inhabitants, using in that role an unemployed man—a development which constitutes an infringement on the people and is within the domain of matters within the jurisdiction of responsible authorities. Among these matters is his pledge to the people that he will guarantee their security and safety if they obey his commands, his statement that he will rearrange the world and expand the effects of the spell gradually, and his assumption of responsibility for the entire citizenry. Please take cognizance and advise.

Some Zafarani Incidents

It is obvious that the sheikh's commands are not fully carried out as soon as they are given. Some of them appear, at the beginning, to be difficult to abide by. Some people declare their disobedience openly while others harbor it secretly. Continued resistance, however, is difficult in the shadow of the spell. Disobeying the sheikh leads to greater anger on his part. After the ban on quarrels, some little incidents take place—two of them at the sergeant major's house on the same day.

The first of these takes place in his apartment. He couldn't care less about the spell or about the whole alley's impotence, nor could his wife, for that matter. The sergeant major is now approaching his seventy-fifth year. His life is now totally tied to his wife, his years are a living part of her days. He cannot stay for one hour without her: If she goes out to buy vegetables or meat, anxiety attacks him. He stares out of the window and when he sees her approaching he shouts out, asking her to hurry up. He spends his time talking about his old friends and their wives and their habits, or looking for an old box to take apart then put together again, or nailing down the frame of the window, or hanging a picture. When he tries to fool around with the electrical wiring, his wife begs him to stay away from it and keeps begging him, but he responds only when she invokes the name of the crown prince.

As the days under the spell passed, they began to worry; something comparable to what had happened to the other inhabitants might happen to them as well. They couldn't guess what might befall them. That Oweis was living in the same house scared them. It seemed to them

166

that they could hear noises late at night. When that occurred the sergeant major would slightly raise his head and then assert that the jinn had come to the baker's room. He would tell his wife never to admit to anyone what she had heard and she would nod her head in agreement. He would then say that he knew her and how, with her loose tongue, she couldn't keep a secret. On those occasions she didn't answer him; she would ask him to be quiet when he continued to insult her. She would tell him that Sheikh Atiya would be angry if he knew they were talking in the middle of the night.

They both obeyed every order that Owcis announced, fearing the punishment that might be visited upon them if they didn't. This morning, however, the sergeant major displayed open disobedience. After he got up, his wife asked him to go get their share of fuul and milk. He asked what she was talking about, and she said if he didn't go down at once they would not have a single bite to eat and would go hungry. He stood up suddenly. Was it conceivable that the time had come when the sergeant major, cook to kings and princes, would have to stand before a woman with a disgusting smell and that she would give him a handful of beans and a glass of milk?

His wife's eyes were wide with consternation and she said, "Calm down. Are you crazy?" Had he forgotten the sheikh's instructions? She remembered the two stones standing in front of the bakery. The sheikh could transform them, and then years would go by without being able to move; they would see everything around them, hear the whispers and the shouts, but they would never speak. The sergeant major stiffened, declaring that he feared no one and that he would not under any circumstances get food that was prepared so quickly. His wife tried to muzzle his mouth, she could ignore anything except what was taking place right now, since it affected the sheikh directly. She knew her husband; he forgot himself when he carried on this way. When her hand approached him he grew furious; he shouted at the top of his voice, declaring that he was now certain that she didn't respect him. Things deteriorated further when she tried to restrain his hands; his varied and extensive life couldn't stand humiliation for a single day. He rushed through the hall to his room. His wife forgot everything as she saw the danger; her screaming was heard quite distinctly. Tahun expressed his exasperation with those fools who violated the sheikh's blessed teachings as if the matter concerned them alone, forgetting that all would pay for the infractions of any individual.

As the sergeant major's wife began screaming, Rummana the politico was going upstairs carrying a plate covered with a loaf of bread and a small glass of milk. The woman's screams made him go up to the second floor. She cried out, "The gun!" Rummana listened to the sergeant major talking about his life, the princes, the great foods, and this age of humiliation that was now forcing him to stand in line to get his food. Rummana said that the sergeant major's history was well known to everybody, that no one denied it. But Zafarani was passing through strange times, which surprised him personally. In his view, what was taking place in Zafarani right now was the nucleus of something strange that had yet to be fully explained, that the subject was much more comprehensive and much more profound than it appeared on the surface. He didn't think the sheikh's food procedure was harmful or bad; on the contrary, for himself personally, it was useful, because he hadn't found a job since coming out of jail and had very little money and wasn't expecting any more money from any source any time soon. The regime was still at the beginning and things at such a stage usually appeared difficult; as time went on things would return to normal.

Rummana leaned against the wall, assumed a relaxed posture, ignoring the gun that the sergeant major was pointing up at his own head. He said his life was full of situations similar to this one. When he went into solitary confinement for the first time in his life, he had been struck at how small and narrow the cell was; he spent the first night weighed down with grief, and was certain he would die if he spent three days in there, where life was impossible, where he couldn't take more than two steps in a straight line, where he couldn't sleep fully stretched out, where nobody talked to him. He was surprised when the days began to pass; time was compressed inside that cell, perhaps because he didn't move around. A week passed; some time later he forgot the difference between one day and another. All time was the same: no difference between Friday, Saturday, Sunday, or any other day. He began to scratch little lines on the wall of the cell. Did the sergeant major know how many days passed? The sergeant major shook his head. Rummana noticed that the hand holding the gun was coming down. For six months and four days he hadn't spoken to a single soul.

Rummana paused; he said he would mention another incident that had a more profound significance. On his first day in jail, when he went to the ward, one prisoner brought in a big pot filled with a green liquid, with green leaves and cylindrical bodies floating on top. He looked at the food in disgust and turned his back; he noticed that his fellow prisoners, who had spent varying periods of their lives in jail, attacked the food with gusto; he noticed how voracious they were. He remembered telling himself at that time that prison taught the human spirit to be coarse. In the evening supper was brought to them. It was fuul, the likes of which he had never seen before: the shells had to be removed and then the mealworms had to be extracted before the beans could be eaten. He gulped down several of the beans. On the second day he voraciously devoured that insipid green soup, and later on he even enjoyed it.

The hardest things softened with time. What the sheikh did was not without its good side. As Rummana was standing in line he had heard Tahun describing how he had once gone out to buy breakfast for

169

his children and at the alley entrance had seen a divorced woman who was going through hard times. She prayed that he might never be in need and asked him for two piasters to buy some food. Rummana said that the recent procedure saved women from having to go out to the greengrocers and the butchers and standing in front of the co-ops. This was particularly opportune since in the last few days the vendors and salesmen at the stores had begun using bad language with them. Of course a decent woman like the wife of the sergeant major . . . . At that point the sergeant major made a threatening gesture with his hand saying that whoever dared to say anything like that to his wife—he would empty the gun into him. Rummana realized that the timing was now right, so he asked the sergeant major to put his royal gun back where it belonged. The sergeant major looked to his wife and said that for the sake of the man who had suffered and who had been imprisoned for many years because of his convictions, he would reconsider his present position.

Rummana went back to his room. Since the spell had been cast, he hadn't gone out. He spent a great part of his time reading books or reliving the old days. A few days ago a young man from Zafarani had visited him; he said he was Hassan, son of Hasan Anwar, that he had learned of Rummana's release and wanted to get to know him better. Rummana said he would like that, but secretly he was suspicious. The dark days full of spies had taught him to suspect anyone who approached him with interest. He talked to Hassan cautiously. Two days later he was certain of the youth's genuine enthusiasm and thirst for knowledge. He remembered his own green days when he sat down with Badr, who taught him socialism and love for the people and showed him the first steps in clandestine political action. Rummana was waiting for Hassan today. So far they had only talked in general terms. Rummana wanted to know about the new generation; he wanted to discuss many matters with him, such as the university and what was happening there, what was taking place in Zafarani, and his father, about whom he had heard so many contradictory things.

Rummana couldn't continue his musing. He heard a child screaming upstairs, and because the most trifling incident could now acquire significance, he hurriedly opened the door of his room and looked out across the banisters. He saw a huge woman bending over a small child, raising her hand to shower blows on him. Rummana shouted, "Have pity, lady!" The child sought his protection and through his tears cursed the woman. Rummana was surprised when Sitt Busayna came up close to him, her huge bosom touching him; her eyes gleamed through the mesh veil with its golden clasp, two big eyes expressing all the desire with which this huge body seethed. She said the boy's name was Yusif, son of Umm Yusif who lived below Radish-head. As she was going out she had seen him standing outside Oweis's room and, since she was an honorable and decent woman, she couldn't stand for that kind of thing. So she had told him to go away, but he stuck out his tongue at her, and that was when she began to beat him. Rummana asked what sort of thing it was that she could not stand for. Lowering her voice in such a way that a tremor ran through his body she said that Umm Yusif was a greedy woman, always in need of a man to cool her fire; that stupid woman thought that Oweis was the only one who could do so, in view of his closeness to the sheikh, so she had begun to stake him out and now she was sending her son to him. Sitt Busayna slapped her bosom and said, "Has anyone seen a catastrophe worse than this?" Rummana shook his head in disbelief. He was surprised that this woman was being so forward and talking to him about such matters in such direct terms. Her glances and the gestures of her hands said more than her words, as if she wanted Rummana to blurt out that he was the one to whom Sheikh Atiya had referred. She said she would never accept that kind of hanky-panky and went downstairs slowly, turning around to look at Rummana after every flight.

Nobody knew how the news reached Umm Yusif, who tried immediately to rush out, but Tahun stood up to her firmly and, in a low voice, reminded her of the possible consequences; she was disobeying the sheikh! The blood rushed to her face. He was certain that her foolishness would make her fly out to the alley. The people of Zafarani had always relished the quarrels of Sitt Busayna and Umm Sabri, followed closely by those of Umm Suhair and Umm Yusif. The quarrels in which any one of these women participated were major spectacles for the inhabitants; each was blessed with a voluminous lexicon of insults and similes, but each had her own specialty.

Sitt Busayna accompanied her insults with clapping, incessant moving of her eyebrows, and choreographed steps. The people of Zafarani attributed this to the fact that she had at one time been a professional dancer. As for Sitt Umm Sabri, she depended on her deep voice and on the baring of certain parts of her body. It was said that during one quarrel she had spread her melaya on the ground and begun to take off her clothes, and when she became absorbed in what she was doing, the inhabitants who were leaning out of the windows and balconies to watch were surprised to see her take off everything until she was as naked as the day she was born and then to begin turning in every direction. Umm Sabri was often invited to take part in quarrels in other alleys; her mere appearance on the scene silenced all the adversaries. It was rumored that she had fans who followed all her quarrels, traveling to alleys near and far.

Umm Suhair was known in the alley by the dignified declamations she recited at the beginning of every quarrel: "God is great! God is great! God is great! you daughter of . . . ." Then she would loose a stream of abuse without looking at the other party in the quarrel. She

172

would shake her fists several times, paying particular attention to the constant movement of her middle finger. Despite the dignified beginnings of her quarrels, the alley usually would settle down to listen to a great many stories full of sexual insinuations. When things got a little out of hand, she would leave her apartment and storm the place where her opponent would be hiding, then attacked her physically. The alley remembered how she had gone to Mahasin, Ali the ironer's wife, and sat on her and showered her with blows using an old slipper. As a result, Ali the ironer couldn't have sex with her for a month.

As for Umm Yusif, she usually started quietly, addressing her neighbors as she always did. Usually the other party did not cease or desist either, and thus the intensity of the shouting increased. At that point, Umm Yusif would disappear for a few moments, then reemerge carrying a tabla on which she beat, arranging her insults in rhythm.

Tahun now had to hold her arms and push her into the inner room and he was quite taken aback. It was the first time he had touched her in days, her soft skin sent a tremor through his body. He remembered the numerous times they had made love, and sadly he remembered his moments of boredom, of being tired of her body. Now all he wanted was to embrace her. But then what? It was as if he had been running a long distance then had suddenly come up against an invisible barrier; screaming didn't help. What if he were to beat his breast, pluck out his eyes, or bite the dust? But it was as if he were bound up, his thoughts casting thick shadows on his eyes. His wife's voice was hoarse, faint. She begged him to let her answer the slut. Tahun said he didn't want to incur the sheikh's wrath. She freed her arms, beat her breast, threw herself down on the tiled floor, biting her hand and pulling her hair. Strangely enough, her voice was getting louder despite the intensity of her feelings. Through her hoarse gasps she said she couldn't put up with her own son being beaten and she herself being unable to respond.

173

His voice crept up, begging her to have patience and assuring her that the sheikh would not tolerate what the foul-mouthed Busayna did.

Umm Yusif did not go out that whole day; she did not even look out the window. Sitt Busayna, however, did not calm down; she couldn't stay in one place for five minutes. She went out to buy the silliest things; at eight o'clock she went out to buy a needle. Later she walked all the way to Bayt al-Qadi and then came back very slowly. Her heart was burning like live coals in her chest for various reasons. Never before had such a long time elapsed without her making love with a man. She now remembered her nights with Usta Abdu and the way he had shown her certain arts that he had mastered. And how when he looked at her and noted her satisfaction, he had been very happy. He would leave the bed, go to the kitchen, squeeze some limes, and offer her limeade as she lay down, relaxing. Despite his virility, he had been afraid to disturb her if she overslept a little. He left the house frequently without taking his pocket money. He never kept the money he earned, but handed her his entire salary on the first of every month. She had taken care of everything. Gone now was the man she used to order about and whom she used to see sitting in a corner in the hall waiting for her to come out of the bathroom. Many times now she hoped that he would knock on the door and come in, but she hadn't even bothered to ask about him herself; she hadn't gone to the station manager where the bus line began. Abdu had no extended family and she didn't know his father or mother or sister. He never spoke of an uncle, on either his father's side or his mother's. He never went to visit relatives on Eid days, nor did he visit the sick or offer condolences to any relations. She suddenly remembered his impotence and could not even bear to visualize him. And yet she felt very lonesome on those still and silent Zafarani nights.

At the end of the day, her loneliness became too much for her. She looked out and saw no one but Latifa. She called out to her. Latifa

174

would come up soon. Busayna figured she'd be tempted by the hope of some food; she was needy. Was this woman worth talking to? Well, what else could she do? She could find no one else, and at least this way she would get some attention and someone would listen to her. She duly expressed her resentment of the debauchery of certain women. Latifa agreed by nodding, then said the world was going to the dogs; that it wasn't the same good old world. The sheikh had been right when he replaced all greetings with one phrase. It was indeed the time of flight— flight from love, goodness, and sincerity. The truth was that Latifa never let a chance go by without praising the sheikh's works for fear that he still might harm her son who was away from home, on the grounds that he was of Zafarani stock. For the first time she hoped her son would not come while the alley was still under the spell.

Sitt Busayna moved to other topics; she bad-mouthed several women; Latifa nodded. Sitt Busayna attacked the men of the alley who had given in to this fate. Latifa was silent; agreeing with this kind of talk was risky. Busayna attacked Nabila the schoolmistress, said she was full of hot air and arrogance; she thought she was so important because she was going to college. But no matter how high a position she might ultimately attain, she would never be able to rub shoulders with Busayna's acquaintances of the old days. Latifa said today's girls were arrogant. Busayna tapped her on the knee and said that arrogance was only skin deep. Nabila's salary was ten pounds a month; she fixed a big pot of macaroni every day at home and took it to school where she sold it in sandwiches to the pupils, and woe to those who didn't buy from her! She really persecuted them. She said Nabila's family was having trouble making ends meet. Their apartment was immediately facing hers, and she had never once smelled onions being browned in ghee. Only the smell of oil came from their kitchen. They ate meat only once a month. Latifa was annoyed; she looked thin and haggard and had a decent meal only when those rare money orders from her son arrived. She was sensitive about anything that had to do with poverty. She told herself that Busayna didn't really mean what she said.

All Busayna's thinking was now focused on Nabila, who filled her with a sudden anger. Nabila was the only Zafarani woman who never got involved in a quarrel. Even her mother was hardly ever heard, except for her negotiations with street vendors before they had stopped coming to the alley. Slowly Busayna headed for the balcony; it was approaching sunset. Her mind was empty now apart from the need to pick a quarrel with that girl and expose her arrogance. Circumstance didn't make her wait long. Some children began to toss a ball back and forth to each other—these were clearly Zafarani children, since the mothers in nearby alleys had warned their children against playing there. The boys began to fight, and Nabila appeared, holding a book. She told the boys to stop playing ball so she could review her lectures. It was a suitable pretext. Busayna asked loudly and sarcastically about the level of noise the boys were making. Was it necessary to fabricate situations to remind people that the snotty princess was in college? Nabila was completely taken aback. The tone of an all-out offensive was so obvious that a number of women scrambled to the windows; some of them swore that the day would not end well. Nabila puckered her lips in surprise. Busayna shouted that she could no longer stand seeing such a skinny girl, a twenty-eight-year-old spinster, an elementary schoolmistress dying of desire to smell a man's sweat, bathing only once a month, an impolite girl, chasing men and trying to dictate to Zafarani. Wasn't what had happened enough without this skinny girl coming and saying do this and don't do that?

The whole alley was surprised by this blitzkrieg, which Busayna had mounted with no preliminaries. Nobody had noticed any earlier tension between Busayna and Nabila. Nabila hurriedly went in, calling her mother in a scared, tearful voice. Ahmad the carpenter loudly asked Busayna to cool it; what she was doing was bad for the whole alley. For the first time the voice of Atif the college graduate was heard loudly, "That's not done, Sitt Busayna!" Boiling water was now coursing through her veins. This was her chance to attack two people whom nobody had offended before. She asked whether Atif was poking his nose in because she was going to the university from which he had graduated or because there were something else behind things? Nothing that took place in Zafarani escaped her. There was no need to speak about that now, but if the two of them thought they were superior to the people of the alley, they were mistaken. Busayna had the highest status among the inhabitants. She had often caused torment in men with whom Atif could not even dream of associating, and perhaps that scarecrow of a girl was now studying the history of these men.

Atif shook his head and disappeared into his apartment, as did Ahmad the carpenter. Even Khadija the Sa'idi woman did not come out to watch. Busayna's voice died down and the lonesomeness of the sudden quiet weighed heavily upon her heart, now trembling with fear. She wished she could see Abdu now. She was terrified by the bare tiled floor, the old walls, the pictures in pale frames, the door which she expected no one to knock on, and the loneliness of the night. Her sudden irritation had now turned into fear. A secret voice kept repeating a strange idea to her: that if she closed her eyes, she would never open them again. She watched the gray light that approached with cruel determination. Her past appeared to her as if it had belonged to someone else: the war, the nightclubs, the English men, the sudden blackouts, and the sad tunes of the qanun. She couldn't remember the names of any one of those foreigners. All she remembered was her naive thought before the first of them had touched her: Would she find him different from the Egyptians? She remembered the way his face had contracted. She had departed from her habit of keeping her eyes closed. One of her Egyptian friends had told her that, as men, the English were weak. Her own experience, however, proved the contrary to be true. The sighs of ecstasy, the bright lights of the halls, the exploding noise of bottles being popped open—how insignificant it all appeared now! She had known dancers and singers who were full of life and vigor but who nonetheless had died suddenly. She was afraid of death. How horrible it seemed, to close one's eyes and then never to open them again, never to have dreams, never to be awakened by noises. No one would know she had died until her body had decomposed and begun to stink. She saw the people of Zafarani trying to break down the door and heard voices saying, "Yes, we haven't seen her for days." "Since she yelled at Nabila, nobody has heard her voice." "This is a just punishment for her sin against that poor sinless girl."

Busayna now sat in the hall succumbing to a cruel coldness. All evening, until the Zafarani bedtime, no one saw her on the balcony or heard her voice. This, however, did not mean that quiet had prevailed in the alley. At around seven o'clock there was news of strangers appearing at Daturi's café. Ali the ironer asserted that they had come from India bringing a solution to the problem. Tahun said they were officials who had come to investigate the matter. The situation in Zafarani was no longer a secret, and the state was supposed to protect the citizens. Maybe they would summon the inhabitants one by one. What should they be told then? He sought out Oweis to request he convey to the sheikh this question about how the strangers' questions should be answered. The truth of the matter was that over the last two days, Tahun had gone to Oweis several times to inquire about small matters in order to guarantee that his name would duly be repeated to the sheikh several times.

Oweis promised to convey Tahun's inquiries, and he always kept his promises. Everything that he heard from the inhabitants he repeated to the sheikh but he didn't expect a quick answer. He had already heard about those strangers. Perhaps somebody from his own village had come to ask about him. Perhaps Me'allim Abul Ghait had sent for him. No one would reach him, ever. He began to forget, gradually, the features of his faraway village, and Me'allim Abul Ghait, and the baths with its respectable effendis. Being alone for long periods of time made him constantly revisit various aspects of his past. He had often dreamed of a small room, the smell of a home-cooked meal waiting for him, and a wife. The outlines of the dream became much clearer after he came to Cairo, despite his sleeping at the bakery, the stifling steam of the baths, and the dampness of the pavement around al-Hussein Mosque. He considered all of these to be merely passing matters that paved the way to the day when he would settle down. He had to bear those temporary inconveniences. When he rented the room he felt very hopeful and spent his first few nights a happy man, gazing at the room's slanting ceiling, which was the underside of the staircase.

He could hear all the footsteps going up and down. Sleep was difficult, since his work at the baths required him to stay up late and exert a vigorous effort with the effendis. Despite the annoyances of the constant traffic up and down the stairs, as soon as he had finished his work he returned to his room with light steps. For the first time in this big city he owned a key to a closed space in which he could take off his clothes, go naked, laugh, cry, and feel as homesick as he pleased, with no fear of policemen, or thieves, or pickpockets.

During the last few days, however, Oweis had looked with fear upon the past years of his life: thirty years he had spent trying to survive, sitting silently while others talked, going to weddings not as a guest or participant in any way but to offer his services. During wakes, nobody paid any attention to him, and those who served the coffee skipped him. Who knew how many years would now pass before the sheikh would release him? At the beginning he had thought he was going to be cured quickly in view of his special status. As time went by, however, a burden began to weigh upon him: Whenever he visited the sheikh's room, he left a part of his life there. The thought that he might spend the rest of his days in this condition was no longer strange; he had fallen captive to something unknown. At certain moments he would still be struck by a painful desire, thin and sharp as a razor's edge, to go to Abul Ghait's café, meet people from his village, and inquire about what was happening there. Yet his wish to own that pushcart: why had it diminished so? Would the sheikh release him easily? Whenever he went to there he was gripped by fear, anxious to carry out properly all that was required of him lest he should be turned into a cat or a stone.

The people of Zafarani no longer ignored the black cat that had appeared a week earlier and stood near the food line. Umm Sabri swore that she had heard the cat speak a human language but couldn't understand what it said because she was so afraid! Everybody treated the cat kindly and prevented the children from chasing it or throwing stones at it. Each inhabitant had a secret fear of meeting the same destiny. A rumor of unknown provenance spread about, saying that the cat was Amm Mustafa the grilled-corn vendor transformed; nobody had seen him for some time. It seemed that he had angered the sheikh by making certain threats after he had fallen under the spell upon entering Zafarani the first day. Umm Sabri asserted that Tekirli would meet a similar fate.

Oweis felt an interest in the strangers. The thought made him aware of how lonely and cut off from the world he was; his interest in those men was tinged with longing. The sheikh must be told of them, especially since they didn't seem to be in a group; according to the inhabitants, they were all sitting apart and didn't know each other. At about 7:15 p.m. news spread of a fight taking place in front of Daturi's café. It happened as Tekirli and his wife were coming home that one of the strangers—an effendi—confronted them. Tekirli chided him quietly but the man didn't stop, so they came to blows. According to another version, when the stranger saw Tekirli coming along, he got up and shook hands with him and invited him to sit down, but Tekirli seemed embarrassed, as he pointed to his wife who was a few steps ahead of him, whereupon the stranger walked in her direction and pointed to Tekirli, saying he could make a fortune if he would listen to him. He said the alley was now without men and they could work together right away. The blood rushed to Tekirli's head, his fingers trembled; he shouted, ordering the effendi to bug off. The effendi shouted that Medhat Bey hadn't forgotten the ten pounds that had been stolen from him in Tekirli's house. The eyewitnesses were unanimous in reporting that Tekirli erupted in rage, as if his whole body had turned into a fist that he aimed at the man. He jumped toward him, knocked him to the ground, bent over his ear, and sank his teeth into it. A number of passersby hurried to separate the two men. Two other men got up and moved away from the café without trying to save the effendi who, only moments before, had been sitting with them. They didn't want to get involved in a fight that might end up in the police station, where both of them would be exposed for what they really were.

Among the crowd, Tekirli's wife was the most afraid. She knew how vicious and bloody her husband could be. Under circumstances like these he could easily kill—it was the same ease with which he had been receiving clients for many years, spreading the bed sheets for them, sitting and waiting for his wife, watching from the keyhole as she writhed in the arms of total strangers. She knew the number of times that, as the two of them walked together, he had flown into a rage and started a violent brawl after overhearing just one word of flirtation or catching some deliberate caress. She screamed and called out his name several times.

It was at that moment that Ali the ironer and Ahmad the carpenter appeared, pushing through the crowd to where the two men were fighting and showering blows on the stranger. Ali the ironer had heard that some pimps had come to Daturi's café and had bad-mouthed Tekirli, his wife, and the alley. Ahmad the carpenter had chanced to drop by just then to have a galabiya quickly ironed. Ali told him what was happening and the two dashed to the scene. Daturi didn't move from where he was sitting, but kept blowing the smoke of his hookah, as if the altercation were taking place on a different street. This thought occurred to everybody who looked at him. In truth, however, he felt wounds reopening within him, unseen by anyone. Days were passing and the calamity persisted, and as the new state of being settled over the alley, people's relationships with each other became ever stranger. He remembered how Sitt Busayna had come to him, sat for a while, and then suddenly asked him whether he was the only one left. She begged him to be honest with her, not to hold back. She was afraid of going to sleep.

Busayna wasn't the only one who suspected him; some of the men also looked at him suspiciously. Tahun had approached him twice, beating around the bush, but he only answered with a nod or shake of the head. And now they were fighting and passersby were watching as the children began to mimic the movements of the wrestlers. The café's regular customers had deserted it since what was happening in Zafarani became known. Who knew what might happen? Perhaps what had happened to Zafarani men could happen to others too: impotence spreading like a contagious disease through touch or proximity. The customers of a lifetime who had filled the café for many precious years, playing cards and dominoes, telling stories, or listening to the concerts of Umm Kulthum, had now migrated to the cafés of Bayt al-Qadi and al-Hussein. In the carefree days he had been so used to seeing them that if one failed to show up several days in a row, he used to send the café servant to his house to ask about him. Even casual customers no longer came to the café to drink some tea or smoke a hookah before rushing off.

As for the owners of stores and shops, they had stopped ordering tea and coffee after lunch, and he no longer sat watching the yellow brass trays go out of the café balanced on the palm of a waiter in astonishing equilibrium. He used to sit there guessing who was going to drink that full glass, what feelings he would have as he sipped its hot contents. He would look at the empty glasses, noting that some customers left a few sips of the tea, while others chewed up the very dregs of the leaves. A new breed of customer was coming to the café nowadays, besides the pimps. He couldn't throw them out: the café was open to the public. A different kind of stranger also appeared. This morning a young man in his thirties had come in. He had ordered a cup of ground fenugreek, which he drank slowly as he looked all around him, then called over Amm Muhammad the old waiter. Muhammad had pointed to Me'allim Daturi; the young man had got up and walked toward him. Daturi wished he would leave; he had no desire to speak to anyone. The young man said he was a journalist for al-Yawm newspaper, had heard of what was happening, and just wanted to know more about it. A subject of this kind was quite sensitive and could not be published until a number of reports had been made and interviews conducted.

As he talked, Daturi's mind was preoccupied with one question: Should he answer the young man's greeting using the traditional words or should he respond, "Time to flee"? It was a question of extreme importance. Committing an unintentional mistake might, in the sheikh's view, be equal to a deliberate, premeditated violation. Daturi was afraid. The journalist might hear whatever he liked, but for the me'allim to speak of what was happening in the alley—that was not done. The young man fell silent, then began to ask whether it was true that there was a general in the alley. Daturi raised his eyebrows. The young man said in explanation that according to some rumors there was a high-ranking officer of unknown nationality in the alley. Was it true? The me'allim did not say a word. The young man smiled and said his name was Hamdi, that he would now be coming to the café often and would be happy to get to know the me'allim.

As Daturi was returning home he had stopped by Oweis's room and asked him to convey his question about greetings exchanged with strangers and whether or not they could be told what was happening. He looked up at Hasan Anwar's balcony; they thought he was a general. Zafarani had become accustomed to the way he stood there. The sheikh's answer was not long in coming. Oweis in his nightly announcement declared that the same words of greeting must be used; no matter how strange they sounded, there would soon come a day when others no longer wondered about them, even if they spoke a foreign tongue. There was no harm in speaking about the affairs of Zafarani, for what was remote to others today would be close to them tomorrow.

Now Daturi was watching the fight, which had come to an end. The effendi moved away and Tekirli took his wife and walked toward the alley. Ali the ironer and Ahmad the carpenter came up. They said "Time to flee," and the me'allim returned the greeting. They sat down. Daturi looked at Muhammad the waiter. He could say the most complex things with his eyes; he spoke only rarely, but Muhammad the waiter and Zuqla, who stood behind the counter, knew exactly what every glance meant. A few moments later Muhammad brought the tea. Ali and Ahmad said they were requesting that no strangers be allowed to frequent the café; they didn't want threats to the honor of the alley or its exploitation. Ali said the café was very close to the alley and it was easy for strangers to follow home whomever they liked. Daturi noticed that some passersby were stopping to look and then hurrying away. The fact that three people from Zafarani were sitting together was unusual. He remembered what Oweis had said about the day approaching when Zafarani affairs wouldn't seem odd to strangers. Ali the ironer pointed out that Daturi would not accept just anyone as a tenant in his building, which he would be building soon, God willing. When he talked about his prospective tenants he had spoken of the importance of being particular; he had to be particular about his customers as well.

Daturi felt a heavy burden weighing on his heart. Since the customers had deserted him, he no longer spoke about the building; no broker brought him a customer who begged to be accepted as a tenant. He hadn't even given the building a thought in two days. He was filled with a grief that rose in his throat until it choked him, killed the words on the tip of his tongue. He no longer added to the details of the structure of his building; the number of floors; the color of the paint; the floor on which he was going to live; how the entrance would look. He looked at his two neighbors with tearful eyes and did not answer. They were so confused that they were unable to get up when they saw the tears, while his full face remained blank. Had they made a mistake? Slowly they said, "Time to flee."

A quarter of an hour before the collective bedtime, Basyuni al-Hagrasi went out of his room and loudly addressed the inhabitants of the alley, telling them that he was disowning his son, Luli. The ingrate bastard was counting the few morsels that the father ate. His voice grew even louder as he said that he was going to hand his son over to the police because he was working against the State: his son was a member of a Muslim Brotherhood ring. Luli came out, looking tired. He approached

185

his father, tried to kiss his head; the old man grew even more furious. He repeated that he was going to inform the police, for whom he had worked a whole lifetime. He wasn't going to stand silently by while his son plotted acts of sabotage. Luli was no longer his son. Had it come to this? Counting how many crumbs of bread he ate? That same night, immediately before bedtime, Oweis had declared that it was necessary to resolve disputes before they could even arise, or violators would be severely punished. Sufficient trespasses had already occurred and, until the day came when every problem had been solved, all should be one, like the waves of the sea each pushing the other, each supporting the next. He also announced that the sheikh would one day speak to a select few people from Zafarani. When Oweis fell silent, the night seemed to grow deeper. An unknown voice said, "Time to flee." Another voice answered, "Time to flee."

"Excerpts from a Strictly Confidential Memorandum, Submitted to the Director of the Special Security Authority"

Information began to reach us after we assigned Detective Sabet Abdel Gabbar, of the Superior Security Force, to the political prisoner Mansur Suleiman, a.k.a. Rummana, during the first three weeks of the month of March. The detective informed us that he couldn't keep up with the subject; when he arrived at the alley, more than one person cautioned him loudly that if he set one foot on Zafarani soil, he would be put under a spell. And despite the fact that Detective Sabet had a great deal of courage, he hesitated, then decided to get to the bottom of the matter in case it was a trick devised by the subject and some of the inhabitants. However, it became clear to him that strange things were indeed going on.

He went to Daturi's café (owner lives in Zafarani Alley) and decided to place the subject under surveillance from there. He didn't see the subject go out at all during the first three days. Asking about him discreetly, it turned out that he had stayed in his room all the time, leaving it only to obtain food, which was prepared for the whole alley without exception. Nobody visited him, because it was impossible to enter the alley. Detective Sabet tried to obtain additional information, but his efforts were thwarted. He noticed a young man who regularly frequented the same café; it emerged that he was a reporter for the newspaper *al-Yawm* and went to the café to keep up with what was going on in the alley. After reviewing his record, it was concluded that he was not politically active.

Before addressing the role of Mansur Suleiman, a.k.a. Rummana, we would like to call attention to what is taking place in Zafarani and which can be summed up as follows:

There is indeed a Sheikh Atiya in the alley. A search, however, revealed that the Authority has no files on him, nor is anything known about him. We have neither pictures of him nor a description. Searching through the archived records of al-Azhar University, the lists of the hafizes, the muezzin, and the students of elementary and intermediate religious schools for the last hundred years yielded nobody by that name. His name wasn't in civil records either. A source from al-Azhar told us that in the past they used a different educational system; students were not registered in classes but were free to move from one course to another. Many attended those courses without obtaining an academic degree.

Confirmation of the spell: According to reports received from various sources, many citizens have begun to refer to Zafarani and the spell. In the daily register of jokes there is more than one about Zafarani; the most recent was registered on 4/3 to the effect that a man was unable to make love to his wife, so he insolently said that he had passed through Zafarani. Another goes: a person asked the Sphinx why he had been silent for five thousand years. The Sphinx winked, saying, "You think I'm crazy? If I opened my mouth the sheikh might think I was from Zafarani and take away my sexual prowess."

The crux of the matter is that Sheikh Atiya cast this spell on the entire alley (with the exception of one individual, whose identity he had not revealed) in order to impose certain conditions that could result in his control of the alley's residents, subsequent to visiting upon them a tremendous failure in their most private affairs. The impotence caused by the spell creates concrete, incontrovertible facts. As the sheikh says, man's memory is poor and people easily forget the most serious of matters. Human beings learn nothing from their experiences and indeed miss self-evident truths; they are dominated by conditions fixed in place by forces that must be defeated, as the sheikh himself puts it, so that the world can be changed and humanity returned to its pure, unsullied elements. It is for this reason that the spell cast on Zafarani was only the first of many steps. Those affected by the spell would be awakened, after the initial shock wore off, and would then be forced to acquiesce to the sheikh's demands. It was said that he promised everyone good things. He declared he would not make promises that could only be realized in future generations or coming eras. All those alive in our world would witness the fulfillment of his prophecy; each human being would experience a time when he or she could breathe easily, when grudges would disappear.

Among the thoughts reported to us are the following:

- True equality among human beings. About that, the sheikh notes that it is common to say there is one human race, yet how can the poor, the sick, the disabled, and those with hopes that will not be realized be placed in one group with the rich and the overfed? He calls for correction of the human condition.

188

- Ending all disagreements and disputes among human beings. In this connection are cited many examples—attributed to the sheikh—of the infighting of the followers of the same ideology or sect.
- Elimination of all hatred and malice.
- Eradication of the causes of pain.

There are other thoughts about which we have not received sufficient detail, but it is no secret what these thoughts, and the measures taken in the alley, imply: infringement on the authority of the State, threat to the values of society, violation of the freedom of others, and undermining of existing foundations and structures. It should be noted that the spell has almost completely isolated the alley from the rest of the country—a fact that facilitates the committing of acts within that parameter. Here we can refer to the former political prisoner Mansur Suleiman, a.k.a. Rummana, whose influence on many of the ideas advocated by the sheikh is unmistakable. His presence in the alley for several consecutive days is a clear indication of his role. And since we are responsible for combating subversive communist ideas, we call attention to what the said Mansur might do in these new and recent circumstances, for example, acquiring a mimeograph machine to print leaflets or an illegal radio transmitter, or sharing documents with the international communist apparatus. We, for our part, will take all possible measures to counter his subversive activity, and we hope the various departments of the State will collaborate with us in these measures.

Special File Detailing the Affairs of Hasan Anwar

Excerpts from the Newspaper that Hasan Anwar Issues
before Going to Bed Every Night:

Four things you should never trust: money, no matter how plentiful; rulers, no matter how close to you; women, no matter how long you have lived with them; and Time, no matter how good it has been to you.

These lines occur repeatedly and serve as a heading for the paper. They are followed by the headlines, which he always displays in bright red letters. The following excerpts have been taken from various issues over several days.

Headlines:

- SEARCH FOR SAMIR FAILS: SAMIR LOST
- SEARCH OPERATIONS SUSPENDED
- ENEMIES GATHER
- ENEMY FORCES UNITE UNDER SINGLE LEADERSHIP
- MY VENGEANCE HORRIFIC, HASAN ANWAR
- CHALLENGE ACCEPTED, HASAN ANWAR REVEALS

- FIGHTING IMMINENT
- SHEIKH ATIYA LEADS OFFENSIVE
- SPORADIC BATTLES AMONG INHABITANTS

Excerpts from the Editorials

It has become obvious that Samir has joined his father's enemies. It is not yet definite which side he has chosen, though. Has he chosen to join Sayyid Bey Abul Mu'ati or the forces of Abdel Azim al-Gawahiri? Or has he joined the general command where Sheikh Atiya presides? The Chief is facing a rare and tragic situation: the son is divulging his father's secrets to the enemy; he may even lead the main offensive. It is usually quite horrible when each is ignorant of the other's identity; for instance the Chief, in his early youth, meets a woman who begets him a son, who in turn grows up away from his father; circumstances make the son an enemy commander; father and son find themselves fighting each other without knowing their true identities. How unspeakably awful it is then, in the present situation, when each knows the other! What one would like to affirm here is that the Chief will never retreat; he has suffered a great deal and his misery has been boundless, but he will rise above his wounds. The moment, years awaited, has come.

Among the conclusions to be drawn from this analysis is that Sayyid Abul Mu'ati has, over the years, conducted a campaign of cold war, that he has used the method of indirect intermittent hits, aimed at curtailing the Chief's ability to dream and hope. In his offensive he has combined underhand and direct tactics. Among the former are the circumstances surrounding the Chief's family, his inability to obtain a university degree, and his dreams for the world. Regarding the latter, there are many. The Chief has put up with a great deal, including the irritations caused by his colleagues of the same intermediate level of education, the likes of Gawahiri, who has been able, by crooked means, to obtain a glass-topped desk, then his own office, then a telephone and a messenger to stand at his door. When the Chief requested that a telephone be installed in his home, it took forever; the excuse given was a shortage of available lines. But of course Sayyid Abul Mu'ati was behind it all. The Chief had ignored the small skirmishes in order to direct his energies to the more comprehensive battle: to make of Hassan a doctor and of Samir an engineer.

The sheikh has combined all the plots that were engineered at different times and has thus dealt a skillful blow. Here we must record the Chief's testimony as to the force of the blow and the skill involved in dealing it. Samir's running away from home has come as the result of superb military action. Here we also have to point to the courage of the Chief and his ability to face even the most painful facts objectively. He respects the traditions of war—the same traditions which his enemies have contravened. But no matter how cruel and ruthless the adversary, the Chief's forces are getting stronger and his military resources are boundless. He has a famous maxim: so long as the commander has decided to fight, he has absolutely no excuse if he doesn't fight well. He will find that there is no shortage of battles to fall back on, hence he must fight and win.

Excerpts of Interviews with Hasan Anwar, the Last One
Conducted Hours before the Fare-up of Battles:
"War is ugly and hateful and so long as it exists it proves that humanity is not yet human. It is, however, a necessity when there is no other way to fend off evils and crimes or when war threatens."

"All my life I have hoped to live among allies who would support me and whom I would support in turn. I am now discovering, however, that my whole life, since birth, has been a series of battles. The smallest private situations are battles that have all the elements of the biggest military conflicts. Buying something is a little battle; the seller tries to make more money while you try to pay less. Isn't this a battle between two wills? Your attempt to get to know a certain woman is a battle in which you try to win her heart. At the beginning of the relationship and as it goes on we find each of the two parties trying to dominate the other. A politician spends his whole life chasing strange illusions, which he sometimes sums up as gaining a position. People's lives are made up of hundreds of tiny battles—tiny when compared to the totality of the general objective. The objective remains relative."

"I do not mean to do away with conflict. I just want to prove that life is a series of battles, the most dangerous of which is the fight against death. True, death vanquishes man, the individual; but humanity vanquishes death. As soon as I finish my wars, I am going to wage a merciless fight against death."

"I will take up arms against enemies that no one has fought before. I will attack evil. I will crush disease. Wickedness will become my prisoner and I will never release it. I will assassinate poverty wherever it exists. These are the objectives of my wars."

"On the contrary, I will answer it: my wounds are deep, and deep wounds always bleed quietly."

News Item

All the Chief's fighting gear has been prepared. Radish-head, the president of a friendly nation, has supplied him with a full military uniform, some gear, and food supplies. A uniform for the parades planned for

193

the night of final victory is under preparation. A field library has been set up; it includes biographies, epics, and plans. A collection of precisely drawn, unique maps of the battlefield extending from Zafarani to include many outposts and many years has been prepared, as have binoculars which reveal that which is concealed.

Before the Battles

He stood long in front of the mirror; he had to inspire awe and respect among his troops. His close aides and the troops in the front trenches would comment on his appearance, his facial expressions, and the way he thought during the moments preceding a decision. General appearance is very important, especially since his troops include the best warriors. Now he is going to devote all his time to waging decisive battles. He has cut off all the relationships he had been strengthening for many years. He has stopped going to the Department; the time of quaking before Sayyid Bey and kissing his boots was gone for good.

Now he is pacing back and forth in his apartment, his wife sitting at the end of the hall not uttering a word. Last night he had asked her to make a definite choice between two options. One was to stay with him as his life's companion and support him in times of hardship, giving him comfort especially when he sought her out in the quiet of the night. These hours usually revealed the commander's human weaknesses and she would have to keep secret everything he said or did. The second option was for her to decide that she was not qualified for such a role, in which case she should leave him for her parents' house and join her traitor son. He was strong and could face solitude. However, deep down, he hoped that she would not leave; he undoubtedly needed her. She bowed her head and cried bitterly. She said that she would never desert him; they had shared this beautiful lifetime together. How could she desert him in a time of hardship?

He was moved; he almost cried, but he saved his tears for more painful situations. The strongest commanders did not cry when their armies were destroyed, but wept like children when faced with a simple human situation. He saw in her a steadfast, loyal woman. He approached her, pulled himself together, puffed out his chest, and raised his hand in a salute. He would note in his diary that he gave his wife a military salute when she decided to stay with him. One must write down these little things that collectively constitute one's private life. One day these things would provide fertile material from which artists would draw inspiration for their work and would also shed light on his character when the scholars and the historians dealt with it. His wife said that their life had been quiet, that what was happening now was like a bad dream. Time had stabbed them everywhere, everywhere. He patted her on the shoulder saying she would forget everything when they tasted the sweetness of victory. He appreciated her stand, and that was why he promised to give her a woman's medal as soon as the war was over and to make her stand next to him on the dais at the victory parade.

Hassan did not utter a word. When Hasan Anwar saw his son, he became all tenderness. But he didn't trust even those closest to him, not even his own ideas; he reviewed an idea several times before putting it to the test. Even his own wife he didn't fully trust. Who could tell? Maybe she was secretly aiming a blow against him. He remembered now: ". . . and women, no matter how long you have lived with them." To avoid a repetition of what Samir had done, Hasan Anwar assigned to his elder son a direct responsibility that made him accountable to his father at all times. He would notify his son of his post before the fighting erupted. He wrote a few lines—the first of the daily orders that he would address to his lieutenants and their units. A few moments later he stood up, his shoes shining, with his wide leather belt and medals covering his chest. He had given those medals a lot of thought:

Should he wear them all, as many commanders did, or should he declare that they be removed? He opted for wearing them all; seeing them would give his men confidence. Slowly he crossed the hall, went out on the balcony with a short stick under his arm and a pair of field binoculars hanging from his neck. The subtlest thoughts that occurred to people like him in similar situations remained unknown.

A heavy silence had enveloped Zafarani; the windows were closed; the floor tiles were shining under the rays of the sun; distant music was heard. Images began to pour in on him. Bagpipe music reminding him of distant feast days in a faraway childhood that now seemed like a safe, blessed castle, with secure doors on which hung spells that were far stronger and far more potent—spells that kept worries at bay and banished fear and poverty. Unfortunately their potency wore off with the years. The bagpipe music grew louder, shriller. The players now stood opposite the balcony, followed by the standard bearers, displaying the colors of armies, divisions, and battalions, a forest of multi-colored flags now fluttering before him. It was time for the bloody struggle to hoist these flags atop the enemy castles—the flags of the commanders he recalled from the recesses of the years to lead the armies on various fronts: Hannibal, Genghis Khan, Julius Caesar, Lucullus, Crassus, Von Moltke, Sidi Ahmad al-Badawi, the Duke of Wellington, Khalid ibn al-Walid, Napoleon, Zhukov, Bismarck, Frederick the Great, Rommel, Goering, Antara ibn Shaddad, Sayf ibn Dhi Yazan, and Abu Zayd al-Hilali, all masters, geniuses in the art of war. Some had fought until they finished each other off. Here, now, he was uniting them in one outfit. He could see their faces, knew which qualities distinguished each of them and in what capacity he would make best use of their unique talents. He was now raising his hand in salute as they paraded before him. Zafarani was empty for some moments as a faint, thin music rose, heralding huge numbers of oppressed infantrymen from all eras, bearing all kinds of arms, including cudgels and shields, swords and spears, even rockets and armored troop carriers. Arduous days were awaiting him, and awkward moments too. He saw days in which people were celebrating victory; he saw that he would enter cities he had not yet seen and look at blue seas that spelled serenity.

Order No. 1

Hassan Hasan Anwar shall be appointed General Chief of Staff; he shall assume his duties as soon as the battle erupts.

Order No. 2A

Joint command shall be formed to coordinate the efforts of the forces in the following manner:

Field Marshal Rommel, Commander of the African Brigade in the old times: now Commander of Desert Forces; Attila, Leader of the Huns in the old days: now Commander of the Vengeance Corps, to be given the title of Field Marshal; General Himmler, Chief of the Gestapo in the old days: currently Director of Intelligence.

First Clash

As circumstances would have it, the fighting began earlier than he had estimated. Hassan, the Chief of Staff, came to headquarters and handed the Chief a strongly worded letter signed by Sayyid Abul Mu'ati. The letter was phrased in an obscene way; it ignored the Chief's titles and ranks, addressing him by name only, putting only the honorific 'Mr.' before his name. He described him, mockingly, as an "employee, fourth class." He threatened to refer his case to Legal Affairs because of what he described as "unauthorized absence." Hasan Anwar jumped to his feet. How could Hassan accept such an ultimatum? Hassan was hesitant; he trembled, saying, "Dad." The Chief said he wanted to see his son in the best shape: from now on he would find himself supervising the most efficient warriors; he would deal with Napoleon, von Moltke, and Rommel; he would draw up plans for them. He was responsible for running the war. The Chief asked him to go to headquarters, not to stare at him like that, and to instruct Goering to mount concentrated saturation bombing raids. He turned toward the balcony; his wife did not dare follow him. He thought of assigning some tasks to her, for example, making her Head Supervisor of the Committee for Dressing Deep Wounds, or Head of Profound Grief Therapy. She shouldn't spend the whole time crying over her son, the traitor. He would settle the matter for good by a resolution to be issued today. For the time being, he had to fly over the theater of operations: there was thick fog covering the northern regions of Zafarani. The binoculars showed him slow movements, shifting feet, wheels, flags, citizens in military uniforms carrying bags and files, buttoning their jackets, some sipping coffee and discarding cigarette butts. He noted smiles and bows, shiny shoes and people scribbling on paper, messengers bowing and elevators opening quickly, brooms sweeping rugs, pictures in gilded frames, telephone switchboards, telephones ringing, black and red telephones, telephones with dials, extension telephones, mouths saying hello, and wires quivering. He turned the binoculars around and focused; Sayyid Bey was hiding in a deep trench of files. He paused on the incidents of a distant life: hopes of going to college, the means to a respectable job, to being called "Hasan Bey"—then the alternative hopes: the years of a life filled with the hope of getting a monthly one-and-a-half-pound raise. Sayyid Abul Mu'ati was leading the front, assaulting his dreams, assisted by Abdel Azim al-Gawahiri, another traitor.

Sheikh Atiya was leading the main front for the destruction of life and everything in it. The dust was heavy; he turned aside. Each gesture of his hand or nod of his head was immediately translated into a significant act. That slow turning around meant his wish to summon the Director of Intelligence. General Himmler came carrying a file containing the latest reports on the situation of the enemy. He noticed on his face a glimmer of gratitude: the Chief had assigned him to direct Intelligence after the years of cruel unemployment he had suffered since Hitler disappeared. An order from the Chief also permitted him to look for Hitler. As soon as Hitler was found, the Chief would appoint him Supreme Advisor for Armed Forces Affairs and he would appoint Marshal Zhukov co-commander, thus bringing together divergent elements of history. He asked General Himmler to brief him on the position of Sayyid Abul Mu'ati's forces. The general opened his confidential file. The Chief leaned with his hands on the edge of the table.

"Since Sayyid Abul Mu'ati sent his recent ultimatum, our agents have reported that his armies have begun to move. The main blow is expected to come from Personnel, with support from Legal Affairs and Investigations."

"And the Sheikh Atiya front?"

"For three days, calm prevailed. Suddenly his armies issued a succinct proclamation calling for an end to all ongoing quarrels and immediate surrender. He ordered that a number of inhabitants go to his head-quarters to receive the teachings, and indeed Sergeant Major Sallam went over and held a seven-hour meeting with him. Our intelligence will try to discover what was discussed after you authorize necessary expenses for updating modern weaponry. Following the bilateral meeting, Oweis, the military spokesman and Sheikh Atiya's press secretary, declared that Atif, Radish-head, Qurqur, and Daturi were to go to the sergeant major's house to hold the first exploratory session. That session is scheduled for one o'clock tomorrow afternoon following the distribution of lunch."

"How about our forces now?"

"Field Marshal Rommel is making a wide circle around the wickedness of Abdel Azim al-Gawahiri; he is being aided by Field Marshal Genghis Khan. As for Sayyid Abul Mu'ati's attack, it has done nothing except cause fear—factored in the loss column."

"I demand a report every hour."

General Himmler gave a military salute. A few moments later the Chief shouted, calling the Chief of Staff. His son came, impassive. The Chief gave him a small piece of paper containing a few lines that explicitly ordered an immediate offensive against Sayyid Abul Mu'ati's front, and a freezing of the situation on the Sheikh Atiya front.

The Teachings

An attempt to put together some material for an investigative news report:

At 11:00 a.m. Qurqur the musician went out, heading for Daturi's café to meet Hamdi the reporter. It had come to Qurqur's attention that among the patrons of the café was a young reporter who had been trying for two days to meet one of the men of the alley, without success. Qurqur introduced himself, saying he was a musician, a qanun player, and a Zafaranite. Hamdi the reporter looked interested and clapped his hands, but Qurqur restrained him, saying he was a guest. Hamdi offered him a cigarette; Qurqur said he didn't smoke. Hamdi knit his brows, saying the name was not unfamiliar and trying to remember. Qurqur fished a piece of paper out of a black leather briefcase. The paper was white with a clipping from an old art magazine in the middle. It was a news item published about him in 1952: "Among those taking part in providing entertainment for the party is Sayyid Qurqur, the most famous qanun player in the dancers' circles." He offered Hamdi an issue of *al-Ithnayn* magazine that had yellowed with age and turned the pages quickly, stopping at the "Quick News" column, pointing with his finger to a few lines in the middle of the first column, the full text of the news item. Hamdi nodded his head. Qurqur took out an old photograph that he held carefully by the tips of his fingers: it was of Abdel Halim Hafiz in the early days of his career. Around him were several men; in the second row was a smiling face, that of Qurqur in person. Hamdi said that many genuine talents did not have much luck and never entered the limelight.

It seemed like an encouraging beginning to Qurqur. He had long dreamed of meeting a journalist who would listen to him play and recognize his genuine talent. He had never stopped hoping throughout all the many years that he had spent performing at weddings, playing for dancers in the alleys, on the roofs of apartment buildings, and in remote villages. At long last the opportunity was here: he was meeting, face to face, with a young reporter. He had been afraid of going to newspaper offices: Who would know him there? And who would stand up for him? He remained lost among the members of the orchestra, no difference between him and the drummer, the flute, or the tambourine players. It was often the case that even the tabla player stole the show because of his movements and histrionics while accompanying the dancer. Qurqur had never played a solo, and never known a journalist or anyone to introduce him to one. Even if such an introduction were to be made, did he have the wherewithal? He had heard that all kinds of exorbitant expenses and banquets were required to entertain journalists.

As time went on his conviction that the established stars were conspiring against him grew. He just needed one chance and he would soon be out there, instead of them, accompanying the most famous of songstresses. He was so much more deserving of fame than they were. Who else had made such sacrifices for the sake of art? He had never married and had had no children. If he were to fall sick now he would starve to death. He traveled third class by train in pursuit of weddings all over the country and with his colleagues took all kinds of transportation in order to arrive at some village where they got no appreciation or respect. The big stars, on the other hand, traveled throughout the Arab countries, were summoned by kings and taken by airplanes to royal palaces. A few of them maligned him quite openly, but all of them obstructed his progress with their connections in the press and the broadcasting service.

And now here was his chance! This made up for what had happened to Zafarani, as far as he was concerned. He said that he had wasted his life for the sake of art, that he had sacrificed everything to provide enjoyment for people, but they had denied him his chance. Hamdi interrupted him, saying it was time to separate the genuine from the fake, that he knew exactly what was taking place in artistic life and the values prevailing there. He wondered why a talented musician like Qurqur did not occupy his rightful place. Qurqur said that he had a unique style of playing and that was why they had fought him, to prevent him from getting ahead. Qurqur said he had composed some pieces in which the qanun played a major role, and Hamdi said he would love to hear them. Qurqur invited him to his apartment.

Hamdi the reporter, visibly taken aback by the invitation, fell suddenly silent, then asked whether the rumors about the alley were true. He told Qurqur he would gladly go, because it was not every day that one discovered a great artist, but it was rumored that any man whose feet touched Zafarani was changed into a woman. He apologized for those last words, but the whole city was talking about it, and the authorities were not allowing the news to be made public for reasons of their own. Qurqur began to experience a sinking feeling. Would the reporter give up on him because of what was happening in Zafarani?

Suddenly Hamdi the reporter asked, "Had Qurqur said he had never married?" Qurqur's enthusiasm quickly returned and a gleam came back to his tired eyes. He said his life was replete with scores of incidents that could provide material for an entire book, never mind a report. Indeed he had never married. Hamdi asked abruptly, "Why?" His sudden interest in whether the man had married or not was the result of various factors. First, he didn't want to appear interested only in what was happening in the alley, nor did he want to lose the one man who had agreed to talk to him after he had been rejected by the other inhabitants. Second, he had been visited by an apparition of his own wife. He wished he could just get up and go; the desire to sit down, however, returned as soon as he began to get up. He had a personal motive in coming to gather material about the affairs of Zafarani. When that journalism student intern at the paper had told the editor in chief what was happening, the editor in chief had held a meeting with the staff of the features department and asked them to consider the matter strictly confidential so that rival newspapers would not get wind of it. He said it was necessary to use this strange incident to raise circulation. It was possible that the censor would not permit publication because of the subject's sensitive nature, but it was nonetheless necessary to get the features ready for publication. The editor in chief assigned two reporters, Abbas and Khalid, to go to the alley that had no men, but they came back the same evening saying things were not as the editor had portrayed them. The Zafarani phenomenon was quite well known: any man stepping into the alley became impotent; it all had to do with some mysterious working of magic. The editor offered them a generous bonus, but they both turned it down.

The next morning Hamdi had learned what had been happening and said he was willing to go to the old neighborhood. It was agreed that he would work full-time on the assignment, that no deadline be set, but that he would submit the feature as soon as it was decided to go ahead with publication of the story. The editor in chief pledged all kinds of treatment in case any damage actually occurred. Hamdi didn't know why he had volunteered for this experiment; his colleagues would make fun of him. They would say he had nothing to lose. Six months earlier he had asked some friends to witness his divorce papers. Some of them had been surprised. He had been married only four months. Why divorce now? It was incredible; he had to give his marriage more than one chance to make sure the relationship could not work. He said, as the hole in his heart grew bigger and bigger, that he and his wife had already agreed to divorce. His colleagues said that their love throughout college had been an ever-burning fire, that they had been held up as a model. That kind of response pained him. He remembered a whole life that had been born the moment he had met his wife: the tentative, thoughtful beginnings, then the fast, hot acceleration tearing down all obstacles; her father's threat to cut her off, the long walks, the saving of a few piasters to pay for two glasses of lemonade, the saving of some pounds to look for a small apartment, joining savings groups, shopping for things for their apartment; the joy in her eyes as she came back from the market having bought something for the house.

When the cabinet maker finished making the armoire she had pointed joyfully to the shelves inside, "This is where your shirts will be." When they went out into the city, she had leaned her head against his arm as they walked to a treelined street near the Nile; there she had stood on the tips of her toes and kissed him. She said she was defying the city that was watching them the entire time.

He remembered the way she had hugged him before he went to work, putting her arms around his body; the sleepiness in her eyes and how they opened wide in the dimly lit room; the peace that followed satiation, her body seeping through his. How could love last seven full

205

years, end in marriage, and that marriage end after four months. Why? He couldn't answer that. At home he had tried to uncover the reason. She said that their life couldn't go on because she wanted to travel, see the world, go about taking part in changing the world. She wasn't going to turn into a food preparer and a babysitter waiting for him to come home every night. She had discovered this after having been married a month. She had resisted the idea of separation for a long time, but she came to realize that if they didn't part, she would turn his days into a living hell. If he didn't agree, she would try to travel anyway; she was going to tour the world.

Hamdi knew the strength of her will; he didn't show his reaction. He was used to her sudden decisions and the way she later changed her mind. He talked with her, discussed the whole thing in full, but she just seemed terribly determined. She said she cared for him a lot, respected him, and believed that he would find plenty of other women; the world was a big and crowded place. Just as he had met her, he would meet other women. He did not express his anger, but waited for the sudden idea to spend itself. He remembered that he had often loved these sudden projects of hers, her sudden enthusiasm for things. She'd be so enthusiastic about something that she seemed ready to sacrifice her life for it, then a short time later she'd discover that she had made a mistake or rushed things, or she simply changed her mind. Late in the afternoon one autumn day he felt as if a hand had grabbed his spine and yanked him back. He looked at her and it was as if he was seeing her for the first time; as if he had not lived with her, slept with her; as if they hadn't shopped together to furnish their small apartment, hadn't pictured their future baby together. He turned his eyes away and looked at the curtain. Later he wondered: Had Shuhrat ever walked around the house in her nightgown while he was there? He almost heard the threads of their relationship snapping.

In the yellow, tired daylight, he had realized that what had existed between them was over; resistance was impossible, arguing useless. He lived through those moments when the lover didn't exchange loving glances with the beloved, when neither cared for the feelings of the other. Something inside him was being snatched and thrown away. He thought sadly: How people change! Shuhrat was no longer his, she was no longer part of his world. That very night he crossed the hall and knocked at the door of the room where she had taken refuge from him. She said, "Coming," and came out to him. He almost broke down when he saw that presence of hers which he loved so much, the sweet wonder in her eyes. He said he was going to give her what she wanted. She said, "Thank you." He returned to his room, broken, a ruin.

On the following day his friends asked him: Why? He couldn't answer. He went to see some people from his village and they said that divorce was the most hateful thing to God, that the very heavens shook when it happened, and they asked him: Why? As he was walking downtown he remembered a store owned by one of his classmates from secondary school. They reminisced about the old days. His friend said that he followed what Hamdi wrote, was proud of it, and made a point of reading it. The old schoolmate listened to his story in surprise and asked if divorce was necessary. Hamdi said both parties had agreed and was careful not to let his tears flow. The old schoolmate said he and his brother would act as witnesses.

They made an appointment. They took a four-passenger cab. Hamdi and Shuhrat sat in the back seat while the two witnesses sat in front. From the window he saw stores, traffic cops, motorcyclists speeding past the taxi, vendors of jasmine necklaces; one of them looked in and waved a necklace. Hamdi didn't know what to do and Shuhrat turned her face away. When the taxi arrived at the marriage registrar's office, the schoolmate insisted on paying the fare. They sat down on a long wooden bench facing three men wearing peasant attire, their small hats made of felt and wrapped in brown scarves. There was a poster with the words, "My faith in God protects me," cleverly written. There was silence for a few moments. Shuhrat focused her eyes on the poster, and to his surprise Hamdi found himself smiling and then he laughed and she laughed. He tried to hold on to that tone of her voice so he could recall it from time to time, and also her laugh. She smiled with her eyes, lips, nose, and mouth; the laugh seemed as if it would never end, an everlasting laugh. The two witnesses looked on, surprised.

After the proceedings ended, Hamdi went over to the jar of cool water, removed the glass that served as its cover, and drank it to the last drop, then sat down. He saw that the glass was not put back right; he rose again, put it back in its place. Shuhrat said he still drank too much water. Her words brought back to him her interest in small things. Signing the divorce papers hadn't shaken him, but her sudden interest in him almost knocked him down with an unstoppable flood of sadness. She said she was planning to stay with him her last few days in Egypt, until her travel preparations were finished, but if her presence bothered him she could go to her friend Salma's house instead. He said it would be no bother, but if it were, he could leave the house himself.

He was surprised at her talk of leaving. He didn't ask her for the details; she was no longer part of him. He wondered when the idea of traveling had first taken hold in her mind. Where was that moment in relation to her past days? He remembered a conversation they had had a few days earlier, after supper. He said he didn't like chewing gum. She said she disliked people who made a noise eating watermelon. In the morning they left together; as she crossed the street she held his hand. He thought: She is killing me softly. When the metro started moving he noted its number: 819; it carried a whole cross-section of his life and neither the conductor nor the passengers knew a thing about it. The most painful thing he experienced during the following few days was seeing her preparing her papers: her passport, her leave of absence, and other papers he knew nothing about.

When he saw the yellow immunization card from which a long airline ticket stuck out, gloom took hold of him. She had separated herself from his life like the final flight of a rocket that had lost its way without finding its orbit. He looked at her as if he were a dead man who had somehow remained conscious and watched his own burial. Whenever he heard her movements at night he felt as though he were in a city where he had lived a long time and was suddenly being forced to leave. He paced back and forth in his room, unable to sit or lie down or stand or go out. He couldn't bear to go to work at the newspaper. At midnight he knocked at her door; she wasn't yet asleep. "Come in." He pushed the door a little. The night and the winter seemed as cheerless as if together they belonged to the early days of the creation of the world, when no man, animal, or ant moved. His silence lasted a long time and she asked him in fear, "What do you want?" He begged her not to leave him. The silence was as heavy as being on a mountain peak or being lost and alone on the high seas or after a forced landing in an unknown desert. She didn't answer; not a word. He went back to his room like an orphan.

The first night he spent alone he talked to himself in a loud voice. Defeat. He had to hold on until he could gather the fragments of his life once again. Was that why he had accepted this difficult assignment with the siege tight, the chains in place, and the wounds raw? Had he been wrong when he loved her sudden enthusiasm, her insistence on carrying out whatever came into her head, that insistence which laid bare, destroyed, and exterminated?

He returned from that distant voyage and noticed Qurqur, who was still continuing to talk. Perhaps he had decided to keep going so as not to embarrass the reporter. Qurqur was speaking about the woman he loved, how he played for her at all the weddings where she sang, the long years during which she had hurt him, paying no attention to his feelings, whenever she deliberately talked about her lovers to his face. She would sit late at night, smoking the hookah, watching the expressions on his face as he opened the door of the room. Qurqur said she was irreplaceable, one of a kind.

Hamdi thought to himself sadly: Every man thinks the woman he loves cannot be replaced. Qurqur said she was a real artist, had had many chances to be famous, but that she lived for the present moment alone, never wore herself out seeking anybody, never thought of tomorrow. Every day it seemed she was living her last day. When she laughed, she laughed hard, and when she cried it was as if it was the last thing she would ever do, as if she were crying in advance for several years to come. She always said she would never fall in love; if she did, that would be the end of her. She would die if her lover deserted her. When he was away from her he would go to his colleagues and begin to talk. Any subject he ever touched on would eventually lead back to her. He would talk about her or perhaps sing some of the songs he had composed for her and tell them anything that might have to do with her, and little by little he would talk about his feelings for her.

He remembered a question that had been asked of him several times, "Does Sukkar love you?" He would fall silent. Me'allim Subhi, the famous oud player, had once told him such love was a drain on his art, and Qurqur had replied that most artists lived through unsuccessful love affairs. Me'allim Subhi countered, "Not always. Look at Abdel Wahhab and how women chase him!" Now he was looking at Hamdi and telling him that a woman usually liked a man who chased her; that if he ever learned that some woman loved him but he didn't reciprocate her feelings, he'd be unable to get close to her because women were different. A woman liked to keep a pool of admirers while offering her real affections to someone completely different.

Hamdi smiled absently and wondered: Had he appeared weak? On the contrary, their feelings were always glowing, her tenderness, her interest in him. He had told her that his emotions expressed themselves silently, that she shouldn't worry if he didn't use words of love frequently. She hastened to hug him, saying she wanted to feel his closeness to her. When had they exchanged these words? A month before she left? Twenty days before the divorce?

Hamdi was asking now, "Could a one-sided feeling live on for many years?" Qurqur nodded. Because Sukkar caused him so much pain, she had become part of his life; a whole life unfolded. He uncovered images that were about to be forgotten and smells that he could no longer remember and a mysterious yearning he could not define. After years of being in Sukkar's company he began to see in her something that was more than just a woman. Everything that had to do with her, even the aggravation she caused him, he had grown accustomed to. He liked her cruelty to him and her rejection of his overtures of friendship. Didn't her cruelty arise from her knowledge of his feelings? He never had a single thought that wasn't tinged with shades of Sukkar. How should he answer this reporter who seemed amazed that his love had lasted so long?

Qurqur said he was not going to give a direct answer to the question, but asked Hamdi Bey to ask him about Sukkar: Where was she now? Hamdi had not expected to be answered with a question. He remembered a few lines in a letter from Bakr, a friend who was now living in Europe. He had not complained to any of his friends nearby; whenever he felt his heart was about to break because of a certain memory or thought, he would write a letter to Bakr. His friend had said, "Since she is the one who left you, don't be sad. Try to forget her. Time is a great healer; it is also free. Help it by having affairs with many women. You're still a young man. . . ." Did Time undo everything? Even if the wounds healed, wouldn't they burst at some point and sweep away everything, break one's spirit? Was it easy to forget? A whole lifetime, seven years and several months. Didn't forgetting require double that time?

Qurqur was saying, "Ask me." Hamdi smiled, "Where is Sukkar now?" Qurqur replied that she turned sixty-two weeks ago, that she wasn't aware of anybody, and that when she saw him she didn't recognize him, but called him "God's guest." He didn't know what that name meant to her. She no longer sang, and whenever she grew loud, the nurses would punish her either by beating her or by giving her tranquillizing shots. They called her "the forgotten one"; nobody visited her except Qurqur. The Sukkar of the old days was gone, but he went to visit her as if he were migrating to the cherished years of his life.

The sad smile returned to Hamdi's face. How would he meet her in twenty years? Would he recognize her easily if they met by accident? He was seeing her now in his mind's eye, wearing the same clothes she had been wearing when she left: a pullover and slacks, even though it was now hot and she was probably wearing a summer dress.

Qurqur said that several questions occurred to him whenever he visited Sukkar: If she had lived with him, would she have become as ugly as she was now? What about her children? How would they have grown up? What would they have become? Each time he left the hospital he resisted the urge to cry. Hamdi nodded. He understood what Qurqur wanted to say. But weren't there other reasons for his not marrying? Qurqur slowed down somewhat: the arts had occupied him to a great extent; the constant travel, the concerts. His mother, who had died three years ago—God's mercy be upon her—had never let him suffer the usual hardships of bachelorhood. He had no knowledge of buying or selling or laundry or cooking. After she passed away he had been confused; she had always taken care of him as if he were a child and had kept encouraging him with her good words and prayers. Until she died, she had dreamed that one day she might see him play for Umm Kulthum. The taste of his days was different now that she was gone. He could no longer eat at home or sleep restfully.

Qurqur stopped suddenly and asked, "Are you thinking of getting married, sir?" Hamdi was silent for a moment. Daturi fixed his eyes on him. Lifting his head, Hamdi said, "I was married." Qurqur had not expected this answer and was at a loss how to resume the conversation. Some children began shouting; they pointed at Qurqur, Daturi, and Hamdi. "Zafarani, Oh woe is me, look what happened to me." Hamdi was lost in thought; beads of sweat were forming on Qurqur's forehead.

Daturi was being pricked from the inside out by tiny needles. The grocers were refusing to sell anything to anyone from Zafarani. Had it not been for the sheikh's instructions, the residents of the ally would have suffered a great deal more. The task of purchasing was assigned to one resourceful person who could obtain staple items from the market or from the government co-ops. For a week now Daturi had been thinking of closing down the café; even the Coca-Cola and soda distributor would not give him his consignment. He resisted the idea; staying home meant death. All his life he had walked that short distance between the house and the café, sat there near the street, which was freshly sprinkled with water, smoking his hookah, looking at the passersby and the customers who were not regulars, watching the changing light on the buildings and the eternal slow-creeping shadow.

In the evening he was surrounded by the backgammon players' laughter and the customers' jokes. He would keep himself busy by observing the faces and trying to guess what they were hiding. Where had the good times gone, when the afternoon customers used to come to the café after lunch? He remembered Ustaz Mansur Ba'issa and Ustaz Zanhuri the Algerian coming after school was out, wearing pure white galabiyas; they would nod to him and he would return their greeting and give the waiter a look. In a few moments two hookahs would be placed in front of them and they would puff calmly away. Where had that serene time gone, whose light was brighter and more translucent? If Ustaz Mansur passed by now he looked lost, wearing a short jacket and socks with holes in them. He no longer wore a white galabiya, and the skin of his neck was now thin and wrinkled. As for Ustaz Zanhuri, he had left for Algeria, his homeland. Real estate agents would come to Daturi with their clients, and sometimes he would break his silence and ask the client about his job, his name and family. Then he would take out a blue notebook whose leaves were held together by a thin rubber band. He would remove the rubber band and with indelible pencil take down the information. He would ask the client to come back again in six months and would turn down any money he was offered, saying he wouldn't charge a penny in key money.

Many of the links around his life were now broken. He wouldn't close the café even if he himself were the only patron, even if Muhammad the waiter left him to follow Zuqla and he was forced to fix the hookah himself. He faced a lot of pressure from his neighbors, but he said he couldn't bar any customer, that he wasn't going to close down the café unless Sheikh Atiya ordered him to. Wasn't it enough that he closed the café early in the evening so that he wouldn't miss supper and bed-time? The smokes had also changed. Where was the genuine tobacco and its endless varieties —Persian, Azmir, Aden, Turkish, Indian . . . ? Now there was nothing but garbage. In the good old days an ounce of tobacco was never more than three piasters; now it was closer to a pound. He remembered his years as a waiter in the big Ukasha café. For years he had dreamed of owning a café, but just when his dream had come true, the customers had changed and the whole thing turned insipid.

Oh, how he took care of his café: new paint every year, oil paintings that he bought from that art student hanging on the walls. A café was a place for sharing worries and longings. He kept looking over at that young effendi sitting with Qurqur. Daturi felt he already knew him. Such familiarity with one customer was not an easy thing for a café owner to come by; it needed time. He knew the regulars and gave them special attention, little things that pleased them, made them feel apart from ordinary customers. For instance, when the waiter saw one of them coming in he would shout, "A hookah for Usta Ahmad!" or "Where is Me'allim Farag's tea?" And when he brought coffee to one of them, he would bring with it a glass of water with a little piece of ice.

Daturi considered this effendi a regular even though he had come to the café for the first time only two days before, perhaps because of his gentleness and politeness and the good milieu he obviously came from. Daturi learned his name and his profession from Muhammad the waiter. He was not in a rush to learn the purpose of his visit; he would know everything in good time. Many strangers had come to the café in the last week; some, such as the pimps, had created problems. Others had asked in general about the alley and he never saw them again. This morning a policeman from the Special Security Authority had come to him. He said that his name was Sabet Abdel Gabbar, and that he belonged to the Department for the Suppression of Subversive Ideas. He made several inquiries about Rummana the politico, wanting to know all his movements in the alley and his role in recent events. He said the Department was taking measures that would ensure the resolution of the present problems—which Rummana the politico was probably behind. Daturi answered in a few words: he had nothing to do with Rummana. The policeman seemed to be in a hurry and left after warning Daturi not to mention anything about his visit or their conversation to anybody.

An hour later, a man wearing civilian clothes had come in. He asked Daturi, "Are you from Zafarani?" Muhammad the waiter replied that he was, and he pushed his chair back a little. He said that he belonged to the Special Security Authority, Department for the Suppression of Religious Fanaticism. He inquired about Nadir Basyuni al-Hagrasi, a.k.a. Luli, and about his friends and visitors, manifestations of his secret activities, and his relationship with the sheikh. He said Luli's role in the events of the alley was not unknown to the Department for the Suppression of Religious Fanaticism, that honest citizens had sent numerous letters alerting the authorities to his activities. Daturi said his relation with the younger generation of Zafarani was very weak. The officer left after asking him to observe the movements of Nadir al-Hagrasi, a.k.a. Luli, so that the measures being taken by the Department to combat the Zafarani calamity might bear fruit.

Daturi was now aware of Qurqur: he was saying loudly how much pleasure it gave him to introduce the famous journalist Hamdi to the me'allim. Daturi rose very slowly and Hamdi could hear the air inside his lungs; his movements required enormous effort. Qurqur said the me'allim was the most noble man in the whole neighborhood; no problem, no matter how big or small, was ever solved except through his efforts. He wanted to do good by everyone and was among those who believed in Qurqur's talent and encouraged him. Whenever anyone asked his advice about a wedding, he would counsel them to hire Qurqur. Until recently he had taken it upon himself to awaken people at dawn and lead them to al-Hussein Mosque to perform their prayers, but his health no longer enabled him to do so. Qurqur raised his hands heavenward, asking God to confer good health and vigor upon the me'allim. Daturi puffed at the hookah. Qurqur's words pleased him and he was moved. Qurqur said that Ustaz Hamdi was one of the most honest journalists, that he had a clean pen, was motivated neither by self interest nor by subservience to anyone. Hamdi said that Qurqur was exaggerating a little, that all he practiced was the pursuit of truth, and truth could be found in a genuine talent such as that of Ustaz Qurqur, or in a current event taking place somewhere in the world.

Qurqur got up, the blood rushing to his head, and pointed at Hamdi; he had never seen a more honest man. He had led a very hard life, but he never lost hope that one day an honest man would come and introduce him to the world, unveil the truth. Even if he were to die, somebody would eventually come who could appreciate his work; but he was lucky, as Ustaz Hamdi had come before his departure from this world. He sat down, excited. In his mind's eye, he saw huge crowds applauding his music and making all kinds of comments, such as: "Where was this talent buried? The world is still a good place so long as it has finally surfaced. . . ." He bowed to the audience, insisting that Ustaz Hamdi be at his side. He was struck by a gentle sadness: how he wished for Sukkar to see his success. He would visit her tomorrow in her eternal exile and give her a transistor radio; she would listen to it and weep over the years she hadn't lived with him. The art magazines would write about his great love. He looked at Hamdi with genuine love and gratitude as if what he imagined had actually taken place.

Hamdi asked how many years Daturi had lived in Zafarani. The me'allim's eyes flickered. Qurqur looked on, ready to answer, but Hamdi gestured that he wanted to hear the me'allim himself. Daturi said he couldn't remember. Hamdi said he wished he could see the house, but the circumstances of the alley prevented that. Anyway, he felt comfortable in the café; the room inside and the walls covered with huge mirrors and oil paintings gave the café its special flavor. Qurqur pointed to Ustaz Hamdi: "Look how he appreciates art!" Hamdi said that he loved the old neighborhood, then suddenly fell silent. He saw Shuhrat, her arm in his, walking to the old wall, ascending the high, broad stone steps. She had seemed anxious to know everything: Who owned the place? Who built it? Who restored it? She had cried out, "Look!" And pointed at the stones of the walls, where in the shadows some hieroglyphic writing was hidden: "They must have torn down some pharaonic monuments and used the stones to build these fortifications." They had looked from the narrow opening down onto the big square: hand carts and passersby. The guard had not followed them. They were alone. He had a desire to possess her; the tips of their fingers touched and their breaths mixed. She felt him with her adventurous lips and gently passed her hand down his back. When they came out into the light, happiness flowed through their bodies as an ancient monument flows in time.

Now, every trace of their ecstasy was gone. If he were to go up that street a few yards now, he would still be able to pinpoint the spot that had contained them. Daturi was looking at him with a heavy, slow gaze, while Qurqur was silent; perhaps both were wondering at his sudden withdrawal. Hamdi said he wished he could live in the neighborhood and hoped that his wish might be granted by the me'allim; he had heard about the me'allim's apartment building. Daturi let out a dense puff of smoke; the effendi was silent. It was a subject that never bored him, and he broke his silence and reserve. He would build the apartment building, God willing, but several obstacles had caused delays. One of these was that he had no confidence in the architects who designed modern buildings. He wanted a design reminiscent of the sweet old days: big rooms, little fountains in the halls, mashrabiya screens instead of windows. Money would be no object. The building must stay there after his death, a landmark in the neighborhood: the Daturi Apartment Building. He wanted respectable families that would keep the building and preserve it, but what had happened in Zafarani had thrown up another obstacle. He paused, waiting for some sign of enthusiasm from Hamdi after his mention of the affair in Zafarani. The effendi's lack of interest disappointed him, but at the same time increased his sense of familiarity.

Qurqur said that what had happened would not affect people's projects and, as the sheikh had said in his recent meetings with some of the inhabitants, he meant no harm, that what might appear to some as damage was simply a general pause after which humanity's affairs would be put in order for good. What had taken place was just a means to an end. Daturi said the end was not yet clear but it was enough that the sheikh had said what he said. Hamdi intervened by asking, "Couldn't the sheikh find any means to his end other than making men impotent?" Daturi looked at Qurqur, and Hamdi realized that he shouldn't have said that. He recalled Daturi's tone of voice, which seemed to be defensive of the sheikh. Was such a tone compatible with impotence?

It occurred to him to ask Qurqur about his artistic activity during the last few days, but he postponed those questions until another time. He wanted to get to know them better, so decided to return to the subject of Daturi's apartment building. Qurqur had told him that the key to talking with the me'allim was to talk about the building. Daturi had neither the money for it nor the land to build it on, but he had been dreaming of it for years. Hamdi didn't know what else to say or ask about the building. He would ask about the building permit: had he got it yet or not? But Qurqur stood up and walked toward a tall man wearing a suit. He greeted him, "Time to flee!" and shouted with great enthusiasm, "Ustaz Atif, the college graduate, one of the respectable inhabitants who appreciate art and are moved by good music!" Hamdi shook his hand: "Hamdi Rashwan, lover of the old neighborhood first, and reporter for *al-Yawm* newspaper, second."

Excerpts from a Memo Submitted to Chief of the Special Security Authority by the Department for the Suppression of Religious Fanaticism

. . . What further supported our initial evaluation were the letters we received about the activities of Nadir Basyuni al-Hagrasi, a.k.a. Luli. One of those letters was sent by the subject's own father. This, by the way, has been established only as a result of our own investigations, since the father didn't sign it, and we are trying to contact him. It must be mentioned here that he is an old plainclothesman who worked for the secret police.

There is no doubt that his old commitment to his job and his loyalty to his oath compelled him to inform on the activities of his son. All evidence points to the direct responsibility of the subject. Through the teachings that we were able to collect, we can discern some of Hagrasi's ideas and fanaticism, and their incitement against State and Society. It should also be pointed out that this information was gathered with great difficulty. The following are broad outlines of the sheikh's ideas, which he conveyed to a number of inhabitants of Zafarani, including our subject:

The sheikh asked those at the meeting to put aside their doubts: the process of change had already begun. They should rejoice because their lifetime would witness the decisive turn: he that was promised to humanity had appeared after an absence of many eras behind the thick veils of majestic might, after enjoying countless attainments of perfection, after indescribable patience toward what he had seen and what he had heard. He would uncover the sources of earthquakes and lift the chains and the yokes. He was no more than a single letter from a great book, a single drop from a sea that had no shore. All his life he had concerned himself with humanity. He had spent his life contemplating the world: what had been, what was, and what would be. He was overcome with longing to see humans cooperating. Now, however, the time of harmony was at hand. He was taking the pulse of the world and seeing the days which, with no doubt whatsoever, were to come—days in which he could hear songs and anthems of love rising whenever humans congregated: he was penetrating into a happy future with his piercing vision. It was not a guaranteed future—for man, since his creation, has been living a promise yet to be realized—but a future to be achieved.

He said that he had banned quarrels as a prelude to eradicating wars: man should be tolerant of his brother. After the ordering of human lives, enmities would disappear; love and kindness would be real. Instead of quarrels, each man would recognize his own uniqueness and that of others. Man had been created rich: why was he poor? Man had been created proud: why was he humiliated? Man had been fashioned from the clay of love: how could he hate? He had emerged from the womb fed and satisfied: how could he go hungry in the world?

The sheikh had thought a long time about how to accomplish his goal. After much erudition and superior suffering, he decided to deprive humans—for a time—of fruit. In the beginning he had thought of depriving them of bread, but that way they would have perished and crumbled away. The best option, he deemed, was to deprive them of fruit. He knew that a sterile human was like a leafless tree; such trees could be softened by the heat of fire. He had, however, damaged this ability to procreate only for a limited time; it would create a shock that would awaken the human race and would be far less harmful than the shocks of hatred and fighting. After the shock, people would obey him. If obedience did not ensue, strife and upheaval would continue; people would go on fighting one another. Humans were now using a great deal of their power to frustrate their brethren rather than working together to remove pain, visible and invisible. Enough had been wasted since the creation of the world in fighting and warfare. Immediately after the shock, all human conditions would be equalized perfectly and entirely, and would later change collectively, totally: the whole human race would be like leaves of the same tree, like equal gems in a necklace, like stars, and like gazelles in the same pasture.

He said the whole world would listen to the voice of truth, all the media that convey man's voice and his image would speak it, conveying it by air, river, sea, and land.

This is what we received after the sheikh's last session with a select group of the alley's inhabitants. It was rumored in the old neighborhood after the meeting that, as a prelude to the propagation of his ideas, the spell would affect all those who work in radio, television, and other news media. He chose a person from the alley called Sergeant Major Sallam and gave him the title of First Warner, or, according to other versions, Messenger Number One of the Charter.

The World Falls Apart

Rummana the politico says he has been jailed altogether fourteen years for the cause—ten in one stint from 1954 to 1964, on top of this last sentence. Hassan repeats, "Ten years in a row?" His face shows surprise, reflection, and an attempt to visualize such a time in a man's life. How old was he in 1955? Mere months. Rummana had gone to jail when Hassan was still a baby and had come out as he was entering eighth grade. In 1964 he had found his way to the school library and to Sheikh Tuhami, who sold used books. He would go to him after school, pay him five milliemes, and sit on the curb. His heart would leap with Arsène Lupin as he attacked his rivals, his weapon drawn, taking from the rich to give the poor. His imagination was ablaze with the adventures of the honest thief. He saw himself wearing a black suit and mask, putting his hand in his pocket, taking out jewels and gems, handing them out to Zannuba the divorcée, to al-Bannan and his wife Latifa so they could buy a ticket and join their son. He saw himself putting money under his father's pillow to protect him from the anxiety of the last few days of every month, giving each person around al-Hussein Mosque a whole pound. Oh, how full of hope those days had been!

As the years went by the imagination began to wilt and wither; day by day one gave up one's dreams, until in the end one had given up life itself. He now remembers those feelings of 1964: he mocks them. In ten years' time would he be making fun of his present thoughts? But what have those long years done to Rummana? Can he still dream? Hassan says aloud that he cannot imagine himself locked up for one week. Rummana laughs: despite the long time in jail, he still recalls some of those days as beautiful memories. There is no end to man's ability to adapt. Rummana falls silent. The quiet is weighing down heavily upon them. Hassan wonders. The alley is usually filled with screaming children and women talking across the balconies at this time of day. He remembers that the silence has now lasted for days. Rummana says that what he fears, as far as the alley is concerned, is man's ability to cope with trying circumstances. What is happening is puzzling and strange, beyond logic, ungoverned by law. The people of Zafarani are facing metaphysical forces and live in the hope that the spell will be lifted and the "shock," as people are calling it, will be ended. Every day a new rumor spreads about the sheikh's decision to lift the spell from a certain number of people, but this doesn't happen. It reminds Rummana of the rumors of release that the prisoners used to spread in jail. Sometimes they would even give the names of those about to be released and fix the time for their release. Days would go by, no one would be released, and the rumors would die out, only to be revived once again: they lied and believed their own lies. These rumors usually got stronger before or during religious or national holidays, such as the Prophet's birthday, Revolution Day, and Mother's Day. This was now occurring in Zafarani.

Hassan observes Rummana closely, slowly, his mind dominated by one idea: this man has spent fourteen years in jail. The word 'jail' evokes dark caverns, cells so small a person cannot even stand, days without end, savage dogs, cruel jailers.

Hassan says that those who have protested are now silent, especially Tekirli, whose behavior recently has been rather mysterious. There is another observation: over the first few days, each man tried to suggest that he was the one exempted from the spell, but now they are all hiding their affliction. The people are growing more and more afraid lest the sheikh divulge their secrets, in the meantime wondering: how does he discover these secrets? Rummana wonders: Have the people of Zafarani forgotten that they are the source of all that the sheikh knows about them? He is simply repeating what they all told him when they went to him with their problems. Hassan says that the sheikh has spent seven years in seclusion, not meeting anyone on earth. Rummana says that what has happened in Zafarani during the last few years is very mysterious to him.

Hassan thinks: Rummana is one of those who are trying to change the world— arrested at the age of twenty-eight; released at thirty-eight; arrested again; no children, and no secure future. After their first meeting Hassan realized: Here is a man who has wrestled with life; at the beginning Rummana worked as a bookbinder, then as a waiter in a café owned by his mother, who died while he was still in jail.

How Hassan wishes his father were able to cope with the calamity! But his father has suffered much and confided in no one. All his hopes were centered on his two children; he saw his peace in their success. That was why Samir's running away from home was like the collapse of the foundation on which the two-story house was built. His father was condemned property. He feels a lump in his throat when he remembers his father. Even before going to bed, his father never takes off his shoes.

He often stands at attention in the hall, and if Hassan or his mother try to talk to him he shouts at them, ordering them to shut up and give him a chance to receive the report of Ibrahim Pasha, Commander of Cavalry, or listen to Rommel's problems. Hassan goes to his room and cries. Here was his father, in a condition he had previously heard of only in stories told about other people. To see it in his father was painful.

Hassan is certain there is a connection between what is happening to Zafarani and his father's condition. Rummana asks him what he is going to study in college. Hassan recalls his father during his moments of serenity on Friday afternoons after coming back from al-Hussein Mosque, saying that he has recited the opening chapter of the Qur'an for the spirits of the dead and prayed to God to accept his prayers that Hassan get good scores in his exams and go to medical school. Rummana asks, "What does Hassan know about socialism?" He says he has read some books about socialism and that one of his teachers at school has talked to them at length about the three years he spent in a socialist country. He says that his readings are disconnected, that there is no method or coherence to them. At the beginning he was enthusiastic in a childish way. He doesn't remember exactly where he read that socialism brings about justice. It was in that moment, however, that he began to see socialism as something mysterious that did exist somewhere. He became so enthusiastic whenever he spoke about it that one of his teachers cautioned him. His mind at that time did not grasp how hard the path to justice was and he didn't know anything about the arrests of 1959. He had not yet reached the age of eight. He remembers that when he was given some money to celebrate the Eid, he went out to al-Hussein Square. He was attracted by a book with a glossy cover, *Les Misérables* by Victor Hugo, and he brought it home. His father said the book was difficult and that he had to go to college before he could understand it, and took it away. Later, however, he noticed that his father was showing the book to one of their relatives, and he heard him say, on that quiet evening, "Look at what my son is reading!" He still remembers some lines from *Les Misérables*: "I fell, face first, to the dust; farewell, my comrades, for meet again we must."

Rummana says that first things—the joyful and the painful—are never lost from one's memory. He has spent many days in jail, but the first is still fresh in his mind, with all its details, so much so that he can almost see before him now the jacket of the detective who was acting as a jailer in the detention center of the secret police, which was missing a button—the second one up, he thinks. Rummana is silent for a moment, saying that he will try to find some books for Hassan to read, and that he is not sufficiently well educated. His political work has mainly been concerned with direct action, but he does know some essential, indispensable books. Hassan says this will help him crystallize many of his ideas.

Rummana looks through the window: the houses of the alley are sick. Zafarani has grown used to the silence since the sheikh's ban on quarrels took root. He remembers Hassan's father's strange posture and asks, "Did his father work for the army?" Hassan shakes his head; he doesn't want to talk about it. Rummana falls silent. At first Hassan wishes for their conversation to go on, but, among the people of Zafarani, no matter what subject is being discussed, it always leads to the alley's predicament. Several questions oppress his mind. Now that Rummana has found out about the spell, what does he think the solution should be? Does the situation affect him?

Similar questions are also on Rummana's mind. He and Hassan talk about a number of issues and inevitably turn to personal matters, considering the peculiar circumstances of Zafarani. Hassan is not afraid of the subject, but he is annoyed whenever anyone reminds him of his father, especially since his condition has become more alarming.

This morning two children climbed onto the roof facing their house, having evaded their families; they began to point at his father and take up a rhythmic chant: "Lo-ser! Lo-ser! Lo-ser!" He shouted that the enemy was waging a ruthless psychological campaign on the radio. One of the boys threw a stone at him and he called out to his son, the Chief of Staff. He said there had been an attempt on his life by a trained unit and shouted, saying that the gaps had not been filled properly. He had called Himmler, the Director of Intelligence. Hassan nodded his head and turned away, but his father grabbed him and slapped him hard, saying he had to give a proper military salute before leaving, that it was just such lack of discipline that was responsible for Hannibal's difficulties in hiding the movement of his troops across the southern section of Zafarani. He told his son to observe discipline both in appearance and in action. Hassan nodded sadly and raised his hand in a military salute.

At the door his mother stood weeping in silence. She whispered, "Our house is ruined!" and asked him where he was going. He said he would go up to the roof of the opposite house and prevent the boys from throwing stones at his father. Should he go to Oweis and beg him to inform the sheikh of the boys' trespasses? So far Hassan had refused to admit that the spell was real, even though he was under its influence. But he might go to the sheikh regardless, since he represented the real power and authority in the alley. He didn't find the two boys on the roof, but when he looked down they were standing in the alley, pointing up at the general on the balcony. He went down quickly but couldn't find them. He was overcome with embarrassment; he wasn't used to entering other people's homes. Now he was chasing a couple of kids. He overcame his annoyance and gave his father a military salute, submitting the report required of him, to the effect that the assassination squads had been liquidated.

Rummana looks at Hassan and sees again his own early years, his work at the print shop under the supervision of an Alexandrian worker named Badr, from whom he learned bookbinding and politics, how to print leaflets, how to evade surveillance. He had been healthy, untouched by the turmoil of political action; he didn't get embroiled in disputes or argue with a comrade who, although he held the same point of view, disagreed so violently with his fellow comrades that they became enemies more hostile than the reactionaries or the forces of exploitation. At that time, Rummana was motivated only by his enthusiasm and desire to challenge the unknown, to eradicate the old conditions. Life seemed long enough and reality appeared willing to submit to the forces of change. In prison his hopes grew feeble. Sometimes he thought how difficult, almost always impossible it was, to do anything; how tiny man was vis-à-vis the greater goal. Now, however, he remembered the old man who had died in jail at the age of ninety. He had been a founding member of the first party in 1921, and he remained loyal to the cause until he died in the Oases Detention Center. He recalled the magnificent funeral: the man's body wrapped in a red blanket with a black ribbon running from one end to the other; the funeral procession, and how the guards stood still—those guards whose official uniforms could not disguise their peasant features and their origins in the villages and hamlets. He remembered Mao, who was the leader of eight hundred million people and who was approaching eighty. But how few were those who lived to see what they fought for made real before their very eyes! Here, it was a strange secret that kept people apart from each other, kept differences and bloody disputes alive for years and years, made everyone suspect his own comrades. Was it a disease caused by a microbe that could only live in a climate like Egypt's, that was mild both in winter and summer?

He looks at Hassan, trying to prevent his thoughts from being reflected in his eyes, where this sharp, enthusiastic, young man might detect them. Since his release, weakness has begun to creep into every-thing. Even what is taking place in Zafarani seems like the result of years of disagreement, dissension, disunity, and aimlessness. He turns to Hassan; his eyes gleam. He has no child of his own, but his feelings toward the young man are bigger and more complex than fatherly feelings. He experiences a strange feeling of relief: here is someone who will carry on his old enthusiasm, who will speak of him to his closest comrades, who will tell them that the cause renews itself, that the years they have spent will not be in vain. When he objected to the dissolution of the party, it had not occurred to him that there were young people in the world who were still inspired the way he had once been, and who would one day build their strong edifice. He is overcome with emotion. Will Hassan stop the world from falling apart?

Report from the the Department for the Investigation of Leads to the Supreme Information Authority

On 3/28 *Der Avoniaz*, the Austrian newspaper, published an item very prominently on its front page. The story identifies a strange phenomenon in Egypt's capital and tells of a certain sheikh who has cast a spell that takes away men's sexual ability and has declared his intention of extending the spell to the entire world. Spanish satirist Barios de Fuega, currently residing in Austria, wrote an article from which we excerpt the following:

It is exciting that this should happen in the twentieth century. If it is true, preparations should be made to face a world without men; women should hurry and partake of some pleasure before it becomes hard to get. We do not know what science thinks of all this, but the subject raises several issues, since the man behind the spell seeks to achieve certain ends. According to news agencies, his intention is to change human nature by means of shock to make way for a world free of strife and conflict, a world whose borders will be eradicated and whose languages will be unified, where differences and hatred will no longer exist. The sheikh says that our world in fact comprises several divisions, that it is not true that the human race is one: there is the rich race and the poor race; the black race and the white race; man against man. This is what he wants to eradicate by making man work for mankind, by causing humanity to be united in one condition that will awaken it so that he can change it as he pleases. This is what those strange news stories are saying. I hereby and henceforth declare that I will be the first missionary to spread the sheikh's creed, in the hope that he will protect me from the spell. . . .

After the publication of this comment, a political affairs reporter in West Germany called for an urgent appeal to our government to take a firm stand and to issue an official communiqué that would put matters in the right framework to preserve the human race. The same author called upon his government to consult with its global counterparts to address this serious matter. (It is no secret that this suspicious call is in fact a prelude to foreign intervention in our country's internal affairs.) The hostile mouthpiece hastened to repeat this news and called upon tourists to think twice before coming to our country. Their aim is to strike at our tourist industry and thereby sabotage an important component of our national economy. . . .

After a number of foreign journalists addressed questions to the official spokesman about Zafarani Alley, the chairman of the Information Authority issued an official communiqué, the text of which follows:

Some foreign newspapers have recently attempted to disseminate false allegations to the effect that certain incidents have taken place in Zafarani Alley, located in the old neighborhood of our great capital. These stories contain outlandish fabrications that no civilized mind in this, the last quarter of the twentieth century, would accept. We emphatically deny the truth of these allegations and hasten to add that the people of Zafarani are leading normal lives, as are all the inhabitants of the capital and elsewhere. In the face of these allegations, we can only laugh at those who spread them and who mislead world public opinion. . . .

Fear of the Loss of Doubt

In the beginning, Atif hid his feelings; he was cautious and suspicious. It had been a year or more since he made new friends, and he had begun to see his old friends in a new light, and therefore stayed away from them. He wouldn't seek out Farid or Wagdi unless he was completely overcome with loneliness and felt on the verge of dying alone, or unless he wanted to experience a family atmosphere for a brief moment. At such times, a brief but painful sadness would take hold of him after he had spent time with Farid and his wife, watching their merriment, Farid running to the kitchen to get the jelly dessert his wife had made, or making juice using the blender he had bought from the duty-free shop at the airport after his return from Italy last year. His friend's apartment was small and neat and he knew the story of every piece of furniture in it. Peaceful married life produced in him delicately ambivalent feelings: not envy, not hate, but a consciousness of his raw wounds. He would see himself in Farid's place, and Rahma in Safaa's.

He would see himself sitting with Rahma talking about matters of concern to them both, things they had to buy, a visit they ought to make, a new movie they must see. Now he imagined Rahma in another city, glancing, in a way that had once been exclusively reserved for him, at one of his closest friends. Nabil would be surprised to discover how much Rahma knew about him. She knew his most intimate affairs: how many shirts he had, the address of the tailor who made his jackets, the movies he liked, the songs that moved him. She would not tell him that she had come to know him through Atif who, when they went out, would talk to her about Nabil, his friend, telling her his latest adventures, his ideas, where he was that day, and what he was doing. Before Atif had introduced them to each other, he had already talked to Rahma about his friend. When he introduced them for the first time he had been filled with happiness. Rahma had sat there, shy. He encouraged her to speak and was touched to the point of tears: his best friend and his beloved. He left more than once to use the telephone and leave them alone. On his way back he saw her. Rahma was turning a glass in her hand and looking at Nabil. He was very moved. At the end of that meeting he declared that he was happy that a friendship had started between his beloved and his life's brother, his soul's twin. He said that he had told each of them enough about the other that their relationship had invisible roots. He held her hand and Nabil's. He still remembered every detail of that first meeting, as he remembered the phases through which he kept track of the betrayal as it unfolded: the special tone in which she used to ask about Nabil; her saying a short time later that she had met and talked with him; then the falling out.

Atif has not trusted anyone for months now. Perhaps that is what transformed his formerly outgoing manner into constant silence. But he thinks a good deal about Hamdi the reporter. The way he had welcomed him reminded Atif sadly of the way he used to respond when he was introduced to somebody: that outgoing manner which had rusted over. He used to consider his friends as extensions of himself. He had noticed or imagined, however, a certain affectation in Hamdi's manner. Perhaps that came from his work with the press, which required him to appear friendly in order to get what he wanted, even though he had stressed his personal motivation in coming to the alley. Atif listened, wished him good luck, then insisted on leaving. On his way home he reflected that what was happening in the alley was becoming common knowledge, that it had reached the press. He felt terrified whenever he thought he might be summoned by one of his bosses and asked about the spell. Could he ignore his bosses then? The whole country, he felt, must know about it by now.

At the beginning, every Zafaranite had tried to conceal the matter from others, but now everything had come out into the open. Days were passing and nobody knew when relief might come. It seemed that the authorities were keeping an interested eye on what was happening: many mysterious men came, gathered information, and asked questions. He had learned from Rhode that it had all been thanks to the influence of Sayyid Tekirli. As for Ali the ironer, he stopped Atif more than once to assure him that India was interested in the matter, that a number of Zafarani residents had been invited to India to be examined and cured.

Atif hid his annoyance over how long the spell had been in effect and grew even more annoyed at the rumors spreading through the alley declaring that the lifting of the spell was imminent. The guessing would start and names would be suggested. Rhode was now coming to Atif's apartment at regular times; he no longer feared that. And of course Sitt Busayna, who had grown weak and thin, noticed that Rhode was going into Umm Muhammad's house, where Atif the bachelor lived. She noticed the close relationship between the two, and assumed that Atif was the last, unchanged, man. She went to him, offering to wash his clothes and prepare his food, but he wasn't interested. She couldn't shout, since that was against the sheikh's teachings. So instead she went from one woman to another, talking about the illicit relationship between Rhode and Atif, but they were all indifferent. Nobody listened to her anymore, perhaps because everyone had enough worries of their own, or because they assumed that she had gone crazy ever since she had left her own house and begun to sleep in the alley. She feared that if she slept in her apartment, death would catch up with her. Tahun Effendi met her one day as she was running through Bayt al-Qadi Square; she looked terrified and grabbed him by his clothes. He calmed her down and she trembled like a wet dove, saying she was running away from death; if she stayed in one place, death would catch up with her.

Zafarani was not upset that Rhode was visiting Atif or that the two would stand together on the balcony. Atif noticed that only Nabila the schoolmistress would get upset and close the shutters whenever he appeared. Rhode said that jealousy was devouring Nabila, first because she had been working as a schoolmistress for six years and was said to have saved two hundred Egyptian pounds; and second because even though she was going to college she had got no response from the only person in the alley who was suitable for her. She hadn't given up hope until she saw Rhode and Atif together on the balcony with her own eyes, and she wondered at the effendi who ignored the college girl and chased an ignorant divorced woman. She later said more than once that what had happened to Zafarani was fully justified, and that its men deserved even worse.

Atif listened to Rhode as her soft body nestled in his arms. He smelled her hair and looked at her splendid breasts. When she visited she gave him the news of the alley, looked in his armoire, took out the dirty clothes, cleaned the apartment, and mopped the floor. He watched her as she bent, showing her knees as her dress traveled up, revealing luscious thighs. He followed the clear contours of her body as she moved about, deliberately remaining before him for long moments. The curves of her body veiled by her dress were more naked than the exposed skin. He imagined himself getting up suddenly, laying her on the floor as she said in frenzied desire and ecstasy, "Take me, take me!" then yielded all her feminine charms to him, holding him inside her. A little while later he would bite his lips: his desire had come under the influence of the spell. The burning lust was fast extinguished.

At first he had almost sent her away because he wanted to flee his impotence. But when he stopped his daily outings, he began to grow accustomed to her; he became so familiar with her energy and enthusiasm that he suffered intense anxiety one night when she didn't appear. He had got used to her. She came to him like a tide that was sometimes calm, sometimes tumultuous. He fantasized that she had been with him for the last three years; with her he evaded treachery and the searing pain of separation. When he saw Rahma on the street, it was no different from seeing any other woman. He tried to remember how many times he and Rhode had met by accident over the course of their relationship. Once, on the main street, he was so happy to see her he almost hugged her; she pursed her lips to caution him. Had Rhode come into his life three years earlier, Rahma would not have met Nabil, and destinies would have changed.

On one of his walks, he stopped before the same store as before and bought the same perfume and gave it to Rhode. The corners of her lips trembled: he saw her as a child, a happy woman. She said, "May God preserve you! No one has ever bought me anything before." His gifts kept coming: a galabiya, slips, a shirt and a pair of pants for her child, and she cried when he gave them to her. She whispered, trembling, that she wanted nothing except to be close to him. He could see that she was telling the truth. He was consoled by the thought that what afflicted him afflicted all the men of Zafarani. Sometimes their eyes would meet. Then what? She didn't let the moment freeze but hastened to kiss him, and he gave in, hoping in vain the miracle would take place. She hoped to find in him the only man left, but he doubted that such a man existed. Where was he? Was he married or single? Or was he an infant, still at his mother's breast?

Atif was also skeptical about what had been conveyed by Sergeant Major Sallam. When the sergeant major summoned him together with Tahun and Radish-head, he was secretly worried and sarcastic; was this man, who forgot a face he had seen an hour before, capable of being the First Warner? Atif noticed a new seriousness in his manner of speaking, the rhythms of his speech: it was an unmistakable change. He told them that the sheikh wanted to convey to them, in the name of the Prophet's intercession and al-Kawthar, the blessed river of Paradise, that his love for the inhabitants was such that if he were to reveal it, it would overflow and outstrip the waters of the seas. He loved them and pitied them. The substance of his love was everlasting; its warp and woof were his concern with their affairs before they came into the world. He knew that everybody secretly hated what had befallen them. The time would come when each would realize the unparalleled advantage and the great hope. The sheikh's love was vast, boundless; it went beyond people to the flowers, stones, animals, and cliffs extending into the sea; its vastness was like the distance between the stars; it was as transparent as the water of the sea. What the sheikh wanted was for everyone to open up with their hidden love. Atif strained his mind to comprehend what the sergeant major was trying to convey: he had a vague feeling, deep down, that he was witnessing a profound event that would change the course of time. The sheikh said that men's impotence was the first step on the path of his love. How would the other steps appear? At the end of his talk, the sergeant major said that what had befallen them

237

was not a secret, that the world was beginning to know, to pay attention. The sheikh's words would find their way to different races and to the most isolated of ethnic groups.

All that day Atif gazed at Rhode; she bowed her head shyly. He loved her rosy cheeks and the shyness in her eyes; she looked like a virgin, untouched. He said the sheikh did what he did because he loved the people. She was about to make a sarcastic remark, but since the conversation had to do with the sheikh, she had to be careful. She asked when he was going to lift the spell, then. Atif fumbled with a button on his jacket, haunted by a sense of being captive, imprisoned. He offered her his lips; she raised her eyes in supplication: "May God deliver us soon!" It was an impassioned prayer. Atif was embarrassed. He said he would go out for a while. She didn't object, either for fear of upsetting him or because she wasn't sure she could convince him. As he crossed Zafarani he remembered something he had once read about a city in Asia being quarantined after it was stricken with the plague. Merchants had stopped coming, as had visitors; if someone lost his way here, and was about to enter the alley, he would now be warned off by the scores of neighborhood residents who were constantly gathered some distance from the entrance to Zafarani, and whose curiosity was voracious.

Umm Muhammad no longer sat in front of the door as she used to; she stayed in her room with the door closed. She no longer found anybody to watch. Atif didn't see her. He felt embarrassed before Rhode: he had to find some way to appeal to her, as a man. What could it be?

As Atif passes in front of the café he sees Daturi sitting on the chair, his hands clasped in front of his belly, his head bowed. He catches a glimpse of Hamdi the reporter. He decides to ignore him but he hears the reporter calling his name. Hamdi says he would be very happy if Atif joined him. Atif hesitates a little, then agrees, saying he will not stay long. He greets Daturi, who smiles calmly. When Hamdi calls Muhammad, the old waiter, Atif says that he shouldn't. Hamdi laughs; he now considers himself one of the inhabitants of the neighborhood. Atif is about to correct him: But you are not from Zafarani. Hamdi says that since their first meeting he has been fascinated by Atif, an impression difficult for one person to create in another. He will be frank; he has felt Atif's hostility toward him. He asks to be allowed to call him Atif, and he begs Atif to call him Hamdi. He feels that Atif's rigid face is hiding an extremely tender spirit. Atif smiles and nods gratefully. Hamdi's voice gets louder; he really means what he says and would like to speak to Atif as a human being. What is happening in Zafarani has been reported by the news agencies, but the censor is forbidding it from being discussed locally for higher undisclosed reasons. Atif's interest is piqued: Are Zafarani's tribulations well known? Where? Abroad? But he doesn't want the conversation to go on. Hamdi asks, "Has Atif lived in Zafarani a long time?" Atif narrows his eyes: "Five years." Hamdi grabs Atif's left hand, then the right one: "You're a bachelor?" Hamdi says that he too is a bachelor, but with one difference: he was married once, for four months. For the first time, Atif seems interested. Has Hamdi been gathering information about him? But nobody in the alley knows any details of his relationship with Rahma.

Later on, Atif was unable to pinpoint when he had begun to get closer to Hamdi. Was he reverting to his former self: to being enthusiastic about people the very first time he met them? Years would pass, but he would still be under the influence of his first impression, ignoring anything that contradicted it—ignoring faults, dealing with values and characteristics within himself, until catastrophes led to calamities. He always blamed himself for forgetting the simple proverbs that he had learned when he was very young.

Hadn't he studied the story of Cain and Abel? He didn't reach the conclusion that it was impossible for one human being to open up to another until he was bitten by the serpent. He realized that each human was a locked fortress, no matter how much love there was and no matter how hearts seemed, by illusion, to be bigger. There always remained closed enchanted doors hiding nobody knew what. He remembered a story from the *Thousand and One Nights*. The hero arrives at a magnificent castle filled with all kinds of treasures. It has seven doors. The owner of the castle says to the hero, "Open any door you like and enjoy whatever you find behind it, but beware the seventh door." There was always a seventh door in every relationship that, when opened, caused all the treasures, all the bliss, to disappear. Atif chose not to enter the castle itself at all so as not to have to grapple with his weakness in front of the seventh door. What drew him to Rhode was that no matter how strong the relationship between them grew, each would have his or her own past world. Sitting with Hamdi a few times would not take away what he had surrounded himself with. The ability to communicate and lay oneself bare was something a wounded person could not do. A healthy body could run, swim, and dive, but how could a sick body do any of that? He shouldn't worry then; the barriers would remain in place.

Rhode was now in Atif's house. Before he went out she had said, "I may spend the night with you." He remembered the old dream of his adolescence: to spend the night next to a woman and to have her whenever he chose. He was struck by an unsettling thought: Perhaps Rahma knew what had happened to him, perhaps she was making fun of him or having a painful discussion about him with Nabil and both were wishing him a speedy recovery. Perhaps she was going to move away altogether, as Hamdi's wife had done. But the story was reported in the foreign newspapers. How would he face Rahma if he were suddenly to meet her? He had not seen her since that spring night, that April night. Perhaps she looked different now. After that sad night he had been convinced for a while that if they were to meet by accident, that hateful dream would come to an end. She would smile and their sweet moments would come back to life, blooming and bearing fruit. It was only later that he learned that the light coming from her room and which he saw from the street was the one that enabled her to see her suitcases, to pack the clothes that he had touched and smelled many times: the yellow dress with red roses, the green dress scattered with yellow leaves, her black evening ensemble, the nylon hose, the greenish slip edged with lace—all of that was being prepared for another man whose blow had proved fatal, created a gap, and demolished a building. If Rahma were to meet him suddenly, if she were to notice that he looked different, she would forget the alley's impotence under the spell; she would smile, trying to discern in his look the effect of this unexpected meeting. Clouds of regret would hang over the sky of her soul; she would look at him closely, notice that he didn't look merry, that his eyes were smaller, as if they had withdrawn a little. She would ask him what was wrong and he would say that he was preoccupied with important matters, that his schedule was very tight and that was why he couldn't stay long.

She would look at his shirt, at his front pockets from which protruded pieces of colored paper and card. She would stop at the wide leather belt around his waist and she would gasp as she noticed the brown leather holster attached to the belt; "Atif, what is that?" He wasn't going to tell her that it was a very modern gun, loaded with bullets: twelve of them that could be shot with one squeeze of the trigger. What would shock her was his new appearance with a gun, which added mystery and awe; the way that gun dangled from the leather belt highlighted his graceful figure. He wouldn't make any comments on her surprise or her questions. Perhaps she would discuss the matter later with Nabil, who would be scared that Atif might shoot him.

In his mind, Atif walks slowly; he meets Hamdi the reporter and answers his questions about the gun. He tells him how hard it is to get one like it, how powerful it is and how accurate, what a sharp shooter he is. Daturi is scared; he asks him loudly to put it back in its leather holster. The whole alley is afraid of him. At home Rhode eyes him with even more admiration than before.

Atif is now standing in front of the window of a gun and sporting goods store: huge double-barreled shotguns, spears, diving gear, ammunition belts, stuffed birds; in the background a colored poster of a foreign man aiming a pistol at something on a snow-covered mountain. Atif takes his time looking at a long line of guns of different sizes and shapes, brown wood, black barrels. Some guns have feminine features; he shudders in disgust. Their appearance contradicts their fatal reality. A gun is a masculine noun even if a feminine sounding word is used to designate it. His eyes are glued to a gun with sharply defined contours, a straightforward barrel, rectangular handle, resting in a wooden box lined with red velvet. He looks long at it, lifts his head to read the name of the store, looks at his watch. It is seven o'clock. He has half an hour to get home and another half an hour to get ready for bed. Tomorrow he will come back to stare at that well-defined metal body, sleeping like a landmine, that is seen countless times a day by passersby. But they are unaware.

Excerpts from a Brief Report

to the Director of the Information Authority on
the International Developments of Zafarani Affairs

According to reports from news agencies and press attachés in the country's embassies, Zafarani affairs have begun to attract attention throughout the world. It is interesting that a small French-language newspaper coming out in La Paz, the capital of Colombia, should mention Sheikh Atiya, describing him as the saint of this age who is going to change the world. Such coverage means that his reputation has reached faraway countries. As for the leading European newspapers, no day passes without detailed stories appearing on their front pages. *Le Monde* has devoted a regular twenty-five-line column printed in boldface letters in the right hand section of the front page. In its most recent weekly edition, it published an article by Professor Corteau, the sociologist; in it he wrote of what he called, "The Thoughts of Sheikh Atiya" and where the sheikh stood in relation to world thinkers who have brought about great revolutions in human history.

The professor ranked the sheikh at the top of the list because he had the practical means enabling him to realize his ideas. He answered those scholars who were skeptical about the sheikh's ability to castrate men by talking about the power of suggestion: illusion could be quite effective if a powerful personality operated under certain conditions. He said the masses' fear and respect toward their leaders were constituted for the most part by suggestion and illusion.

Greek, Italian, Spanish, and Canadian newspapers have published what they claim to be the sheikh's thoughts. Each section is called a 'perspective.' So far four perspectives have been published. The first deals with the power of the all-embracing universal love; the second with wars, plagues, and famines, and how they have persisted since the creation of the world and the futility of all efforts to end them, and how feeble the collective human memory is. The third talks about the hidden truth and deals with some obvious facts, which are as clear as day; political regimes are able to twist these facts and convince people of the futility of things that are good for them. He gives examples of wealth and poverty, and how millions of people submit to the rule of a few or to a misleading ruler for many years or whole lifetimes. The fourth perspective bears the title, "The Beautiful Illusion," and revolves around the illusions that prevent people from seeing the truth or demanding their rights. These perspectives have been translated into several languages and have appeared in various editions, especially in India and Afghanistan, where groups have formed announcing their allegiance to the sheikh.

Last week, the permanent ambassador of Malandia lodged a protest containing his government's objection to what he called foreign intervention in the internal affairs of his nation. He pointed out that a huge organization had come into being suddenly and was receiving instructions from Sheikh Atiya. That organization had held several mass rallies in which a number of its leaders, mostly elderly men, delivered speeches announcing the birth of an invincible power that was going to resolve all forms of conflict and wars among men and between each man and his ego. Meanwhile, extensive riots had broken out resulting in violent clashes between the police and demonstrators in the major cities of India and Malagasy: thousands gathered in the main squares and started cheering and calling upon Sheikh Atiya to extend his influence all over the world and to change and to alter, for humanity had already waited too long. These calls were accompanied by brutal acts of violence, and several institutions and business centers were ransacked. A group of sailors in the Indian Ocean seized the oil tanker *Owansha*, owned by a Dutch company. They announced the end of a long illusion and that they would no longer permit their blood to be sucked. The foreign news agencies played up these reports, and some international broadcasting services have begun to talk about Sheikh Atiya.

The first broadcasting service to do a story on him was Radio Mont Cafry; the first service to broadcast a special feature about him was Radio Ankara. Radio Roxana, directed to the Arab countries, and Rossania Radio, which broadcasts in Arabic and is directed to the Orient, have begun to report about him. According to public opinion polls covering the period 6/7 to 12/7, submitted to the Committed Security Groups, Federations of Security Authorities and Bureaus of Combating Sarcasm and Jokes, all point to the public's interest in the sheikh. For all these reasons we propose the following: that our newspapers publish news stories about a man making certain claims (our media will mount a strong campaign showing the sheikh as an insane charlatan). A parallel campaign should be mounted about a local incident given extensive coverage, such as a murder case or an escaped lunatic threatening to strangle or kill innocent people. Our writers and journalists will make fun of the foreign newspapers and the pro-Sheikh Atiya organizations and the publishing houses that print his works. Broadcasting and publishing news about him will absorb much of the current furor.

Text of a Comment on the Summary of Several Reports on Zafarani Affairs

A Supreme Committee shall be created for the monitoring of Zafarani affairs, comprising the following:

- Headman in charge of citizens;
- Chairman of the Supreme Thought Authority;
- Chairman of the Supreme Health Authority;
- Coordinator of Security Affairs.

An Escape Attempt

Tekirli's voice was heard again after an interval. As the inhabitants stood to receive their breakfast, he began to shout when he saw them looking at him. He saw Nabila come out onto the balcony, Khadija the Sa'idi woman look out her window; even Umm Muhammad shielded her eyes from the light with her hand and looked at him. He started yelling, calling all the inhabitants cowards, saying that as long as they agreed to do nothing, even more horrible things were going to happen to them. Tahun hastened to interrupt him before anyone else to prove that he was the first to defend the sheikh. He asked Tekirli to be silent and not to forget that he was from Zafarani. At the top of his voice, Tekirli shouted that he was moving out that very day; he had waited in the hope that some men might join him in resisting the corruption perpetrated by the sheikh, but could find no men. Why? Because even before the spell had been cast, Zafarani didn't have any men!

From the food line came the loud voice of Radish-head, slightly nasal, saying that the alley knew the truth about Tekirli, thanks to the sheikh. If it were true that the alley had no men, it was because they had allowed him to stay among them until that moment. Tekirli shouted sarcastically: Had it come to this, that Radish-head, with running saliva, was talking back at him? He knew things about his wife that if he were to tell, Radish-head would be paralyzed where he stood. Radish-head screamed, "Shut up, pimp!" A female voice was heard saying, "May it be our turn!" Tahun recognized his wife's voice; he left the line, looked up at the window where his wife was leaning out, wearing a red nightgown. "Go inside! Go inside!" She made a gesture with her hand as if to say "stop it."

Tahun's silent anxiety was compounded. His wife no longer let any chance go by without visiting the neighbors or talking to men from the window, paying no attention to him, her glances taunting him on account of his affliction. When he told her of his project for achieving justice by means of tunnels, hoping to gain her respect for thinking about lofty subjects, she made fun of him, saying that if anyone were to open his head they would find a sewage network there.

Tekirli ended his diatribe by spitting on the whole alley. The news of his leaving prompted several discussions in all directions. After breakfast almost every man and woman began to wonder whether Oweis would touch upon Tekirli in his announcements. They listened for it, but he never even mentioned or hinted at Tekirli. The announcement contained a short reply to some queries made to the sheikh expressing the inhabitants' confusion about matters having to do with their religion. Should they fast for the month of Ramadan, which was soon approaching? The sheikh replied that the alterations he was going to make in man and the world would not touch the essence of religions, dogmas, or sects; his teachings had to do with quintessential matters that did not conflict with higher truths. When the world understood what had come about and responded to it, that which was invisible would be made visible, and everything would appear in all clarity.

At about nine o'clock, Umm Suhair wondered, in the course of her conversation with Umm Nabila, how Tekirli was going to move his furniture. Who was going to risk his virility and enter the alley to move the furniture? In fact Tekirli came to face this problem in a very terrible and concrete way.

As Zafarani was having breakfast, Tekirli went out, heading for Baydaq Street, where there were many moving companies. He was surprised at the absolute refusal that met him, the questions addressed to him, and the mocking glances. The spell on the alley was well known to the truck drivers. He had to leave quickly, especially after a great number of drivers, movers, and passersby gathered around him and began to scrutinize him impudently. Several shouts were heard: "Watch out! Here's a Zafaranite. . . ." He went to Sayyida Zaynab Square in an attempt to rent a horse-drawn cart, but he was equally unsuccessful. He went to Darrassa, Abbasiya, Kubri al-Qubbah—everywhere he went, he was met with refusal and fervent curiosity. One cart driver said he wasn't about to accept a similar fate.

He finally succeeded in getting a cart owner to accompany him— an old, deaf man standing in Matariya Square. He didn't argue about the price. He took the man around a longer, back road so that none of the alley's inhabitants might see him by chance and ruin everything. His arduous search lasted seven hours, and he returned to the alley around four o'clock. As the light faded, his wife heard the sound of wheels on the alley's cobblestones. When she looked out the window, she saw all the inhabitants looking out of their windows and balconies. Tekirli pointed up and the cart driver nodded. Some of the inhabitants shouted but the driver didn't look around him. Tekirli was now pushing him upstairs while he looked back over his shoulder and made threatening fists at the watching people.

Nadia, Tekirli's wife, was in pain; their leaving made her unhappy; she had lived here a long time. It was true that she never objected to anything her husband did; even if he left her for days without food she wouldn't show her displeasure but would look at him in the same shy way. Usually he didn't let her keep any money; he bought her whatever she needed. She never asked him to take her out or go to the movies without him. But when he told her he intended to move out of Zafarani, she asked him why. He was very much alarmed because he had hardly ever heard her question anything he did and because she was oblivious to her surroundings. As for her question, he took it as an implicit insult. She said that the sheikh's warning made it clear that the spell would still have its effect whether inside the alley or out of it. He was angry. Was she going to believe that crazy sheikh? He came close to her, put his arms around her, and whispered that he was longing once again to stay up nights with her and tell her stories. She bit her lip, afraid lest she should let her face reveal what she was feeling.

A few days earlier she had gone out, exposing herself to the eyes of Zafarani and to the possibility of suddenly meeting her husband. Going to Nabil at the other end of the city was one of her most dangerous adventures. But she met him, embraced him, kissed him, cleaned the room, arranged the books, insisted on washing his clothes, and he begged her to sit with him. She turned to him with a face that was dark with desire; she tried to arouse him, but in vain. She moved away from him and wept. Nabil didn't speak, but as she was leaving he said that they should respect what the sheikh said. She said she feared for him, but couldn't stay away from him. She asked him to write her a letter and she would answer it and eventually she would have a collection of love letters that she would read after Tekirli had left.

Nabil did not say the words that she had longed to hear, that she had heard neither from Tekirli nor from any of the men who had had her. In the beginning she had seen their desire and heard the sounds they made. As they emptied their desires, she felt that each of them wanted nothing but to get away. Some never exchanged a word with her. As for Nabil, he seemed to take his time despite his youth. The last thing he wanted was her body. When Tekirli had shouted at him to hurry up, he had kissed her hand—the first time that any man ever had. Then he had left. She had asked him to come during the day so they could spend as long as possible by themselves. What terrified her during her last visit to him was her feeling that he was shying away from her; perhaps he saw in her a threat to his virility. That was why she had begged him passionately to write to her, but she received no letters. She consoled herself by thinking that no mail carriers had entered the alley after one of them was afflicted by the spell in the first few days. The same was true of electricity meter readers, street vendors, Department of Health nurses who sprayed insecticide to fumigate houses and who secretly sold quantities of it to those who wanted more.

She decided to make another secret visit to Nabil after moving to her new house. If Tekirli found out he would probably kill her. She was now saying goodbye to part of her life. In the bedroom, with its glossy paint, he had smiled at her for the first time, whispered sweet nothings in her ear. She thought a lot about childhood; she kept flipping through the years of her life in the hall during Tekirli's absence. Fear was slowly paralyzing her. What awaited her in the new house? The neighbors, the new men, their failure, puzzlement, resentment . . . . Perhaps Tekirli would give up on her and seek to marry another, throwing her out. She had a secret desire. She wished she could go to the sheikh and tell him her worries. She still remembered his reference to her through Oweis, that she was a good woman and that he wasn't going to say bad things about her. In spite of all that had taken place, she was leaving behind a place that was dear to her. Every piece of furniture that was being taken apart and moved downstairs by the deaf driver was like a piece of her flesh being cut away. She looked sadly at her husband, moving about energetically, carrying suitcases, chinaware, and glasses. He was impatient to leave. She was saying goodbye to security and predictability, to

Tekirli's coming home every day, by himself or accompanied by a man. As every chair was moved, its place looked empty, the tiles on the floor colder, and the whole apartment like a decayed mouth whose teeth had been pulled out.

The inhabitants were watching the furniture being stacked onto the cart, as was their custom whenever a neighbor left or a new inhabitant arrived, trying to figure out the social status of either from the value and quantity of the furniture. Some were now visualizing what had taken place on the bed, which was dismantled and stacked on the cart. Others were watching the deaf driver, imagining what was going to happen to him that night if he attempted to be with a woman, who might be waiting for him somewhere. Radish-head was pacing on the balcony, anxious. Farida had gone out early that morning with her daughter Nashwa and had not come back. An hour before, Radish-head's mother, who rarely came down from the roof, had come to him and said in her tremulous voice, "Look out for your house," and returned upstairs, her legs shaking, inspiring fear like a bad omen. He decided to have it out with his wife that very night: no more of these English lessons that were making both of them, his wife and his daughter, go to the house of a stranger. He was also anxious because he wanted to speak secretly with Tekirli, to beg him to send word if the spell wore off after he left Zafarani. If that proved to be the case he would try to do the impossible, to move to another lodging, no matter how much he had to pay for key money or rent in advance; he wasn't going to worry about the monthly rent. What mattered was saving himself and his household from Zafarani and its spells, even if he had to spend a painfully large amount. He didn't leave the balcony, and when the cart was almost filled he began to get ready to go downstairs to talk to Tekirli.

Sitt Busayna was also watching the neighbors who were about to move out. She was much thinner now, eating only occasionally; she shielded her eyes and narrowed them. She slept only very briefly, afraid of dying if she were overcome with fatigue. Throughout her waking hours mysterious footsteps echoed in her ears, breath touched her skin as she began to fall down an endless spiral precipice, shackled by invisible chains, and she would awaken, panting. She had left her apartment, afraid of dying alone, and sat in the alley, resisting sleep. Her mind was filled with images; she saw the houses with posthumous eyes. Things would still be there after she was gone; thousands of women were going to enjoy moments of pleasure after she was gone. She was never going to give death the chance to attack her alone in the apartment. What did Tekirli's leaving mean? He must be the only male unaffected by the spell and wanted to save himself. She was clutching at straws.

The inhabitants saw Sitt Busayna, her hair disheveled, her feet bare, going to Tekirli's house. She met him on the stairs and with a soft smile, in contrast to her hard features and the confusion in her eyes, she said to him, "A word, if I may." He looked at her in surprise; a wariness close to fear showed in his eyes. He jumped away on the stairs: "Yes, lady." She approached him calmly, slowly: "Five minutes in my place, if you please." Tekirli's voice was heard loudly. Khadija the Sa'idi woman said that perhaps Sitt Busayna had lent Tekirli some money and now wanted it back. Umm Suhair asserted that something mysterious was afoot. Zannuba said she had heard Busayna's screaming at night. But Umm Yusif was closest to the truth when she said that Busayna wanted to check Tekirli out before he got away. The inhabitants now saw her rush out after the driver, who was carrying some mattresses, go to the middle of the alley, fending off unknown persons, standing on tiptoe on first one foot, then the other, as if she were performing a strange, mysterious dance. Her eyes were gleaming, and she was biting her lips. Tekirli shouted, "Crazy alley!" When the driver harnessed the mule to the cart and it began to move off, Busayna ran after it and clung to it like a child. The driver looked over his shoulder, raised his big stick, bent his body, and brought the stick down first on her head, then on her hands. She fell down. Some children shouted mockingly, but their mothers chided them.

Busayna's torn clothes, her wild running, and her swollen face created a strange fear, a sadness in Zafarani. Umm Suhair couldn't hold back the tears that she was shedding for this, the best of women, who always wore the most magnificent clothes and who drowned the whole of Zafarani with the scent of her perfume every time she went out. Even Umm Yusif watched her calmly and with fear. Nobody remembered who it was who said that she perfectly deserved what she got because she had begun by making trouble for the alley, and because she had openly called the sheikh names more than once when she went out in the early spell days to buy fish or vegetables in the nearby market. She may have thought that what she said would not reach him, but he saw everything, heard the whisper, knew the truth about a sigh and what it signified. To hide a thought from him was futile; he knew everything, understood all languages and dialects, knew all the mysterious signs, could establish connections with all kinds of animate beings and inanimate objects. That was what the inhabitants discussed that same night. They predicted a horrible fate for Tekirli. Busayna remained outstretched in the alley until the compulsory bedtime arrived. But in truth she didn't sleep that night in Zafarani; nobody could protect her from death. She was going to keep moving through the streets and squares, escaping death from city to city and town to town.

After the cart had left, Tekirli appeared down in the alley, arm in arm with his wife, walking slowly, carrying a small briefcase, his head held high in open defiance. He didn't greet anyone and his wife bowed her head shyly. They avoided the outstretched Busayna. The day was drawing to a close. The women could go back into their houses, wash what dishes were left, and get ready to receive supper. The voice of Basyuni al-Hagrasi was heard briefly shouting at the wife of his son Luli: "Stay away from me! Stay away from me, whore! I am like your father!" She ran out in tears after this outburst and sat for a while in front of the house, then she went back in.

Hasan Anwar didn't leave the balcony and kept pounding his fist on the little table where he kept his map. He had lost a considerable portion of his forces; one of his most important fronts had collapsed. Ruin was galloping through the regions his forces had evacuated a short while before. He summoned Rommel and reprimanded him; the great German commander made excuses that sounded convincing: lack of supplies and fuel. But when have arguments and reasons alleviated the bitterness of defeat? He summoned his son, the General Chief of Staff, and gathered the field marshals: Himmler, Director of Intelligence; Goering, Commander of the Air Force; Zhukov, Commander of the Central Division; the Duke of Wellington; Napoleon; Von Moltke, Advisor for the Central Front; Lord Allenby; Montgomery; Eisenhower; Rokossovski; and Doenitz. He shouted at them, waving his baton. He must know the reason for defeat. How did the word 'defeat' ever worm its way into his terminology and language?

Developments

After the formation of the Supreme Committee for the Monitoring of Zafarani Affairs, the issue was discussed on several levels; several chiefs discussed it with their subordinates, and the various departments showed great interest in this urgent affair.

As for the Supreme Security Authority, they were interested in several important matters, among them finding a way to watch Usta Rummana and Luli al-Hagrasi. The Department for the Suppression of Subversive Ideas insisted that the former was responsible. The Department for the

Suppression of Religious Fanaticism, however, presented many letters it had received that described Luli's activities. It was decided, at the highest levels, to place these two under surveillance. To begin with, a Supreme Committee was set up comprising those in charge of the Supreme Security Authority, each division represented by a colonel. A dispute arose between the Subversion and the Fanaticism divisions when it was decided to employ the only expert in the country who had a PhD in scientific methods for the unearthing of forgotten ruins. Each division insisted on employing him, and each presented powerful arguments.

The matter would have reached conflict proportions whose consequences would have been hard to measure had it not been for the personal intervention of the Chief of Supreme Security, who resolved the matter by assigning the expert primarily to the Suppression of of Subversive Ideas Department, in view of the dangers posed by Rummana and the possibility that he might establish contacts with foreign agents. At the same time, the expert was to be assigned for one hour every day to provide consultation and advice to the Suppressors of Fanaticism. After a six-hour meeting, the committee decided to set up a subcommittee to study what Usta Rummana might do in Zafarani. This was followed by a series of meetings, wherein were consulted the files and reports of the wardens of the prisons and detention centers where he had been held for varying lengths of time, in addition to the remarks of prison guards and informers. Specialized scientific reference books were also used, one of which was purchased and flown in from Italy. It was considered possible to determine what kinds of subversive acts he could perform. These, in a nutshell, would be the attempt to spread his ideology in the alley—a conclusion confirmed by the committee by what was described in the confidential report submitted to the Supervisor of Secured Security, based on sources recruited from among Zafarani inhabitants.

According to that report, one of the alley's inhabitants, a student, was a frequent visitor of Usta Rummana, and their meetings were getting longer—proving that Rummana planned to work in student circles. A second conclusion reached by the committee was that conditions existed for the harboring of a secret press. The third hypothesis was that he was collecting weapons that would enable him to carry out acts of sabotage should he decide to progress to the stage of armed struggle. The subcommittee concluded that sincere efforts should be exerted and means be found to place Rummana under surveillance by a competent expert or to arrest him as he left the alley and isolate him in a remote detention center.

At the same time the committee discussed the case of Luli al-Hagrasi, and information about his life and activities was compiled. It was possible to put him under surveillance since he went to work at the factory every day. The reports detected a puzzling phenomenon: he did not perform his prayers—a fact that caused the committee chairman to be skeptical about the letters they had received—but the division representative asserted that the subject's own father had sent one of the letters, his allegiance to both his nation and his old profession as a plainclothesman having taken precedence over his fatherly feelings. Hence, it was decided to continue with surveillance in Luli's case.

That was what happened in Security circles. At the same time, directives came from on high to include representatives of all government departments, authorities, agencies, and organizations in the subcommittee emanating from the Supreme Committee to Follow Up on Zafarani Affairs. A request was made by one of the members of the Elected Assembly to announce the truth about what was really taking place in Zafarani Alley. He predicted this would prevent all the complications and whispers that were becoming unauthorized cries. The delegate from Information, however, rejected this argument.

Publication of the news would be considered an official admission of what had previously been denied. The story had been published in more than one international newspaper before the authorities in the country had even heard about it and nobody knew how the story had leaked out. But in today's world nothing can be hidden and everything can also be hidden.

The members of the committee were amazed and asked for clarification on that last point. The delegate from Information said that what happened in Zafarani had been taken up by foreign quarters and hostile adversaries to destroy the reputation of the country and harm the tourist industry, and thus it came about that the name of the small alley had leaped to the front pages of international newspapers, splashed in sensational headlines. This could all, however, be denied. He then proposed that an official declaration be issued and distributed to our embassies abroad denying the existence of a Zafarani Alley in the country. This had to be carried out simultaneously with an emergency plan, for which immediate allocations had to be made and which consisted in notifying all the inhabitants of the alley that they must vacate their homes, upon which they would be moved into government housing in different, distant places in such a way that no two families would be close to each other. Then a new plan would be drawn up for Zafarani in such a way as to preserve the old style in new buildings. The Information Authority would cover the project, thereby giving the impression that it was no more than a manifestation of interest in the preservation of old neighborhoods. Thus many internal and external goals would be met.

The proposal was received with skepticism. The delegate from the Supreme Authority for Buildings Built with Red Bricks replied scientifically and objectively by saying that what the colleague was asking for took into account only informational considerations, without the least regard to other considerations. There was, for instance, the impossibility of tearing down and rebuilding the neighborhood in a matter of days. Choosing one alley would cause more astonishment and suspicion than conviction. From the practical point of view it was impossible to finish the project in under six months. First, a technical architectural committee had to be formed to draw up the new plans; then the committee had to make an onsite inspection—an insurmountable task in view of the spell on Zafarani. The delegate from the Supreme Authority for the Conservation of Monuments spoke next, vehemently attacking the proposal of the delegate from Information, calling him shortsighted because he wanted to sacrifice the nation's legacy for the sake of the glitter of a false reputation: tearing down Zafarani was a crime against civilization, since it contained ruins of a house dating back to the first Mamluk era. At that point, the delegate from Information objected, saying that although the Archaeology Authority was generally negligent in the conservation of the nation's monuments, leaving them exposed to decay, the Honorable Delegate would get angry only when it came to the tearing down of a wall on which the nation's reputation depended. The archaeological delegate replied by citing the insufficiency of funds allocated to the Authority, and pointing out that despite this state of affairs, the Authority was exerting great efforts to preserve the legacy of the nation. He read out a list of the jobs done by the Authority during the last fiscal year, demanding that the list be published and accusing the delegate from Information of ignoring the efforts of the Supreme Archaeology Authority.

The first meeting ended without the committee making any specific resolutions. At the same time the listening reports prepared by the Supreme Department of Eavesdropping, entrusted with following Zafarani affairs in all the broadcasting services of the world, contained new developments. According to the news broadcasts of the B.B. Zdenogras, a group of men who called themselves 'Followers of the

Sheikh Atiya,' who believed in his thinking, declared that they intended to send a delegation to the city that had been honored by hosting him. A radio service that broadcast in the Indo-Asiatic language announced that great numbers of citizens in Himacuala stood in long lines, walked for hours under the rain, and rallied in the main square in the country's capital. There a man delivered a speech in which he said that the time had almost come: that what was distant had drawn near and what was hidden would now appear; everything would return; things would be simple again; cracks would heal; valleys would close up; the clouds and the earth would embrace; mercy would prevail and the absurd would disappear from the life of man; order would be restored to the system, which was confused and chaotic. The broadcasting service of Maqdiliano, Kobenshu, and Halloran transmitted lengthy excerpts from the old man's speech. The Supreme Department of Eavesdropping sent a confidential report of this news to the Supervisor of Information and the Chairman of the Public Authority for the Preservation of the National Reputation. Then the Philosophical Subcommittee, comprising the professors of philosophy in the country's four universities, held a meeting to study the goals of the sheikh.

During the first session, an officer with the rank of general in the Special Security Forces, who apologized for keeping his name to himself, joined them. He then read to them a report containing an outline of the sheikh's objectives contained in what were called 'perspectives.' First, the general said the sheikh loved the world; second, he declared that the sheikh pitied the world; third, he reviewed some of the various kinds of misery human beings suffered; and fourth, he described steps to be taken in order to correct the direction in which humanity was proceeding. In respect of the fourth perspective, it contained a description of some of his steps for correcting the direction in which humanity was proceeding. His means to that end were to rob mankind of that which they held most dear, up to a certain time, and by bringing about a situation in which conflicting and discordant conditions would be made into one uniform condition. The professors listened profoundly, then the oldest one among them got up, thanked the general for having taken such pains to come to the meeting, and assured him that the committee was greatly interested in what he had read, but that there were matters that had to be discussed in total freedom before reviewing the sheikh's thoughts. Among such matters, for instance, was determining who the sheikh was. Was he a reality or an illusion? A means or an end? A cause or an effect? Once agreement had been reached on the main outline, they could then move on to discuss the thinking itself, and try to approximate it to a specific philosophical school of thought or determine a clear definition. These were matters that required some time, since each of the professors belonged to a different philosophical school of thought from all the others. Then, in a polite fashion, he requested the general to leave the meeting so that his presence might not constitute a threat to the freedom of thought. The general acquiesced, but the Supreme Security Authority suggested that it would be necessary to exert intense efforts to recruit a professor to keep up with what was going on. The chairman of the Authority rejected a proposal to install secret recording devices, saying that recruiting a professor would be more useful, since he could also lead the discussions in certain directions.

However, the influx of secret police into the old neighborhood continued. And the Supreme Authority for the Collection of Jokes and Rumors intensified its activities, keeping track of everything that was being said. This resulted in strangers overcrowding the cafés of the old neighborhood. Some engineers from the Surveying Department suddenly appeared in the streets close to Zafarani, setting up their equipment on wooden tripods and looking through it. One of them took measurements of the main street for four hours. A strong rumor began to circulate about the government's intention to tear down a great number of buildings and streets to prepare a bus route. And in spite of the fact that there were no practical indications confirming or disproving the rumor, it didn't die down—a fact that caused great anxiety among the tenants of old, low-rent buildings.

Some Incidents

Tahun Gharib was going to work as he did every day when he caught sight of a piece of paper folded neatly on the ground. And because he now thought twice before doing anything for fear of committing an unintentional mistake that might anger the sheikh, he hesitated slightly before bending down and picking it up. When he read the few lines written in a slanted hand, in green ink, he didn't know what to do. Should he inform Oweis of what he read? He looked around; nobody was there, no woman or child had seen him.

Should he go back home and begin to carry out the instructions on the piece of paper? If his wife learned what was written there she would surely help him. she would spare no effort if there was the minutest chance of his virility coming back. But if he were to turn back now it would look suspicious. He ought to go back to work, to the winks of his male colleagues and the pitying glances of his female officemates. As one of them raised her head from the ledger in which she was taking down some figures, he would read in her eyes sympathy for his condition, as if she were saying: God help your woman! Perhaps there were scores of men in the department who couldn't get it up, but nobody knew about them. He, on the other hand, was walking around like someone with a sign on his head.

A terrible thing happened. At the entrance to the alley, Ali the ironer met him. He stopped Tahun, asking about his health and how he was doing. Many of his customers had left him, he said, and now he was only ironing the clothes of Zafarani inhabitants, and that did not bring in enough to pay for the kerosene that kept his stove going. Had it not been for the free meals that were being distributed, his children would have starved to death. He raised his hands, praying to God to give the sheikh long life. He leaned toward Tahun: Did Tahun know of anyone who could lend him money? Tahun shook his head. He wished he could leave at once, but Ali the ironer showed no intention of leaving. He said he was thinking of collecting enough money to buy a ticket to India, and there he would find a spell to counter the sheikh's. Indian spells were the best. The solution to all problems could well come from India. Suddenly he dropped his dreamy tone of voice, and said if Tahun could convince the inhabitants to collect his fare to India, he could bring back relief. Tahun opened his hands as if to say: Where could he get the ability to convince the people? At the same time he looked more closely at the ironer; he had heard from his wife that the ironer returned home to the alley drunk every night, that he went to an old bar at the end of Muski Street, where he drank cheap alcohol and then reappeared, staggering, just before the alley's compulsory bedtime, stopping everyone he met and assuring them that relief would soon arrive from India. Zafarani had not known many drunkards, other than Nabila the schoolmistress's father, who drank a great deal before he died. The inhabitants had often seen him on his way home, staggering and sometimes falling to the ground. One night some children chased him, and he kept on turning round to face them, struggling to maintain his balance, then raising his hands and shouting oratorically, "You stupid ones! You don't know what I have in my heart for you. . . ."

Tahun had chanced to be returning home at the same time. He had chided the kids and accompanied the man, who now kept turning to him too and accusing him of not understanding what was in his heart.

Umm Nabila met them with tears and grief. A case of alcoholism in Zafarani was considered a catastrophe. The alley had often heard Umm Nabila shouting at her husband trying to prevent him from going out on the balcony and addressing the alley. Many a time Umm Nabila had argued with her husband. Would people like him go to heaven? Would funeral prayers for him be accepted? It was said that a respectable government employee had come to ask for their daughter Nabila's hand in marriage but had withdrawn when he learned of her father's reputation and the symptoms of addiction that had begun to show during the last three years of his life.

The ironer said that relief was undoubtedly coming and that India would not put up with things for long. Tahun thought he smelled of liquor and was annoyed; he took his leave, saying he had to go to work, and hurried away, clutching the piece of paper.

Tahun saw Daturi's café open, with the waiter sprinkling water on the floor inside. The young man that they said was a journalist was sitting there. None of Oweis's announcements had contained any instructions about staying away from him. The people were used to seeing him sitting with Atif the college graduate, and some had seen them walking together at the end of al-Azhar Street. Tahun considered himself immune to the likes of that journalist. He wondered at the ease with which Atif had succumbed to him, and Qurqur the musician, too. He told Daturi that the coming of such a virile youth to the alley could mean only one thing: he was coveting the women of the alley. He was hiding behind his journalistic work, which protected him from any legal liability. His aims were the same as those of the pimps who tried to get to Tekirli's wife, but he was more dangerous because someone was protecting him. Daturi did not respond.

The journalist continued to come regularly, every day. What puzzled Tahun was that he came at such an early hour. Perhaps he had arranged with one of the alley's women to meet her after her husband went out and have her to himself for the day, then she would go back before two o'clock in the afternoon. He wondered who she was. Was it Umm Yusif, his wife, for instance? Her animal lust had been quite clearly shining from her eyes in the last few days. He tried to keep away, to avoid her eyes. He slowed his steps.

He pictured his wife, wrapping her melaya even more tightly around her body. He saw her deliberately coming to a standstill in front of the café, undoing the melaya, then wrapping it over again to give the journalist a chance to see some of the treasures of her body. He would then get up, follow her to Watawit Alley, or under the archway of Bayt al-Qadi. From al-Hussein Square they would take a cab that would take them both to his house. She would be impatient to be alone with him; he could imagine her in the bedroom. Tahun visualized his wife in lewd positions. Besides, the journalist was still a young man, and that would show her the true measure of her husband's virility; Tahun didn't know why he was so sure that his own ability was inferior to that of the journalist. Even if the spell were to be lifted, she wouldn't forget the effendi easily.

Tahun almost stumbled; a massive sorrow overwhelmed him. He felt the piece of paper; perhaps relief would come after he had carried out its instructions to the letter. He didn't stay long at work. He requested permission to leave early and went back toward the alley. He was relieved to find the journalist still sitting at the café. When he approached Sidi Marzuq Mosque, some children who had gathered there suddenly shouted, "Woe is me! Woe is me, Zafarani!" He was taken aback, and even though the children hastened to hide, he ran toward Zafarani, and only when he had crossed the entrance to the alley did he feel secure; beyond that point no one could follow him. His boss couldn't look at him suspiciously for having been temporarily exempted from driving trains and given a clerical job in the tool workshop. Nor could the journalist enter the alley.

Zafarani was quite calm; the parents had to prevent their children from going out to play with children from other alleys because too many quarrels had taken place. The children's staying at home caused endless annoyances, especially during school holidays such as this one. The houses were small and couldn't take much noise. But now the children left neither the alley nor their homes and were strangely quiet. None of them shouted any more, and none was ever seen engaged in a hotly contested ball game or stone-throwing battle. Most of Zafarani's children now spent their time sleeping. It was a strange quiet that Tahun was not used to, so much so that it now occurred to him that maybe this wasn't Zafarani. Perhaps because he never returned so early, when the sun still shone on much of the alley, and one could hear the slow tasks of daily life being carried out in people's homes, the washing of pots and pans or the mopping of floors.

He knocked at the door; it would be only a few moments before he would hear the sound of slippers on the floor. He didn't hear anything. He knocked again, once, several times. Nothing. A rough hand gripped his heart. Where had she gone? But the journalist was at the café. Was he sitting there deliberately to mislead Tahun, then getting up and going to meet her in an agreed spot? Perhaps he had already come back from an earlier rendezvous and she had tarried a little longer so as not to arouse suspicions among the café customers and the people sitting in front of the shops. Tahun had no key. She always opened the door. He left the alley once more. Whose slippers did he hear? Was it an illusion? Images were coursing through his burning head.

Tahun went to the mosque, performed his ablutions, and began to carry out the paper's instructions. When he was a young man he had never missed a prayer; but now, years later, he only performed Friday prayers. He would go to al-Hussein Mosque every week and then to a café that had not been torn down like other old buildings. During the last two years he had frequently missed even Friday prayers, but he still kept up with the two Eid prayers. The people of Zafarani used to gather at an early hour, greet each other, shake hands, and even if there was some dispute, everything would be cleansed by the pure, cool breeze that blew in their faces as they left Zafarani. All that was now over. Anyone from Zafarani was ashamed to face his neighbor. Should he leave the mosque, the only place where he could sit alone without being bothered? Should he go to Daturi's café? He wouldn't feel comfortable in any other café; perhaps the waiter would ask him to leave because the other customers were afraid of coming into contact with him or drinking from his glass after he had drunk tea or fenugreek tonic.

The people of Zafarani were quite well known in the neighborhood. Before the collective food arrangement was put in place, some of the inhabitants had forbidden their women to go out to buy vegetables or meat. Some of the merchants had shown covetous interest in the women, just like those low-life men who hung around prisons on visiting days, setting their traps for the wives who missed their husbands locked behind the walls. But Tahun's wife paid no attention to what he told her and just went out.

Tahun felt he was the victim of a ruthless plot despite being a good, poor, kindly man who never harmed anybody, never conspired against anyone, and never informed on any of his colleagues. He, in contrast, was being conspired against by the broker who had shown him the apartment, by Radish-head, who had agreed to rent the apartment to him, by Daturi who had chosen for his café a location close to the alley, by all the men who looked at his wife's round buttocks. All were part of the conspiracy. If only they would agree to collaborate with him to carry out the huge project that filled his head: the network of tunnels which diverged yet converged and in which all the hungry people would meet and, at an agreed moment, rise, come out into the light, uproot everything in their path, and change the order of things.

A short while later, several incidents took place in Zafarani that forced Hamdi the reporter to cut short his meditations and, with things being so quiet these days, were also noticed by Daturi while Tahun had to resist a strong temptation to stop writing the 'In the name of God' formula to observe what was happening. Just before midday, a young woman carrying a huge, brown suitcase rushed forth, followed by a girl of about seventeen. Both were confused and flustered. The woman put the suitcase down near the entrance of the mosque and the girl put her suitcase down next to it and returned quickly to Zafarani. The woman stopped and looked about her. Her clothes exuded a subtle perfume and she was clasping and unclasping her hands: no one would stop her or persuade her to change her mind. Her daughter now reappeared, carrying a small brown suitcase. There had been nothing extraordinary about them until now. But moments later an old woman with a very bent back came rushing after them. When passersby saw her they guessed she must be over a hundred years old. Her stumbling gait and her wailing voice attracted the reporter's attention. Daturi turned around slowly to survey the scene. The old woman was shouting, "Whore! Traitress!" and calling on the passersby to run and stop her, and as the distance grew between herself and the woman and girl, her wailing increased. And indeed a passerby approached her to inquire what was wrong, but two screams were heard simultaneously, one from the old woman herself, and the other from someone standing in the street: "Beware, she is a Zafarani woman!" Hamdi inquired about the young woman's identity, and after a pause Daturi replied that it was Farida, Radish-head's woman, with her daughter Nashwa. Daturi was silent again. The old woman stopped, heaped dirt on her head, screamed some gibberish, looking like a spoilt child who had lost something precious and was unwilling to go home without it. The screaming made Tahun stop.

He couldn't continue. For a moment he was afraid that some calamity might have befallen his house. He got up unconsciously, went outside holding a pen without its cap and walked toward Radish-head's mother. Her wailing grew louder; she told him to catch her, return her to her house. Tahun asked in alarm, "Who? Who is she?" The old woman said, "The traitress, the bitch!" Tahun realized that she meant her own daughter-in-law and was relieved. He had a fleeting feeling of derision as he looked at the old woman, who had collapsed to the ground. But his scorn evaporated as he too suddenly found himself screaming like the old woman upon remembering that he had interrupted his writing of the 'In the name of God' formula. He was confused: Should he start again at the beginning or simply continue where he had left off? If he continued, should he perform his ablutions again? Who could counsel him in such a matter? He didn't know, nor did he know who it was who had written the instructions on the piece of paper. Should he beg Oweis or Sergeant Major Sallam, who had become the First Warner, to convey his dilemma to the sheikh? Perhaps that would cause the sheikh to be angry with him.

Tahun had been upset by that piece of paper from the outset. He went back to look at what he had written since he had forgotten how many times he had written it. He cursed Radish-head and his mother, blaming them rather than Farida or the spell. How could such a beautiful princess live with a man who had such a face? He tried to stop thinking, looked at the piece of paper, and leaned his elbows on the table, but his confusion grew.

Radish-head's mother was now crawling to the entrance of Zafarani, which stood on a slight rise in the ground, and there she wailed and babbled at the same time, cursing the traitress bitch, insulting her family and her ancestors, and asserting that the most important consideration when choosing a wife was her family, but her son had not cared in the least about his wife's family. He was attracted by her white flesh. She fooled him with a couple of tricks in bed and the poor man was lost. He didn't cheat on her and had never known any other woman all his life. He had had many chances and many women desired him, but this woman who had no roots had thrown away her blessings, ruined her home with her own hands. She was dirty, cleaned her house only once a month, the smell of her cooking was unappetizing, the smell of perspiration under her arms was so bad it it could choke you. She had never removed her body hair. She had taken her daughter with her; the young man who had seduced her would turn to her daughter as soon as he had had his fill of her. A man who married a child deserved all the consequences: her coyness and playing hard to get, his returning home every day to find no food cooked and dirty dishes all over the kitchen. He had to wash them himself and chop the onions and the garlic. When they walked together she would wink to the young men and the poor man wouldn't even notice. She had no respect for her mother or for her dead relatives, never once went to the cemetery during the Eid; she never gave alms for their souls   not a piaster, not even a cookie. All she was concerned about was finding men. The real pleasure for the likes of this whore came only in the arms of strangers. If she made sounds in the arms of her husband it would just be a ploy to get some money or spend the summer in a resort. Only God knew what happened when she bared her body in front of hundreds of young men. Everything was topsy turvy in these dark days when a woman's femininity would be complete only when she bared everything for men other than her husband. In her young days and in her old days *she* had never dared to look at a stranger. Before she shook hands with any man she would wrap her hands in her shawl for fear of undoing his ablution. Now the time had come when a woman would ruin her home with her own hands.

Radish-head was shaking his mother's shoulders, trying to make her stop; his eyes were bulging and there was a thin line of saliva flowing from the left side of his mouth. Fear was engulfing him little by little, a fear he had never known before. He looked around; Atif the college graduate was watching him. He seemed to have just come back from work; he was silent. Ali the ironer went to Radish-head, saying he had seen his wife going out with her daughter and that they had three suitcases with them. He said he had thought of stopping them but he couldn't: what right did he have to interfere in people's affairs? She would come back when relief arrived from India. Radish-head looked impassively at the ironer, noticing the triangular opening that revealed a large part of his chest, and part of the silk vest he was wearing. He remembered the rumors about his coming home drunk every night. He remembered a scene in a film where the hero asks the heroine, "Would you like to drink whisky?" His woman was looking at a glass in the stranger's hand and was whispering coyly, "No, I am afraid to."

He noticed a crack in the wall facing him and remembered a family that lived in the same building, a pious man called Hagg Bayyumi who owned a paint store in Rashidi Alley. His wife, Sitt Na'ima, was one of the best-liked ladies in Zafarani. He always saw her looking out of her small window, her head covered with a white shawl. Her son Fadil was always seen carrying his books and had recently added to them a long wooden ruler. When he had graduated from the College of Engineering two years before, he had insisted that the family move to another house. Radish-head met Hagg Bayyumi, who was now more advanced in years. He looked clean, without dye or lime stains, his clothes exuding a nice fragrance. He said that Fadil had insisted he retire and rest. He had sold the store and now did nothing but go from the mosque to the house and from the house to the mosque. As for Fadil, he was working in Saudi Arabia and next year would send them an invitation to go on the pilgrimage to Mecca.

Radish-head asked which way they had gone, and Ali the ironer pointed to the street leading to the square. The ironer hid his surprise at the very serious manner in which Radish-head had asked about the direction, as if he believed this would restore the runaways to him. Suddenly, however, Radish-head rushed back into Zafarani, stumbling, behaving as if an invisible man was controlling his movements. He opened the door of his apartment and went directly to the big safe, feeling its handle; everything was in its place except for the armoire whose doors were wide open. The perfume bottles had disappeared from the top of the dresser. He remembered a bottle in the shape of a woman raising her hand, holding a bouquet of flowers in their natural colors, despite their tiny size, with the perfume coming out from the middle of the bouquet. The section for his clothes in the armoire was open and completely empty; the drawers of the small desk, inlaid with mother-of-pearl, were all open and the drawer in the middle was broken: he felt it, pushed the latch with his hand. Its repair would cost a pound and involve a short errand to Khan al-Khalili; this kind of lock required a skillful locksmith. He made a tour of the apartment; except for those things, everything else was in its place. Why had she taken his clothes? he wondered. Who would cook for him? Wash his clothes? Who could he trust to come into his house? For a long time he had objected to having a maid. His mother was an old woman who could not do his chores, although she got up every day at dawn, took a cold shower even in the dead of winter, washed her own clothes, cooked her own food, and was always aware of everything around her. She spent all her time combing her hair, raising chicks and ducklings to sell to a woman who sat in Umm al-Ghulam market.

Time was passing slowly and the light was fading. Farida must now be in the house that had been her destination. Two announcements were made but he didn't pay any attention. The big clock in the cold hall chimed six times, time for the collective supper. He didn't move. His face was calm and, had it not been for that thread of saliva, it would have appeared normal. A breeze wafted through the window and he remembered the rustling of her clothes as she passed near him, her mockery, the way she jumped sometimes to sit on his lap, the way she bit his neck. In the early days of their marriage she would wake him up if she wanted to go to the bathroom, asking him to wait for her in the hall. Strangely enough he didn't think of Nashwa; when he saw her photo, he quickly averted his face. He didn't want to see her; had it not been for her, Farida wouldn't have gone. Nashwa was the one who knew her way to the English teacher. A few days ago, Farida had shouted at him saying she was tired of him and would run away and go to the handsome young teacher. He hadn't paid any attention, thinking she was just teasing.

The pendulum of the clock swung back and forth in empty time. He bent over the edge of the desk inlaid with mother-of-pearl, contorted himself, then straightened up. He would look for the teacher, become acquainted with him, make him the gift of a can filled with hexagonal two-piaster silver coins, telling him that the value shouldn't be measured by the number of coins but rather by the weight of the silver they contained. It was an obsolete coin and the jewelers were collecting it, smelting it, and using it in jewelry. He would also give him a rare antique from the warehouse: an antique sword once owned by one of the Muslim Indian sultans; its handle and sheath were inlaid with emeralds, turquoise, and sapphires. He would make him the gift of a Spanish bull fighter's outfit made in the sixteenth century and would explain their value to him; he would tell him that antique dealers had offered him huge sums of money for both objects, but that he had refused to part with them. It was enough, for him, to sit in front of them and visualize the sultan and the bull fighter: how each had fought against his enemies. Would the teacher turn down these gifts? Would he give up Farida?

Another kind of certainty had been growing upon him slowly; ever since his marriage to Farida he had been expecting this. He had been certain that one day she would betray him and fall in love with someone else and leave. He had tried to postpone it as long as possible. He had heaped money on her, satisfied her sexually—until the spell came. Was it his fault? Farida had run away; the deferred anxiety was over, anticipation was gone. The time for missing her, which he had expected for so long, had now begun. Because he had been imagining it for so long, he didn't find it strange now, it was as if he had lived these moments before. He saw the day on which Farida would die; she would be carried away in a coffin covered with a beautiful colored fabric. He would pray for her soul; he would cry, but he would finally be relieved.

Excerpt from a Report Submitted to the Supreme Committee for the Monitoring of Zafarani Affairs

. . . and indeed a good pious man, famous for his miraculous feats, residing in Qift in the province of Qena was summoned, and he prepared a spell for the protection of those working in the information media, especially radio and television, so that the sheikh would not threaten them and blackmail them into using the government-owned media to disseminate his Zafarani principles. On the other hand, it was established that a number of inhabitants, mentioned hereinafter, were responsible for what happened:

- Rummana, the communist, who is hiding in Zafarani to evade police surveillance;
- Luli, known for his religious fanaticism, informed on by his own father;
- A mysterious general about whom conflicting reports have

been made; it is possible that he is an agent of a foreign power that advocates subversive principles, and that he has somehow been dropped into Zafarani;

- An Indian agent, disguised as an ironer.
- The activities of all these men are being coordinated by the sheikh who is making all this noise. Steps are being taken.

Arrogance

Sergeant Major Sallam now stood for long periods of time on his balcony. A sudden vigor had overtaken him, and he no longer shouted at his wife or made a fuss about his new circumstances. On the contrary, if one of the inhabitants complained or committed an infraction, he was the first to give the warning, and in most cases would offer advice and try to calm people down. The people of Zafarani now knew him by his new title, 'The First Warner.' The sheikh said he was going to choose seven 'warners' from among all humankind. He told the sergeant major that what was happening in Zafarani was only the beginning: the Alif, the Fatiha, the first gasp, the first scream. In the very near future, perhaps, he was going to assign to his First Warner tasks that went beyond the country's borders: everything in its time and season; a little later, when his branches had drunk of the water of knowledge and wisdom, he would leave. Several things about the sergeant major had changed since he met the sheikh. For many years he had not mixed with the people and never allowed his wife to visit her neighbors. If she went out to buy some vegetables or to visit al-Hussein Mosque, he would fix a time for her to be back. When she did go out, his loneliness weighed upon him; he would pace up and down, impatient for her return; he would go and look out from the balcony in hope of seeing her as soon as she arrived. His face would cloud over and he would chide her, accusing her of being late on purpose. He would talk about old women

274

who looked with covetous eyes at young men fit to be their sons. Since the spell had been imposed on the alley, however, his wife hadn't gone out at all. After he came back from the meeting with the sheikh, he reminded her of the dream he had had three times—how the crown prince had come to him, held his hand, taken his arm, walked with him in the garden saying, "We miss your food, Sallam." When he described the dream, he felt her silently accusing him of lying. She assured him that she had done no such thing. But he closed his eyes and said he was sure she had thought he was being untruthful, yet time was proving him right; the sheikh had called him, had sat with him for seven hours. He wouldn't tell her what the sheikh had told him, but she must rearrange the house because he was going to be receiving a number of the alley's inhabitants. When they came, she was to do nothing but close the door and leave him alone with them; she shouldn't disturb them by coming in. He was going to convey to them gems of precious wisdom—a task that could not be compared with what that Oweis boy was doing. Oweis was just a crier; his loud voice and the strength of his vocal chords were his only qualifications for the job. The mere act of comparing the two was an insult to Sergeant Major Sallam. He frowned and asked: Did she mean to insult him? His wife assured him that she didn't.

He thought about this, and despite repeatedly having said that he had no intention of revealing any details about his meeting with the sheikh, that night, before they went to bed, he told his wife about the sheikh's room, the smell of incense that permeated it even though he had not seen any incense burner with live coals, of the sheikh's voice and how it came from behind a brown partition but sounded as if it came from above, from below, and from all corners of the room. It had been awe inspiring, but he was used to sitting with great men, which made him more capable of handling awe.

Three days later, Oweis announced that Tahun, al-Bannan, Atif, and Daturi had to go to the First Warner and advised them not to be late. Sallam turned to his wife and said that the time had come when the alley would realize his worth. Oweis did not mention his own name among those invited because he was the crier. The truth is, nobody much cared whether Oweis came or not. Oweis himself was never impressed by being with Atif the college graduate or Tahun in the same meeting. Nobody really knew Tahun's exact job; his wife said that he was the engineer of a deluxe train, but the women, during quarrels, taunted his wife about her husband, the stoker of engines. Oweis didn't care. Nothing mattered to him now. He would often run into one of the inhabitants after delivering an announcement but would not stop to talk. He just gave the Zafarani greeting, "Time to flee." He no longer cared to talk even with the head officer of the police station. The huge city that had dazzled him at the beginning was now much smaller; all he saw of it was that strip between the sheikh's room and his own. He, in particular, was not permitted to leave Zafarani. He had succumbed to a strange condition: he would go to the sheikh, then walk down the alley slowly, making his announcements. Now he quickly absorbed whatever was dictated to him. He would go to his room, eat his collective meal and, still in his room, watch the houses, the faces, and the light disappearing. He recalled images of his life both near and far, as if it all had nothing to do with him, as if the person making the announcements or walking along or going to meet the sheikh was someone different from himself. Sometimes he would even look at the movement of his arms or legs, or his fingers as they held the plate of food, and he would imagine that these appendages belonged to somebody else. He often woke up from his tired, intermittent daytime sleep and looked at his body as if he was seeing himself in a dream where he could see his eyes, his head, and the back of his neck. When he got up he would feel no desire to meet the new day. As for food, it all tasted the same. He was not eating to enjoy food but simply to fill a gap that had to be filled.

He remembered faraway days that belonged to a man he no longer knew. His life in Zafarani was just one day repeated many times over. There was no room for dreams or hopes. If he did return to his village he would be renounced by all who saw him. "The city has polluted him," they would say. It had stripped him of everything without giving him a safe place to sleep or good food to eat. He no longer even felt sad when he remembered giving up on his dream to own a pushcart or a white cart decorated with pictures of flowers, faces of smiling women, women wearing melayas, a nightingale, and the name of God. At the beginning he thought that following the sheikh would be the best way to realize his dream, but little by little he began to stop dreaming. He remembered sadly how as a child he had sat in the train station in the town he went to on market days, anxiously awaiting the passing of the fast train, whose gray cars blurred into a single line and whose wheels shook the earth. After the last car had passed, the noise came to an end, just as if it had never existed.

He tried to recall the days before he had come to Zafarani, Abul Ghait's café, the me'allim's questions about the village streets, its palm trees, its every brick. He was beginning to forget what it looked like, but he never gave up on his dream to go back one day, to look for a good bride who would return with him to the city; he would ask around, choose, select. How happy the bride! All her friends would envy her; she was going to live in Cairo and visit all the members of the Prophet's family, and the sheikhs and the saints, and she was going to return to the village once or twice every year, wearing a melaya like the women of Cairo, with a veil and a clasp on her face. Oweis might even allow her to paint her lips all kinds of colors. He could imagine them now grooming her and making her clothes and running hither and thither getting her

277

this, getting her that, preparing the henna. They were secretly envious despite the joy they displayed. Oweis himself was sitting, wearing a white galabiya and a white turban, smoking cigarettes and talking about the big buildings, the bridges, the streetcars, the women of Cairo and how loose they were and how, if he had given in to them, he would have been lost; which was why he had decided to come back to his village to choose a good wife who would share his life and fix his clothes and his food.

A sharp, cruel grief gripped him now: He had never wanted to own a store or a café or a boat on the Nile or to work in trade or as a messenger in the government. All he had wanted was enough to avoid the humiliation of depending on others, to guarantee his bread today and tomorrow. What had obstructed him? Who had done this to him? What hatred he bore toward someone he didn't even know! Who? Yet as the days passed, the pain no longer mattered. What could matter when each moment was like every other? Time brought nothing new. Deep inside he had a strong conviction: everything would stay the same; no change would ever come; he would never see his village again or own a cart.

Tahun looked silently at his neighbors. He didn't know what the title 'First Warner' meant. Sergeant Major Sallam had not yet begun to speak. Not one of those present had entered his house before except to calm him down as he threatened to shoot himself. Tahun wished he could convey to the sheikh how upset he was about what had happened to him. He now spent most of his time away from home. At work he wished he could hide from everybody. The Zafarani affair was well known across the country. One of his colleagues said our country was peculiar in that many things were widespread and common knowledge to both young and old alike, yet they were totally ignored by the press. Tahun trembled; he wished he could disappear from his colleague's sight. The desire to hide was getting stronger. Two days ago he had wished to drop down a manhole when he heard two men jesting with each other on the street and one of them had said to the other, "Oh you Zafaranite!" One of the messengers at work yelled at the cafeteria worker, saying that he walked as softly as a Zafaranite.

Tahun had requested several times to be referred to the department's physician to get a leave of absence, but each time the doctor ordered him back to work. The whispering around him increased: someone wished him speedy recovery even though it was impossible; on several occasions, co-workers came into his office for no reason whatsoever accompanied by strangers who wanted to have a look at the Zafarani man. A visitor once came to see one of his colleagues, who then invited him to see the man from Zafarani. The visitor stood in front of Tahun, expressing sorrow and saying in a loud voice, "Only God has power . . . yet the man has a beard!"

Tahun was even more resentful after his repeated failure to write the 'In the Name of God' formula a thousand times. He did not quarrel with his wife when she returned; he talked to her. She didn't mock him, but begged him not to wear her down, because he lit a fire inside her then left her alone. He smiled a smile that she thought had something behind it; he embraced her and fondled her breasts, but nothing restored life to the wasteland. He turned on his back as her breathing became a hiss and she said in a hoarse voice that pained his heart, "Calm me! Relieve me!" He spent the night away from her. Now he wished he could ask First Warner Sallam to convey to the sheikh his resentment and his question: How long was it going to last?

The First Warner welcomed his guests. He said he was going to talk to them about higher matters. Those present had no inkling who he really was, even though he had been their neighbor for many years, but people like himself who were used to performing difficult tasks that could be done only by the select few were usually hidden away from prying eyes until a certain moment arrived. Few among the inhabitants knew that he had spent decades preparing food for kings and princes. Time, which left nothing untouched, had changed and altered things in such a way that he was brought to Zafarani. And because he only undertook large deeds, he was chosen by the sheikh to convey to them what he wanted. The sheikh wanted good for humanity and loved the whole world. Each person in Zafarani thought the sheikh was doing something bad, but, if they were to think on the matter a little more profoundly, if they were open to what his strong vision revealed, they would know that what appeared like calamity was at its core boundless good, benevolence, and righteousness. The people of Zafarani would be distinguished forever because they were the first to follow the teachings of the sheikh. The sheikh had studied the affairs of the caliphs, the annals of nations, the lives of the great, and the stories of the ancients and all their legacies and books. He had delved deep into religions and creeds, absorbed sects and cults, examined the reasons for wars, famines, catastrophes, and maladies of the human spirit. The sheikh said unto the people of Zafarani, "Let each of you look at himself! When he is born, his infant imagination has desires and dreams; it teems with images. Everyone has at some time looked forward to becoming a great person, changing and altering things. Some were confident that one day they would become kings or famous physicians. As time went on, their hopes grew smaller, their wishes became more modest, their dreams contracted. The person who has had these hopes will himself at a certain stage in his life wonder in disbelief: Did I once hope to become a chief or a leader or an engineer or a pilot? How foolish I must have been!"

The First Warner was silent for some moments. He looked at them with his narrow eyes, perhaps to ascertain the effect of his words or to remember what the sheikh had told him. Atif was looking at an old picture of the sergeant major hanging on the opposite wall in an ornamental wooden frame inlaid with ivory and mother-of-pearl. There was little resemblance between the picture and the old man sitting before them. A man's very features were subject to change—his physical features. How then could the non-physical, intangible, and invisible escape it? Atif wondered: Was he himself going to live forty more years? What would he look like then? If he read Rahma's obituary in a newspaper sometime far in the future, would it fail to elicit any feeling of sadness from him? Maybe he would meet her relatively soon—in five or six years—pushing a small carriage with an adorable baby boy in it, and not be moved or stirred. Forty years, thirty, ten? What an illusion it all was! Had he ever imagined, ten years ago, what was happening to Zafarani now? At the same moment, ten years ago, parallel with the one he was experiencing now, had it crossed his mind that he would be sitting with men like these, each aware of the other's problem, all brought together by impotence and a man whose own awareness of his surroundings was doubtful, conveying teachings to them? He was speaking very arrogantly. Nobody knew when the present conditions would end. According to what this dried-up old man was saying, the condition in Zafarani would expand to include other parts of the world. Did that mean that things would continue as they were now, or would the nightmare here end as it moved somewhere else? Nobody knew.

Atif remembered Hamdi the reporter now waiting for him at Daturi's café. Atif liked him, but it wasn't the same as what he felt for his friends. For years he had seen them every day: Nabil, Abdel Rahman, and Farid. They had stayed up together, roamed the city streets together at night. He had consulted them about his most intimate affairs. He hid nothing from Nabil. It was Nabil to whom he confided his joy at his first meeting with Rahma. And when she had told him she loved him for the first time, his happiness had reached its height. He had bought a bottle of brandy, they clinked their glasses, and he had talked a long time. He had wished then to tell his friend everything that was in his heart and on his mind. He spoke of his childhood, of his classmates from elementary school to college, and about this tender girl who whispered when she spoke, as if looking far into the future. She was his classmate in college. He raised his glass: he had asked Nabil to drink to the health of her smile, which had so long perplexed him. He now sent her warm greetings where she was living these days, in the Hague. He had never seen the city, but it seemed to him that it was a tender capital, like the girl—its streets whispering to each other, the roofs of its buildings touching. He had spoken of his mother, of the feminine shyness that stayed with her until she died at the age of seventy. He hadn't thought opening his heart was enough; he had wanted to show Nabil everything connected with himself. He took out his wallet and showed him what it contained: a little pocket calendar, a train ticket, a piece of paper with telephone numbers on it, a picture of Rahma on which was written, "to my only love in the world, now and forever, Atif."

He was on the point of smiling now: "forever" had lasted a few months. That night he hadn't stopped talking until morning. His friend had listened to him. He told him about Rahma, about her habits, the rhythm of her speech. That late night their friendship had seemed eternal, everlasting. After every night out with his friends, he used to talk to her about them, about their evenings in the café, their group songs, their jokes, what each of them said after he got drunk. Her eyes would gleam; she wanted to share their freedom, to see the birth of sudden wishes. He had promised to set aside one evening every week for her to spend with him and his friends. He had made her live others' lives more than his own. She knew their habits, their temperaments better than she knew his. When they met he spoke to her of others. She would ask him: How is Farid doing? Did Nabil get his clothes from the tailor? Did he pay his overdue telephone bill? Did he get the new refrigerator?

He tried to introduce her to Nabil, his closest friend. He told himself that as she came to know Nabil, she would know part of his own personality, since his friends were, at that time, natural extensions of himself. He couldn't remember which day it was that, when they met up, Rahma had told him Nabil had called and asked how she was doing. She said he seemed to be gentle. At that moment he was all enthusiasm. That same day he called Nabil and begged him to keep calling her; when Nabil talked with her it was as if he himself had done so. He didn't remember, now, at what point he had begun to worry. When did he begin to wonder: Was it Nabil who called Rahma or the other way around? He didn't know when he had discovered that she didn't know as much about himself as she knew about the others, especially Nabil. Even his emotional attachments—she knew all their details. He had made himself into a bridge without knowing it. Did anyone love as he had? He had loved the walls, the streets, the trees, the stores, and the houses among which his acquaintances and friends moved. Then what happened happened, and now the sheikh was talking about all-embracing, captivating love. What kind of love was that?

Atif felt irritated to be sitting there, but there was something that compelled him to follow all the teachings of the sheikh. Rhode did not require anything of him. She never explicitly gave voice to that desire that her womanhood so loudly proclaimed. What she wanted was to be next to him. He grew accustomed to her company, but he was disturbed by her body clinging to his. As he smelled it, felt its softness, and felt the life within it, he tried: perhaps a miracle would result or an exception be granted; perhaps the spell would forget him for one night or one hour. His kisses would glow and burn. He would cling to her, but eventually he would realize that it was no use. His energy would be gone but she wouldn't calm down; then she would awaken to the reality of the alley and her voice would clear of the choking desire and she would whisper that all she wanted was to be near him. Silence would shroud them. Atif would imagine himself standing before her, naked apart from the leather belt from which dangled that black gun with the sharply contoured handle, a little red circle centered on each side and a pyramid-shaped piece of incendiary over its barrel. This would make him appear mysterious; men who wore guns were rare.

The First Warner was ending his presentation, suggesting that each perspective released by the sheikh be memorized. There was still a while before the compulsory bedtime, but Atif had no desire to go home; Rhode was washing his clothes right now, sitting there with her arousing knees whose lusciousness made him ache. Al-Bannan was waiting for him outside the house; Atif no longer liked talking to others, but he had taken pity on the old man, who had produced a letter and begged Atif to read it to him. The letter had arrived that morning and he couldn't find anyone to read him the words that he couldn't decipher for himself. If he went out on the streets, young and old would flee his presence because he was an afflicted Zafaranite.

Atif looked at the rectangular envelope with its multicolored edges. It had four stamps, three of which were the same, each bearing the head of a woman with a beautiful neck who looked on with dignity. The fourth had a bouquet of flowers held up by a hand, though he couldn't tell whether it belonged to a man or a woman. He could not immediately make out the words, although the numbers indicating the value were quite clear. They were neither in English or French. Perhaps the stamps came from a country to which Rahma was moving right now. Perhaps she had sent her family a letter with just such stamps as these, after having moistened each little piece of paper with her tongue.

She most certainly did that. His heart was gripped with pain, an old sickness revived by flashing reminders.

He began to read the letter, written on light, transparent paper. The son had written from a port whose name he didn't mention, but which was at the other end of the world. Night would fall there as the people of Zafarani were getting up. He was all right, was working on a Greek ship. Some months ago he had sent them twenty pounds sterling, a piece of fabric, a coat, and dates stuffed with almonds. He begged them not to worry about him. They could write to him at the address of the headquarters of the company in Athens, where he would be arriving four months after the date on the letter. Atif stopped reading to say this meant that he would arrive in Athens two months from now, adding that the letter was late.

Al-Bannan said he had been quite worried about his son these last few weeks, especially since the mailman had stopped coming after what had happened to Zafarani, so he had decided to go to the main post office on al-Azhar Street. There he found all Zafarani's mail put to one side, and the head of the office, after telling him to stand at a distance from the barrier separating the employees from the public, threw the letter to him as if he were kicking a ball into goal. The old man looked quite upset as he asked Atif if he knew anyone at the post office who could help him find the parcel that had never been delivered. Atif thought for a few moments; he didn't know anyone, but he would try; perhaps he would succeed. Al-Bannan said that whenever he heard about his son's visit to some country, it was as if he himself had been there and seen it with his own eyes. The whole thing puzzled Atif: When the son had played in this alley and shared his parents' poor room, had it ever crossed their minds that he was going to travel around the world as a sailor? The strangers who saw him in every port, the women he slept with, the customers of the taverns he went to on land, all of those people: did any of them place him in Zafarani? Could anyone in the whole world even dream that a woman like Rhode existed? All she wanted was to be near him—her greatest hope was just to go out with him and sit beside him on the grass, in the sun. How many women in the world were like her? He extended his hand to shake the old man's.

He was sure that al-Bannan would also stop someone else and ask him to read the letter aloud as well. Yet here he now was, hoping that his son would not return home until the calamities were over. For years he had been hoping to see his son, but now and with the same tongue and heart he was fervently wishing him not to come. He was at a loss how to tell him what was happening. Could a letter do his son any harm? Perhaps he would think that something bad had happened to his parents; he would hurry back, his feet would touch Zafarani, and the catastrophe would follow.

Atif approached Daturi's café. He made his way toward Hamdi the reporter, thinking that he would be bound to have acquaintances in the postal service. He had a desire to build bridges with Hamdi. The distance had shrunk, but caution was still holding him back. Ten minutes after they began talking, Atif felt a strong urge to leave and be by himself again. In the midst of the crowds he laughed at the masses who surrounded him in the thousands yet couldn't reach him. He looked at them from inside a closed glass case with invisible walls. After several meetings with the reporter, he felt sure that Hamdi's interest in Zafarani affairs wasn't purely professional. He didn't detect in him that indifference which made a journalist treat all matters in the same detached, uncaring spirit.

He told the reporter that the First Warner had held a meeting with a number of inhabitants, during which he conveyed some of the sheikh's thoughts. Hamdi replied that he would be interested to know those thoughts, unless the sheikh had banned their dissemination. Atif looked at his watch; time itself was subject to the spell, chained. There were still three and a half hours before bedtime. He could go back to that store in an hour and look at the gun. He told Hamdi that he understood the sheikh to desire the establishment of peace and equality. Hamdi was interested. Atif remembered how he used to rush headlong into his relationships with his friends, as if he were seeing himself in a faded picture like that of First Warner Sallam, imprisoned in that wooden frame inlaid with mother-of-pearl. Atif said that the sheikh saw humanity's desire for equality, for an end to war, for everybody rising above narrow self-interest, for the first to be like the last—but none of this had been achieved, despite the succession of generations and the rhetoric of every leader or thinker who expressed a sincere desire to bring it about. Every generation would say, "Things are going to be better in the future!" But nothing changed for the better. True, there were some changes, some adjustments, but they were changes in form and not in substance. He gave the example of wars, people becoming accustomed to famines, and the persistence of poverty. He spoke of the soul and its suffering and how many matters were not yet resolved, how many desires were not yet fulfilled, and how many wishes were not yet realized. He spoke of a pamphlet containing one of the sheikh's 'perspectives' with the title: "Guide for the Perplexed to Knowing Mankind," which he planned to distribute some time in the future. Atif said the sheikh had spent many years preparing his spell; that what had happened in Zafarani was only the beginning; that he was going to expand the spell to cover the whole world, and then he would be able to achieve what history could not.

Hamdi was interested. He said, "The press has to start alerting people to the danger. What happens if the sheikh dies before he undoes the spell? What does science say about such a phenomenon? Does the sheikh depend on invisible or visible powers to carry out his plans? Or does he depend on the power of suggestion?" Atif was skeptical about the latter, since cases of impotence had appeared prior to anyone ever having heard of the spell. He said that the sheikh would issue a new calendar so that, in the distant future, he could unify all the different calendars in all the different countries. This calendar would begin on the day the spell had been cast on Zafarani. Its days, months, and years would be divided up according to the steps taken toward the realization of everything mankind had ever dreamed of.

Hamdi laughed: So they would find themselves in a world ruled by a spell? Atif said this meant an impotent world, and through that impotence the sheikh would rearrange things. Hamdi asked: Had Atif seen the sheikh? He said he never had, as the sheikh had been in seclusion. He didn't go initially to complain about his affliction, and when he went later on he heard a strong voice, but didn't see the sheikh because the curtain dividing the room kept him out of sight.

From a chair opposite, Daturi watched them, his hands clasped over his belly. Some passersby stopped to point at him and at Atif. Atif didn't care, he felt so certain that he would one day see them all Zafaranized when the sheikh's will was done. Hamdi asked how he was doing. Should he tell the reporter about the gun that he had decided to buy? Should he tell him how much he missed Rahma? Should he tell him about that old faded photo of First Warner Sallam? Instead he said, "Nothing out of the ordinary." Hamdi said without any preliminaries that he had received a postcard from his ex-wife. Atif was interested. How? What did she say? He stopped the torrent of questions as suddenly as he had begun it.

Hamdi said that the postcard was very beautiful, that it was made of magnificent paper the likes of which he had never seen before, that it was almost sky blue, with slim green branches painted on it. Each branch had a thin white line in the middle. She had written one line to say she was thinking of him and that she had liked the postcard, so she had sent it to him. She didn't include an address, perhaps because she didn't want a one-sided conversation to start; perhaps she desired no dialogue at all, and it was just the flutter of a passing memory that had made her send the postcard. He said that the postcard was like the beats of the meseherati's tabla in the night, but that he didn't attach too much value to it. He knew that she wasn't going to come back to him, and even if she were to knock on his door one day, would he find her the same person? Would she find him the same?

Atif smiled. Zafarani's real-life meseherati was living a tragedy right now. His wife had fallen in love with her daughter's teacher and gone to meet him. Apparently she was the only Zafarani woman who hadn't come back disappointed, and there were even rumors that she was happy. Every day, Radish-head stood on the balcony watching the entrance of Zafarani as if awaiting her return. He would often stand there in his underwear oblivious to the women of the neighborhood. Some people had heard him speaking loudly to himself. It was said that he would take off all his clothes in his apartment, look at his body, his thin legs and protruding ribs, and be overcome with tremendous sorrow for himself, kissing his own body and whimpering, and wailing like a child, "Don't grieve, Radish-head. Don't be sad, Radish-head," calling himself by the name that he had refused to hear for many years.

Hamdi said that when his own wife left, he had fallen silent. He hadn't made any attempt to convince her to change her mind, except when he went into her room the first night they started sleeping apart. That Hamdi's wife had left him seemed strange to Atif. Travel played a curious role in the lives of lovers. It brought about sadness in any case; it was the last stage in the process of separation. Would the day come when he loved a woman, then left her, making her suffer because of him? He asked, "Don't you want to travel?" Hamdi asked back, "To her?" Atif shook his head. He meant travel for its own sake. He longed to travel. He saw himself stopping in harbors and airports. The travelers would be looking in surprise and admiration at the gun he was wearing; he wasn't going to part with it; he wouldn't put it in his suitcase, but would wear it, even as he slept in mountain hotels or when he went to a quiet, elegant restaurant.

Hamdi said that what he wanted would surprise Atif: he wished he could meet the sheikh and listen to him. Sometimes it seemed to him that the sheikh did not exist at all, that the people of Zafarani had been the victims of a mysterious hoax, by a force unknown. Atif pulled a face and didn't answer. He wanted to leave. Hamdi took out a pen and a piece of paper, perhaps he was writing some of what Atif had said about the sheikh's teachings, or jotting down some remarks.

Daturi was watching Atif. That college graduate effendi must have understood the teachings of the sheikh better than he himself had done. What he heard sounded like the prelude to a catastrophe. What did it mean to place the whole world under the spell? That would turn the order of the universe upside down. Yesterday Daturi had realized something that perturbed him a lot. He wasn't worried because he had very few customers or because the shop owners had stopped ordering drinks from his café. He had enough savings to face hard times. His needs were limited and he had never had any special habits, even though he had spent all his life in cafés. What really hurt him was his discovery that four days had passed without his thinking in the least about the apartment building, not because of the scarcity of customers or because the brokers had stopped visiting him, but because until four days ago he had thought about the building most when he was alone. And despite spending more and more time by himself in these Zafarani days, he had not once thought of the building, had not imagined the materials he would need for its construction, had made no mathematical calculations in his head to arrive at the cost of steel and cement. He had stopped visualizing what would take place between him and the Rent Assessment Committee. Worse still, he had forgotten the names of those to whom he had decided to rent apartments. Some time ago he had asked himself: Would people agree to live in a building owned by a man from Zafarani? Wouldn't they be afraid of falling under the spell? Wouldn't they be afraid of losing their ability? He convinced himself that the housing shortage would make them accept. Besides, there was no explicit stipulation that the spell was contagious in that way. His heart trembled: Had he also forgotten what the building looked like? He had decided after much consultation to make the entrance big and wide, to use rose-colored marble for the floors and the walls, to place marble seats on the staircase landings so that the elderly and the weary could rest as they went up the stairs. He had forgotten the color of the exterior paint, even though this should be left until the very end. These days tenants frequently moved in while the building was still raw red brick or while the scaffolding was still up. But he had decided not to let any tenants move into an apartment before everything had been completed.

What grieved him now was that he had forgotten the color of the paint. The color of the friezes had also totally vanished from his mind. He twirled his fingers around each other as he tried to remember, but to no avail. He wished somebody would come and sit with him. If only one of those people who used to beg him to reserve an apartment for them would come now, so he could talk to them! For the first time, he asked himself: Was he really going to build the apartment building? Was the money he had saved, or intended to save, enough, even if he were to sell the café? Could he now meet the construction costs, which had gone up so exorbitantly? Daturi didn't know what had come over him. Should he take a practical step and buy the land tomorrow? All it would take was a short tour with the brokers and then he could make his selection. He had no conditions except that it be located in the old neighborhood. He could tear down the café and sell it, provided that he leave a big space for a modern café on the ground floor of the apartment building, with many tables, a television set so that the patrons might watch the soccer games and Thursday night movies, and a special corner for chess players. He would also ask somebody who might be going to Lebanon to get him a tape recorder on which to play Umm Kulthum songs. But he would lose a great deal of money if he tore down the café and sold it; the price he could get per meter would drop because he was a Zafarani man. He could always find a buyer—somebody who would think it was a bargain to buy it cheaply now and, after Zafarani had returned to normal, watch the price go up. But the color of the paint: had he forgotten it so easily?

Daturi saw al-Bannan walking slowly, carrying an envelope. He had asked many people to read the letter. Daturi was suddenly moved; he almost cried, visualizing al-Bannan's son sailing all over the world, his father hearing his news from only one or two letters a year. There was a great hole in Daturi's heart. If only he had married and had a son, his son would have been an architect by now. He would have become his best adviser on matters of construction and would have supervised the plans personally. Daturi sat wondering: Never before had he felt the need to be a father. He loved children, played with them, gave them piasters on Eid days; the young men of Zafarani still remembered Daturi's gifts of money from when they were children. He never saw himself as a father. In spirit he was more akin to children; he almost disregarded matters of dignity and played with the boys as they passed in front of the café, shouting, kicking a ball, and exchanging insults. He followed what they were doing with contentment, his feelings remaining hidden behind his friendly face. Now, for the first time he felt the need for a child. A strange fear overtook him and an overpowering sadness almost made him cry. This morning he had met Usta Abdu, Sitt Busayna's husband. He had come back to Zafarani after his wife had disappeared. Daturi asked him about her.

Usta Abdu said she was running through the streets, attempting to escape from death, afraid to sleep lest death should overtake her. She had met several people and told them that she was going to flee from death to Giza, and if she felt it was still after her she would disappear in Minya, in Qena, in Aswan, and if she gave up on her escape in Egypt she would hide in Sudan or Hijaz, but she was not going to die, she was not going to allow death to stop her breathing. Usta Abdu said that as she ran she looked back behind her every minute. He had tried to convince her to go back to Zafarani, but she got away from him.

Daturi's sadness was compounded. He remembered Busayna's evenings: how she would invite all her friends over every Thursday, and the sound of clapping, the playing of the oud and qanun at her house, and the sound of her singing. He was sad over the café, now deserted by its original regular patrons, and over al-Bannan going around with his son's letter; sad over the old waiter who tied himself to the destiny of the me'allim and the café, no family, no shelter, stretching out on the bench at night and then getting up before six in the morning to light the fire and sprinkle water on the floor; sad over Radish-head deserted by his wife after such a long time together; sad over Atif who had left the café a few moments ago, leaving behind this inquisitive journalist; sad over that arrogance newly acquired by First Warner Sallam; sad over Hasan Anwar, the good man from a good family who never left his balcony now, dressed in a military uniform; sad over his son Samir who had run away from home and whose address or whereabouts nobody knew. He was sad over the wasted years of his life; he hadn't married, didn't touch drugs, didn't indulge in pleasures, didn't experience joy, didn't accompany Diyab the paper-merchant and Zanhuri and Ba'issa in their nocturnal outings, singing, listening to music, smoking hashish. Silent tears were flowing down his cheeks as Ali the ironer approached, staggering drunk, raising his hands and shouting that relief was coming from India, relief would come from India.

An Urgent Report Submitted to the Supreme Committee for the Monitoring of Zafarani Affairs

The strenuous efforts exerted by security men, all branches, have resulted in the recruitment of one Zafarani male in return for the promise of a speedy recovery. Thus it can be said that Zafarani is finally no longer a closed area. We have faced several difficulties because of the inhabitants' strong belief that the sheikh knows everything they do and thus can do them harm. But after intensive efforts we were successful in recruiting this Zafarani man.

This development has also made it feasible for us to study the man's physiological condition. We have had him examined by more than one specialist to determine what kind of impotence he suffers from and how it can be reversed. We have submitted the reports of the physicians, who conducted very thorough tests on this Zafarani male, to the Supreme Supervisor of Health Affairs. It has been established that a unique condition actually exists. It can be summarized as follows:

1) Inability to achieve an erection;
2) Semen completely disappeared;
3) Reproductive organ intact—neither inflammation nor disease.

Because of the uniqueness of the case, the doctors have named it "Zafarani impotence syndrome," and a complete medical team is now studying it. This Zafarani inhabitant has provided us with invaluable information, which we outline below:

- The sheikh is putting forth certain thoughts by means of which he aims not only to undermine order in our society, but to destroy all human order.
- The sheikh claims that the human mind is still in a primitive phase and that despite the achievements of science it is still backward, that the important factors which determine human destiny are non-rational and incomprehensible. He uses war as an example, saying that mankind has been dreaming of eradicating war, but that human memory is short and therefore wars break out anew. He says Cain and Abel are still alive.
- He uses the example of justice. He says justice is a relative concept changing according to different systems, that it is nothing but an opiate of which humanity has dreamed since the dawn of its existence. But has it been realized? Anyone looking at the current state of the human condition will see that bringing about justice is impossible. It is no good for a thinker or theorist simply calling for justice. This is, moreover, one of the things that proves the futility of the human mind and its shortsightedness. People are born equal, but then differences emerge; to each person a path is plotted out as a result of circumstances over which he or she has no control. Humans are easily convinced by circumstances, to the extent that they accept even the most blatant aberrations as normal: thousands starve to death, while many others die of overeating; skyscrapers rise high and tin huts sink low; justice is something that can be achieved only by an extraordinary act, an act that strikes human consciousness and causes it to face a danger threatening existence and eternity. In a case such as this, the goal can be reached.

These are some of the general ideas that we obtained from the Zafarani man. Due to the gravity of the matter, we have seen fit to deal with it in strictest confidence. It has come to our attention that a member of our Legitimately Elected Assembly has decided to pose a question in the Assembly to the Supreme Official in Charge of Human Resources concerning what is happening in Zafarani and the vicious rumors being spread at home and abroad. It has further come to our attention that this member, elected from the old neighborhood, intends, should the requested response not be clear, to call for the creation of a fact-finding committee to uncover the facts about Zafarani affairs.

Remarks written on above report:

- Consolidate secret police force around alley;
- Concentrate on surveillance of former political prisoner Rummana and suspect Luli; make sure that neither has any connection with a foreign power;
- Contact Supreme Head of Legitimately Elected Assembly and prevent any discussion of Zafarani in Assembly.

An Attempt to Save the Situation

From our Military Correspondent:

Chief Hasan Anwar has devoted a great deal of attention to what has been happening on the central front as the sheikh amassed his troops for an offensive and aimed a major blow by warning the people of Zafarani through his First Adviser for Intellectual Affairs, Marshal Sallam. The warning implies that the condition will persist until a near but indefinite date. Sayyid Abul Mu'ati has sent a third ultimatum to the Chief and Leader, stipulating that he be fired for good from the Department. Meanwhile, the Chief himself has gone this morning to the field command post on the central front, where several ruthless, savage battles are taking place.

A Press Cable

It has been learned that more than one attempt has been made on the Chief's life. The most notable of these took place as he was moving from the main command post on the balcony overlooking the battlefield in Zafarani to the small window in the room adjacent to the hall, which houses the fortified field command post. Following this, Marshal Hassan, Chief of Staff, pursued the assassination squads.

Confidential Order

Push shock troops under Marshal Attila to the depths of enemy.

Defeats Begin

Hassan's efforts and those of his mother were not successful in stopping the children from provoking Hasan Anwar. His standing there day after day tempted them to engage him, especially when he loudly reprimanded the commanders who committed acts of negligence. Yesterday some children began watching him from the opposite roof. One of them threw a stone at him, hitting him on the shoulder. He shouted, "Where is Himmler?" He was not afraid of assassination attempts, he had to be a role model for his men; the least cowardice that he betrayed would be reflected directly on all the troops in all the battlefields. The photographs taken of him by the news agencies and the newspapers must show self-control and strength, no matter how trying the circumstances. Hassan had had to go himself to the families of the children, but that proved useless. It seems that the children, in harassing Hasan Anwar, had discovered a source of entertainment that made up for the loss of their previous forms of recreation after it proved difficult to visit other alleys or takes trips to the desert or to old mosques. Besides, their parents or guardians had kept them at home in view of the harassment they faced at school, which reached such a point that a group of pupils had held down Yusif, son of Tahun, and removed all his clothes to see whether he looked like them or was different as a result of the spell.

Hasan Anwar summoned his son and asked him to stay by his side all day. Hassan was irritated; he wouldn't be able to stick around all day long. Hasan Anwar was surprised; he had given an order and had to be obeyed. Hassan was capable of going along with his father for a very long time; sometimes he would take part in reviewing the minutest details to do with the progress of the battles. He got excited and expressed interest, but it hadn't occurred to him to stay with his father the whole time; he had to keep up with his studies and look for his brother. He wouldn't be able to go to Rummana.

Time for Rummana passed faster than he had imagined it would. When he had been Hassan's age, thirty had seemed quite far off. He had been preoccupied with his work and with evading the police; then came the long years of detention. All of that had prevented him from forming any real relationships. He didn't regret it, but that was one of the main factors depriving him of the right to choose a wife and settle down. The older one got, the fewer chances were available, not only in marriage but in everything. Sometimes when he was feeling down he thought that everything he had worked for was lost.

When he went to jail for the first time a friend of his had come and told him, in a whisper, not to talk more than was necessary or give away information, because some of the inmates were working for the management and informed on everything that took place in the open wards to help with the investigations. Rummana hid his surprise: How could there be somebody working for the authorities among the comrades? The thought of it gave him several sleepless nights. Later he learned how a man could change from one extreme to the other. It was easy enough to say that people changed, but it was horrible to watch them after the change and the fall. Rummana was silent for a moment. He said there was no limit to man's capacity for change. This was often painful. He saw many turn their backs on the movement and when he objected to the dissolution of the party they informed on him. But getting to know Hassan was quite a consolation. Hassan's meetings with Rummana had meanwhile become essential to him, as had those times when he went out into the rough terrain nearby and sat on a stone, or went to a small café frequented only by truckers.

Hassan was irritated with his father. He made a point of picking the right pretexts for refusing his father's requests. During the last few days the Chief had felt an emptiness: his massive troops, led by the greatest commanders of history, the bravest, couldn't inflict painful losses upon his adversaries. Abul Mu'ati was still mounting one assault after another, sending letter after letter. In an admittedly smart move, Abul Mu'ati had blocked the Chief's main supply route by cutting off his monthly salary. As for the sheikh, he too was tightening his grip. But worst of all was his son Samir's collaboration with the enemy. He only trusted Hassan; that was why he had summoned him and asked him to remain close by. He said he was not shaken by the recent changes in the situation. He was going to mount concentrated offensives against the Abdel Azim al-Gawahiri front, the owner of the opposite house, and the Chief of Personnel. All Hassan had to do was assume his responsibilities.

Hassan said that he was loyal to his father and his Chief, but that he couldn't carry out this last command in view of many things that had to be done. Hasan Anwar sprang to his feet; he shouted in a trembling voice, "This is an order!" Hassan had become more and more irritable lately. At first he had thought that his father was going through something temporary that would end in two or three days, but since then he had watched as his father traveled farther and farther down a road from which there was no return. He remembered what had happened before they went to bed the night before; it had made him weep. He had never expected to see his father in such a state. It was easy to hear of so-and-so's insanity, but to see that in the person closest to him was unbearable. He couldn't take it any more, so he got up and went out. Had he stayed one more moment he would have broken down again and wept.

He didn't know where to go. Sit a little at Daturi's café? Go for a walk out in rough terrain? But Zafarani bedtime was approaching. He went upstairs to Rummana's room.

At home his mother rushed into the room when she heard a rattling sound; she saw her husband's face rigid, his lips trembling, and heard muffled sounds coming from him—sounds that the ear couldn't exactly place or identify as either human or animal. His soul was deeply wounded. Several loud voices were demanding that he surrender. Here was his Chief of Staff, his eldest son, deserting him in his most critical hour. The hostile broadcasting services would repeat it and his men would be demoralized. His lieutenants would run away. Rommel had committed suicide by taking poison after the failure of his desert offensives. Genghis Khan had been captured. Goering's planes were falling like flies. His soul was shaking. Should he do what other great leaders had done in such circumstances, and aim his last bullet at his own head? But he had to fall standing up, and suicide was an escape. He would have the courage to surrender. He shook his wife to stop her crying and make her face with him the destiny of a great commander.

Special File

Revolution

Over the last few days, Oweis the baker had conveyed several instructions from the sheikh to the people of Zafarani. Some of these sounded mysterious, and others seemed disturbing even though the inhabitants had become accustomed to a number of measures that had gradually changed their lives. Yesterday Oweis had announced that the sheikh intended to reorganize Zafarani's affairs; each inhabitant was to prepare to leave his house for another lodging. On the same day, Sallam the First Warner held a meeting to which he invited a limited number of Zafarani people: Atif, Hassan, Daturi, Ahmad the carpenter, and al-Bannan. He said that very soon he would give them the good news, for in a short while, in just a few hours, they would find themselves part of a whole; the people of Zafarani would occupy the most prominent place in the world. It was not only to share this news, however, that he had invited them to this meeting; he also wished to convey to them some lofty ideas.

He talked at length about the currents and paths of human life, and how some of these diverged from what man really wanted. What the sheikh desired was to grant mankind the freedom of choice. He recited texts and read out lines revolving around the right to make new choices. Before the meeting ended, he asked Atif to communicate to Hasan Effendi Anwar the sheikh's anger at his failure to attend the three meetings to which he had been invited.

Atif left and headed for Hasan Effendi's house. He was fairly familiar with his condition, having observed him in the alley and seen him standing on the balcony wearing an old military uniform. Atif was aware that he was taking part in strange goings-on in Zafarani. He had passed through a mysterious phase and didn't know what awaited him. This was why he was feeling dejected. Hasan Effendi's wife opened the door, her eyes swollen from crying, her shoulders bent as if a weight was pressing them down. It seemed to him that there was a momentary gleam in her eye when she saw him. She asked him to wait a few moments while she told her husband, who said that he didn't mind meeting Atif. She was overjoyed, whispering that this was the first time in a long while that her husband had agreed to receive a guest. His condition had worsened over the last three days, but she hoped this visit could help him somewhat.

Hasan Effendi stayed sitting as he received his guest. Atif's heart sank; he could see that the man was unraveling. Hasan Effendi was leaning forward on the edge of his chair, his uniform unbuttoned, his shoelaces undone, his fingers stretched out on a galvanized steel table, his beard unshaven, and the floor covered with sheets of paper, maps, pencils, and colored pens. He got up slowly and looked at Atif so submissively that it seemed to Atif that it would just take the smallest movement of his finger to push him this way or that. Hasan Effendi said in a faint voice that he accepted everything; all he begged from the gentle delegate was a guarantee that he would be treated properly.

Atif was dumbfounded. The sight of his neighbor made him deeply sad. A life that had proceeded normally for many years was collapsing and deviating from its natural course to follow difficult paths in uncharted terrain. At that moment, Rahma appeared to him, distant, blurred. He tried to recall her features. Rhode then appeared with her kindly face and her modest wishes and her loving submission. He didn't know why he now suddenly recalled walking one night near a green kiosk. Two youths had suddenly rushed over to bend down by the ground next to the kiosk, their laughter getting louder and their mirth ringing. They had stretched out their hands toward a man sleeping on a blanket. Atif could only make out the man with difficulty as he screamed in utter misery; he felt overpowering sympathy for him.

Life appeared to him strange and incomprehensible; what happened to him or to Hasan Effendi, who had once been held up as an example of cool-headed thoughtfulness, was utterly unbelievable. He said that many people sent their greetings to the good man. Hasan Effendi snapped that he wasn't going to accept any pity, that he had agreed to hear out the conditions for surrender only to protect the lives of his loyal troops, that he wanted the sheikh and Sayyid Abul Mu'ati to know that. Atif heard someone crying softly: the woman whispered, "We are finished; our house is ruined!" Atif asked her about Hassan, and she replied that he only returned at the compulsory bedtime, that he spent all day with Rummana the politico. She begged Atif to ask Rummana to let their son go—he was the only son they had left. Atif said he would, but hoped Hasan Effendi would attend the meetings called by the sheikh. Once again Hasan Effendi shouted that while he might be defeated, he would remain standing and would never fall to his knees.

Atif descended the stairs slowly; he left Zafarani. He didn't think about how much time remained before bedtime. He crossed the crowded streets to the weapons store; he had been there many times during the last few days. He had stopped in front of the little gun seven times on one day. As a child, as he lay in bed watching the walls, the lamp, and the chairs, he had thought that inanimate things could hear and see, and so he could have a silent talk with the tables and the walls. He was sure the gun knew him, was appealing to him to end his reluctance, to wear it and show it off proudly. Yesterday Rhode had lain down next to him, bent toward him, kissed him, passed her hand over his hair. When she felt his anxiety she embraced him and asked him to hold her close, preventing him from an attempt that would inevitably fail and lead to resentment. She whispered her news to him; her sister no longer threatened or hassled her—not because of the spell but because of her relationship with Atif, because she now had a man around whom her attention revolved. She said that as she was hanging the wash out to dry, an old towel fell on their neighbor Khadija, the Sa'idi woman. Had this happened in ordinary times Khadija would have shouted and raised hell. She was very fond of quarrels and watching fights; she rewarded any child by giving him half a piaster or a piece of candy if he told her that a quarrel was going on outside Zafarani. Then she would wrap her melaya around her, leave the food on the stove, and hurry to find a good spot to watch the quarrel. Umm Suhair claimed that Khadija the Sa'idi woman would be sick if several days passed without a quarrel to watch. Rhode said that when Khadija quarreled, she typically reverted to her own dialect and refrained from hurling insults or obscenities. She usually screamed loudly, addressing herself, calling herself names and saying her luck was perverse for making her deal with so-and-so or live under so-and-so or buy things from so-and-so. Rhode said that she was quite annoying with her endless screaming, but that a single sentence could make her stop: if anyone said she had come to Zafarani from behind the water buffalo, meaning that she was an uncouth villager, who didn't belong in the rarefied city. The length of her strange quarrels gave the macaroni vendor a chance. . . .

Atif asked in surprise, "Who is that?" Rhode narrowed her eyes as if to ask: Do you really not know? He denied any knowledge of her identity, so Rhode admitted it was Nabila the schoolmistress, daughter of the drunkard. She cooked a big pot of macaroni every day and stuffed loaves of bread with it and sold the 'sandwiches' to the pupils at her school against their will. Umm Suhair had figured out her secret when she suspected Nabila of loitering on her balcony whenever Umm Suhair's husband went out onto their balcony opposite. Umm Suhair made the insinuation loudly when she addressed one of the kids down in the alley by describing his mother as a macaroni vendor, whereupon Nabila immediately went inside for fear of Umm Suhair's tongue. Usually Nabila used Khadija the Sa'idi woman's quarrels as an opportunity to flaunt her university education, asking her to stop shouting so she could study. Rhode's voice was calm as she said that she frequently noticed Nabila standing there, watching Atif or calling loudly to her sister to buy her some notebooks for her university lectures, or chiding street vendors when they came into Zafarani to lower their voices because she couldn't study her university subjects. Rhode said she had noticed Nabila's glances, so much so that she often wanted to reach out and push Atif back into his apartment, to keep him away from Nabila.

Atif had listened in surprise. He couldn't imagine himself as the object of female jealousy, especially after the rejections he had suffered. Oh how close Rhode had become to him! How beautiful, kind, and sweet! The pores of his soul opened to her as she lowered her eyes in shyness before his. Did she realize what was going on in his mind at this moment? He had decided to ask her to marry him. He wanted to ask her to share his life, but the words had stuck in his throat. Would his desire to own the gun remain forever latent?

Atif looked at the metal body. He stepped inside the store; a short husky man was talking to an old lady. He appeared to be an Armenian or Greek who had lived in the country for some time. Atif examined the diving masks, the shotguns, a small motor for light boats, the picture of a handsomely dressed man in a hunting outfit and a big hat, with one eye closed and the other open, aiming his rifle at some target outside the frame of the photograph. "Yes, sir?" Atif was startled; he smiled quickly saying he wanted to inquire about the price of the little gun. The man asked, "The Browning?" Atif went outside to the window and pointed at it. The man removed the wooden back cover and nodded. Atif came back into the store. The gun was looking at him through its narrow barrel. The man offered him the gun. Atif was about to flinch; he was frightened, and wanted the metal body to be pointed away from him. He swallowed hard as he took the gun. The metal body filled his hand; it was heavier than he had imagined. He aimed it, then returned it quickly to the man and asked how much it was. The man asked, "When are you planning to . . . ?" And, having determined that the customer was just asking and would not buy at once, he said curtly, "Forty pounds."

Atif left quickly. If he spent forty pounds, he would deplete his savings by almost a fifth. After Rahma left he had begun spending without restraint, without control. He could buy the gun; he could buy a wide leather belt. The people of Zafarani would see it. He would aim it every now and then at some empty spot. He would go to a remote spot and shoot at the rocks. He would clean it every week. He would certainly get a little pamphlet explaining how to use it and how to clean it. But . . . "Atif dies as he cleans his piece." "Man sleepwalks on seven-story ledge." "Atif shoots himself in his sleep." "Strange accident: Victim so full of ideas that he acts in his sleep." "The truth is that he got up while he was sleeping—he is a sleepwalker—calmly took out the gun, aimed it at his own head . . . ." Rhode was crying, looking at his body, the pooling blood destroying her hopes of a pleasant outing together, of sitting next to him in a park overlooking the Nile.

He was walking quickly now; he was half an hour late for bed. Strangely enough, he was neither afraid nor confused. He actually had a desire to stand right in the middle of Zafarani and shout. He didn't know what he wanted or what he might say, but he was going to make a noise. The people of Zafarani would gather around him; they would understand. He didn't possess what he desired because he was afraid of it. Had the sheikh cast a special spell that had made him incapable of buying a gun? He went to a small café near Zafarani, ordered a cup of fenugreek, and felt pity for a man wearing a galabiya stained with lime and dye. Rhode appeared to him: Should he tell her what he had thought the day before? Should he ask her to marry him? Should he bend down, kiss her, cry, and propose? The first marriage in Zafarani! Hamdi would be happy with this piece of news.

How far away Rahma was now! Of one thing he was certain: she would never mention his name, no matter what she heard about him. She would hide her interest so that Nabil would not notice, because she was anxious not to upset him. How would she know he had bought a gun? Even if she met him by chance, would she stop and talk to him? Would she ever have a chance to see the gun he was wearing? He was full of sorrow; he searched his soul to find some justification for his inability to buy the gun.

Atif got up. He didn't want to sit down. He didn't want to walk. He didn't want to go home. He didn't want to stay away from Rhode. He was afraid of being close to her. There were now fewer passersby, lighter traffic. How would the sheikh know that he had arrived home late? Daturi's café was closed. A faint electric lamp gave off a pale light. He imagined that he saw shadows moving in the dark corners. All the houses were closed. He remembered winter and the cobblestones shining in the rain beneath the light of the single lamp and the little patch of sky that was visible between the houses, which stood close to each other and were tired and old. Would the people of Zafarani gossip about what would happen to him because he had deviated from the instructions? He was overcome by a strong feeling that somebody was watching him, following him, which he couldn't shake off until he was well inside his apartment. He even opened the doors to each of the three rooms, looked under the bed, spun around more than once to catch whatever was following him. On the bed he saw a slip Rhode had left behind. He wished he could see her now. He smelled the slip, the particular scent of her body. Did he hear footsteps in Zafarani? Had the sheikh assigned some of his followers to make the rounds, or were these the normal sounds of the place? Two years ago he had gone to Alexandria, seeking calm and quiet. He had borrowed a colleague's apartment, and when he returned there the first evening he heard whispering voices, then a sudden shout, the sound of heels hitting the floor tiles, a strong exhaling, the rustling of clothes, the whistling of a train. On the following night he realized that these were the sounds of the place: the wind passing through the openings of the house or the sounds of vehicles on a nearby street.

In the silence of Zafarani, all of that was being rearranged. The apartment was lit, anyone looking at it from the alley could see it. For the first time since the era of the spell had begun, lights were burning in a Zafarani house past bedtime. Atif Effendi did not take off his clothes immediately; he was more and more convinced that he had to go to Umm Sabri's house now and bring Rhode back with him so they could spend the night together.

Nabila the schoolmistress was watching Atif's apartment from the window of her room. She pulled the shutters to, closed them and turned on the light. She was filled with a mixture of irritation, disgust, and sorrow. For days now she had been asking herself: What now? She was approaching twenty-six, and nothing she had done, nothing she had forced herself to do had borne any fruit, had led to anything. Before she was twenty she had suppressed her feelings for Shaarawi, owner of the herb shop. She didn't pay him any attention or respond to his calm glances, though they used to release currents of warm water under her skin. She knew the way all eyes watched a girl. She in particular was being watched more closely because of her father's reputation as an alcoholic toward the end of his life. He had left no café or house without stopping in front of it and shouting, demanding that people understand what was in his heart. When a suitor came for her after she obtained her secondary school certificate, she turned him down. Her mother said, "Nabila will finish college and will not marry now." She thought a B.A. would be her ticket to a better marriage and a young man who would take her out of Zafarani. But there were lots of university girls around. Her numerous, cautious efforts had failed to attract the attention of the one bachelor college graduate, who made no effort to hide his relationship with that fallen woman, Rhode. She didn't understand these men. When she was seventeen, she had said a man would take her in his arms when she was eighteen; when she was twenty-one, she had said it would happen when she was twenty-three. Whenever she came upon glasses or towels or spoons, she would buy them for her future home. But so far, no man had proposed to her, no man had taken her in his arms; she had never been kissed, never embraced. When, then?

She closed the door to her room, stuffing newspaper in the keyhole so her younger brother would not look through it. After a short pause in front of the wardrobe mirror, she stuck out her tongue several times; she began to walk, sway, swing her hips. She whispered, "Turn off the light." Moments passed; she whispered again, "I am not going to take off my clothes in the light." She clicked her tongue, making the sound of the light being switched off. She whispered in feminine coyness, "Be gentle." She took off her slip slowly, bending backward and forward, to the right and to the left. She heard steps approaching, two arms circling her waist.

"I asked you to wait," she says weakly. She turns around, undoes her bra, looks at her breasts, sends them flying kisses. "No, wait." She discards the last piece of clothing and goes to the bed, which she had moved some time ago to face the mirror. She climbs onto the bed, and crouches there on all fours. She looks at her buttocks through the gap between her thighs. Suddenly she flips onto her back—"Don't be so rough"— she makes her fingers caress her back . . . she makes short, muffled noises. She looks at the mirror; she is alone drowning in the cold light of the room, her hair disheveled, panting, biting the edge of the pillow. Till when? Until when, then? She is not concerned that she is late for bed. Grief is breaking her heart. She bites the pillow and cries.

❖

Hasan Effendi had not yet left his balcony. His wife's pleas were to no avail. He now saw the siege closing in tighter and tighter around him. The last phase was Hassan's desertion. But he no longer greatly cared about his elder son or where he spent his days or who his friends were. His thoughts in these last two days had turned entirely on the ideal way to effect his surrender. He had decided to surrender to save the lives of thousands of his troops. At the same time, he decided not to take his own life; millions of hearts were attached to him and believed in his ability to rid them of the sheikh, Sayyid Abul Mu'ati, and their allies. At a certain moment, somewhere a call would be made and the scattered remnants of his army would rise from the four corners of the earth. That was why he had decided to surrender under the best possible conditions.

Now he was wearing his full uniform, with all the medals and decorations. This morning he had told his wife to take care of his papers and not to hand them over to anyone. She asked him where he was planning to go. He said she would learn everything soon. She tried to stop him, but he forcibly pushed her aside. Thus it was that that morning, Zafarani witnessed a strange spectacle as Hasan Anwar walked through the alley, wearing his old military uniform, looking at the women staring from their balconies and giving them a military salute. The sight of him tempted a number of Zafarani children to chase him and throw stones. He ignored the pain and kept walking.

As he passed Daturi's café some strangers tried to argue with him. His heart trembled when he thought he saw his son Hassan. A few moments later he was certain that his son was looking at him from the midst of a group that had gathered to watch him. The passersby around the mosque considered him one of the newly possessed who covered their chests with medals and bottle caps. But he would not stop on his chosen path, even if Samir himself were to appear, kiss his hand, and announce that he would continue his studies until he graduated as an engineer the way his father had once hoped he would.

Hasan Effendi decided not to stop. And like the great commanders who, when they were going through grave and decisive moments in their lives—which were also of great import for thousands and millions— remembered little details of their private lives, he recalled with sadness how he and his two sons used to go to the mosque on the mornings of Eid days. On their way back they would stop to shake hands with neighbors and friends. They used to stop in front of Radish-head's store; on those occasions, he used to bring toys and balloons out of his warehouse and sell them. How far away it all seemed now!

The messengers looked at Hasan Effendi with great surprise as he entered the Department. He went to the office of Sayyid Abul Mu'ati's assistant and asked to see the bey immediately. The assistant looked at him in silence. He crossed the room to the door covered with green felt. He didn't wait long. He must have told the bey about Hasan Effendi's appearance and aroused his curiosity. When Hasan Effendi entered the office he saw three men, one of whom looked Japanese or Chinese. Sayyid Bey said he had interrupted a meeting to see him. Hasan Effendi was certain that the men in the office had come especially to watch this final scene. Abul Mu'ati smiled; he looked at his strange uniform, said something to his guests in English. Hasan Anwar was going through the most excruciating time, but true courage revealed itself in the enduring moments of defeat. He took off his sword, took it to Abul Mu'ati and said, "I surrender to you." Sayyid Bey pushed a button and asked the secretary to call the chief security officer. After a few moments, he arrived. Hasan Anwar began to breathe the air of captivity. He bade farewell to a familiar past to begin an unknown future. Perhaps he would be given the death sentence. The chief security officer called two of his men; when they grabbed his arms, he insisted on maintaining his dignity in these, his last moments. He refused to be manhandled; he would go in any direction they wanted. He remembered that Napoleon in St. Helena never bowed his head; even when they built a low door in the route he took every day, as he approached the door he bent his legs a little, thus passing through with his head held high.

The news of Hasan Anwar's arrival in his strange outfit spread among the employees. Some of the old employees who had been his colleagues for years were alarmed; others saw it as a break in the monotony of their day. The older employees gathered in Abdel Azim Effendi's office. Each expressed an opinion, but they were unanimous that some of them must intercede with Sayyid Bey to have pity on their sick colleague and take him home. One of them said that he might commit acts that posed a danger to society. Another said he looked quite docile and peaceful, that what had befallen him was the result of what was taking place in Zafarani. They were unanimous in delegating Abdel Azim Effendi because of his efficiency. And indeed the man did not fail them: he walked in confidence, his body leaning backwards, his belly protruding in a manner that his colleagues remembered noticing only once before—the day a telephone was installed in his office. He never revealed what took place between him and Sayyid Bey, but before entering the security office he turned to his colleagues saying, "I swear by God that Sayyid Bey is irreplaceable."

A special car was dispatched to give Hasan Anwar a ride home. He was accompanied by Abdel Azim Effendi and two employees from the technical division. From the window, it seemed to Hasan Effendi that his son Samir was walking on the sidewalk or riding in a car coming from the opposite direction. If only Samir would come close to him, that would rekindle his fatherly feelings. Samir's running away had been the first sign of treason, the first step toward the end to which he had finally been driven and the humiliation of being accompanied by Abdel Azim Effendi rather than Abul Mu'ati himself. He blamed Director of Intelligence Himmler and Rommel, because they hadn't carried out their mission with the dispatch necessary to allow Hassan to graduate as a medical doctor and Samir as an engineer.

In front of his café, Daturi did not hide his tears. He had lived to see the day when people described Hasan Anwar, his neighbor of a lifetime, as "not dangerous," as if he were an animal who was harmless if kept as a pet. Silently he accompanied his friend into the café and turned to the crowd. The old waiter understood what he wanted and shouted at the crowd to disperse; there was no need for scandals.

Hasan Anwar observed his surroundings. So, they had chosen Daturi's café for his prison? He tried to remember any commander who had suffered a similar fate, but couldn't. It was really an end that wouldn't occur even to the most vindictive individual! Several people looked on; a young man stopped, took a small camera from his pocket, and pressed a button several times. The waiter brought him a tray with a demitasse of coffee. He refused to receive any affected show of attention lest it be used for propaganda purposes against him. These simpletons; they wanted to publish photographs of him as if he were an ordinary prisoner of war being given a glass of water.

Before Daturi could say anything, Hasan Anwar said he had agreed to everything they wanted and of course although he couldn't impose his conditions, he still demanded proper treatment and a fair trial. Daturi motioned him to sit down. He said the whole neighborhood knew Hasan Bey as a decent man who made no trouble and hardly any noise. Daturi's words irritated him: to strip him of his titles and call him simply "Hasan Bey," that was all right; but to say that he lived without making trouble or noise, that was a falsification of history! So they had begun to distort the facts already? Was it a virtue for a man to live without making trouble or noise? They were beginning to insult him; this was something he had to suffer.

Daturi said he hoped Hasan Effendi would go with him, that whatever he wished would be done without delay. He raised his eyebrows: What end were they plotting for him? He shouted at Daturi to shut up and stepped outside. The old waiter caught up with him; several people crowded around him and someone tried to touch him, others shoved and pushed. Hasan Anwar unsheathed his sword and brandished it at the crowd, then began to run. A boy threw a stone at him and a man yelled at the boy. Hasan Effendi entered Zafarani, still running. He refused to talk to his wife or leave his room. His wife had not left the balcony since early evening.

Now he seemed to have decided on something; he crossed the hallway and carefully opened the door. He left Zafarani and went straight to the police station. He asked the guard, "Is the commander in?" The old government building came to life. That morning an order had been issued to arrest that Zafarani general who had left the alley after puzzling the security authorities for so long but, before the special task force could arrive to arrest him, he had re-entered Zafarani and now, here he was, in person. He was finally standing in front of the enemy's military commander, foiling the conspiracy of both Abul Mu'ati and the sheikh to treat him with contempt.

"Here I am. I surrender. I demand a fair trial."

He began by taking off his military uniform. His surrender must be decisive; later on, fair-minded historians would find an excuse for him; he did what he did out of a desire to end the unequal battles between his troops and their enemies. The officer asked his name. He didn't answer right away. One policeman slapped him on the back of the neck; another smiled as if it were a perfectly natural thing to do; they could do anything to him without risking an adverse reaction. Despite the cruelty of the insult he answered, "Retired Field Marshal, Supreme Commander of the Forces Allied against Injustice, Hasan Anwar."

The whole place erupted in laughter. He had taken off the jacket of his uniform and was now unbuttoning his trousers. The walls around him were blank, concealing things taking place behind them. He was stark naked. The officer was shouting into the telephone.

As the new Zafarani day began, Umm Hassan began to scream and cry without cease; she declared between her sobs that her house was ruined. Umm Yusif was shaking with fear. Tahun stopped chewing the food in his mouth. What was happening seemed terrible and no one in Zafarani was safe from it. During the last few days he hadn't stopped thinking about his project for digging a huge network of tunnels: Was it madness? He dismissed the idea; his project was perfectly realistic. He even thought of buying some big sheets of white paper on which to sketch out his plans. Hasan Effendi's wife would not stop wailing. Tahun whispered in fear, "God protect us." Umm Suhair sighed in pain, asking loudly, "What has happened to the world, to people, to

Zafarani?" She was outraged. The people of Zafarani noticed that she was hinting at what the sheikh had done, especially when she said that Zafarani had been quiet throughout its existence.

Nabila the schoolmistress stood calmly on her balcony. She hadn't slept at all the night before; she was dressed to go out, and in her hand she held the notebooks she had taken from her room as she went out, turning the pages randomly rather than keeping her finger on a specific page in order to give the inhabitants the impression that she was constantly busy, and had had to interrupt her reading or studying to come out on the balcony. She acted as though her mere appearance was a call for them to be silent. Today there were several reasons why she couldn't ask them to be quiet so she could study: the day was just beginning; the apparent confusion reflected a far more serious calamity; Atif was not yet on his balcony, and, most importantly, she was bored and felt that it was no use, that she had never behaved naturally but had always worn borrowed moods, never once her own.

Sitt Khadija could be heard crying loudly for the good man, the best of neighbors. Umm Sabri declared that there were not now and had never been any men in Zafarani, either before the spell or since. Everybody was listening, and gradually they realized that Zafarani was beginning to talk about the sheikh himself. Umm Sabri said that no man in Zafarani was worth anything. If they were, then why were they all silent? What more could happen to them? Umm Yusif answered her in agreement. She added that all Zafarani homes would be ruined, one after the other, while everybody looked on and no one did a thing, or uttered a single word of protest. Umm Yusif cried out, "Why don't they say something? Why?"

Tahun asked her to stop, but she paid no attention. He swore to divorce her if she didn't go inside. She pounded on the window in resentment, mocking him loudly: "Divorce? Hello Mr. Divorce!" Tahun felt as if some one had slapped him on the back of the neck, that he was completely passive and couldn't react. Hadn't his wife been late in coming home more than once without him asking her where she had been or him objecting to her lateness?

Hassan rushed to the police station: they told him that his father's condition was serious, that a special agent from the Ministry of Health had taken charge of him after determining that he was from Zafarani, to conduct necessary tests on him. He was also under the supervision of officers from the Security Authority. They advised Hassan not to resume his search or to try to see his father, as it would be difficult. Hassan was not convinced. He contacted Abdel Azim Effendi, who expressed alarm, saying he would talk to Sayyid Bey and ask him to intervene, even if things had become difficult now that the matter had reached higher official levels. Hassan called Abdu al-Burtuqani, who had become a member of parliament, but couldn't find him. He thought angrily: All these calamities began with the spell. He went back to the old neighborhood, exhausted and aching. He didn't know how he would handle his father's absence. He remembered sadly how he had been irritated with his father over the last two weeks and wished he had listened to him and stayed with him.

How would things have gone had the spell not affected Zafarani? All these calamities had come with it, and meanwhile the First Warner was still talking about the coming happiness and the justice that would be done. The strangest thing he talked about was the sheikh's love of the inhabitants, who would always be credited as pioneers in building the new, just world. What love? What justice was that? Should he go to the sheikh himself, tell him what had happened to his father, and ask him whether he liked that? But the sheikh was in seclusion and wouldn't meet anyone. There were even those who whispered that he wasn't actually in the room, that the voice the inhabitants had heard when they visited

317

the sheikh in the first days of the era of the spell, the voice Oweis and Sergeant Major Sallam heard now, didn't come from anywhere. Others said it was a conspiracy by Oweis and the sergeant major to take control of Zafarani, and that their next steps would be to extort protection money from the inhabitants and try to seize Radish-head's fortune.

Although Radish-head had heard these stories, he neither moved nor changed his posture, which people had recently become accustomed to: his head hanging down all the time, his saliva a constant stream. During the last few days, his mother had frequently been heard screaming. Three days ago, Radish-head had had a bad nightmare: he was about to choke but nobody awakened him. He thought of asking his mother to leave her room on the roof and come and share the apartment with him, but he was afraid that she might disturb him by getting up early in the morning and taking a cold shower, as she did even in the dead of winter.

Besides, she wouldn't leave him alone for a moment or give him a chance to think of Farida at all. Yesterday she had grabbed him as he was going out; nobody knew where she got the strength that enabled her to knock him down, punch him in the ribs, then put her hand in his pocket and take out five ten-pound notes. Then she began slapping her own face, screaming, calling on the people to come to her aid, to save that good-for-nothing spineless son of hers. She said the whore who had ruined her house and taken her daughters to live with her lover had had the gall to ask him for money just as she had had the gall to ask him for money in order to spend the summer in a resort. She held the money up, waving it about toward the windows and the balconies.

Khadija the Sa'idi woman, who had never seen fifty pounds in all her life, expressed shock. Umm Sabri declared that she was sorry for the men of these days. Actually, Radish-head was increasingly relieved that his wife and daughters had left. Sometimes there were moments

318

when he felt as if he had never married at all and had never had children. Her desertion and betrayal had been recurrent ideas and images in his mind throughout his marriage until they had now finally come true. There were, however, certain disturbing thoughts that upset him and developed alongside his feeling that he was well rid of them. He kept wondering where they were living. He imagined Farida looking at the teacher, not making fun of him, kissing him on the mouth, and whispering to him, "My darling." When she had an orgasm, the teacher would ask how Radish-head made love to her.

Radish-head was ashamed when he visualized the teacher making fun of him after hearing what had happened when the spell was cast. He now stopped going to get his Zafarani food regularly. When he stood in line after the way Zafarani people glanced at him, he wished the earth would open and swallow him up. Zannuba the divorcée whispered something to Qurqur. Radish-head was drenched in sweat. When he reached Luli, who was in charge of distributing breakfast that day, in accordance with the Zafarani rotational system, Luli said, "Don't get upset, Master Hussein." He raised his round eyes, murmured something and asked himself: Had any of what Farida was saying about him reached Zafarani, or Luli? He went home, carrying his plate, with uneven steps, wishing to hide himself as quickly as he could. Farida was bound to talk about him. He would make a gift of the sword and the bullfighter's outfit to the teacher, not to get his wife back, but to contradict her if she talked about the failure of her old husband. No. He would send her something. He had to silence her.

He thought of going to Oweis to beg him to tell the sheikh that shame now prevented him from sleeping, and to ask if he could cast a spell to stop Farida's mouth if she made fun of him to the teacher. He thought of writing a letter to his wife, reminding her of how he had treated her, how he had given her whatever she desired, given in to her strange whims. Then he decided to send her money regularly, hoping the teacher would not be able to keep up with her extravagant ways, or that he would ask her for money and she would have nobody to get it from except Radish-head. He would set only one condition: that she not make fun of him. So intense was his shame, however, that his heart nearly stopped whenever he imagined what she might say about him.

Just as Radish-head had been returning from his store the day before, a stranger had told him that Rummana the politico was the cause of all that had befallen Zafarani—that he had created a state of confusion so that he could "pounce on" society. That same night, a group of strangers met up with the inhabitants and repeated the same claim to them. But the people of Zafarani refused to accept it. Tahun shouted at the man who was speaking, telling him to shut up and stop sowing discord. He said Rummana was one of the bravest men in Zafarani. He had been about to say he was one of the most "manly," but he was too ashamed. In the alley, Basyuni, Luli's father, yelled again at his daughter-in-law more than once, telling her that Luli was responsible for what had happened in Zafarani. He kept trying to incite Atif, Tahun, Oweis, and Sallam against Luli, but nobody would believe him; they were indifferent. So he went to Daturi's café and wrote a new report about Luli's subversive activities. The people of Zafarani were not convinced; what had happened could not be attributed to one person alone. There were all sorts of other ideas in circulation about the ruin of Zafarani and how calamities were going to descend on people's lives.

When Hassan returned to the alley after visiting several acquaintances to see what could be done about his father, he was surprised to see Daturi's café crowded; he saw Tahun, al-Bannan, and Umm Sabri's son-in-law. They asked about his father, and he told them that everything would be cleared up within the next few days. He was quietly surprised at what he now saw and wondered whether new instructions had been issued permitting them to stay up beyond bedtime. Tahun said no such instructions had been issued on that point, but other instructions had been issued which no rational being could accept. If they remained silent much longer, all their homes would be ruined.

Hassan was exhausted, heavy of heart, and heavy of tongue, not knowing what he would do the next day or the day after. How was he going to find his way in that maze of departments, closed doors, cruel guards, hospital signs, and police stations? But what he now heard grabbed his attention, and little by little he began to comprehend the new developments that were taking place in Zafarani. The truth of the matter was that unusual activity had begun during the last part of the day, after the meeting that First Warner Sallam had had with a number of Zafarani people, and after the mid-afternoon announcement made by Oweis. They had all discussed the enigmatic texts that spoke of the chance to make new choices: the choice of a profession or life partner, hopes and capabilities, choosing one's ambitions anew, reviving hopes that had died. Then Oweis had announced that houses 1, 3, and 5 would be assigned to the men and boys of the alley, and houses 2, 6, and 8 to the women. At a specific time, each of them would exercise his or her right to make fresh choices. The inhabitants of Zafarani all went to their windows or out onto their balconies. Their collective reaction seemed to defy the approaching night, especially when Umm Suhair uttered her famous battle cry, "God is great!" and declared that she would not move one inch from her apartment and, if push came to shove, she would storm the room of that accursed sheikh. Let him do his worst! She was not afraid.

Radish-head rushed out. His mother appeared, stumbled, and in broken words declared, "He has gone to her." There followed a noise that Zafarani had not experienced since even before the spell, an uproar that occurred only in times of sudden drama, such as a husband beating

321

his wife at two o'clock in the morning, brandishing a knife in her face, threatening to cut her throat. On those occasions the wife would rush to the window and the people of Zafarani would wake up, asking what was going on. As soon as they found out, the wise among them would intervene by going to the house where the fight was taking place, and the husband would usually refuse at the beginning to open the door. Then from window to window, the neighbors would start talking to each other about things that had nothing to do with the quarrel. For a time indistinct voices would be heard, interspersed by a child's cries or odd words here and there, like individual beads in a rosary that had just broken apart. The present uproar in Zafarani was just like that kind of sudden awakening of the alley. It was accompanied by a number of people going outside. Tekirli, it was said, had appeared in front of Daturi's café, trying to incite people and stir them to action. His wife had apparently left him for a student whom she loved. Nobody knew how Zafarani got its news, but in most cases it got the truth. Zannuba the divorcée said she liked what Tekirli's wife had done and wished her happiness. When Tahun heard the news, he thought to himself that things clearly didn't change when someone from Zafarani simply moved out of the alley.

Khadija the Sa'idi woman sighed in sorrow: Where was Sitt Busayna now? Umm Sabri replied that she was running from town to town, afraid of death. She sighed again. As night fell the uproar grew louder. Rummana was seen leaning out of his window. It was said later that a mysterious smile never left his lips. One of the inhabitants of Zafarani must have conveyed this tidbit to the security people, since the official in charge of Suppressing Subversive Ideas wrote a memorandum in which he described how Rummana had leaned out in silence. He exaggerated the details that he attributed to "a certain source," perhaps to one of the inhabitants, or to stories heard by the plainclothes policemen in the old neighborhood, his purpose being to show his success in cultivating sources of his own in the alley on the one hand, and, on the other, to lay the lion's share of blame on Rummana.

At about 10:00 p.m., the people of Zafarani, who had now violated every one of the rules, saw Radish-head returning from outside the alley, creeping along on all fours and looking all around him. He stopped near the door of the warehouse and looked carefully about as the inhabitants held their breath. He removed the steel bar and then, after shutting the door with a clang, he disappeared. It seemed that his old mother was watching him or following him in close pursuit; she suddenly appeared outside the door of the warehouse, shrieking in shrill tones. But the door remained firmly shut. After a while her voice grew hoarse. She sat herself in front of the warehouse, placed the bag that hung from her neck down in front of her, shook her finger in the air, as if addressing someone standing before her, and said in a tearful voice, and a childish tone, "My heart gives me no comfort."

Report No. 1: Urgent; Submitted to the Supreme Committee for the Monitoring of Zafarani Affairs

. . . it has been reported that an insurrection has taken place in Zafarani. Secret forces spread across the old neighborhood have been promptly reinforced. All cafés have been ordered to stay open twenty-four hours a day, and foreign correspondents have been placed under surveillance to ensure that they do not approach the old neighborhood. The Bureau of Search and Camouflage is currently looking for reporter Hamdi Abbas, who began frequenting the neighborhood some time ago and was successful in establishing close connections with the people of Zafarani, but who has refused to cooperate with any security organization. The editor in chief of his newspaper has notified us that he is not responsible for reporter Hamdi Abbas's frequenting of the old neighborhood and that he has been considered absent without leave for four days. Our information indicates that there is no connection between the reporter and the leaking of Zafarani news abroad, feeding this international uproar. We hope the committee will approve the following measures that we, in our capacity as an authority responsible for Supreme Security, have decided to take:

- Address a public message to all the people of Zafarani, requesting that they storm the sheikh's room and arrest him alive;
- Ask them to get ready to vacate the alley altogether; the Governorate will relocate them in its housing facilities;
- Allocate a sum of money from our secret expense account to reward any inhabitant of Zafarani who takes part in securing and handing over the sheikh, the crier, and the First Warner.
- It should be noted that most Zafarani people are poor and, as such, the sum of one hundred Egyptian pounds will constitute a tremendous inducement, in addition to the promise of a cure for all Zafaranites.

Signed: Head of Supreme Security

News of a Youth Rally in Paris

A huge number of young people held a massive rally in the French capital. It seems the rally was held as an advance response to the rally that the followers and supporters of "le Zafaranisme" plan to hold tomorrow morning. Speaker after speaker denounced the charlatan from the East, all agreeing that humanity had reached a stage at which such ideas were unacceptable. For justice to prevail on earth and for conflicts and wars to end, a process of natural evolution, not suspect miracles, was needed.

Bloody clashes erupted when a large number of Zafaranistes who support the sheikh arrived. Meanwhile the daily *Le Grillon* commented in an editorial that European civilization had reached such a degree of high-tech industrialization that Europeans were now prepared to embrace any metaphysical or irrational cause whatsoever.

N.B.: This story, like all stories touching on Zafarani affairs from overseas, was not published.

Text of an Urgent Report from the Supervisor of Good Neighborly Relations and Permanent Friendships to the Chairman of the Supreme Committee for the Monitoring of Zafarani Affairs

Our permanent representative in Moscow has sent us an important report: The General Information Committee of the Soviet Communist Party has issued a statement published in the third column of the front page of *Pravda*. It seems that the statement had been circulated among the cadres of the Party before its publication. The statement referred to talk among the people about so-called Zafaranism and rumors that a spell would be cast worldwide as a prelude to changes that would ultimately lead to absolute equality. The statement summed up human attempts to create a world without class distinctions, until Karl Marx came to crystallize the theory of class conflict, when capitalist society had attained a certain degree of evolution. Marxism is the theoretical weapon of the working class as it wages the ultimate social struggle; this is the natural evolution. If attempts are made to accelerate the eradication of social and human conflict using metaphysical forces, they must be rejected from a scientific point of view. Only a continual struggle against the exploiting classes and for the building of socialism will succeed in eliminating social conflict. *Pravda* concludes the article— the first reaction by a socialist country—by saying that conflict will not be expunged by quick fixes or miracles, and that such a claim could only be made by the insane. Hence, the Soviet Communist Party will struggle ruthlessly against any propagation of Zafaranism.

Comment Inscribed by the Official in Charge of Suppressing Subversive Ideas on His Copy of the Report

We have to take what *Pravda* has written with a grain of salt. We do not consider it unlikely that the article is an attempt to cover up Rummana's role in the incidents occuring in Zafarani—a conclusion supported by all the indications, in particular his steady nerves, his remaining in his room, and the smile that has been referred to in the reports that have reached our attention. We must be careful.

Report No. 2: Very Urgent

As soon as the incidents to which we referred in previous reports had taken place in Zafarani, we reinforced the detail stationed in the old neighborhood. The special groups undertook to gather information, which can be summed up as follows:

- Up until the time this report was completed, there was no news about Radish-head; his mother was still in front of the warehouse, crying and repeating words we were unable to make out.

- There were cautious rumors in Zafarani to the effect that a stone found in front of Radish-head's house—a stone resembling a carrot or a radish—was none other than Radish-head transformed by the sheikh into a stone that could not speak, but was aware of everything taking place in its vicinity. This was taken to be a warning to the inhabitants that the sheikh was going to transform them all. Nonetheless, Ahmad the carpenter announced in a loud voice that he preferred transformation to his present condition. Then he went to the stone, looked at it briefly, and slapped it hard. Following this, a number of children from Zafarani gathered around the stone and began to slap and spit on it. It was reported that a moaning sound could be heard coming from the stone and that saliva began to flow from it. When people told Radish-head's mother that her son had been transformed into stone, she refused to believe it, pointed at the locked warehouse door, and said he was hiding in there and she was waiting for him to come out.

- Reports indicate that Atif Hasanain no longer lives alone. We do not mean Rhode, who has been his frequent visitor since the casting of the spell, but are here referring to the fact that a young man is staying with him. None of our sources could positively identify this person, who is considered to be the first stranger to enter Zafarani. It was also noticed that the said Atif does not try to hide his relationship with his neighbor Rhode. They were seen together this morning, holding hands as they went out. They were followed and seen entering Hurriya Gardens, where they sat on the grass in the sun and laughed, played together, and ate cheese, soft pretzels, and hard boiled eggs. Rhode poked the above-mentioned Atif three times in the chest, and he pinched her once on the arm.
- At ten in the morning, Tahun Gharib loudly exhorted the people to dig a number of tunnels leading to a space under the sheikh's room so that he might be attacked and the spell deactivated. Tahun said tunnels would solve all problems.
- Abdu al-Bannan and his wife made the round of all the cafés in the neighborhood, begging the patrons to prevent

their son from entering Zafarani, should they see him; he had sent them a letter informing them that he would soon be arriving. They have stationed themselves at the entrance to the alley to prevent their son from entering.

- Two hours ago, two persons entered the alley: an unbalanced man named Radwan and a cotton candy vendor. They announced that they were going stay in Zafarani, as the spell had already hit them.
- So far, First Warner Sallam has not taken any further action; nor has Oweis made his announcements on time.
- One of our task forces installed a loudspeaker through which they made several appeals to the inhabitants of Zafarani in a bid to strike while the iron was hot and utilize the agitation felt by the people. The appeals advised them to force their way into the sheikh's room, arrest him, and hand him over.
- Ahmad the carpenter loudly called upon the one person exempted by the sheikh from the spell's effect to step forward so that the people could regain their peace of mind and truth might prevail. This is a summary of the overall situation until 3:00 p.m.

Directive from the Supreme Authority Supervising Information:
It has come to our attention during the last twenty-four hours that stories concerning Zafarani affairs have been pouring in from around the world. The gag rule remains in effect.

Report No. 3: Extremely Urgent
Late in the afternoon, a Zafarani delegation emerged. The delegation comprised the following:

- Me'allim Ahmad Husni Hanafi al-Daturi
- Tahun Gharib
- Atif Hasanain

They told our men that the people of Zafarani rejected all appeals being made to them, that they considered whatever happened in Zafarani to be their own business, that they themselves would handle their affairs with the sheikh, and that they would not permit any external actors, official or unofficial, to interfere. We include a verbatim transcription of Tahun Gharib's words here: "If you take the sheikh, who will guarantee the undoing of the spell?"

The leader of the task force asked Tahun Gharib to help, in view of the fact that he was an employee of the state, but Tahun said the matter was out of his hands and that whatever promises were made or inducements offered, the people of Zafarani were determined to handle it themselves.

Flash Bulletin, Reuters, Buenos Aires

Thousands of men have converged on doctors' offices, clinics, and hospitals in the capital complaining of a strange sexual impotence.

Flash Bulletin, AWN News Agency, Paris

A reliable source at the French Ministry of Health has stated that sexual impotence has reached epidemic proportions. He further announced in a statement addressed to the French people that the epidemic was being studied by scientists on a large scale. He tried to reassure the masses, but was unable to stem the chaos and turmoil that ensued. The streets filled with men trying to test their virility on any woman they could lay their hands on.

Cable from Malawanda, AS News Agency

All tonics and aphrodisiacs have disappeared. The opposition has issued statements accusing the government of negligence in confronting the epidemic that is sweeping the country. Throughout the day the radio has continued to broadcast lewd and lascivious music and pornographic songs to help the men.

Cable from Galantia

The newly formed Zafaranist organization has declared that the whole country will be subject to the effects of the spell beginning the first night of the full moon, and that from now on history will take a new course. Humanity must wake up.

Cable from Isteffendial

All ports and airports have been closed by Presidential decree in an attempt to stop Zafarani epidemic.

Urgent Bulletin from the Capital of Kiriliana, India

Supporters of Zafaranism today organized a massive rally that marched downtown. A thin man got up to address the crowd. He described himself as the Second Warner: after reciting some texts of the well-known Zafarani perspectives, he released part of a new perspective heretofore unknown. It contained news for the Zafaranists that the time had come: the blow had been dealt to mankind to wake up for good, change things, and correct conditions. In the beginning there would be chaos, just as the kneader of the dough mixes flour, milk, and water so that cakes and biscuits can be baked, or as furniture is piled in a corner in no particular order before being put in its proper place, according to plan. Thereafter, hearts would rest in contentment. He said the world would be divided into seven parts, each entrusted to a warner who would inform, alert, explain, interpret, clarify, and organize relationships and destinies and set things right. He said that everything would be completely transformed: negative conditions would be corrected; inanimate matter would speak; the seas would overflow with love; the great day when justice prevailed would without a doubt arrive. He concluded his talk by saying, "Farewell, old time, eras of darkness and distortions of truth; farewell to death by starvation, to miserable love, to frustrated hopes, to suppressed desires, to deferred promises, to unjust systems, to relative justice, to complicating that which is simple and making difficult that which is easy. It will not be long now. The era of the spell is here, to change the world."

Glossary

athar a personal possession of someone for whom or to whom an act of witchcraft is performed—for instance, to draw him or her to fall in love or to render a man impotent.

basbusa a popular pastry made of semolina wheat flour, ghee, sugar, and topped with roasted almonds.

bastirma beef cured in a mixture of fenugreek powder, garlic, and paprika.

'ifreet a member of the jinn 'species' known for frightening children and superstitious adults.

kushari a popular dish made with rice, macaroni, lentils, caramelized onions, and usually topped with hot sauce.

mesaharati someone who beats a drum and calls on Muslims during the fasting month of Ramadan to wake up for the predawn meal.

qanun a stringed musical instrument resembling a zither.

Translator's Acknowledgments

I would like to thank the following for help with various aspects of the translation: Eric Christensen, copyeditors Klara Banaszak and Jenefer Coates, and, from the American University in Cairo Press, Neil Hewison, Nadia Naqib, and Abdalla Hassan.